PERIMETER

A Levi Yoder Thriller

M.A. ROTHMAN

Primordial Press

ISBN-13: 9781983357213

ALSO BY M.A. ROTHMAN

Technothrillers: (Thrillers with science / Hard-Science Fiction)

• Primordial Threat

• Freedom's Last Gasp

• Darwin's Cipher

Levi Yoder Thrillers:

• Perimeter

• The Inside Man

• Never Again

Epic Fantasy / Dystopian:

• Dispocalypse

• Agent of Prophecy

• Heirs of Prophecy

• Tools of Prophecy

• Lords of Prophecy

For Sandi, Ryan, and Aaron.

CONTENTS

This page purposefully left blank.

TO: Bradley Hinshaw, Deputy Director - CIA
SUBJ: NARA Query Response – Broken Arrow

A search of the Central Records System has not found any evidence of Broken Arrow incidents over the Mediterranean within the last sixty years. However, there was a match to your search parameters in the National Archives. I've attached a scan of an unclassified memo from the JCAE.

Sincerely,

Kaitlyn Shaw
Archives Technician (3A)

~

Joint Committee on Atomic Energy
Washington 25, D.C.
March 28, 1956

Honorable Carl Walske
Assistant to the Secretary (Atomic Energy)
Department of Defense
Washington, D.C.

Dear Dr. Walske:

I am forwarding three copies of the transcript of the executive session before the Joint Committee on Atomic Energy on March 20, 1956, at which you and representatives of the Defense Department testified that on March 10, 1956, an Air Force B-47 went missing somewhere over or near the Mediterranean Sea.

1

It has been confirmed that the aforementioned aircraft was loaded at MacDill AFB, Florida, with two Mark 15 nuclear capsules. The combined explosive power of the payload is estimated to be equivalent to 3.4 megatons of TNT. The aircraft and its payload remain missing.

It would be appreciated if you would arrange to have the testimony reviewed for accuracy and for a corrected copy to be returned to the Joint Committee.

Your assistance in these matters is appreciated.

Sincerely yours,

John T. Conway
Executive Director

CHAPTER ONE

"Mr. Yoder, I'm sorry to have to tell you this." Dr. Cohen looked concerned, hesitant, but he spoke quickly, as if to get it over with. "You have stage-4 pancreatic cancer."

That was certainly not how Levi had expected his nine a.m. follow-up visit to go. A chill spread through his chest and sent a shiver down the middle of his back.

The gray-haired doctor sat across the table from Levi and nudged a box of tissues in his direction.

As if tissues could help anything.

"How can I possibly have cancer?" Levi's fingers dug tightly into the arms of the padded red leather chair as he leaned forward. "I'm only thirty, and I've lived a clean life. I don't drink alcohol or do drugs. Are you sure?" He realized it sounded like denial.

Dr. Cohen stood, walked around his large mahogany desk, and put a wrinkled hand on Levi's shoulder. "Son, I'm genuinely sorry." He sighed, his breath smelling of peppermint tea. "Unfortunately, the early stages of pancreatic cancer have almost no symptoms. I sent the biopsy samples to two different labs, and they both came back with the same results. The radiology scans we took last week also confirmed the level of metastasis. The cancer has spread into your lymphatic system."

Levi took a deep breath and let it out slowly. The tautness of his muscles dissipated as a feeling of resignation came over him.

"Stage 4? What does that mean? How do we treat this? What's the next step?"

Pulling a chair closer, the doctor sat across from Levi, their knees practically touching. "Stage 4 simply means the cancer has spread to other organs. In your case, we've detected the cancer in your pancreas as well as your lymph nodes. As to treatment, Sloane-Kettering and a few other research hospitals conducted clinical trials in 2005 that dealt with this type of cancer. Nowadays there are experimental radiation treatments that we could try, coupled with multiple rounds of chemotherapy, but at this stage of your disease, I'm afraid the odds aren't good." He leaned forward and with a solemn expression said, "My best estimate would be that without treatment, you might only have four to six months to get your things in order. And even with treatment, I'll be frank: only one percent have survived five years. Nonetheless, I've already made some calls and we've got world-class treatments that can hopefully improve those odds. I'll do everything in my power to help you get through this."

Levi's mind raced as he absorbed the doctor's words.

He'd always been known to those in his line of work as a fixer. He took care of sensitive issues when the mob bosses needed someone with a deft hand and not just pure muscle. He also fixed issues that the cops couldn't or wouldn't fix.

For this, he had no fixes.

However, he knew there were a few things he needed to take care of right away.

He stood and shook the doctor's hand. "Dr. Cohen, I know it must be hard to deliver this kind of news. Thank you for being honest with me. I'll be back in a couple weeks, after I've set my affairs in order, and we'll talk."

"But Mr. Yoder, you really should start the treatments right away. I called Sloane-Kettering and I've gotten you into one of their treatment programs—"

Levi waved dismissively and turned toward the exit. "I appreciate it, but I'll be back."

As Levi opened the door and left the doctor's private office, all he could think of was Mary.

~

When Levi walked into the bedroom, Mary, already in her night-clothes, shot him a brilliant smile while she placed a record on the turntable. "I just found this in an old record shop. You have to hear it."

The sound of Nat King Cole, one of Mary's favorites, came over the speakers.

"Love me as though there were no tomorrow…"

The haunting lyrics of the ballad brought a lump into his throat.

Mary danced toward him with a dreamy smile on her face, enraptured by the music. Just as her gaze met his, she froze mid-step. Her smile faltered, and lines of worry formed on her forehead.

Levi had never been able to hide his feelings from her.

He stepped closer, cupped his wife's face in his hands, and stared into her beautiful dark-brown eyes. Her face was framed by a thick mass of jet-black hair and she looked as beautiful as the day he'd met her.

As he explained what the doctor had told him, his mind flashed back to when he'd first laid eyes on her. It was only five years ago when she'd arrived in America as Maryam Nassar, a twenty-two-year-old refugee from Iran. She spoke passable English and had responded to one of Levi's ads for a personal secretary. The moment he first saw her, it was like he'd been struck by lightning. His skin had tingled, and he'd barely managed to catch his breath.

They were married nine months later.

His chest tightened as a storm of emotions flashed across her face: disbelief, hurt, anger. Her dark eyes glistened with tears and her chin quivered as she exclaimed in her strong Persian accent, "B-but you prom—"

She pulled in a deep, shuddering breath, and Levi wrapped her in his arms.

"Honey, I know…"

He pressed her to his chest and rubbed her back as she sobbed. Mary was the only person in her family who'd chosen exile after the Iranian revolution. None of her family had any deep religious convictions, yet the moment she left Iran and married a non-Muslim, she'd sealed her fate. She couldn't go back. Mary had nobody else in this world, and that's what made telling her about his prognosis so difficult.

She also wasn't the type of person to let her emotions out freely— yet now she trembled in Levi's arms.

His throat thickened with regret. He could only imagine the fears she had going through her head. "I'll make sure that you never have to worry about anything for the rest of your life," he said. "This will always be your home, no matter what happens. Do you understand me?"

"I don't need *things*. I don't need Levi Yoder, the businessman. I *need* my *husband*." Mary fiercely grabbed both of Levi's wrists and stared at him with bloodshot eyes. "I love you."

He'd only heard her say that a handful of times. Each time had been a euphoric experience. Yet this time, it pained him to hear it.

He'd helped hundreds of people in the past. But this time, when it mattered most, when the person who needed help was the one person he cared more for than anyone in the world … he couldn't help. He couldn't fix this.

"I'll stay with you as long as I possibly can—that much I promise you." He wiped the tears from Mary's cheeks with his thumbs. "I love you more than you'll ever know."

She grabbed Levi tightly around his chest and they held each other in silence, knowing that no words would fix what they were going through.

∼

Yousef Nassar's skin prickled with anxiety as he watched the laborers empty the ancient burial chamber of an early-Egyptian priest. It had been only two days since Yousef had discovered the long-forgotten chamber, and already it was nearly empty.

Thieves! These men were all thieves, and knowing that he was in some way enabling this … the guilt gnawed at Yousef's stomach.

Trying to ignore the men who were stealing irreplaceable artifacts, he turned back to the wall with the faded hieroglyphs and continued transcribing them into his notebook. With his mind focused on the task, the world and its goings-on vanished.

"Dr. Nassar?"

Yousef flinched as he heard his name spoken in English, but with a heavy Russian accent. He turned to see one of Vladimir's men. Despite the heat in the underground chamber, the man was dressed from head to toe in a black suit. His chiseled face and stone-gray eyes showed no emotion.

"Yes?"

The large man stepped closer, and a small, precious, amber bead cracked under his foot. He pointed across the tomb toward the six-foot statue of Anubis with its arm extended. "Vladimir had instructions in case such a statue was found. Has the ankh been packed properly?"

Yousef's pulse quickened, and he struggled to keep his face neutral. "We didn't see anything near or on the statue."

The man's jaw muscles clenched and relaxed. "You're certain of this?"

"I am." Yousef hitched his thumb toward the wall. "When you talk to Vladimir, let him know that some of what is written here needs to be preserved—"

"I'll inform Vladimir of what's been found."

The broad-shouldered man turned, and the workers scattered out of his way as he walked stiffly toward the tomb's entrance.

Yousef cleared his throat, and the sound echoed off the stone walls of the chamber.

Despite the oppressive heat, he felt a chill race through him as he began unraveling the meaning of a few of the images. The scenes depicted in the pictographic messages told of a time when southern and northern Egypt had yet to be unified.

"Yousef," a woman's voice whispered. "Have you gotten further in the translation?"

He glanced over his shoulder at Sara. In Farsi, he asked, "Did you…?"

She nodded.

Breathing a sigh of relief, he gave his wife a brief kiss and smiled. "I really think this might be one of the earliest tombs we've ever encountered. This is definitely from the early First Dynasty."

Sara peered at the notebook in his lap. "What do you have so far?"

He flipped to a prior page and scanned his notes. "Like you suspected, this is definitely a tomb of an early priest, but I don't see the markings of Atum, the sun god. It's something else. The messages are talking of a great war with the south. Here, listen to this."

"The land is aflame with disease and pestilence.
    "A piece of the sun came down and it was a man—"

Yousef put his finger on the next symbol and frowned as he wracked his mind on how to best translate it into something meaningful.

"Glowing like many stars in the night, his breath was like a crocodile."

"What does that even mean?" Sara asked.

He shook his head. "Your guess is as good as mine. It doesn't make sense. We'll need to research that when we get back to the university. In fact, the next several passages seem nonsensical."

Yousef shifted his gaze to the remaining symbols he'd yet to transcribe. He tensed as he recognized one of the hieroglyphs. "My God, what could *that* mean?"

Sara pointed at two of the symbols on the faded wall. "The catfish and chisel … doesn't that depict Narmer?"

Yousef nodded as he tried to glean meaning from the other nearby symbols. "It does, but it almost seems like the message is saying that this man who was a piece of the sun gave something to Narmer."

As he leaned in closer to the wall, the sound of something metallic clattered behind him. He whirled to see a grenade rolling over the sand-strewn floor, like a cluster of dark grapes.

Yousef's yell was trapped in his throat as the grenade exploded.

"I guess today's a banking day for the Yoder family. Your wife was in a few hours ago."

Never having been one for small talk, Levi simply nodded and showed the man his key.

The well-dressed, gray-haired bank manager glanced at Levi's safe deposit box key and returned his nod. "Follow me, Mr. Yoder."

The manager turned, stiffly walked into the bank's vault, and panned his gaze across the metal wall. He moved toward the right-most section of the vault, and paused in front of the safe deposit box that held the number found on Levi's key.

Pulling a second key from his vest pocket, the manager inserted it into one of the keyholes on the front of Levi's box.

He held out his hand. "The key please, Mr. Yoder."

Levi handed the bank manager his key, and the manager inserted it into the remaining keyhole. As the manager turned both keys at once, Levi heard the snick of a lock disengaging. His box slid out half an inch from the wall.

The manager returned Levi's key to him. "Mr. Yoder, allow me to lead you to a room where you may go through your belongings in private."

Levi pulled on the handle of his safe deposit box. It slid smoothly out of its alcove.

Moments later, Levi found himself in a private room smelling faintly of wood polish and leather. The bank manager closed the door behind him as he left, leaving Levi alone.

Levi withdrew a thick envelope from his suit coat pocket and placed it in the metal container. Within the envelope were several legal documents regarding the house and his assets. Upon his death, everything would be placed in a trust, and Mary would never need to worry about anything from here on in. Their home had been paid for, and monthly expenses would automatically be debited from the trust.

Levi felt some small comfort that he'd done all that he could to arrange for Mary's needs.

Placing his hands on the safe deposit box, Levi bowed his head and sighed. The lump under his armpit, which he now knew was a tumor, had grown bigger over the last few months. It was the first of many that had spread through his body, but this one in particular was hot and throbbed angrily, keeping pace with his heartbeat.

He wasn't going to have much more time with Mary, and that was what he regretted the most.

His throat tightened for a brief moment, and he allowed himself to feel the sadness that he normally didn't dare show in public. He'd overcome so many things in life, yet this was going to be the end of him.

Levi wiped his eyes with the back of his hands and took a deep, shuddering breath. He gave one last glance at the contents of the box, and just as he was about to close it, he spied a package he didn't remember seeing before.

He pulled it out. It was a bit larger than his hand and about the same thickness, but heavy for its size. It was addressed to Maryam Nassar—that was Mary's maiden name—yet the address on the package was their current place of residence. Heavily laden with postage markings, it had come from far away, yet it was still sealed.

"What in the world?"

Levi retrieved his folding knife from his pocket. With a press of a button, the blade sprang open. The box had been wrapped with many layers of adhesive tape, and it took some effort to hack through the seal.

When at last he lifted the cover, a hand-scrawled note lay inside the box, on top of something wrapped in cloth. It was written in the feathery script common to many Middle Eastern languages, which he couldn't read.

He set the note aside and flipped open the cloth wrapping.

His eyes widened.

Nestled in the bed of gray cloth was a gold object unlike anything Levi had ever seen. It was nearly the size of his fully extended hand, and looked very much like a cross, but instead of a vertical line running through the horizontal, the upper portion was an upside-down tear shape. Almost as if it was meant to hang from the overly large loop.

It seemed like a very strange thing for Mary to have received. After all, she was an atheist.

Levi furrowed his brow. "Why would anyone have sent you such a thing," he said aloud, "and why didn't you open it?"

He sat back and stared at the golden object. Somewhere in the back of his mind, he recalled seeing such a thing when he was in the city. It was in an Egyptian museum exhibit. What was it called? An ankh?

It was probably a trick of the light, but for a moment, the golden ankh shimmered as if it were alive.

Levi lifted the ankh out of its box, and almost dropped it. It had an unexpected greasy feel to it that made it hard to hold on to. He tightened his grip. It became oddly warm to the touch.

"What the hell's this thing made of?"

The world seemed to slow as Levi's neck and face flushed with heat. His heart began thudding loudly. A burning sensation crawled up his arm, and he felt a searing pain in his hand. It was as if the thing was attempting to burn through his palm.

It suddenly dawned on Levi: *drop the stupid the thing.*

His hand unclenched, and the heavy object dropped onto the wooden table with a loud thud.

Levi's chest was tight, and he struggled to pull in a deep breath. He winced at the throbbing pain climbing up his arm and spreading across his chest and the rest of his body. There was no blistering yet on the palm of his hand, but he knew that it would soon follow. The flesh there was red and angry with whatever it was that the ankh had slathered on it.

Levi began to sweat as he wiped his hand with a handkerchief, wondering aloud, "Mary, why did someone send this to you?"

He looked back at the object where he'd dropped it on the table. To his shock, it looked different now. No longer did it have a shimmering golden hue, but instead, it held a look of dull silver.

As the heat from the palm of his hand pulsed in time with his heartbeat, Levi wondered if the gold coloration had been some type of poison.

He snorted ruefully and shook his head. *What difference does it even make at this point?*

Bring it, he challenged the dull, lifeless object.

Using his handkerchief, Levi carefully placed the ankh back into its box and slid the cover back onto the container.

Driving home from the bank was torturous. His eyes felt sticky and began to burn, and his mouth was parched. He desperately needed a glass of water. His body ached; a high fever was taking hold.

Either he was getting a terrible case of the flu, or this was some unadvertised symptom of the cancer nobody had told him about. Could that ankh really have been coated with poison? Whatever it was, it seemed dead-set on making him as miserable as possible. By the time he'd driven into his neighborhood, Levi was sweating profusely and his eyes were drooping.

The flashing lights of a police car parked in front of his house brought him out of his stupor.

Levi pulled into the driveway and climbed painfully out of the car. An officer standing at his front door turned in his direction.

The policeman glanced at a photo in his hand and then at Levi. "Lazarus Yoder?"

"Yes, officer. That's me." Levi's heart thudded heavily in his chest as he wiped the sweat from his brow. Lazarus was his given name, but ever since he'd come to New York, he'd used Levi instead. "What's wrong?"

"Mr. Yoder, can we talk in private? I'm afraid there's been an incident."

Levi glanced toward the garage; it was empty. Levi couldn't fathom where Mary might have gone. She was a diabetic, and always came home at this time of the day to take her insulin shot. The muscles around Levi's chest tightened like iron bands, and he felt short of breath. The world began to spin.

The grim-faced officer placed a hand on Levi's shoulder. "Mr. Yoder, you're not looking well. I think you'll want to sit down for this."

Levi glanced at the photo in the officer's hand, and the blood in his veins turned to ice. The photo was blood-stained and torn, but he recognized it. It was his wedding photo.

The same one Mary carried in her purse.

It had been a week since Mary died in the car accident, and only a day since her funeral. Levi only remembered pieces of the ceremony; he'd passed out sometime in the middle, evidently due to dehydration from the flu he'd been struggling with.

Now he lay in his bed at home, a nurse hanging a bag of clear fluid on the IV pole.

"I've pushed an anti-emetic through the IV's access port, so the nausea should get under control soon," she said. She set a large plastic bottle of water on Levi's nightstand. "Please try drinking as much as you can. If you can't tolerate taking in fluids to maintain your hydration, Dr. Cohen says you'll have to be admitted."

Levi shook his head. "Alicia, you seem like a nice enough lady, and I know you mean well …"

His head fell back onto his pillow, his energy completely drained. His muscles ached as if he'd been working out nonstop for a week, and his joints seemed particularly affected. He felt like an arthritic old man. And that was nothing compared to the burning he felt in the tumors where his cancer had spread.

It reminded him that the flu was the least of his issues.

Alicia, the dowdy middle-aged nurse from Dr. Cohen's office, studied him with a sympathetic expression. "I *do* mean well, and I'll be back in the morning to check on how you're doing."

"Okay." It was the only response Levi could muster. He closed his eyes, trying to ignore the pain wracking his body.

He must have fallen asleep, because when he awoke, the sun had broken through the gap in the beige-colored bedroom curtains and blazed its early-morning welcome onto Levi's face.

His fever was gone.

The bed was wet from nighttime sweats, his eyes weren't burning anymore, and the aches had subsided. Yet he still felt … odd.

The sounds of the morning seemed somehow louder than ever before, as if he'd previously had cotton balls in his ears. Birds called to each other in the front yard, and somewhere in the distance a school bus's air brakes engaged. The old-fashioned wind-up clock on the nightstand ticked loudly with each movement of the second hand.

Suddenly, the sounds vanished, and for a moment it seemed like the world had paused … and then everything started right up again. The clock continued ticking, the birds chirped, and the bus disengaged its brakes.

As Levi yawned and stretched his arms over his head, he felt a tug on his arm, and the IV pole fell on top of him. He lurched into a sitting position and ripped the IV out of his arm. He flinched as the tape that held the clear tube in place tore from his skin. The odd slithering sensation of the plastic tube withdrawing from his vein sent a shiver of revulsion through him.

His skin tingled as he swung his legs out of bed. Blood had begun oozing down his arm, so he grabbed some gauze from the nightstand and pressed it against the site where the IV had been.

The bottle of water on the nightstand was empty.

"What the hell's wrong with me?" Levi shook his head to clear the cobwebs. He hadn't slept more than two hours at a time since Mary's death, and suddenly twelve hours had vanished in one go.

He stared suspiciously at the empty IV bag, now lying on the ground, and wondered what else the nurse had put in there.

He stood, feeling remarkably steady for a person who'd felt like death warmed over just the night before. Levi touched the burning lump under his armpit and winced.

Can't I ever catch a break?

For some godforsaken reason, his tumors now all felt like red-hot pokers.

Levi turned back to the nightstand, and the world seemed to pause yet again. This time, as the clock's second hand was frozen, Levi counted aloud. "One … two … three … four … five."

The hand began ticking again.

"I'm losing my mind."

Throbbing pain issued from more than a dozen points in his body. He grimaced and took a few deep breaths.

He knew what he needed to do.

Moments later, Levi was dressed and headed out the front door.

Dr. Cohen had some explaining to do.

As Levi raced along the Northern State Parkway toward Dr. Cohen's office, the frustration within him grew.

"After all I've been through, he should have leveled with me."

Something had happened to Levi last night, but he couldn't quite make out what it was. Dr. Cohen must have had Alicia put something more than anti-nausea drugs in that IV.

Everything around him seemed more intense. Colors were more vivid than ever before, and the sounds—birds flying overhead, the noise of the cars on the highway—were clearer, more distinct. His skin tingled annoyingly as the wind blew across the hair on his arm. It was as if he could feel each individual hair stirring.

Is this what it feels like to be high?

A car raced past him on the left, and he heard the whoosh of its six metal cylinders plunging in and out of its engine in near-perfect harmony.

Levi scratched at the burning spot near his armpit and frowned. It had been the place where he'd found the first tumor. But the lump now felt … different. Smaller? And it was even hotter to the touch than ever, like a burning ember buried under his skin.

"Damn you, Doc. What's going on?"

As Levi walked into Dr. Cohen's office, the blonde receptionist looked up from the novel she'd been sneaking a peek at and smiled brightly. "Good morning, Mr. Yoder. I don't think you have an appointment today."

"Is Dr. Cohen in?"

"He's working on his charts, but—"

Levi strode past her and barged into the doctor's private office.

Dr. Cohen was busy scribbling in one of the many patient folders stacked on his desk. When Levi walked in, he looked up from his stack of work, and his eyes widened.

"Mr. Yoder. Alicia told me you were stuck in bed." The pen fell from his hand and rolled off the desk. "I was going to come over this afternoon to check on things. Are you okay?"

The heated tingling in Levi's body fueled his anger. "What the heck did you have her put in that IV? Everything feels strange, almost like I'm high or something."

The old man stood and leaned heavily against his desk. "What are you talking about? You were given a saline drip for your dehydration and a drug for your nausea."

At the old man's confused and earnest expression, Levi began feeling foolish for suspecting something nefarious. "I'm sorry, maybe it's just … I don't know." He rubbed at the burning sensation coming from the tumor on the side of his neck. "First things first. Why does it feel like I'm on fire?"

"I don't understand." Dr. Cohen walked around his desk and closed his office door. He put his hand on the side of Levi's face, and the furrow between his eyebrows deepened. Turning Levi's face to the side, he probed at the lump on his neck. "That's not right …"

The old man lifted Levi's left arm and probed with his fingertips along several spots, up to and including the armpit, which was throbbing painfully with heat.

"What's not right?" Levi said. "Don't tell me—let me guess. I'm dying."

The elderly doctor took a step back and donned a pair of rubber examination gloves. "Take off your shirt." The doctor's humorless expression brooked no argument.

Levi stripped to the waist. As the doctor prodded under his arms and the sides of his chest, Levi asked, "What do you see? What's wrong?"

"You haven't taken any radiation treatments or any chemical infusions since your diagnosis?"

"No. I didn't exactly see the point."

"I don't understand," the doctor muttered. "Levi, it seems as if the tumors infiltrating your lymphatic system have all shrunk since the last time I saw you. The few I'm detecting are very hard and warm to the touch, and the others … well, some I'm unable to find at all. I want to biopsy some of these to see what's going on."

Levi sighed. "Go ahead. Do what you think you have to."

Pacing back and forth in the wood-paneled waiting room of the Sloane-Kettering Institute, Levi couldn't figure out what could be taking so long.

His visit to Dr. Cohen several days ago had yielded nothing but full-body scans and needles. And at the doctor's insistence, Levi had spent this morning being prodded by still more doctors at Sloane-Kettering. It was now late afternoon, and he was still in the waiting room, already having read every magazine available.

From somewhere in the distance came the faint sound of raised voices—one of which sounded like the voice of Dr. Cohen. Curious, Levi left the waiting area and followed the sound through the hallways. He stopped outside a set of closed doors labeled "Radiology and Histology." Two voices argued on the other side. They were muffled by the doors, but Dr. Cohen's nasal tone was unmistakable.

"Frank, all I can tell you is this. Three days ago, that patient entered my office complaining about a burning sensation. I palpated some of his lymph nodes and confirmed the presence of abnormal growths, which I biopsied and brought here."

"Dr. Cohen, I'm telling you there's no way those biopsies you brought me and the ones I took this morning are from the same person. I don't mean to be rude—after all, you *were* my histology professor in med school. But are you sure you didn't mix something up? I couldn't feel any swelling or anything out of the ordinary in my exam. I felt bad putting that man through another biopsy, yet I did it anyway based solely on what you said."

Levi removed the bandage from his neck and touched the spot where the Sloan-Kettering cancer specialist had biopsied him. He couldn't find a hint of swelling where the biopsy had been taken.

As the doctors continued to argue, he leaned against the yellow cinder-block wall. The room wavered unsteadily. Levi shoved his hand into his shirt, accidentally popping off a button as he felt along the crook of his underarm. He couldn't feel the hard burning nodule there, either. It had been there only a couple of days before.

How is that possible?

The second doctor was speaking again. "Based on the biopsy and the PET scan results, all I can tell you is this: that man in the waiting room doesn't have a thing wrong with him."

CHAPTER TWO

Madison frowned as she suited up for her role as the mission's standby diver.

"Maddie, calm down," Jim whispered as he shrugged into his own diving gear. "It'll be okay."

It had been only fifteen minutes since they'd transferred onto a nameless ship off the coast of Turkey, but from the moment she'd set foot on the deck of the diving vessel, Madison hadn't liked anything about their mission.

There were five others on board. All of them seemed to be Americans, but it was pretty obvious that the ship was well shy of a standard Navy dive crew.

She clipped on her weight belt and leaned closer to Jim, who was adjusting his dive vest. "This is crap," she whispered. "They're expecting us to do a mixed-gas dive at four hundred feet and they don't even have a full crew. That's just a slap in the face."

With a slight shake of his head he tossed her a lopsided grin. "It'll be fine. This looks like a pretty typical commercial dive setup."

Did it? Madison was used to the standard twelve-man crew that the Navy employed, but she trusted Jim. He'd been an explosives specialist, diving everywhere in the world for over fifteen years. He'd seen it all.

She took a deep breath and released it slowly, trying to rid herself of her pre-dive jitters.

Jim snorted. "Sometimes the spooks take shortcuts."

Spooks?

All of the travel under the cloak of darkness, skirting the spotlights in the Bosporus Strait, the lack of specifics regarding their mission … it all suddenly made sense.

Madison turned her gaze suspiciously to the others on the ship. Most of them were dressed like merchant marines, which meant they looked like a ragtag bunch of civilians. But they clearly knew their way around a boat, expertly scrambling from one station to another. They were taking care of business. Two of them were handling the platform while another operated the controls of the winch it was attached to. Another crewman operated the dive console.

But one man stood out from the rest of the crew. He was in his forties, blond hair, in khakis and a dark polo. He was no sailor. Madison wasn't sure about the rest, but if there was a spook on board, it was him. This guy screamed CIA.

The spook stepped forward and addressed them all with an authoritative tone. "Divers, we've got an old airplane wreck lying directly below us at about 380 feet. It's been down there a long time, and it has a pretty narrow cross-section. It looks like there was a landslide and part of the entrance is covered by the debris. If it weren't for that, we'd have used an ROV to survey the interior."

"What are we looking for?" Jim asked.

The spook pressed his lips together and hesitated. "I'm sorry, but the exact nature of the aircraft's payload is classified."

"Classified?" Madison scoffed, feeling a rising sense of indignation. "You're asking us to do a technical dive onto a wreck we know nothing about and you're not even telling us what we're looking for? How the hell—"

"Enough!" the agent barked. "I'll be asking you to be my eyes down there and tell me what you see." He picked up a box-like device that resembled a metal detector and pressed a button on its handle. When a green LED on the box turned on, he handed the device to Jim. "Take that down with you."

Jim turned the box over in his hands. It looked like a sealed metal box with no markings, a telescoping handle with an already depressed button, and the now-glowing LED.

"What is it?" Jim asked.

"If it starts flashing, I'll want to know right away. It probably means you're near one of the items we're looking for."

Jim hooked the device onto his dive belt.

The agent addressed the full crew once more. "All right, let's move. We've only got five hours until dawn breaks."

Jim donned his dive helmet. One crewmember began reeling out the umbilical that would be Jim's lifeline and sole means of communicating up from the depths, while another man, at the console, yelled, "Comms check. Chief Uhlig, can you hear me?"

Jim's voice echoed through the dive console's speaker. *"Roger Topside, hear you loud and clear."* He gave a thumbs-up and stepped onto the metal stage. The stage swung over the side of the boat as the men called out instructions to each other.

Just as the winch operator began lowering the stage into the water, Madison made eye contact with Jim, and he shot her a thumbs-up.

She returned the gesture and recited the same prayer she did for every dive. "Guide us. Keep us safe. Let us live to dive another day."

Madison worried as she sat in her gear. As the standby diver, she'd only be getting wet if there was an issue.

Ten minutes passed.

Finally, Jim spoke. *"I'm at 375 feet. Panning the spotlight all around me and I'm not seeing anything yet. Just water in every direction."*

The man at the dive operator's console leaned in to a microphone. "Diver, the current has pushed you 75 feet away from the cliff's edge.

If you turn to 255 degrees and move in that direction, you should see the ledge and the target."

"I need more slack on the umbilical."

"Roger that."

One of the crewmembers reeled out more of the thick cable containing air and communication lines.

Focusing on staying calm, Madison listened to the waves lapping against the side of the boat. The speaker crackled with the sound of Jim's breathing.

He must be swimming.

"Topside, I've spotted the wreck. It looks like the front half of an airframe got sheared off and fell to the ocean floor. The back half is barely visible with all the debris covering it."

The agent walked over to the console and pressed the microphone button. "Diver, I'll need you to clear a passage into it. The structure should be fairly wide open once you get in."

The sound of Jim's grunting echoed across the deck.

The console operator announced, "His heart rate has increased to 140 beats per minute."

"Topside, I've cleared a wide enough opening. This must have been a recent landslide—"

"Why do you say that?" the agent asked with a worried tone.

"The debris was only loosely stuck together. It just sort of pulled away as I picked at it. Topside, I need more slack. I'm standing at the edge of the drop-off."

The spool unreeling more of the umbilical made a loud clacking sound.

Madison licked the salt crystals off her lips. She closed her eyes and imagined herself down there with Jim.

Jim spoke again. *"Okay, this is obviously the remnants of an old bomber. I see the crumpled remains of the bomb-bay door lying on the floor ten-feet ahead.*

"There's lots of growth in the interior. Sponges and hints of coral. I see some rails attached to the floor, and we've got two large metal racks on either side of the doorway."

"What do you see on the racks?" the agent asked, his voice tense.

"Nothing. They're empty."

Madison opened her eyes and studied the agent. He seemed to deflate just a bit, his shoulders sagging.

"Topside, the box you gave me. Is there anything you want me to do with it?"

"Yes. What light is showing on it?"

"You mean the LED? It's still glowing green, if that's what you're asking."

"Wave it along the racks and the bottom of the cabin. See if the light changes at all."

"Roger that."

The agent paced back and forth with his head down. The frown on his face made him look as if he'd swallowed a lemon.

"No change in the LED," Jim said. *"But it looks like the lockdowns on the racks were sheared off, and not that long ago. The metal looks like it was pinched off by bolt cutters or something. There's no encrustations or remnants of paint, and it has no patina. Definitely way after this thing crashed."*

"Damn!" The agent turned away from the console and dug into his front pocket.

"Sir," said the sailor manning the console. "Is there anything else you want from the diver?"

"Just bring him back up." The agent retrieved a satellite phone from his pocket and walked toward the front of the boat.

The console operator flipped open the dive chart. "Diver, you've given us the data we were looking for. Start your scheduled ascent. First stop at 260 fsw for one and a half minutes."

"Copy that. Leaving the wreck and starting my ascent."

As Jim began the slow ascent with the scheduled decompression stops, Madison studied the agent, who stood twenty feet away with the sat phone pressed against his ear. He was still pacing and talking animatedly to whomever was on the other end of the line. When a light breeze blew in her direction, she caught fragments of his conversation.

"… B-47 …"

"… stolen cargo."

"… Russia … Turkey."

"… no detected radiation."

Madison's stomach did a somersault at the word *radiation*.

When the agent put the phone away and walked back toward the others, Madison waved him closer.

The blond man approached, his eyebrows furrowed in frustration. "What?" He didn't even look at her; it was as if his thoughts were a million miles away.

"Are you seriously telling me that you asked us here to dive on a missing nuke?"

The agent stiffened, and his gaze focused laser-like on hers, his expression turning to stone. "I don't know what you're talking about."

With a sudden surge of fury, Madison shoved the man, pointed at the ocean, and yelled, "You asked for Navy divers to go down onto a crash site that could easily have exposed us to radiation—and you didn't tell us!" Her heartbeat thundered in her head as she pulled in a deep breath and stared daggers at the agent.

He returned her gaze unblinkingly and said nothing.

"This is a Broken Arrow incident, isn't it? Does the Navy know?" *Broken Arrow* was the military term for an incident involving a nuclear weapon.

Glancing at the other men on the deck the spook shook his head ever so slightly. "I'm sorry, but this isn't something I can talk to you about."

Madison took a step back. She felt the rage drain from her, replaced by a cold chill that crept up the middle of her back.

Could the US have actually lost a nuke?

Worse yet, did we lose a nuke and someone else reclaimed it ahead of us?

"Diver," said the console operator, "you're now at 180 feet. Your heart rate is just a bit above normal. I'll be switching you from heliox to air at 170 feet and then to a fifty-fifty mix at 90 feet."

"Roger that, Topside. Pausing at 180 feet."

Jim was fine, and he'd be back up on the boat in another forty minutes or so. No harm done … this time.

Madison returned her attention to the agent. "I'm sorry I shoved you," she said. Her temper was one day going to get her in some serious trouble.

The agent's expression softened. He cracked a smile and rubbed his chest. "Hey, I understand. And I'm sorry, it's just…" He left the sentence unfinished and chuckled. "Join the agency someday, and … aww hell, even then I'll probably never be able to say anything. You know how it is."

Madison nodded. She'd been read in on more than a handful of highly classified matters before, and he was right. The list of people she could talk to about any of those things might as well have been zero.

She took a seat next to the dive platform and shivered.

A nuclear bomb is missing.

Levi had prepared himself for death; what he hadn't prepared for was having the rest of his life ahead of him.

Without Mary.

He'd received a copy of the final accident report, and its details haunted him. Mary had taken an off-ramp too quickly, her car had flipped, and she'd died at the scene.

It made no sense.

She'd always been a hesitant driver—in fact, Levi had been the one who'd pushed her into getting a driver's license in the first place. He'd never seen her speed. Mary had been frustratingly predictable, always driving five miles per hour under the speed limit.

Guilt weighed heavily on him as he considered an alternate explanation for the accident. She'd repeatedly told him that she wouldn't want to live without him. Did she commit suicide to ensure she wouldn't have to?

Perhaps the reason didn't matter. Either way, here he was—alone, with constant reminders of her everywhere he looked. His home, the city, even the clothes he wore reminded him of Mary. Her absence left him with a gaping wound that was too much for him to bear.

He found himself going on ever-lengthening walks. The smell of the spring air calmed his nerves. As he wandered farther from home, into residential areas he'd never seen before, the sense of unfamiliarity struck a chord deep within him.

He needed a change.

A dramatic one.

As he set foot onto the tarmac in Okinawa, Levi found himself surrounded by many unfamiliar sights and sounds. The roaring of aircraft engines thundered over the airfield as military transports took off to parts unknown; from somewhere in the distance came the chop-chop sound of a helicopter landing; and closer in, a hundred boots marched on the hot black asphalt in perfect lockstep. The drill sergeant's voice rang loudly for all to hear.

"Sound off, one two! Sound off, three four! Cadence count, one two three four, one two … three four!"

Someone placed their hand on Levi's shoulder and spoke loudly over the surrounding din. "Mr. Yoder, welcome to Kadena Air Base. I wasn't given any instructions on what else you might need; it's not often we get civilian visitors. I can arrange for a bunk in the officer's hall and—"

"No." Levi shook his head at the officer who'd come to meet him. "I'll be fine, Captain Lewis."

Levi had gotten here by calling in a few favors from people who owed him—although the New York senator who'd arranged the flight had tried to convince him to go somewhere more "civilized" than a backwater island. The senator had warned him, "Levi, the locals harbor resentment for us having a base there. They actually think that our being there is corrupting the island's culture. That and a few bad eggs with discipline issues have led to some serious tensions. Hell, it doesn't help that some of their elders have some awful memories of our occupation in World War II."

The senator's characterization of the island had only hardened Levi's resolve. The people of the island were scarred; that was exactly how Levi felt. The idea that Mary might have taken her own life because she refused to live without him was too much for Levi to accept, yet it was the only thing that made any sense—and he'd carry the scars of that survivor's guilt forever.

"Just point me to Okinawa City," he said to the captain. "I'll find what I'm looking for."

The captain pointed southeast. "It's about five miles in that direction. I'll get one of the men to drive you in."

"No need." Levi waved the captain away as he began walking toward the gated entrance to Kadena. He yelled over his shoulder, "Thank you for your help!"

Levi knew that the captain probably thought he was nuts. A lone man, walking into a foreign country with nothing more than a backpack of clothing hoisted over his shoulder.

Wiping a bead of sweat from his brow, the morning sun beating down on him, Levi felt a sense of satisfaction in finding a completely new environment. Ages ago, when he first heard the term "walkabout," he'd been intrigued by the idea that a person might just travel as a rite of passage. To break from one's past life, do something different—see other places, experience other cultures.

To not look back.

It was time for Levi to start over.

During his twelve years in New York City, Levi had experienced all manner of problems as he built his own connections—but he had proven himself repeatedly as someone who could take care of almost any bad situation. Sometimes, he'd found himself squaring off with people who were more than willing to use violence to stop him from getting what he needed, and many times he'd had to fight for his success.

The feeling he'd had after those fights was … extraordinary. Other than when he was with Mary, the sense of exhilaration he'd felt as he overcame physical obstacles was probably the most alive he'd ever felt. Being a fixer was a mental game. If you were prepared, you almost never had to pull your hands out of your pockets. But when he was forced into a confrontation, he never pulled a punch.

Sure, there was plenty of pain, and once even a broken arm. But Levi had never backed away from a challenge. There were entire shelves in his library devoted to the prowess of the Japanese fighting spirit. He needed to experience that sort of life-giving energy once again. Immerse himself in it.

Hence Okinawa.

His first challenge was learning the language. He spent the first three weeks trying to find a karateka who would take in an American as a live-in student. But even though he was more than willing to pay for lodging and lessons, he was repeatedly rejected. The senator's warning about the resentment of the islanders was proving to be well-founded.

So Levi decided to take a transport from Kadena to Tokyo. It was there that he was introduced to Mr. Saito, a local friend of the Yokota Air Base commander.

As Saito drove carefully through the busy streets of Tokyo, Levi explained what he was looking for.

Saito, a fifty-something Japanese man, frowned. "I know of such a place. It teaches something called Kyokushin, which is roughly translated to 'the ultimate truth.' But I worry for you."

"As long as you believe they would take me on and they are masters in their style, why worry?"

Saito slowed the car as he turned into a narrow street. "The dojo has a reputation for being severe with its students. I fear you may be injured if you aren't careful. It is very—"

"Perfect." Levi nodded grimly. "That's exactly what I'm looking for."

The car slowed to a stop in front of a building with a placard featuring images of girls in ballet tutus executing pirouettes, and the two men got out. Levi was about to ask about the sign when Saito motioned for him to follow, and scurried around the back of the building.

Moments later, Levi was in the presence of a stone-faced Japanese man wearing a karate gi. While Saito spoke to the man in Japanese, presumably explaining Levi's odd request, Levi looked around the dojo. Two dozen students sat in a wide circle while two others sparred brutally in the center. Punches were blocked, kicks were batted away, and students were tossed heavily to the dojo's floor.

Feeling a tap on his arm, Levi turned back to Saito. "Yes?"

Saito motioned to the man he'd been talking to and gave him a slight bow. "This is Sensei Yasuda, one of the dojo's senior instructors. He finds your request extremely unusual, but he believes your story might be compelling to his master. He is willing to take you on, but you must take your lessons seriously or you'll be immediately ejected from the school."

Levi nodded.

"And there is another thing. As a *gaijin*, you'll be required to pay twice what others would pay."

"*Gaijin*?" Levi asked.

Saito paused, with a pensive expression. "It means outside person. It is what non-Japanese are called."

Levi turned to the instructor and bowed. "Sensei, *doi suru*."

Levi thought he'd said "I agree," but Saito immediately corrected his pronunciation and chuckled. "You have good pronunciation for a *gaijin*."

With a loud harrumph, the instructor, looking unimpressed, turned and yelled, "Tomiko!"

A woman jumped up from the sparring circle and raced to the instructor.

He spoke in Japanese to her while nodding toward Levi.

Saito bowed to Levi and said, "It was a pleasure meeting you, Yoder-san. Best of luck." He turned and walked out the door.

The short woman pointed at Levi's feet and barked in broken English, "Remove shoes now!"

As Levi began to unlace his shoes, the woman grabbed a white karate gi from a table and threw it at him. She pointed to a folding screen that separated a section of the dojo. "Dress there!" she yelled.

After yanking his shoes off, Levi grabbed the gi and jogged behind the screen. His heart hammered as the excitement of something new warred with the uncertainty he felt within.

At first, he was one of the many students watching the others grapple and fight, with the instructor occasionally yelling instructions, and Tomiko translating for him.

But then it was Levi's turn.

The moment he stood and walked into the ring, he knew he was going to get his ass handed to him. But for each hit he took, and for each time he was slammed to the floor, he learned just a bit more.

Levi remembered someone telling him that it was easier to learn through making mistakes than to be shown how something is done. If that was true, he learned a lot on that first day. He was tossed, kicked, punched, and otherwise taught lessons of humility from nearly half the class.

Tomiko was the last—and would soon prove to be the worst.

Licking the sweat from his lips, Levi stared at the pale-skinned woman. She had an ageless quality about her, and he couldn't tell whether she was twenty or maybe even twice that. She couldn't have been more than five feet tall, and he was twice her weight. Despite his lack of training, Levi felt a bit of confidence. He had done better than he'd expected against the others. On occasion, he'd managed to land a few blows, and as he was larger than most of the other students, he could absorb a lot of punishment without receiving any real injuries.

Tomiko stared defiantly at Levi and growled, "Attack."

She circled him, not making any sudden movements. It registered with him that she moved almost like a dancer. No … a cat. A cat that was probably toying with him.

Rolling his shoulders, Levi took on the ready stance he'd seen employed by the others, and leaped forward with the intent of landing a kick. But Tomiko sidestepped him, dropped to the ground, and swept his legs out from under him.

Levi landed heavily on his back, his breath whooshing from his lungs. He scrambled back to his feet, tiny sparks of light dancing in his vision as he struggled to catch his breath.

He moved much more cautiously around the ring now, searching for an opening.

With near-blinding speed, Tomiko leaped forward with what would surely have been a devastating kick to his groin.

But for a split second, it was as if the world slowed, and Levi ducked to the side and rolled out of the way—just barely.

Tomiko's eyes widened slightly.

Was that a look of surprise?

The tiny woman came at him again, and Levi managed to block her swift front kick—but before he could even appreciate his minor victory, she followed up with a spinning back fist that came out of nowhere.

The next thing Levi knew, he was on the bamboo mat spitting blood from a split lip and what felt like loosened teeth.

That was the end of the match.

After the sparring, Levi suffered through group exercises on the use of proper form. At the beginning of each form, he'd try to emulate what the others did—and inevitably, one of the instructors would race to him and shout a string of Japanese that needed no translation. They'd roughly correct Levi's form until they felt he was doing it properly.

Then came strength conditioning exercises that at times were beyond what Levi was capable of. As he was larger than the others, it took much more strength for him to maintain the stances that he was asked to perform. The muscles in his legs felt like they were on fire. But he gritted his teeth and pushed through the pain, even when the instructors walked by, pushing and pulling at the students, trying to knock them off balance.

By the time the sun had set, and Levi realized that he'd managed to survive his first day at the dojo, a great sense of relief flooded through him.

He'd survived.

The students ate their communal meal together. It consisted of rice, some kind of grilled fish or possibly eel, and a large bowl of pickled vegetables. As Levi ate, the others talked in Japanese. Tomiko wasn't among those who remained at the dojo, so Levi had no one to translate. He focused on his meal and listened to the foreign sounds of Japanese being spoken all around him.

When he and the other students had finished clearing away the meal, Levi walked slowly to the back of the dojo, trying not to make it obvious he was in a lot of pain. Following the lead of the others, he stripped out of his uniform, splashed water on his face and body from the faucet, and grabbed a change of clothes that had been provided for him. In a back room, some of the other students rolled out their tatami mats to sleep, and with a barely suppressed groan, Levi lay on the wooden mat he'd been assigned.

As he stared up at the ceiling, the throbbing aches he felt reminded him that he'd pushed himself far beyond anything he was used to.

He wasn't sure if the pain was an affirmation of life or a punishment for having lived when Mary didn't.

His first day at the infamous dojo had been a lesson in pain. So when Levi woke early the next morning, he fully expected to feel his entire body bruised, battered, and non-functional.

Yet as he sat up and stretched, he felt only the slightest bit of stiffness. Even lying on a wooden mat for the first time hadn't stopped him from getting a good night's sleep. He licked his lips, and barely felt the cut that he'd received from Tomiko.

He hopped up onto his feet, rolled up his mat, and set it in its place.

He walked out of the sleeping quarters, weaving past a half dozen of the other students, who were still asleep. As he entered the main area of the dojo, he saw Tomiko stretching with some of the senior instructors, along with another man he hadn't seen before.

Levi bowed and began stretching like the others. Sensei Yasuda looked up, stone-faced, and said something to him in Japanese.

Tomiko translated. "Sensei Yasuda wants know why you not resting with the others."

Levi stretched his legs and reached for his toes. "I feel rested, and didn't want to risk missing any lessons."

Tomiko translated for Yasuda. The instructor's face registered no change in expression, but he gave a slight nod.

The new man said something in Japanese while giving Levi an amused smile.

Again Tomiko translated. "Master Oyama hopes that you continue to show excellent attitude. He says that only intense focus will purge that which haunts you, and he will ensure that you're pushed harder from now on."

Levi was unsure how to respond to that. He bowed his head to the master, and silently wondered what he'd gotten himself into.

CHAPTER THREE

As Madison walked into a wood-paneled conference room at the CIA headquarters building in Langley, the air thick with the scent of leather and lemon wood polish, she was greeted by a man wearing a dark suit and glasses. He looked to her like a grown-up version of Harry Potter.

He shook her hand and motioned toward the conference table. "Miss Lewis, have a seat."

She glanced at the CIA badge clipped to the man's lapel. "Mr. Walker, is it? I'm not exactly sure why I'm here. Two days ago I got a call from the Office of Personnel Management letting me know they'd processed my clearance paperwork, and everything looked fine, but this morning I was told there's an issue with my clearance. Needless to say, I'm a bit confused."

"Miss Lewis, we've processed your SF86 paperwork, and we have a few remaining questions before your application can be finalized."

Madison sat down, and Walker sat across from her. As he riffled through some manila folders, she tried not to let her anxiety show. This was the second time she'd applied to the CIA. The first was soon after the night-time mission on the Black Sea, but she'd never heard back from them. This time, she'd already been put through a polygraph, medical, and a psych screening. Now, sitting here with this agent, she realized just how badly she wanted this job.

Walker pulled a folder from the stack, opened it, and flipped through the papers. His expression soured. "Miss Lewis, you were born in Okinawa. Can you go over once more how you came to be here?"

"Well, I'm a Navy EOD Lieutenant out of—"

"Stop." The interviewer looked up from the papers. "Tell me about your childhood in Okinawa. How did you get here from there?"

"Oh…" Madison was surprised by the question. "Well, to be honest, I don't really know much about my parents. My father was an American serviceman who died in some kind of training accident. My mother was a Japanese citizen who couldn't raise me by herself, so I ended up at an orphanage."

"Didn't your mother have family that could help?" Walker asked.

"Well, I'm sure she did, but … well, with my father being a black American, and me obviously not being like the rest of the kids, I'm guessing they didn't want a mixed-race child. Anyway, I ended up at the orphanage—"

"How does that make you feel? That your family didn't want you because of your race?"

Madison's back stiffened. "Are you serious? What kind of question is that?"

The well-dressed, adult Harry Potter tilted his head and shrugged. "Well, how did that make you feel?"

"I don't know, I suppose I learned to deal with it."

"How?"

Madison huffed, and her mind drifted back more than twenty years. She recalled a dingy orphanage in Kadena and remembered how much she hated some of those kids. "I fought. A lot. I learned to take care of myself. But eventually, I learned who my father was and I decided to visit the air base to see if I could find anyone who knew him."

"How old were you?"

"I was eight when I first met Major Brown. He knew my dad and remembered hearing about Dad's girlfriend being pregnant. I suppose he helped change my life. He arranged for me to get in contact with my nana in the states, Dad's mom."

"And how was living with your grandmother?"

Madison couldn't keep the smile off her face as she thought of her grandmother. "She was awesome. Why?"

"How was your early life in the states compared to Okinawa?"

"It was a bit of a struggle," Madison admitted.

"Oh? How so?"

She shook her head and sighed. "Think about it. My first language was Japanese, my English sucked, and it's not like I fit in with the kids here any better than I did when I was in Okinawa."

"Why? What was the issue?"

Madison frowned. This guy was really getting on her nerves. She took a deep breath and let it out slowly. "Well, just think of it this way: I'm half Asian and half black, and I look it. Too dark to be Asian, too Asian to be black, and the rest of the kids didn't know what to make of me."

"What about your family? How did they treat you?"

"They're awesome. They didn't give a crap about what I looked like, and—" She paused as emotions bubbled up within her, and it took everything she had not to let them show. "I love them, and they love me back. That's all that matters."

Walker flipped to another page. "You've had a good run with the Navy. Top scores in your EOD training, several remarkable missions with Special Operations Command, including some rather technical dives, and by your records, it looks like you're one sea tour away from being eligible for promotion to lieutenant commander. Why would you want to come to the agency? Don't get me wrong, we could use more women in our ranks, but with your record, you'd probably be able to rocket up the chain and make commander in another handful of years. You realize that would make you one of the few female commanders in Navy EOD. Have you given that any thought?"

"Are you kidding me?" Madison felt a surge of indignation. "I'm nobody's diversity hire, *Mr. Walker*. I'm either a good fit or I'm not. My being a woman or anything else isn't the issue."

Walker seemed unfazed by her outburst. "It isn't?"

"It sure as hell better not be!" Madison heard her words echo off the wood paneling, and realized she'd just yelled at the interviewer. A chill raced through her, and she forcibly unclenched her fists and set them on her lap.

"So why do you want to come to the agency?" the man asked again.

"I want to make more of a difference."

"Is that because you feel inadequate due to your mother abandoning you?"

She stared at him, stunned, her neck and face growing hot. Just as she was about to tell the guy to go screw himself, a sudden sense of understanding washed over her.

He was messing with her. It was a test.

She shook her head and replied in a calm voice. "I don't feel inadequate, but maybe I want to prove that I can make a difference."

"How so?"

"If someone like me, an orphan who struggled for everything, can make a difference for my country—well, that's what the American dream is all about, isn't it? I suppose I want to be here for the same reason you or anyone else does."

"You want to be a role model, then?"

"No … I mean, sure, but it's not like a goal of mine. I figure I can maybe do more for my country here than I can as EOD."

"So you're a patriot?"

Madison smiled. "Is that so bad?"

Walker pushed his Harry Potter glasses higher onto the bridge of his nose and cracked a smile. "No. It isn't."

At just over three thousand feet above sea level, Levi breathed in the crisp cool air as he crouched on the uneven stump of a fallen hemlock.

He'd spent years learning from the senior instructors at the dojo, and only when he'd surpassed what they were capable of teaching him had Master Oyama taken over.

Levi then quickly learned that his previous instructors' skills and speed were nothing compared to Oyama's. The master was one of the top martial artists in all of Japan. He was a legend. For Levi, it was almost like that first day all over again. The stress and pain of those lessons were burned indelibly in his mind.

Now, as he balanced easily on his unsteady perch, his mind wandered back to that time.

When at last Oyama motioned for Levi to stop, Levi, sweat dripping heavily from his face, collapsed onto the floor. His muscles burned from the nonstop strain they'd undergone.

"It feels like my entire body is on fire," he groaned in Japanese.

The master made a clicking sound with his tongue and nodded solemnly. "Good. The fire you are feeling is not unlike the fire a sword-smith uses to purge the impurities from his steel. For you to overcome what brought you to me, you must also purge yourself. Never forget what brought you here, but don't let it hold you back. Let those memories feed the fire. It is the only way."

It wasn't until Master Oyama had spoken those words, years after Levi's arrival at the dojo, that he realized he'd been training not as a way of healing, but as a way of punishing himself. Mary's death had been a yoke weighing heavily on his soul.

But something inside him changed after that lesson. Somehow, he learned to use those feelings of guilt and pain as a fuel to propel himself forward. He'd finally understood that allowing himself to self-destruct was never the answer—even after a tragedy like the death of his Mary. The way he interacted with his own feelings and the world around him had forever been transformed.

He stayed with Oyama for another two years, and during their lessons, the master had spoken of a concept known as chi, a life energy.

When he first mentioned it, it seemed to Levi like one of the many Asian beliefs that, although quaint, had no bearing in reality. But in time, Levi discovered otherwise.

Whether it was Mary's memory that revealed some hidden reserve of energy, or it was something else, he couldn't be sure. But as Levi closed his eyes and extended his senses beyond the clearing, he was able to detect things that would normally be just beyond the reach of his ears. It was almost as if he felt the vibrations through the ground as a deer stepped across the autumn leaves of the forest forty yards to his right. Levi knew that a bird had just rustled its feathers and was preening on a perch fifty feet above him.

Levi sensed footsteps approaching from the downslope of his mountain hideaway. Without even having to look, he recognized the pattern of footfalls and knew who it was.

Soundlessly, Levi shifted himself from the stump and stood erect, a slight smile crossing his face as he cupped his hands to his mouth and yelled in Japanese, "Tomiko, I know you're out there!"

Her steps paused, then she picked up her pace. Moments later, she crested the slope in a multi-colored hiking outfit. She still had that ageless appearance of youth that so many Asians had, but a few lines now marred her near-perfect complexion.

Levi motioned toward the edge of the clearing where he'd set up a primitive camp for himself. Turning one of the larger logs on its side, he patted at it and said in fluent Japanese, "Please, have a seat."

Tomiko sat on the log and gazed at him with incredulity. "You look nothing like the uncertain *gaijin* I first met."

Levi sat cross-legged on the forest floor and smiled up at her. "Why do you say that?"

Tomiko panned her gaze across the clearing and looked up at the trees that rose over a hundred feet into the air. She shared a smile with Levi and shook her head. "You seem at home here in Aokigahara, but Master Oyama said you are moving on. Is this true?"

The scent of pine and earth filled Levi's nostrils as he breathed in deeply. He gave a slight nod. "Aokigahara, the Sea of Trees, is a beautiful place. I've become accustomed to its comforting embrace more than I thought I would, but I don't belong here. I'm feeling restless and need to continue my journey. It's time." He sighed as he stared into the forest. "I'm not sure where I'll be going, but I do want to thank you for your kind teaching."

Bringing her hand up to her mouth, Tomiko laughed. "You remember things in a different way than I do, Yoder-san." She tilted her head and leaned forward, her expression one of curiosity. "What is your given name? All these years, and you've never shared it with me."

"Lazarus is the name my parents gave me."

"Lazarus. What does it mean?"

Levi's eyes widened at the unexpected question, and he pursed his lips in thought. "English names normally don't have much meaning, but mine does have some history. My mother told me that when I was born, they were afraid I was dead. When I first came into this world, I didn't cry, and I wasn't breathing. And no matter what they tried to do to revive me, nothing worked. It was just at the moment when they'd given up that I suddenly let out a cry. For my parents, it was as if I'd woken from the dead. In the Christian Bible, it is said that Jesus raised someone from the dead—a man named Lazarus. My parents were religious people, so choosing my name was easy."

"Lazarus…" Tomiko said the name as if somehow savoring how it felt on her tongue. "That's a beautiful story, and a handsome name." She opened her backpack and extracted a nearly foot-long, cloth-wrapped object. She extended it toward Levi with both hands and bowed. "This is from Master Oyama. It is a parting gift that he wishes to bestow upon you."

Levi hopped up onto the balls of his feet and bowed his head as he retrieved the package. Sitting back down in *seiza* style on the forest floor, he weighed the object in his hands, trying to imagine what the master would have given him.

"Open it. It is for your travels."

Curiosity flooded through Levi as he untied the twine and carefully unwrapped the green cloth. When he lifted the last layer, he revealed a remarkable dagger. A *tanto*.

Levi pulled the blade from its wooden sheath; it was perfectly balanced. He'd trained for years with poor imitations of just this type of weapon, but what he held in his hand now was beyond anything he'd ever used before. It was a true fighting weapon.

Tomiko smiled. "May it keep you safe on your travels."

Near the desolate border crossing into Afghanistan—he'd traveled south along the road from Duschanbe, a city in the former Soviet Union—Levi managed to barter for some traditional clothes to replace the near-rags he'd been wearing since leaving the Australian outback.

His new outfit served him well in this area, since it matched the color of the terrain, which was almost universally a mottled beige. The pants were pajama-like, with lots of room in the thigh, and tapered at the ankle, and the shirt was a long pullover with an open neck and a western-style collar. It was relatively lightweight and cool despite the one-hundred-plus-degree heat.

Topping the outfit was a squishy round hat that reminded him of a beret, but it wasn't worn in the style that the American Special Forces wore them. The brim was rolled up and fitted so that it rested comfortably on the crown of Levi's head.

He felt uncertain about having snuck into Afghanistan. He'd explored the wildest and most untamed parts of Australia, China, and Russia, and had lost track of how much time had passed since he'd left Japan ... yet at no point during these travels had he once felt the anxiety that he felt coming from the citizens here.

As he continued south, he spied the occasional flash of reflected sunlight from a concealed military-style weapon shifting under a billowing Bedouin robe.

A hot breeze blew over the burnt land, and the smell of tanned leather, cinnamon, and other spices wafted through the air as Levi cautiously approached the outskirts of Mazar-i-sharif, a relatively large city in northern Afghanistan.

The outer market was very similar to markets Levi had seen in other parts of the world. Unpaved dirt roads dominated the area, and the shops that weren't built on top of movable wagons were typically made from what looked like scraps of ancient plywood held together with nails, rope, or whatever was available. Shoppers haggled loudly with merchants who battled mightily to gain the highest price for their goods.

Levi sighed with relief as it became obvious he could understand what the people were saying. He'd learned Farsi from Mary, and even though the language the Afghanis were speaking was Dari, the languages were fundamentally the same, they simply employed different accents.

At one side of a ramshackle market stall selling men's clothing, a mirror stood propped up, and Levi saw himself for the first time in ages. His blue eyes were a stark contrast to his dark hair. Despite having been in the elements for years, his skin had remained relatively pale. But it was his dark beard that dominated his appearance. Mary had hated the beard when they'd first met—she'd said it reminded her too much of the family and people she'd left behind in Iran—so he'd shaved it off and hadn't worn one the entire time they'd been together. Yet now, it seemed fitting that the man who stared back at him looked nothing like the one he remembered.

"You're not the same Amish kid that left the farm all those years ago," Levi muttered to himself in Pennsylvania Dutch, the language he'd grown up speaking.

A clatter sounded behind him, and he turned to see a woman, clad from head to toe in a black burqa, exclaiming something unintelligible as a half dozen cans of food spilled from her over-filled canvas bag. She cursed under her breath and scrambled after the cans as they rolled away.

Without thinking, Levi scooped up one of the cans that came to rest near his foot. He approached the woman and handed the metal container to her. "Here you go," he said softly in halting Farsi.

The woman's eyes widened through the narrow slit in her burqa, and the background sound of people haggling over prices at the nearby stalls suddenly grew quiet.

An Afghani man who'd been standing next to the woman yelled at Levi in Dari, "You pig! How dare you!"

The woman backed away, and three men approached, two of them wielding knives.

It dawned on Levi that he'd probably made some huge cultural faux pas that he was about to pay for—in blood.

With his body tensed, he dropped the can and backed away.

A man's arm snaked around his neck from behind.

Without thinking, Levi grabbed the man's wrist with his left hand, raised his right shoulder as he'd done thousands of times before, and ducked forward, escaping the grasp of his assailant. With a quick twist of the man's wrist, something snapped, and the attacker screamed.

From the corner of his eye, Levi caught sunlight glinting off metal. He ducked just as another man slashed at him with a foot-long knife.

The blade came within inches of Levi's face, but he swept the man's feet out from under him. The man hit the ground, his breath blasting from his lungs.

Levi slammed an elbow into another attacker's face and felt the man's cheekbone crack.

Suddenly the sound of boots racing across the rocky ground echoed all around him, and American voices screamed warnings in multiple languages. "Hands up! Drop your weapons!"

Within seconds, Levi and his attackers were surrounded by a dozen soldiers, all aiming assault rifles at them.

Levi raised his hands and began to protest in English, "These guys attacked—"

He was cut off as his arms were roughly pulled down behind his back. The soldier binding his wrists with zip ties hissed in his ear, "Just keep quiet, and we'll sort this out."

Another soldier knelt next to the huge, barrel-chested Afghani Levi had struck in the cheek. The man lay sprawled on the ground. "Captain Sanderson, looks like this big guy had the right side of his face smashed by a sledgehammer. He's going to need surgery. The other …" The soldier waved at the Afghani whose wrist Levi had broken; he was being held up by two soldiers and was glowering at Levi as he cradled his arm. "His arm is definitely broken; he'll need x-rays to see how bad."

The captain glanced at Levi, frowned, and yelled over his shoulder, "Sanchez, help Therien get that big guy on a stretcher, and let's clear everyone away from the market and sort this out. Jensen, see if you can reach any of those Red Crescent aid workers. Looks like we need them."

Ten minutes later, his wrists still bound, Levi sat on his heels, leaning against an abandoned stone building near an unnamed village a few miles away. He shrugged his shoulders, trying to relieve some of the ache, but to little effect. He could have freed himself by now, but they'd confiscated his knives, and the best he could do was strain at his restraints and wince as the hard plastic cut into his wrists.

The soldiers were still with him, and he wasn't sure what they had planned. They seemed professional, but you could never be too sure.

One of the soldiers walked by, his weapon at the ready as he scanned the area, looking for signs of trouble. Only a few feet away, the comms officer spoke to the captain in hushed tones. "Captain, there aren't any nearby aid workers, and that big hajji is going to need some serious facial work. His cheek is the size of a grapefruit, and he's bleeding out of one ear. It's not good."

Another soldier pointed in the distance and said, "Anyone got anymore candy? That same kid's come back."

Levi squinted at the approaching child, who was about one hundred yards away. The hairs on the back of his neck tickled a warning. The boy's gait seemed odd. An injury? A glint came from a partially open doorway in a small stone building behind him. A pair of eyes peered in their direction.

Quickly scanning the area, Levi caught a wooden shutter on another building open slightly, then close.

A sense of panic rose within Levi's chest. He pushed himself up to his feet and yelled at the soldier approaching the kid with a small bag of candy. "Watch out! That kid's carrying something—"

A near-blinding flash erupted from where the boy had been, and a shock wave slammed Levi into the wall of the building.

Through the resulting smoke, Afghani soldiers poured from the surrounding buildings, and shots were fired. Levi's ears rang. Chaos exploded all around him, with soldiers yelling over the sounds of automatic weapons fire.

But before he could even gather his senses, the fighting was over.

As the ringing in his ears subsided, and the smoke began to clear, Levi heard the comms officer yelling into a handset.

"Any station, any station, this is Rosebud Five Actual, need immediate assistance, over."

The radio crackled, and a deep voice reverberated through the handset's speaker.

"Rosebud Five Actual, this is Hawkeye Thirteen, send it over."

"Hawkeye Thirteen, request medevac, over."

"Roger Rosebud, send your request, over."

"Line One, LZ Flapper 42S UF 31763 63246—Break."

"Line Two, HF 231.45 UHF 114.1 Rosebud Five Actual."

"Line Three—"

Levi was distracted by a voice next to him. "Hey, let me see your face." One of the American soldiers swiped at the side of his face with a handful of gauze.

Levi's heart skipped a beat when he saw the blood that came away on the gauze. Had he been hit?

The soldier gently tilted Levi's head with one hand and ran his other latex-covered hand over his scalp. "Looks like you got nicked by some shrapnel from that kid's suicide vest. I don't feel any open wounds and looks like the bleeding stopped on its own."

Levi strained at his bound wrists. "Can you get me out of these?" he asked. "I didn't start that fight back there. Those guys attacked me."

A gravelly voice behind Levi said, "Therien, go see to the others, I've got this guy." It was the captain. His face was covered with soot and held an inscrutable expression.

One of the soldiers yelled, "Throwing red!" as he threw something toward an open patch of scrub. Almost immediately, red smoke began billowing up into the air.

"Okay," said the captain, "what's your story? Are you AWOL from another unit?"

Levi shook his head. "No. I'm just someone who's on walkabout … I'm just exploring the world—"

"That's bullshit. What American in their right mind—you're American, right?"

Levi nodded.

The captain shook his head. "What kind of nut do you take me for? What unit are you out of? I'll find out one way or another when we run your prints."

"I'm really not with the military. Never enlisted in my life. Heck, I grew up as an Amish farmer in rural Pennsylvania." Levi saw the captain's suspicious expression, and decided he'd better tell the full story. He explained how he'd been lost ever since Mary's death, and talked about the places he'd explored as he wandered the world.

"That's got to be some of the dumbest shit I've ever heard," Sanderson exclaimed. He shook his head. "I saw what happened to you. Why the hell did you approach one of those hajji girls? That's one of the first things you should know about these people. Approaching one of those girls, talking to them—it's almost the equivalent of rape in these people's eyes."

"I didn't realize that. But I couldn't exactly let them carve me up like a Thanksgiving turkey. Even though I made a stupid mistake, you can't exactly blame me for defending myself, can you?"

The captain chuckled and made a turning motion with his index finger. "Turn around."

Levi turned and Sanderson cut off the plastic restraints. Levi turned back around and brought his arms forward. His shoulders burned. "Thank you."

"No, thank you. I should have noticed that the kid had a vest on. You probably saved some lives today. If you're some Amish farmer, how'd you know?"

Levi studied the captain's face. He was in his thirties, and had eyes that were so blue they reminded him of an Alaskan wolfhound. He shrugged. "Kid looked like he was off-balance, or maybe had a limp.

And then I noticed some folks were paying attention to us and that kid. I sort of put two and two together."

"Well, the Taliban is still around." Sanderson tilted his head toward the line of dead Taliban soldiers lying in the village square. "Listen. Even though I think you're one crazy son of a bitch, I think you can be trusted with your weapons."

"Thank you, sir."

The captain waved over a nearby soldier and sent him to get Levi's knives. Then Sanderson extended his hand to Levi. "This place isn't safe. If you want, I can take you on the chopper as one of the wounded, but there'd be lots of questions."

Levi shook the man's hand. "No, I appreciate the offer, but I think I'll head back the way I came. I may be a little crazy for inadvertently wandering south, but I'm not stupid."

As one of the captain's men approached with Levi's brace of daggers, the captain motioned toward Levi. "He can have them back."

Levi gladly took back his weapons and within seconds had them hidden under his clothes.

The captain gave him a sly grin and shook his head. "Well, there's no doubt you can take care of yourself. I watched what you did." He left the words hanging in the air, seeming to imply something that Levi didn't grasp. "What's your name?"

"Lazarus Yoder, but everyone calls me Levi."

Sanderson clapped Levi on the shoulder. "Nice to meet you, Lazarus. Now get out of here before more hajjis come crawling out of their holes."

With a farewell to the captain, Levi began jogging north, skirting past the red cloud of smoke as the chop-chop sound warned of helicopters approaching.

A breeze blew across the Ganges River, bringing with it air redolent with the musty odors of decay, ash, and the fragrant flowers that had been scattered nearby. Levi felt hollow, drained of emotional capacity, as he stood fifty feet back from hundreds of mourners gathered in front of the funeral pyre.

He wore the traditional white linen outfit that Guru Sinjali had given him. The man's father had died at the age of 106—an incredible age. His son, the man Levi had befriended and studied with for the last six months, was easily in his eighties and had the vitality of a man half his age.

As the fire consumed the old man's flesh, Levi couldn't help but think about how it should have been him on that pile of burning wood. The cancer should have eaten him alive years ago. Yet here he was. Alive, alone, and—after many years of mourning his wife—numb.

He knew he'd been given a gift. A gift of life. It was just hard for him to muster the courage to allow his emotions to awaken again. For years he'd been trying to hold down the overwhelming grief, and it had tired him out, drained him of something vital. Maybe his wandering was coming to an end. He had to face the demons of the past and go home.

But go home to what?

Levi was a made man—one of the only non-Italians to be sworn into the code of silence that was the Mafia. But even when he'd walked the streets with his cohorts, he was never like the others. Because he hated the rackets. Yet at the same time, he knew they were an unavoid-able evil, and the best one could do was to minimize that evil.

Take the protection rackets, for instance. Certain stores would pay for protection, and if not protected, accidents could happen. Levi knew that if the family didn't do it, some other family would move in, and they would almost certainly be worse to the owners in every conceiv-able way. It was a lesser of two evils.

But Levi was no street soldier. He was a man who got things done. And nothing made him feel better than when he did something everyone thought could *not* be done.

That was how he became a "fixer." He took care of situations that nobody thought could be taken care of. It was how he became a big earner for the family. Whether it was getting information he shouldn't be able to get, finding people who didn't want to be found, or finding out who was disloyal to the family, he was the best man for the job. He rarely if ever broke the law—but he didn't fool himself. He knew this wasn't a clean living.

He felt the most whole when he found himself helping those who couldn't help themselves. Sticking up for those who were bullied, or making sure that those who'd wronged others got their due. He saw himself as a righter of wrongs, or in the sense of Guru Sinjali's teachings, one who helped keep people's karma in balance.

He turned his gaze back to the funeral pyre. The skeleton was charred and had begun falling apart.

Guru Sinjali walked toward the pyre with a long bamboo stick. He spoke over his father's remains—Levi only caught snatches of his words—while holding the bamboo stick in the air. Suddenly, the old man slammed the stick down onto his father's skull, cracking it open.

A change rippled through the crowd of mourners. Their grief seemed to dissipate. And then, in ones and twos, they began to drift away. None of them looked back.

The guru had taught Levi about the "rite of the skull." It was a Hindu practice that allowed the soul to be released from the body. It was their belief that the moment the soul departed, the body was simply an empty vessel.

A hand touched Levi's shoulder. "Your spirit is still restless."

Levi turned to find Guru Sinjali standing beside him. He responded in awkward Hindi. "I'm fine. I pray your father's soul is at rest."

The old man waved dismissively at the remark and spoke with his singsong accent. "My father is not whom we are speaking of." He gripped Levi's shoulders with both hands and stared at him for a full ten seconds before speaking again. "You are very much like someone I knew a long time ago. You're stubborn, disbelieving, and living in the past. None of those will help you attain peace. You need to seek someone who can help you understand what you are."

Levi canted his head. "I think I understand who I am."

The guru laughed—a rasping wheeze. "There's a difference between *what* and *who*. And knowing the kind of stubborn mule you are, you'll take a long time learning that. It's time you met a proper guru, one who knows what you are better than I." The old man led Levi away from the smoldering ashes. "Amar Van is in the north. I'll show you the way, and I'll pray to Vishnu for your safe passage."

Levi studied the wizened old man, whom he'd grown to respect for his keen insight and wisdom.

Could I really be that clueless about what and who I am? If so, I'll probably need a lot more than prayers to some Hindu god.

A bitter-cold wind blew through the gaping hole in the eastern wall of the abandoned Buddhist temple. Despite the swirls of straw and leaves flying all around him, Levi remained in the lotus position at the center of the courtyard. His eyes were closed, and he was meditating.

His mind's eye flashed back over his travels. He'd been to Indonesia, Australia, most of India, parts of Russia, and China. Each time he'd stopped somewhere, the time would come when something within him spurred him onward once more. And time and again, these explorations reconfirmed that it was from the humblest of people that he learned the most.

Master Oyama's lessons had only been the start.

After Oyama, there was Mawukura, the Australian aborigine who'd introduced Levi to the beauty and dangers of his land. After Mawukura, there was Master Han, a practitioner of ancient Chinese medicine, and then there was Guru Sinjali, who taught him the art of meditation.

At each spot, and with each teacher, Levi soaked up the knowledge and lived as others did.

And now that he was in Nepal, he felt different somehow. Whether that change was something within him, or was something about the world around him, he couldn't be sure. But it was there.

As he'd traveled through remote villages that had no discernible name, he kept hearing about a monk they called Amar Van. The same one Guru Sinjali had mentioned to him. Levi had no idea what the name meant in the Nepalese language, but in Hindi, it meant "the immortal one."

And certainly everyone who knew of this Amar Van held the monk in high esteem. They described him as a cripple, but wiser than the most ancient of monks. The more Levi heard, the more he felt driven to seek him out.

It was the search for this Amar Van that had led Levi to this abandoned temple.

The large stone structure must have been built hundreds of years ago. Its outer wall had become worn and broken over the centuries, and through a gap in the temple's roof, Levi could look upon a cloudless blue sky.

Yet in this cold, broken temple, Levi felt a yearning he'd not had in a long time. It was as if the well of guilt and anger that had fueled his wandering had suddenly dried up. Images of the pastoral life he'd left behind in rural Pennsylvania flashed into his mind. It was the first home he'd ever known, and something within him wanted to go back.

His eyes snapped open at the crunch of footsteps outside the temple. A moment later an orange-robed monk climbed through the broken wall and entered the inner chamber.

The monk bowed. "Master Levi, I must apologize." He spoke in rapid Hindi. "I've checked with others, and the Amar Van has not been seen in many months on this peak. I may be able to reach out to neighboring villages and learn more."

Levi felt a sense of peace settle over him. It was almost as if something inside him had suddenly clicked.

It was finally the right time.

Levi stretched his arms up to the sky and breathed deeply. With a fluid motion, he hopped up onto his feet. "Don't worry," he said. "Perhaps it wasn't meant to be. Anyway, I think it's time for me to return to my home."

"In America?" The monk raised his eyebrows.

Levi nodded. It had been ages since he'd been home. In fact, he couldn't recall the last time he'd had money, passport, or any form of identification. "Do you know where I can find the American embassy?"

The monk crinkled his nose and frowned. "I'm sorry, but I don't know where that is. Maybe someone in the mountain village of Jiri can help you find it. I hear they now have electricity."

Levi pressed the palms of his hands together, fingertips facing upward, placed them against his forehead, and bowed to the monk. "Thank you for your help."

"Jiri is in—"

The monk pointed northwest, but Levi had already stepped out the front entrance of the temple and was jogging in Jiri's direction.

Jiri had evidently grown from the village that the monk had described, and now resembled something more like a small city. This was probably because it was near one of the trailheads for mountain climbers, and indeed the market, though quieter than many of the ones Levi had seen in his travels, seemed to cater to tourists and locals alike. The bright colors of the signs and goods showed that this community at the base of the Himalayas was thriving.

But to Levi, who had grown accustomed to the wilderness, the surrounding buildings, some of them multi-story ones, felt alien.

It was late in the evening, and Levi entered a building with a beer mug–shaped neon light above the doorway. He was greeted by the smell of stale beer and cigarettes. The man behind the bar greeted him in Nepali

Levi hadn't learned the Nepalese language. "Do you speak Mandarin?" he asked in the common Chinese dialect.

The bartender frowned, but one of the men at the bar turned. "I speak it. Do you need help?"

Levi barely heard the man; he was suddenly transfixed by something he'd never seen before.

High up on the wall behind the bar was a color television that was as thin as a pizza box. Levi remembered seeing advertisements for "plasma" TVs when he'd begun his travels, but never before had he encountered one.

A calendar on the wall showed the year, and Levi's mouth hung open as he realized that he'd been wandering the world for over a decade.

His mind raced, and he wondered aloud, "If some backwater place like this has a television like that, what else has happened while I was gone?"

CHAPTER FOUR

A hiss of steam erupted from the barrel as Levi dropped the red-hot forged steel into the water. A light breeze blew through the barn door, carrying the smell of freshly turned soil and the sounds of his family and the extended Amish community tending the farm outside. The mixture of sounds and smells gave Levi a sense of comfort.

He wiped the sweat from his face and looked into the barrel.

The wavering reflection showed his dark beard, and it made him think of Mary. He'd lived with near-overwhelming guilt for so many years, but in his heart, he knew that it was now time to look to the future once more.

He'd returned to his first home only two weeks ago, and had spent that time indulging in the pastoral existence. The peaceful lifestyle had remained unchanged, as had the people. Oh, sure, some family members had moved, and those few whom Levi had known as children were now grown and forming families of their own. His father had passed, and his mother was aging, but supremely pleased to see him after so many years.

The community seemed puzzled at his reappearance, but to his surprise, they accepted it without too many uncomfortable questions. That was good, especially since he had almost no answers to give.

They wouldn't have understood his life after the farm even if he'd tried to explain. They certainly wouldn't have understood his brush with death and his inexplicable rebirth; he didn't understand it himself. That was why he had reintroduced himself to the community not as Lazarus, but as Levi Yoder. It almost felt as if he'd been born anew.

"Brother Levi, Brother Levi!" Jebediah, a rambunctious eight-year-old boy, ran breathlessly into his father's old barn, yelling for him in Pennsylvania Dutch. "Brother Levi, an English was here! It was the postman, and he left something for you."

Levi dipped his head into the barrel and squeezed the water from his face and beard. *What outsider would even know I exist?* Aloud, he asked, "He left something?"

The excitable blond child nodded emphatically and waved a sealed envelope. "He brought it in a car even!"

Levi wiped his hands dry on his pants, retrieved the sealed envelope and saw that it had come from the bank. Withdrawing the dagger he'd received long ago from Master Oyama, he sliced opened the envelope and read the folded paper.

Mr. Yoder,

There seems to be some complications with the inactive account you'd held at our bank.

Please stop by at your earliest convenience so we can talk about what I've learned from the banking archives.

Levi glanced at Jebediah. The boy stood next to him with a curious expression plastered on his face. He arched up on his tiptoes and tried to read the letter.

"Do you know if anybody's going into town soon?" Levi asked.

The boy nodded enthusiastically. "I just saw Elijah hooking up the wagon to deliver cheese to the Lancaster farmer's market. Should I tell him to wait for you?"

Levi turned to the forge and grabbed one of the metal rakes. "Yes, please. I'll bank the fire and be out there in a moment."

As Jebediah's footfalls receded, Levi wondered what kind of "complications" he had waiting for him at the bank.

Levi sat next to Elijah who flicked the reins. Their open carriage was heavily laden with several hundred pounds of cheeses and other goods for the Central Market. As they rolled along the paved road heading away from the farms, Levi sighed wistfully. He remembered when he was Elijah's age. The mid-teens was when many Amish kids made major decisions about their lives.

Levi had always been a nightmare for his parents. He would often wander past the other farms to see what the nearby town had to offer; on a few occasions he convinced some of the other boys to skip the afternoon chores, borrow a buggy, and watch a football game at the nearest high school. So nobody was surprised when he decided to leave the community. In fact, he was pretty sure that the few who still remembered him were shocked that he'd returned.

Levi turned to Elijah. "You're seventeen, right? What are your plans?"

"Deliver the cheese and the baskets of squash, I suppose." Elijah rubbed at his nose with the back of his hand.

Levi laughed. "No, I meant what are your plans for the future?"

Elijah scratched at the first hints of stubble on his chin and seemed to ponder the question for a moment. "Well, I am seventeen, so I'll get married soon enough, and with God's blessings I suppose I'll eventually save enough to get land of my own." He turned to Levi with an inscrutable expression. "I heard someone say that you've lived with the English for a long time. What are *your* plans?"

Levi was taken aback by the question, and frowned. What *were* his plans? "It's true that I've spent a lot of time with the English. I suppose I'm not yet sure what I'll do. It's something I have to think about."

The wagon's wheels made a smooth rumbling as they entered the outskirts of the town, and they fell into silence. As the wagon moved through the city, Levi worried about whether his instincts had been right in coming back here to Amish country. Sure, it had been his home, but it didn't have the same feel as places like New York or Tokyo—not by a long shot. He tried to imagine living here for the rest of his life, and the thought made his stomach turn. Going back to his old life didn't seem right.

But if not here, then where?

Elijah pulled on the reins and pointed to a building on the right side of the street. "Isn't this where you needed to go?"

Levi nodded and gave Elijah a firm handshake. "Best wishes at the market, and thank you for the ride into town."

Levi sat on a brown leather hard-backed chair in the bank manager's office. The air felt uncomfortably cool.

As the bank manager closed the door and took a seat behind his desk, his wrinkled face frowned ever so slightly. But he cleared his throat and pasted on a pleasant expression.

"I'm very glad you came to visit, Mr. Yoder. These things are best handled face to face. I'll be frank. In my forty years in banking, I've never dealt with a case such as yours. You do realize that as far as our bank's concerned, you dropped off the face of the earth more than ten years ago?"

He'd had the same conversation with the men at the US embassy in Nepal. He'd gone through several days of interviews about his where-abouts and why he'd never renewed his passport or acquired additional visas. It certainly wasn't every day that a US citizen literally went walking through other countries for over a decade, carrying no identifi-cation, before deciding to suddenly reappear.

"Yes, Mr. Cornbluthe, I realize that I've been gone a long time, but I'm back now, and I want to start again where I left off." Levi pressed back against his chair. "What's the problem?"

The manager opened a manila folder, withdrew a printed sheet, and turned it so it faced Levi. "Mr. Yoder, this is a copy of the archive on your account. As you can see, at the time of your last transaction with us, you had a balance of $267,384.05.

"Quarterly deposits were made for the next three years from the Yoder Development Trust—"

"Yes," Levi said. "I'd arranged for regular dividends to be deposited for my wife's use. But she passed away." He pointed at a large deposit on the printout. "What's this? Is this some kind of mistake?"

The bank manager shook his head. "I have to assume it wasn't, since it's in the archive. But yes, three years after the dividends started, there was a deposit of nearly three million dollars—and then no further deposits. Prior to your arrival, I did some research, and could find no existing references to the Yoder Development Trust. Is it possible that the trust was dissolved, and the last payment was somehow part of the dissolution?" He raised his eyebrows quizzically.

"I have no idea." But he had a more important question to address. The last entry on the printout showed a debit of his entire balance—leaving him with nothing. "I never withdrew any money. Why does the account show a zero balance?"

Mr. Cornbluthe ran his finger along the inside of his collar. He pulled another sheet from the folder on his desk and cleared his throat yet again. "Are you familiar with New York abandoned property law, Mr. Yoder?"

Levi shook his head. His mouth became dry and he tightened his grip on the armrests of his chair.

With a deep sigh, the bank manager pushed a printed copy of the New York state abandoned property law statute toward him. "It seems that some official in the state of New York, where your account was opened, must have filed an abandonment claim to revert the funds back to the state. It looks like soon after the last deposit, our bank received an order of escheat for the funds contained in your account." The manager pointed at a location on the printout. "I'm afraid section 4b is what's most pertinent to your situation."

Levi read the statute.

. . .

NY State Abandoned Property Law Section 1406:4B

Such claim for abandoned property may be established only by a person, copartnership, unincorporated association or corporation who shall have had no actual knowledge of the escheat proceeding and who shall commence a proceeding in the supreme court within five years after the entry of the final order of escheat.

Levi had dealt with legal agreements before, and easily picked up the gist of the legalese. "So, New York State wanted my money. They filed a petition, which some judge signed off on, and the bank gave the state my money. And I had five years from that moment to protest." Levi stared coldly at the manager. "And because it's been over five years since that happened, I'm essentially out of luck. Is that your interpretation as well?"

"Y-yes, I'm afraid so. But I'm not a lawyer." The man's voice was strained, nervous. "All I do know is that there's really nothing the bank can do at this point. Our hands are tied."

With a hollow feeling in the pit of his stomach, Levi stared straight ahead, past the bank manager. He was stunned. He'd planned for those funds to finance the next steps of his life, whatever they might be, but now … everything had just changed.

A sense of bitter frustration flowed through him. He wished there was someone other than himself to put the blame on, but there wasn't. It had been his choice to go lose himself out there in the world—and now he was reaping the consequences.

"I have to start over," he muttered to himself.

"Excuse me?"

Levi stood and pointed at the bank statement. "May I keep this copy?"

"Of course—"

"Thank you." Levi grabbed the printout, opened the office door, and walked out.

~

Madison leaned back in her chair, listening on headphones to two women speaking in rapid-fire Russian. One of them was a Russian mobster's wife; the other was the first woman's sister.

"Masha, how's the baby? Does she still have a fever?"

"Sadly, yes, and she's fussing more than you can imagine."

Madison groaned. Her day had been spent listening to a number of conversations like this one, coming from the hundreds of monitored Russian phone lines.

She'd made it. She was finally an active member of the CIA. But the path had been much longer than she'd imagined it would be. She'd spent eighteen months going through the CIA's Clandestine Service Training program, where she'd learned the finer points of covert operations, and that had been followed by an additional nine months in advanced Russian language training, building on the working knowledge of Russian that she'd gained in the Navy.

But even though Madison was now in the Directorate of Operations, one of the few areas that focused on clandestine operations, she'd quickly realized there was much more to the intelligence community than the high-risk activities that an adrenaline junkie like her craved.

Like gathering human intelligence from monitored foreign communications.

Madison smiled ruefully as the conversation shifted from child care to complaints about the mobster's wife's sex life.

"My life as an operator." She chuckled as the phone call ended.

She clicked on the "notes" tab for the call and typed, "No HUMINT."

A light knock sounded on her office door, and Madison turned. A blonde woman stood in the doorway of her office.

"Hey, Maddie, you up for tennis after work? You and me playing doubles against Dennis and that hot cousin of his."

"Hey, Jen." Madison glanced at the clock. It was three p.m. "I'm up for it, but I've got a backlog of calls to go through still. Can we meet at six?"

"That'll work." The blonde agent motioned toward Madison's computer. "Anything interesting?"

Madison snorted. "Oh, the typical stuff. Some drunk Russian mobster threatened another mobster over some botched robbery. I can tell you all about the affair one mobster's wife is having with her not-so-gay hairdresser. It's riveting, let me tell you."

Jen smiled and nodded knowingly. "I know you hate being stuck in the office, but one day we'll get our wish and be up close and personal with some of these dirtbags. Besides, what did you think was going to happen when the higher-ups invested all that DoD Russian language training in you?"

Twirling a pen back and forth across her knuckles, Madison shrugged. "This girl knows all about paying her dues. I'll earn a trip someday."

The computer beeped; another phone call had landed in Madison's queue.

"Hey, let me get out of your hair," Jen said. "I'll come by later and see how things are going."

Madison waved as she turned back to her computer. This latest message had a red exclamation mark on it, indicating it had come from a priority-one location—a prior source of actionable intelligence.

She clicked on the message and leaned back with a notepad on her lap. A gravelly male voice began speaking in Russian.

"Katarina—I sent you the address. The target is Lazarus Yoder."

A woman's voice responded, sounding very cold, almost bored. *"Are you sure he's at the location? The last two times Vladimir sent me after this man, he'd already vanished."*

"He's there. I forwarded you the picture taken at the American embassy in Kathmandu. He entered the US at the Los Angeles airport, flew to Philadelphia, and took a taxi to his parents' farm in Lancaster,

Pennsylvania. One of our contacts drove by only eight hours ago and verified seeing him."

Madison furiously scribbled notes.

"Fine," the woman said. *"We just landed. I should be at the location in about three hours, and I'll be returning immediately after. Does Vladimir want a souvenir?"*

A souvenir? A chill raced up Madison's back as she imagined an ear or a finger being chopped off.

"No, nothing like that. Just make sure you've cleaned up, and for God's sake, don't do anything stupid like speed. We don't need—"

"I know what I'm doing, Dmitri. Tell Vladimir his problem is taken care of."

The call ended, and Madison lurched forward and hit a button on her desk phone.

Her supervisor's calm voice answered. *"Maddie, what's up?"*

With her heart racing, she finished scribbling down the details she'd just heard. "John, we just caught a communication from one of the priority-one lines. It sounds like someone named Vladimir has called in a hit for someone on US soil."

"Whoa, you're sure about this? When did the call come in?"

"It sure sounded like a hit to me." She clicked on the "details" link of the call and glanced at the clock hanging on her wall. "Looks like the call happened twenty minutes ago. Someone named Katarina is the hitter, and she just landed."

"Did we—"

"We've got a lock on the sat phone she was using. It's a Russian military signal that our folks have a decoder for. The GPS coordinates say New York City."

"Okay. Maddie, I need you to e-mail me the voice database number for the call and an exact translation of the conversation ASAP."

"Will do." Madison looked down at her scribbled notes. "They didn't give an address, but the target is someone named Lazarus Yoder, and it's his parents' farm—somewhere in Lancaster, Pennsylvania."

"Great job, Maddie. Turn that translation around to me, and I'll get some resources activated in Pennsylvania."

The smell of autumn was in the air, yet summer hadn't quite given up its grip as Levi trudged through a neighboring field that was lying fallow for the season. He wiped beads of sweat from his brow, his mind churning with what he'd just learned.

"Everything I worked for ... gone."

The idea of having to start over was aggravating, but it didn't bother him nearly as much as the time that had elapsed. It had been over a decade since he left the city. In that time, things would have changed, alliances shifted, friends grown distant.... Were his contacts still any good?

As he psyched himself up to make a decision, he was startled by the squawking of birds. A dozen crows were landing and taking off from the tobacco field between him and his family farm a quarter mile ahead.

Levi quickened his pace. His heartbeat thudded loudly in his chest and he instinctively lowered himself into a crouch, keeping his head below the height of the surrounding tobacco plants.

As he neared the cawing birds, he froze, sniffing the air.

Blood.

He drew a blade from a hidden sheath inside his vest and crept forward on the balls of his feet.

Breathing deeply, he unerringly followed the scent, pressing through the dense rows of green tobacco plants.

The coppery scent of blood was unmistakable as he came upon the body.

The body of a child.

With dread, Levi moved forward and crouched by the body.

His breath caught in his throat as he took in the child's blond hair and open-eyed expression of surprise.

Jebediah!

The boy's neck had been sliced open from ear to ear.

A flame of unmitigated fury bloomed within Levi as he crept past Jebediah and moved toward the farmhouse.

He tightened his grip on the dagger as he pushed through the last row of tobacco plants. Another body lay on the ground not even ten feet from the entrance to the barn he'd been working in hours earlier.

It was one of the neighbor's boys; Levi didn't know his name. He, too, had had his throat sliced open, and his lifeblood was pooled all around him.

Levi panned his gaze in every direction, searching for movement. There was none.

Who could have done such a thing?

Serious crime was practically unheard of in the Amish community.

His heartbeat thudded loudly in his ears as he scanned the ground around the body. When he spotted a footprint near the congealing pool of dark-red blood, overwhelming anger washed over him.

No Amish cobbler had created the shoe that had made that print.

This was the act of an outsider.

The front portion of the footprint was pressed deeper into the ground, clearly indicating a man in motion.

Levi's skin tingled as he sniffed the air, employing all of his senses to help. He sensed the fragrance of lavender. It was too late in the season for lavender to be in bloom. He followed the scent, and soon spotted more footprints leading away from the barn.

The lessons he'd learned from the seasons he'd spent in Australia with an aboriginal tracker were aiding him now. He realized that tracking a murderer was no different than tracking game.

The tracks clearly showed a man racing from the scene. The crushed strands of grass and shifted soil underneath were all he needed. Levi raced ahead. The image of Jebediah's shocked and lifeless face loomed large in his mind.

And then he heard the sirens.

He paused, his eyes tracking the footsteps to the gravel road as three Lancaster County Police cars came to an abrupt halt only fifty yards ahead of him.

A police officer ducked behind the open door of his vehicle and shouted, "Drop your weapon and put your hands up above your head!"

Levi's eyes tracked the footsteps to the gravel road, and from there traced the tire tracks leading away from the farm. He pointed at the road heading north. "Someone murdered two people, and it looks like he got into a car and headed that way!"

"Drop your weapon now!" another officer yelled through a bullhorn.

Levi dropped the dagger and held up his hands. As a pair of policemen, weapons drawn, approached him, he shouted, "Aren't you going to go after the car? A murderer is getting away!"

One of the policemen kept his gun trained on Levi's chest while the other holstered his weapon, pulled Levi's arms behind his back and handcuffed his wrists together. More sirens blared in the distance.

Levi ground his foot into the gravel with frustration. "Why are you arresting me? I just found two people dead, and there are tracks leading from one of the bodies to this road. What the hell is wrong with you people?"

One of the officers approached Levi and took a small spiral-bound notebook out of his shirt pocket and flipped it open. "Sir, there was a murder reported at this location, and we found you brandishing a weapon. You're currently not under arrest, but for now, we're detaining you for your safety as well as ours. You said two murders?"

Levi pulled against his restraints, barely suppressing the urge to release a primal scream of frustration.

As other policemen arrived, one of the neighbors cried out in alarm and yelled in Pennsylvania Dutch, "Holy mother of God, Jebediah!"

"Near the edge of the tobacco field," Levi said, "there's a dead little boy. His name was Jebediah." A lump grew in his throat, and he blinked away tears of anger and frustration.

The policeman's voice was steady. "Do you know a Lazarus Yoder, and if so, when's the last time you've seen him?"

Levi stared dumbly at the man's inscrutable expression. "Of course I know him. I'm Lazarus Yoder."

The officer's expression turned grim. "Oh, well in that case Mr. Yoder, you *are* under arrest."

Levi's back stiffened, and he glared at the officer. "What for?"

The two policemen began walking Levi to the nearest police car.

"Mr. Yoder, we received word that a Lazarus Yoder had gone crazy and had begun killing his family—"

"That's a lie!" Levi dug his heels into the ground, rage surging through him.

The policemen tightened their grips and dragged him forward.

"Who's accusing me?" Levi asked as he was shoved into the back of the police car.

The officers closed the door without answering. One of them walked around to the driver's side and climbed behind the wheel.

Gritting his teeth, Levi tried again. "I know it doesn't matter what I say, but can you at least tell me who accused me of doing this?"

As the officer turned the car around on the gravel road, he looked at Levi in the rearview mirror. "We received an anonymous tip. That's all I know."

Levi wracked his brain, trying to think of anyone in his past who might have had it in for him.

Due to his activities in New York, he'd made his share of enemies, but he never would have thought any of them would pull something like this—and certainly not so many years later.

His shoulders slumped, and he let his head fall back against the headrest, feeling defeated.

Despite his Amish upbringing, Levi had never felt a personal connection to God. But as the police car drove down the road, he closed his eyes and prayed.

CHAPTER FIVE

"Hey, Dennis, great game." Madison bumped fists with her co-worker, a senior agent at the agency.

Dennis was in his late thirties, and his black hair was just starting to get early touches of gray near his temples. He was fit, handsome, and a sweetheart of a guy. Definitely the kind of guy Madison would be attracted to. But sadly for her, he was gay.

He smiled and wiped his face with a hand towel. "Lewis, you need to come out more often. That serve of yours needs work, but damn, girl, your overhead smash is like a bullet."

Jen jogged over. "Hey, she's *my* doubles partner. Don't you get any ideas about stealing her." She draped an arm over Madison's shoulder and led her to the benches where they'd left their gym bags.

"That was fun." Madison grabbed a towel and wiped her face. She leaned against the back of the bench and stretched her legs. "I should probably come out more often. I need the exercise."

Jen waved dismissively. "You're built like a freaking gazelle. I never once saw you stop to catch your breath." Jen had a power-lifter's body, but Madison realized the woman did get winded during long rallies.

Dennis called from the other side of the tennis court. "Hey, you two up for another match next Thursday?"

Jen looked over at Madison. "You said you needed the exercise …"

Madison didn't have to think too hard. It wasn't as if she had much of a social life anyway. "If you're up for it, I suppose Thursday evening is fine with me."

Jen yelled back over to Dennis. "Probably. Let's sync up on Wednesday to make sure."

Dennis waved as he gathered his stuff. His younger cousin was next to him, changing out of his sweaty shirt.

Jen nudged Madison and made a purring noise. "Maddie, look at that six-pack. Oh, what I wouldn't do to—"

"Jen! He just graduated college. You're old enough to—"

"Teach him a few things," Jen said with a laugh.

Madison smiled. They were both thirty, but Jen loved to flirt with pretty much any eligible man she felt attracted to, regardless of age. Madison, by contrast, hadn't dated anyone since she'd left the Navy, and even though she'd welcome someone new in her life, men who were nearly a decade younger than her weren't on the menu.

Her phone buzzed in her bag. She pulled it out. "Hello?"

"Maddie, it's John Maddox. Can you talk?"

She hopped to her feet and walked away from the bench. Her boss never called her. "Yes, I can talk. What's up?"

"I'm sorry to interrupt whatever you're doing. There have been some developments on the case you referred to me earlier today. I'm organizing a team to work on it, and that's about all I can say on an open line. This is time-sensitive. Can you come in tonight? Like, now?"

An electric tingle of excitement rushed through Madison as she walked back to the bench and grabbed her gym bag. "I'm sweating and in a tennis skirt, but I can be there in fifteen minutes."

"That's perfect. Most of us are already here. We'll wait on you."

Madison couldn't keep the smile off her face as she mouthed to Jen, *I have to go to work.*

Jen returned her smile and waved her away.

Madison jogged toward her car. "I'm getting in the car now."

"Great. See you in a few."

Madison stood in front of the conference room door and frowned. The badge reader refused to recognize her ID card.

"Damn it." She wiped both sides of the card on her skirt and reinserted it. The LED on the reader blinked rapidly … then buzzed again, denying her entry.

With a huff, Madison yanked out her card.

She retrieved her phone and was about to double-check the conference room number when another agent walked up. He pushed lightly on the conference room door, and it opened. "Are you going in?"

"What the hell?" Madison pointed at the badge reader.

The agent smiled. "Oh, that. The badge reader isn't working. We called it in."

"Gah!" Feeling like a total tool, Madison stomped into the conference room. The glances she got from some of the others didn't help; she felt more than a bit self-conscious about being at work in an all-too-short tennis skirt.

Maddox was standing at the far end of the room. "Lewis, you made it! All right then. Everyone take a seat and let's get this started."

Madison sat in the nearest chair and realized she'd never been in a conference room with so many other agents at the same time. There were a dozen people arrayed around the long oak table, half of whom she'd never seen before. A screen was coming down from the ceiling behind Maddox, displaying the image of someone's laptop screen—complete with wallpaper of a kitten playing with a ball of pink yarn.

The only person not seated was John Maddox, her supervisor. He was in his early fifties, very high strung and fidgety. He paced back and forth as he addressed the room.

"Okay folks, it's likely that not everyone here knows each other. That's not an issue. I'm John Maddox, senior supervisor, and I'll be point of contact for all details on this case. That means nothing leaves this room. Nothing is shared amongst yourselves unless it's in this type of closed-room setting. Any sharing happens on a need-to-know basis, and I'll be the only one determining the need to know, we got that?"

Everyone in the room nodded.

"Good. You've all gotten the transcripts that Agent Lewis"—he pointed at Madison—"gave us earlier today. We've had a foreign-initiated incident on American soil that has resulted in American lives being lost."

Madison's back stiffened.

Maddox pointed at the agent who had opened the door for her. "Anderson, bring the team up to speed on what we've collected so far."

Anderson nodded. "Yes, sir. As everyone knows, earlier today, a suspect flew into LaGuardia. We've determined that the plane was a Gulfstream G550, a private jet owned by a Saudi corporation named Al-Maseer. We're pretty sure it's a shell company. We're digging further to see who its true owner is.

"I managed to tap into the cameras from one of the neighboring hangars of the private jetway." Anderson typed on his laptop, and the screen at the front of the room showed a blurry image of a woman walking down the stairs from a sleek jet.

Madison studied the image, taking in the woman's red hair. The color was almost certainly artificial. Too red. Too shiny. Maybe a wig? With the dark glasses and ankle-length trench coat cinched tightly around her waist, she looked like a caricature of a Russian spy.

"As you can see," Anderson continued, "it's blurry, and with the distance, we didn't get enough of the face for any facial recognition software to get a hit." He tapped once more on the keyboard, and another image appeared, this one of a black sedan near the base of the stairs. "We did catch the vehicle's make and a partial license number. It was enough for us to ID it on one of the license plate readers on the New Jersey Turnpike. But the car is a dead end. It's a courtesy vehicle provided to the company by the private hangar service in La Guardia.

"And unfortunately, whoever the hitter is, she made it there before our folks could. I'm guessing the target she was after wasn't at the scene. Two youths were found dead. One, eight-year-old Jebediah

Yoder, was found deceased with deep lacerations across the neck, cutting all of the significant blood vessels."

Madison gripped the armrests of her chair. An eight-year-old, being slaughtered? A simmering anger brewed within her. She didn't even hear what Anderson said about the second victim.

"However, our hitter wasn't done with those two," the agent continued. "We intercepted a call originating from the hitter's satellite phone to the Lancaster County PD. The voice used a scrambler, but she pinned the killings on a Lazarus Yoder. He's been picked up by the police and booked into lockup at the county jail."

Maddox stopped pacing and pointed at two of the agents next to him. "Smith and Rollins, have the NYPD and Lancaster PD intelligence bureaus check what they have on Lazarus Yoder. Let's see if they've got anything." He then turned toward another group of agents on the far side of the table. "Hsiung, Calloway, and Radcliffe, reach out to the FBI and Port Authority. We need that plane grounded. But for God's sake, don't let those assholes turn the hangar into a fortress. This lady's willing to kill kids, and I'll bet you she's got other options for escape if we scare her away. Keep tracking her through that sat phone, because right now, that's our priority lead."

Madison's heart raced as Maddox turned to her.

"Lewis," he said, "I need you to do some research. Dig up anything you can on this Lazarus Yoder guy. Scour our files and check with the FBI. Why do the Russians want him? For all we know, it was never about hitting him, maybe it was getting him out of the way. Why would they set him up? There's something we're missing."

Maddox glanced up at the clock on the wall and smacked his hands together. "It's eight p.m., and these are all 'need to be done yesterday' assignments. Any issues, come to me immediately." He glanced around the room. "It's going to be a long night. Any questions?"

No one spoke up.

Maddox pointed at the door. "Okay then. Those of you with assignments, the truth's out there. Go get me some of it. The rest of you, stay put."

The last words the prison guard had said as he motioned for Levi to enter his holding cell were, "A guard will come by in the morning and take you boys to the intake unit for medical and classification."

Levi had been searched, had had his possessions cataloged and stored, and had been put in a holding cell for hours. Now, dressed in blue prison scrubs, he was being escorted by a guard along the edge of an open commons area on the ground floor of a multi-story section of Lancaster County Prison. The lights were dimmed, and the place smelled of pine-scented cleaning detergent, sweat, and urine.

Levi had spent much of his adulthood skirting along the edges of the law, but he'd always managed to avoid doing things that would have landed him in one of these places. Still, he'd associated with people who'd spent years behind bars, and he'd heard their stories. Now, as he walked through the cellblock, their tales all came rushing back.

"Don't you ever let them see you weak. You'll get eaten up, that's for sure ..."

"Avoid the skinheads. They're all pussies and will stick a shiv in you soon as you turn your back."

"Keep to your own kind."

Holding a set of sheets and a blanket for his bed, Levi straightened to his full six-foot height and kept his gaze straight ahead as he walked past the cells. He formulated strategies for worst-case scenarios and paid careful attention to his surroundings.

There were cells all along the four sides of the housing unit, each facing the central commons area. Other than a couple dozen chairs lined up in perfect rows—and probably bolted to the floor—and a few TVs encased in metal cages high up on some of the pillars, the commons area was mostly empty space.

The guard halted in front of a cell and raised his arm. The metal gate retracted. "In you go." The guard placed a large beefy hand on Levi's shoulder and pushed him inside. The electric whir of an unseen motor closed the iron-barred door behind him.

The cell was about six feet by eight, with a metal toilet and sink combination on the left-hand side of the room. On the right, Levi spied a rudimentary metal bunkbed with a thin rubberized mattress.

After dumping the folded bedsheet and cover onto the mattress, Levi sat cross-legged on the bed. He leaned against the cinderblock wall and closed his eyes.

He felt the gamut of human emotions. His fear of being in jail transformed into anger over being falsely accused of murder—and then, as he thought of the dead kids, he was overcome by sadness.

But among the skills Levi had picked up in his wanderings were the meditation techniques he'd learned from Guru Sinjali. Levi used those skills now. He closed his eyes and cleared his mind. He let all of the images and thoughts of the day drain away.

A soothing calm washed over him, and his senses expanded.

He focused on his surroundings.

He heard the steady breathing coming from others in the cellblock. Just beyond his hearing were fragments of sound that he knew were whispers in the darkness—which he'd been told was not allowed during lights out.

And then there were the smells, which reminded him that the place wasn't remotely clean. The mattress he was sitting on smelled of its last occupant. A metallic scent hung in the air. Copper? The plumbing fixtures? Blood? He wasn't sure.

The tension in his body continued to drain away.

He had been put in this cell at around midnight, but as he sat, it was almost as if he could sense the sun beginning to peek above the horizon. And then the click of an electronic circuit announced the slow opening of his cell door, along with all of the other cell doors on this floor.

He opened his eyes. It was morning.

Levi hopped up onto the balls of his feet and stretched.

Some prisoners wandered into the commons area. One tossed a furtive glance in his direction, then quickly looked away. But another walked right up to the entrance to Levi's cell.

Remembering the advice he'd been given, Levi stared directly at the behemoth. He was easily a half-foot taller than Levi, and outweighed him by maybe a hundred pounds. His head was shaved, and two scars ran down the right side of his face. His cauliflower-shaped ears hinted at many prior fights. Maybe he was a former wrestler?

The man's gaze shifted from Levi to his unmade bed. He smiled.

Two other men joined the first, and a tickle of anxiety flooded through Levi. He felt his heart rate increase.

Was he better off inside a confined cell or out in the open?

One of the men whispered to the others, loud enough for Levi to hear, "This will be easy."

He'd spoken in Russian.

"What do you want?" Levi asked in English, his voice steady with a hint of a challenge.

The behemoth glared. "You new here." He spoke with a thick Russian accent. "We have welcome for you."

Two more joined, making five men in total. One of them laughed and said, also in Russian, "So, Vladimir wants this one taken care of? He's a pretty one."

Levi felt the adrenaline dump into his bloodstream. He stepped up to the doorway, which was blocked by the three-hundred-pound, shaved-head gorilla. "Get out of my way," he growled.

The behemoth's eyes narrowed. He growled in Russian, "Let's do this."

Levi didn't wait for the Russians to make the first move. He snapped a devastating front kick to the gorilla's solar plexus. A whoosh of air blew out of the man as the wind was forced from his lungs.

When he bent over, Levi grabbed the back of the man's head and slammed it into his rising knee.

The sound of facial bones cracking echoed in the cell, and warm blood splashed on Levi's pants.

One down.

The other four men immediately rushed into the cell, and for a brief moment, it seemed like everything had slowed down.

One of the men reached for Levi, a jail-made razor in his hand.

Levi caught the attacker's wrist and squeezed hard on the joint.

A look of pain bloomed across the man's face, and the weapon dropped from his hand.

Still holding the man's wrist, Levi smashed his other palm against his attacker's elbow. He felt the tendons pop and tear as the arm bent in the wrong direction.

The man shrieked as he stumbled back over the gorilla's body.

Two down.

A burning sensation ripped through Levi's side. Instinctively, he responded with a back-fist into another attacker's face.

The man wheeled his arms and fell backward. The back of his head struck the steel toilet with a sickening crunch.

Three down.

Levi felt himself smile as he saw apprehension on the faces of the two remaining men.

He feinted toward the man on the left, but instead kicked the other's leg out from under him.

Red lights began flashing, and an alarm rang out across the jailhouse.

Without pause, Levi slammed a kick at the downed man's face and whirled around, smashing an elbow into the face of his last standing comrade.

Four and five down.

Levi pressed his hand against the right side of his chest. His palm came back wet and sticky with his own blood.

His adrenaline abated as guards clad in riot gear rushed Levi's cell and shoved him against the wall. One of them muttered, "Holy shit."

With his face pressed hard against the cinderblock, Levi yelled, "These guys attacked me! One of them cut me with a razor!"

"John," said a guard, "one of these guys is dead. You two, get that guy to the infirmary—he's bleeding everywhere."

Grabbing Levi by both arms, two guards led him from his cell, avoiding the bodies that littered the floor. One of the guards shook his head. "Don't know what you did to piss off those Russians, but you're going to cost us hours of paperwork."

With the side of his chest burning, Levi wasn't about to argue. Besides, he was busy combing his memories, trying to figure out what he'd done to piss off any Russians.

~

This time when Madison inserted her badge into the reader, a green LED lit, and the lock to the conference room door clicked open. It was still five minutes before the meeting was scheduled to start, but she found Jen already seated at the table inside.

"Hey girl," Madison said. "You got invited to the party as well?"

"Yup."

A video was playing at the front of the conference room. It was of a man doing a kata, a martial arts exercise used to hone concentration and simulate combat sequences. Katas were something Madison was very familiar with—she'd been practicing martial arts since she was a kid—and this man's moves were smoother, more fluid than anything she'd ever seen before.

She took a seat next to Jen and nudged her friend, who was staring at the video. "Stop it or your eyes will bug out."

Jen glanced only briefly at Madison before returning her attention to the bearded martial artist. "Oh my god, the guy makes me feel like Sandy in that song 'Summer Nights.'"

"What are you talking about? You mean from *Grease*?"

"You know, 'He ran by me, got me all damp.'"

"Jen!" Madison lightly smacked her friend's shoulder. "Eww! And that's not how that lyric goes."

"Shush. Just look at him."

Madison studied the man's face. "Oh shit, that's the Yoder guy! I recognize him from the passport image I got on him."

"He's delicious."

Madison smiled at her friend's never-ending appreciation of the opposite sex. Yoder was shirtless, and a long bandage covered the right side of his chest. His well-chiseled body was perfectly proportioned, and from what she could see of his face, he was handsome. *Really* handsome. The kind of guy Jen would be all over in an instant—and the type Madison would never have the nerve to approach. Yet this guy was a target of the Russian mob. Almost certainly a shiny apple with a rotten core.

The conference room door opened, and John Maddox walked in with another agent—a stone-faced man Madison had seen before, but had never exchanged a word with.

"Okay," said Maddox, taking a seat in front of the screen, "let's get this started—I've got another meeting right after this. Agent Lancaster, why don't you begin? What happened to our assassin?"

Without even looking at her notes, Jen shifted her gaze to Maddox and explained, "Right, the hitter. She remains a Jane Doe—we still have no ID on her. No identifying forensic evidence was left at the scenes of the murders. She'd arrived in LaGuardia, and we expected her to take the same path back. We alerted the FBI as well as the Port Authority, but the hitter took a detour. But instead of taking the three-hour trip back to New York, she made a beeline for a private jet that was fueled and ready for takeoff in Philadelphia. We knew this thanks to the GPS locator on her sat phone, but before we could scramble any resources to intercept, she'd taken off in a Bombardier Global 6000."

Maddox leaned back in his chair and frowned. "Do we know who owns that jet? That's no run-of-the-mill Cessna. They're more than fifty million dollars each."

"Actually, the Bombardier is roughly sixty million," Jen said, "and the Gulfstream they used in New York was about the same. As to who owns the Bombardier, it's the same shell company as the other, a Saudi outfit called Al-Maseer. And we've confirmed it *is* a shell company— the address is actually the location of a government building in Riyadh. It seems doubtful that the Saudi government would collude with elements of the Russian mob to take hits on US citizens, but we're still working on tracking the ownership."

"Did they file a flight plan?"

"Yes, but that could be changed midflight. For now, the hitter looks like she's heading toward Moscow."

"Thank you, Lancaster. Now, regarding the hitter's target." Maddox hitched his thumb to the video still playing on the screen behind him. "That's the most recent video we have of Lazarus Yoder. It was taken an hour ago in the jailhouse infirmary. Agent Lewis, what do you have on this Yoder guy?"

With that video playing behind Maddox, Madison found she couldn't concentrate—so she looked down at her notes as she spoke. "I'll start from the beginning. IRS records show that he was a self-employed contractor. We don't have anything to show where his income truly came from, but he self-reported roughly eighty thousand dollars per year—"

"Which probably means he was making triple that," Maddox remarked wryly.

Madison continued. "He had no FBI file whatsoever, and as far as I can tell, not even a parking ticket. Roughly twelve years ago, his wife died in a car crash, and that's where things go awry.

"For the next twelve years, we have absolutely no records on him. In fact, he was declared dead by the state of New York, and all of his assets reverted back to the state.

"It was only a few weeks ago when he appeared out of nowhere at our embassy in Nepal and presented himself for a passport to return home. His prints checked out, and as far as we can tell he went back to his parents' farm."

"And that's when we all got involved," Maddox said.

Madison nodded. "Pretty much. I didn't find anything having to do with Russia in any of his records. His wife was an Iranian refugee who'd come here under a humanitarian visa."

Maddox leaned forward, putting his elbows on the table. "Well, he's got ties to the Russian mob or they wouldn't be so hell-bent to kill him. Lancaster, did you manage to get anything regarding the jail thing?" He tilted his head toward the video behind him.

"Yup, it's kind of crazy. I managed to piece together a timeline from the booking records and what I got out of the warden. Basically he got booked last night and he 'accidentally' got placed in general population before even being fully processed. Obviously, he was set up by someone on the inside. I'm checking with the folks in the Utah Datacenter to see if we have any records of the calls or e-mails going into the jailhouse and its staff, but evidently, not everything is recorded as it should be.

"Anyway, as soon as the day started, a bunch of Russians, who are all suspected to have ties to the Russian mob, attacked Mr. Yoder. It didn't quite work out the way they were hoping."

"Is that what the bandage is about?" Madison asked.

"Yes. First thing in the morning, five guys tried to steamroll Yoder in his cell. One ended up dead, another is in a coma and may not make it, and three others have assorted broken parts."

Madison felt the blood drain from her face. She watched Lazarus Yoder practicing a kata. His expression seemed almost serene. How could he be so centered, having just killed someone with his bare hands? Sure, it was self-defense, but still.

"Anything else?" Maddox asked.

"The Russians didn't say much before they attacked him, but Yoder reported to the staff that one of the Russians mentioned someone named Vladimir wanting him taken care of."

Maddox's eyes widened a bit.

"Anyway," Jen finished. "One of the assailants did manage to cut him along the side. That's why he's in the infirmary and not in solitary."

Maddox turned in his seat and stared at the fluid motions of the martial artist. "Lewis, you've got a background in martial arts. What can you tell me about what we're seeing?"

Madison followed the man's movements. "He's trained in multiple forms ... and he's really good. I'm only really practiced at karate, but those exercises he's performing ... well, some of his moves are derived from Wing Chun, which is a form of kung fu. I also see influences from karate, and ... some of those movements I don't recognize."

"With what happened at the jailhouse, it's pretty obvious this guy knows how to fight—"

"No, this guy is ..." Madison watched the prisoner float from low to high, stretching and flowing from a backhand strike to a stylized kick. His motions were effortless, as if gravity didn't affect him. "He's a master of whatever he's doing," she said. "I've been practicing karate since I was a kid. I'm a third-degree black belt, but I've only really gotten to the point where I'd reasonably be considered a sensei, a teacher. This guy doesn't just know the moves, he's mastered their essence, as if he's ... living them. All I know is, I wouldn't want to go up against him. Certainly not without a gun and lots of distance."

Maddox nodded. "Well, considering that gash he got treated for, he doesn't seem too much worse for wear. I think we need to make sure it stays that way."

Madison shifted her gaze back to her supervisor. Was he getting Yoder transferred?

"Lancaster, I assume everything you've told me is in my inbox right now?"

"Yup."

"Okay, I'll make a few calls. We know this guy is sitting in jail for something he had nothing to do with, but we can't jeopardize our investigation. I'll talk to one of my contacts at the US Marshals Service. The Russians wants this guy pretty damned badly. I strongly suspect Yoder knows why." Maddox turned toward the agent who'd walked in with him. "Jenkins, I need you on a flight to Pennsylvania right away. You'll meet up with one of the marshals and accompany him to the jail. I need you to be this guy's tail. Who he meets with, where he goes, et cetera. You got me?"

Jenkins nodded. "Will do."

Maddox turned back to Madison. "Lewis, I'll make arrangements with some contacts in the jail. This guy will have a few different tracking devices on him before he's set free. I'll need you to keep an eye on where he is at all times. You're Jenkins's electronic backup. If he loses sight of Yoder, he'll need help syncing back up with him. You up for it?"

"Absolutely," Madison responded, trying hard to suppress her excitement.

"Okay folks, that's it for now. This guy's our lead on more than just this hitter case, so let's not lose track of him. I'll be expending some credit pulling all these strings at once, so let's not screw it up. Now get a move on. Lewis, I'll forward you the tracking IDs as soon as I have them."

As soon as Maddox and Jenkins had filed out of the conference room, Jen elbowed Madison and whispered, "I wish Maddox would have sent me instead of Jenkins."

Madison smiled at her friend, but her thoughts were elsewhere. She had monitored all variety of scum around the world without giving thought to how dangerous some of these people might be. But this Yoder guy …

Her mind floated back to his serene demeanor. Any man who could kill someone and look as calm as that only hours later … was capable of anything.

She wondered if she'd have what it took to do what Jenkins was tasked with. A shiver raced up her back.

I'm not sure.

CHAPTER SIX

Madison leaned back on Jen's couch, pressed the mute button on the TV remote, and put her cell phone to her ear. "Hi, Nana, how are you doing?"

"Oh honey, it's so good to hear your voice. I didn't call too late, did I?"

"It's fine, Nana. But you have to remember, it's three hours later here."

"Oh my! That means it's almost one a.m. over there! Baby, I'm so sorry. It's just that the day got away from me, and we hadn't talked yet this week—"

"It's okay. I'm over at Jen's anyway. We're watching TV."

"Is that the girl you said you worked with on ... I can't remember, where did you say you work?"

"Yup, we both work at the same place. It's a think tank. We do foreign policy research and stuff." Madison felt bad lying to her grandmother, but it was easier on everyone involved if Nana believed Madison was some kind of political wonk.

"So, how have you adjusted to Washington? Dating anyone yet? I don't mean to pry, but I just worry that you're a girl all by yourself with no family nearby."

Madison rolled her eyes and leaned her head back against the sofa. "I'm fine. And I'm dating now and then, but nothing too serious. How are you doing? How's Uncle George and Aunt Esther and the kids?"

"Oh, we're all just fine. Do you have any idea when you might be coming back home for a visit? We all miss you."

Jen waved at Madison from the kitchen, pointed at a bottle of amaretto, and made a drinking motion. Madison smiled and nodded.

"I'm not sure, Nana. Right now I'm pretty busy. Hopefully I'll get some time during the holidays, but I can't promise."

"Baby, I just worry about you is all."

"I know. But trust me, everything's fine. Hey, Jen and I were about to watch a movie—can we talk later?"

"Of course. Have a good time with your friend ... and you know, I'd understand if your friend was something a bit more. I mean, if you didn't like boys all that much—"

"Nana!" Madison sat up straight. "I told you before, that's not the issue."

"Okay, okay. I just want you to understand that I'd be okay with it. Well, maybe not okay right away, but I'd understand. Your cousin Freddy is that way, and his husband is just a wonderful man."

"Trust me, Nana. I like boys just fine."

Jen approached with two etched crystal glasses filled with amaretto sour. She was grinning from ear to ear.

Madison had to turn away to keep from laughing.

"Well, I love you, baby. Say hi to your friend for me. You'll call next week?"

"I will. Love you, Nana."

"Love you too."

Madison ended the call and laughed as Jen passed her an amaretto sour.

"Let me guess," Jen said. "Your grandmother asked if you're a lesbian?"

Madison took a sip and nodded.

Jen sat next to her and unmuted the TV. "I get the same crap from my dad," she said. "I swear, you'd think being thirty and single was a crime or something."

"Well, we both have pretty traditional parents—and my nana is more so than most."

The satellite TV in Jen's apartment offered one of the Russian TV channels, and it was currently showing a live broadcast of one of the political debates for the upcoming Russian elections.

Madison pointed at the bald-headed minister yelling in Russian. "Which one is that?"

"That's Vladimir Koraloff. He's the one who has almost no chance. He's part of the so-called Patriots of Russia, a real left-wing whacko group that splintered off the Communist Party."

The other man at the podium, who looked like he was about to explode, was handsome despite the scar running along his cheekbone. "And the other one is Porchenko, right?"

"Yup," Jen said. "Vladimir Porchenko is a real asshole. He makes Putin look like Gandhi when it comes to international affairs. He's also ex-KGB and very much into bringing back Mother Russia to its glory days."

Madison shook her head. "I don't know how you keep track of the politics. They all seem nuts."

"It's kind of like a soap opera. Not much different than US politics, really. You just have to keep up with the story as it unfolds. Most of what everyone says is bullshit, but it's oftentimes what they don't say that you have to pay attention to." Jen pointed at Porchenko, who'd just started talking. "Just listen to him; he's the one everyone in the State Department is worried about grabbing power."

The dark-haired man slammed his fist on the podium and yelled into the microphone in Russian. *"The current president and his lapdogs in the Duma can't see what's in front of their faces!*

"The American pigs are not complying with the START treaties! This so-called strategic arms reduction treaty is strategic only if both sides comply, and the Americans cannot be trusted to keep their end of the bargain. They refuse independent observers, and we're supposed to take them on their word? I think not! We must reinvest our resources

into our defenses, or we'll just become their lapdogs like the rest of the world."

"Yup, he's just a bundle of joy," Madison remarked.

Jen pointed her drink at the TV. "You have to admit, it doesn't get much better on a Friday night: two hot babes drinking by themselves, listening to two middle-aged Russian idiots yelling at each other."

Madison laughed and held her drink toward Jen. They clinked their glasses. "I can think of lots worse places to be than here."

"I don't understand," Levi complained as two guards escorted him down a well-lit jailhouse corridor. "Why can't you tell me who I'm meeting?"

Despite the cool temperature, a bead of sweat trickled down the back of his neck. Anxiety washed over him. His wrists and ankles were bound, and he had only enough slack to shuffle along, his chains clanking noisily. And his burly escorts refused to give him any answers.

They passed several guarded checkpoints. This part of the jail was quiet, far away from the raucous noise of the inmates.

Maybe I'm being taken to my arraignment?

It had been three days since the attack in his cell, and Levi had been kept in isolation in the medical wing the entire time. The side of his chest itched, serving as a constant reminder of the roughly ninety stitches they'd used to close the eighteen-inch gash. And now the guards had unceremoniously trussed him up like a Thanksgiving turkey while refusing to say a word to him about why, or where he was going.

"Is this for my bail hearing?"

He'd been told that he'd see a judge the day after he was booked, but then again, he had been told a lot of things that hadn't come to pass. And even if he got bail, he no longer had funds to pay it. He couldn't exactly expect his family to bail him out. As far as he knew, his family believed he'd killed those two kids.

The guards stopped in front of a door, opened it, and motioned for him to enter.

Levi took in a deep breath and let it out slowly. Then he walked inside.

A large man in a dark polo and windbreaker with a US Marshals logo on it sat on the other side of a table. He looked up as Levi entered. "Please, Mr. Yoder, take a seat."

Levi sat on the only other chair. "What's this about?"

The marshal rose and walked around the table. "Mr. Yoder, I'm afraid there's been a mix-up in your case." He retrieved a set of keys from his pocket and began unlocking the shackles around Levi's ankles. "We've gotten evidence that exonerates you, and I'm here to escort you from the premises."

Levi was at a loss for words.

It can't be true, can it?

He'd pretty much convinced himself that he was going to have an extended stay in prison for something he hadn't done.

The marshal proceeded to unlock the cuffs around Levi's wrists. "Unfortunately, I don't have it within my power to address the irregularities associated with your imprisonment and the attack you experienced. Suffice it to say, the state is not bringing any charges against you regarding the incident in your cell. The others involved in the attack will be given due process, but they'll almost certainly see their sentences increased."

The door to the room opened, and a guard entered and placed a package on the table. It was a clear plastic bag with a yellow printed sticker with Levi's name on it, and it contained his clothes and other possessions.

When the guard left, Levi said, "So I'm free to go?"

The marshal dumped Levi's shackles on the table. "Yes. Go ahead and get changed."

Levi began changing out of his prison garb.

"I'm authorized to get you a bus or train ticket to pretty much anywhere you need to go in the area," the marshal said. "If you like, I'll take you to your family's farm myself."

Levi flashed back to the bloody scene at his family's farm. "Have they found who committed those murders?"

"I don't think so. The only information I received on your case was that you'd been exonerated and it had been arranged for you to be released."

Levi shrugged into his black vest and did his best to ignore the discomfort from his stitches.

"So … did you want me to drive you back home?"

Slipping his shoes on, Levi shook his head. If someone was after him, the last thing he wanted was to be anywhere near his family. "No. I've caused my family enough trouble as it is. Can you get me a train ticket to New York?"

"Why New York?"

"It's far from home and a place I'm familiar with." Levi patted at his overcoat and frowned. "I had several knives on me when the police took me in, one of which had sentimental value. Do you know where they might be?"

The marshal shook his head. "I'm afraid not. I can follow up with the arresting officer, if you like."

Levi gritted his teeth as he imagined the cop pawning the knife he'd carried since he'd left Japan. "Please do. I'd hate to … it's just been with me for a long time."

"I'll look into it." The marshal withdrew an envelope from his windbreaker and held it out to Levi. "This'll help to cover the expenses of the ticket—and probably a good couple meals as well."

Levi peered inside the envelope. It contained five one-hundred-dollar bills. He tucked it inside his vest pocket.

"You ready?" the marshal asked.

Levi tilted his head to the side; his neck cracked loudly. He took in a deep breath and let it out slowly. "As ready as I'll ever be."

The marshal opened a door on the other side of the room. "Let's go then. I'll drop you off at the Amtrak station. From there, you should be able to pick up a train that gets you to Grand Central or wherever else you want to go."

Within minutes, Levi was outside Lancaster County Prison. He took in a breath of fresh air and smiled.

Freedom.

~

Levi had nearly three hours to think as the train rolled from Lancaster to Newark. And thinking only increased his frustration.

Someone had killed his neighbors—had killed children. Someone had set him up to take the fall for the crime. And that same someone had tried to have him killed.

Someone Russian.

Levi felt certain that he'd never crossed paths with anyone in the Russian mob.

If it had been the Italians … there might be something there. But the Russians?

Whoever it was, they weren't messing around.

Neither was Levi.

As he stood in line at the Newark train station, a plan began to gel.

He moved forward in the line and handed the ticket agent a ten-dollar bill. "World Trade Center."

The machine in front of her spit out his ticket, and Levi got his change and began walking toward his train.

He had practically no money, and he hadn't talked to anyone he'd known in the city in well over a decade.

It was like he was eighteen again and starting from square one.

Well, not exactly square one.

He knew what the underbelly of the city looked like.

And he was about to dive headlong into it.

~

It was late afternoon when Levi finally arrived in the city. The familiar sights and sounds left him with a warm feeling of comfort.

This was his town.

The honking cars, Columbus Park, the smell of Chinatown as he ambled along Bayard Street, it was all like coming home again.

As he hung a left on Mulberry Street, something caught his eye.

He paused at the street corner and casually panned his gaze behind him, as if waiting for a crossing light to turn.

A crowd of elderly Chinese men were arguing among themselves. But they weren't what had drawn Levi's attention. No, it was the man behind them, his attention on his newspaper.

The man wore a Yankees jacket and a baseball cap. They were common enough clothes for this area, but Levi had noticed that same ensemble on a man who'd boarded the train in Lancaster moments after Levi did.

Coincidence?

Levi turned and continued along Mulberry. He increased his pace, as he passed Canal Street, then ducked into a dim sum joint. He stood at the counter, making a point to eyeball the menu, but really he was keeping an eye on the street.

"Sir, may I help you?"

The old man behind the counter had a strong accent that made obvious his first-generation Chinese immigrant status.

"Do you have a rear exit?" Levi asked in well-practiced Mandarin.

The old man raised his eyebrows and nodded. "Is there a problem?" he asked in his native tongue. He sounded worried.

Feeling a bit foolish for his paranoia, Levi shook his head and smiled. "No, never mind. I'll be back later. Thank you."

Levi left the restaurant. He scanned the street, but saw nothing suspicious.

He had walked along Mulberry Street for another five minutes before he saw the man again.

As a fixer, Levi had spent years observing people, hunting down leads, finding people who didn't want to be found. He'd learned to spot people who were trying to look inconspicuous in a crowd. It was that finely tuned radar that alerted Levi to his observer.

He had shed the Yankee jacket and cap—no, he'd turned the jacket inside out and maybe ditched the cap. But it was him. Levi had no doubt.

Levi ducked into a gap between two buildings, moved past a dumpster, and crouched behind it.

Heart hammering, he turned his attention to the street.

Footsteps approached. Their pace slowed as they drew closer. Into the alley.

A man's breath sounded from the other side of the dumpster.

Levi could almost feel the man's gaze trying to penetrate the shadows near the end of the alley.

"Shit, " his follower muttered under his breath.

The man rushed down the alley past Levi.

In a smooth movement, Levi swept the man's feet out from under him, grabbed his coat—preventing the man from cracking his skull on the concrete—and plucked a gun from the man's shoulder holster.

Ratcheting the slide, he ejected a bullet and chambered a fresh one. He held the gun with practiced ease and aimed it directly at the man lying in front of him.

"Why are you following me?"

The stranger was in his late thirties. His eyes were wide with concern. "I'm not—"

"Bullshit." Levi made a show of tightening his grip on the gun, his finger on the trigger and the barrel aimed at the man's forehead. "You got on right after me in Pennsylvania, switched in Newark, and you just happened to duck into an alley that I happen to know is a dead end. Who are you, and why are you following me?"

The man lay on the damp concrete with his hands up and pressed his lips together.

Narrowing his eyes, Levi growled, "Are you the one who killed two innocent kids? Is that it? You're trying to finish what you started?"

"No."

Levi crouched down and pressed the muzzle of the gun against the man's belly. "You move, and I take out your liver. I promise you, it'll be a painful death."

Levi used his other hand to pat up and down the man's legs. He retrieved a snub-nosed revolver from an ankle holster, and popped open the cylinder. Six bullets fell to the ground.

He tossed the pistol deeper into the alley and continued his pat-down. When he felt a wallet in the man's back pocket, he pressed the gun harder into the man's belly.

"Give me your wallet."

The man slowly lowered his right hand, dug into his back pocket, and handed over the wallet.

Inside were some credit cards, some cash, and a Virginia driver's license. Levi tossed the wallet aside. "Okay, Don Jenkins. I don't know who you are, but I'll give you this one warning. Stop following me." Levi lowered his voice. "You'll notice that I was kind enough to break your fall when you slipped on the wet cement. You could have cracked your skull. Accidents happen, you know. Just stay out of the alleys, and you'll be fine." He pressed the gun even harder into the man's stomach, making Jenkins wince. "Understood?"

The man nodded.

With one quick motion, Levi ejected the magazine and pressed the slide back, ejecting the chambered bullet. He dropped the magazine into the dumpster and threw the empty gun to the far end of the alley.

Without even looking down at the man, Levi strode briskly away.

Levi kept glancing over his shoulder, not sure whether he'd ever lose that feeling of being watched. He walked along Mulberry between Grand and Broome Streets, and aimed for the social hall he'd frequented for years. It was where he'd made many of his acquaintances and first earned his reputation as a fixer.

The smells of Little Italy were everywhere. The aroma of pizza fresh out of the oven permeated the air, as did the smells of garlic and basil. The familiar scents lightened Levi's steps.

Many things in his old neighborhood were still the same. The restaurants and apartments above them looked no different than he remembered them, a generation ago. But sadness and confusion washed over him as he approached the social hall.

It had been converted into an Italian market.

The old hangout was gone.

His mind reeled as he began to rethink his plans.

He couldn't believe that some of the things he'd most counted on had been erased from existence in only a dozen years.

"Levi, is that you?"

Levi looked up. A gray-haired woman was sticking her head out of an apartment window above an Italian bakery named Nonna's.

"Nonna Romano?"

"My god," she said in a heavy Italian accent. "You've come back! Wait there, I'll be right down."

Levi smiled as the light in the bakery turned on and the little old woman he'd always thought of as the neighborhood's grandmother waddled toward the front door, accompanied by a pair of yapping wiener dogs.

She unlocked the door and motioned for him to enter. "Come in, come in. I have some of the limoncello cookies you like so much."

Levi kissed the old woman on both cheeks. The dogs yipped up at him, their tails wagging so furiously that the movement threatened to knock them over.

Nonna smiled up at him as she patted his beard. "You're a handsomer boy without all this scruff."

Levi laughed as he took a seat at the bakery's counter. "Well, I'll see what I can do about the beard." He hitched his thumb toward the new market. "What happened to the social hall? Is Vinnie still around?"

Nonna walked to the other side of the counter and filled a plate with small cookies covered in powdered sugar. She pushed the plate across the counter. "Here. My boys made them this morning."

Levi retrieved the plate and bit into a cookie. The strong tang of lemon took him back to when he was still a teen and had just arrived in the city. Nonna's cookies were the first bite of food he'd had back then, and it somehow seemed right that after all this time, they were his first bite once again.

"What are you doing back in the neighborhood?" Nonna asked. "I thought you'd have gone uptown with the boys. Is there something you need?"

The old woman could no longer sit on the high stools at the bar, so Levi took his plate of cookies to one of the tables in the cozy bakery and pulled out a chair for her to sit on.

"I've actually been gone quite a while, Nonna. But now that I'm back, I was going to see if the old boys from the social club were still around."

"Oh, Levi, you *have* been gone a long time. About five years ago they closed the club and Don Bianchi and his boys all went uptown."

"Don Bianchi?" Levi smiled. "Are you serious? The same Vinnie that I used to play stickball with is now Don Bianchi?"

Nonna laughed. "I remember you boys walking the streets together, laughing and having a good time. But that was a long time ago. Vincenzo does come on holidays. Such a sweet boy." She smiled, and her wrinkled gaze seemed unfocused. "He always asks for his favorite cannolis. The ones with chocolate chips in them."

"So, he's moved uptown?" Levi glanced outside; and noticed it was starting to get dark. "I have some things I need to ask him about."

The old woman reached out and patted Levi's hand. "Of course. Don Bianchi is now staying on Park Avenue, the Upper East Side. The building is called the Helmsley Arms." With a quick squeeze of his hand, she stood and gathered the plate of cookies. "I'll put these in a bag for you. I can tell you're in a hurry. It's very good to see you doing so well."

Levi smiled as the kind old woman filled a bag with all sorts of extra treats. "Thank you, Nonna. I'll be back, and we can talk more."

His mind was on the man who'd been tailing him. Everything about Jenkins screamed cop, but Levi couldn't be sure. How had he managed to follow him in such a busy city? He didn't have a Russian accent, but that didn't mean he wasn't working for someone on that side.

Nonna brought over a large bag. "I packed a little extra for you, and some cannolis for the Don."

"Thanks again, Nonna. You're the best." Levi leaned down, kissed her on both cheeks, and repeated his thanks as she escorted him to the door.

As he stepped outside, the streetlights were just coming on. In his mind, Levi charted the path he needed to travel, and before going to Vinnie's place, there was one more stop he needed to make.

Hopefully, Gerard was still open for business.

CHAPTER SEVEN

"The tracking devices are reporting that he's in Manhattan," Madison said. "By the look of it, he's on foot, somewhere near Chinatown."

Maddox leaned forward at his desk and scribbled something on a notepad. "Okay, well, keep on top of him. Anything new on the hitter?"

"Actually, yes. We received several confirmed pings as she arrived in a city called Chelyabinsk. That's just east of the Ural Mountains, and on the edge of Siberia. It happens to be where that meteor exploded in 2013. You know, the one with all the video of windows being blown out?"

"Interesting…" Maddox leaned back in his chair with a thoughtful expression. "Is she still there?"

"No. We tracked her phone's signal as she traveled southwest. Judging by her speed and the region's topography, she was probably using some kind of off-road vehicle. The signal disappeared as she entered the mountains. The last reported signal came from just outside a place called Mount Yamantau."

Maddox's only response was a slight raising of his eyebrows and some more scribbling.

"You're probably aware of this," Madison continued, "but there've been long-standing rumors of some kind of underground military bunker in that area. It seems like a strange destination for someone working for the Russian mob…"

Maddox's desk phone rang, and he grabbed the receiver and put it to his ear. "Maddox."

He listened for a moment and his expression turned sour. "Shit, let me put you on speaker. I've got Agent Lewis here with me." He pressed the speakerphone button. "Okay Jenkins, repeat what you just said."

Jenkins's voice came over the speaker. *"This Yoder guy made me, and we had a confrontation. He ducked into an alley, and I figured he was taking some shortcut, but when I followed him, he ambushed me and had my service piece pointed at my head."*

Madison stared open-mouthed at the phone.

"I'm assuming you lost track of him after that?" Maddox asked.

"Affirmative, and—"

"Are you okay?"

"I'm fine, but I'm also pretty sure he wasn't kidding about 'accidents' happening if I kept following him. He had me dead to rights, and could have taken me—"

"Jenkins, you've been made, that's enough. Get back here and I'll see about sending someone else."

"Sir, I can maybe … no, I understand."

Madison felt sorry for the man. He sounded defeated.

"Don't worry about it," Maddox said. "Clearly this guy's in his element and has skills we didn't anticipate. Come in so we can do a full debrief and build out this guy's profile. I've got some backup plans, and in the meantime, Lewis has got him tracked electronically."

"Yes, sir. I'll be on the first express tomorrow morning and report in."

"See you then." Maddox ended the call and turned to Madison. "I need your eyes on this guy."

Madison closed her notebook and stood. "In addition to the tracking devices we've got on him, I'll tap into the NYPD's camera system and see if I can catch sight of him on the street."

"Don't lose him."

As Madison walked back to her office, she imagined what Jenkins had gone through, and it sent a shiver up her spine. Outside of training exercises at Camp Peary, she'd never had a gun trained on her.

The thought of it left her queasy.

She quietly admonished herself. "It's part of the job, Maddie. Get over it."

Levi felt a surge of relief as he spotted Gerard's, a dingy old bar that had been one of his hangouts years ago. That, at least, was still here.

The tinny sound of a bell greeted him as he opened the door.

There were only a few customers inside. Places like this usually didn't start seeing crowds until after eight.

"Hey, buddy, have a seat and I'll get right to you."

Levi smiled at the familiar voice. He walked up to the bar and sat directly in front of the man who'd greeted him. He was a black man in his early thirties, wiping down the bar. At the far end of the counter a Hispanic woman was pouring drinks and talking to some customers.

"Seltzer, please," Levi said.

The man looked up with an expression of annoyance—then froze when he saw Levi. His mouth dropped open and a smile bloomed on his face. "Holy crap, Levi? Is that really you?" He reached across the bar, clapped Levi on the shoulder, and laughed. "What the hell are you doing dressed like a rabbi with a beard and all?"

With a snort, Levi shook his head. "It's good to see you, Denny. Rabbi? What's wrong with you? I'd have thought growing up in New York, you'd know the difference between what a rabbi looks like and an Amish guy."

"You're Amish? No shit. How is it that I didn't know that?"

"Your dad knew, but I suppose by the time you came around here, I'd shaved and civilized myself. Speaking of which, is your dad around?"

Denny shook his head as he poured Levi his seltzer. "Nah, he's retired in Florida."

A seed of worry bloomed in Levi's chest. "Last I knew of you, you were off to MIT to get your PhD or something. How'd you end up back here?"

"I took over after my dad retired."

Levi whispered, "Took over for everything?"

Denny tilted his head and gave him a mischievous grin. "Are you back in business?"

"Do you have a piece of paper and a pencil?"

Denny ripped off a blank order form from a stack on the bar and handed Levi a pencil.

Levi scribbled a note on the paper: *I think I'm wired. Can you scan me for bugs?*

Denny's eyes widened. He turned to the other bartender. "Carmen, I'm going in back for bit. You got things?"

"Ya Denny, no problem."

Denny led Levi through a beaded barrier and into a back room. One wall was covered with a tiled mural of a beach scene, the individual tiles were no bigger than one-inch square. Denny pressed on a combination of tiles, and with a beep, the outline of a door appeared. He pushed the door open, and the two men stepped through and sealed the door behind them.

The lights flickered on to reveal a large supply room filled with rows of shelving holding a variety of electronic equipment. "Holy crap, you've upped Gerard's game in a big way."

Denny laughed as he picked up what looked like a police baton. "Dad taught me everything I needed to know, but he was old school. I've added a few tricks of my own over the years. Expanded things." He pointed at Levi with the baton. "Raise your arms, and let's see what you've got."

Denny moved the black wand slowly along Levi's body. As it passed over his neck, it let out a loud squeal. He made several passes with the wand, covering both sides of his body, the front, and the back.

The wand emitted a second, quieter beep near Levi's middle, and a third squeal by Levi's feet.

"That's some metal detector you've got," Levi quipped.

"This is no metal detector. It's a multi-frequency signal distortion detector. Made it myself. Pretty simple, actually—it rapidly runs through a series of signal frequencies looking for distortion fields. That's typically a sign of a transmitter or microphone."

"Okay, whatever you say."

Denny put on a construction helmet with a headlamp attached.

"Toss me your shoes, pants, jacket—aw hell, just get undressed and go have a seat next to the workbench."

Levi did as he was told.

Denny waved the wand over each piece of clothing, tossing aside anything that didn't cause a beep. It took him only a few moments to pry open Levi's left shoe with a penknife and extract what looked like a tiny circuit board with wires protruding from it.

"Well, isn't that special?" He opened a box that looked like it was made of some kind of copper mesh and dumped the item in it.

The wand beeped again over Levi's shirt. Denny began tearing at the collar.

"So, someone's been tracking me?"

"Yup." Using needle-nosed pliers, Denny extracted another device from the shirt collar. "That's number two."

"Do you think the cops might have planted those on me?"

Denny glanced at him. "Cops? Dad always told me your code was to never draw the attention of the authorities."

Levi shrugged. "It's gotten complicated."

"I bet." Denny tore open the seam on Levi's waistband and extracted a third tracking device. He waved it at Levi. "Anyway, cops don't do this." He dropped the item into the mesh box and closed it. "That's number three. No idea where these babies came from. I'll have to take them home and study them."

"How are you going to do that without them tracking you as well?"

Denny waved the wand over what remained of Levi's clothes and tilted his head toward the box. "That thing's a tiny Faraday cage. It blocks any transmissions coming from within it."

"But if you're going to examine the trackers, don't you have to open the box—and when you do that, won't they track you then?"

Denny laughed. "I'll do it inside a room-sized Faraday cage."

"You've got a Faraday cage in your house?"

"Doesn't everyone?"

Levi rolled his eyes.

"Unfortunately," Denny said, "I think your pants and shirt aren't much good to you anymore. You might want to take a look at some of the old clothes my dad left behind." He pulled a cardboard box off a shelf. "They should probably fit you. Your overcoat wasn't bugged, so it's still good to go, and I can put your shoe back together."

"Thanks, Denny. What do I owe you?"

He shook his head and smiled. "Nothing. Just come back when you need something special in the hacking or electronics field. I'll be here."

Levi started digging through the box for something suitable to wear. "Hacking? That's something Gerard never did."

"Yup, but my dad was also never contracted to bypass world-class security systems. Like I said, old school. I went to school with some of the best hackers in the world. They live their lives in that gray area most normal folks don't even know exists."

Levi picked out a flowery Hawaiian print button-down and shook his head. "Damn, Gerard wasn't subtle with his style, was he?"

Denny beamed the light from his headlamp in Levi's direction and chuckled. "Hah, that's all Dad wears nowadays. I suppose it might look better on the beach, but you'll look great."

"You're colorblind," Levi replied sourly. He put on the old clothes and shrugged into his black overcoat to cover them up. At least everything fit him.

As Denny repaired Levi's shoe, he said, "Hey, it just hit me: you aren't packing anything. What's the deal?"

Levi sighed. "It's a long story, but I had a bunch of really nice knives stolen from me, and I haven't had a chance to resupply."

"Knives? I might have something." Denny finished with the shoe, and his lips curled up into a smile. "It's not what I carry, but some douche once tried to jack me with one of these things." He disappeared into the rows of shelves and came back out with a brace of blackened throwing daggers. "They're mostly junk, but better than nothing."

Levi drew one of the knives by its cord-wrapped handle and hefted the weapon in his hand. "What a piece of crap. The balance on this is all wrong." He studied the wavy patterns on the blade and scoffed. "That isn't even a real Damascus pattern. Some moron painted it to look like a forged blade."

Denny shrugged. "Hey, you don't need to tell me what's wrong with it—it's not like I'm trying to sell it to you. If you want it until you get something decent, go ahead and take it. I sure as hell don't need it."

"Sorry, I didn't mean it like that." Levi shrugged the brace of daggers over his head and rotated them so they inconspicuously lay diagonally across his chest. He gave Denny a one-armed hug. "Thanks, man, I really do appreciate it. Compared to the hand-crafted stuff that I made myself, and the knife I got as a gift when I lived in Japan, these blades are crap, but I can use them. Thank you."

"You've been living in Japan?"

Levi put his arm over his friend's shoulder. "It's a long story, and tonight's not the night for that. I've got somewhere to go."

Wandering the streets was a lot less stressful now that Levi knew he wasn't being tracked. As he got off the bus on Park Avenue and walked north past East 86th Street, he took in his new environment. He was familiar with the Upper East Side of Manhattan, but had never had that many contacts here. And after a decade, he no doubt had far fewer contacts here now.

It was a little after nine in the evening when he arrived at a stately old building with a marble column on either side of the entrance. The words "The Helmsley Arms" were emblazoned in gold leaf above the ten-foot-tall doors. The doors looked as though they were made of glass, but as Levi stopped outside, he couldn't see into the lobby.

He hefted the bag of baked goods from Nonna's and took a deep breath. "Here goes nothing."

He walked up the steps to the entrance and pulled at the metal handle. The door swung open noiselessly.

The lobby was immaculate. It was twenty feet long, marble flooring throughout, with a bank of elevators on the far side.

Levi walked over to a call panel with a long column of buttons with names next to them. But before he could even look for Vinnie's name, a door opened on the other side of the lobby, and two barrel-chested men made a beeline for him.

"Sir, is there something I can help you with?"

The man's accent screamed Little Italy, and despite the polite language, the words had been spoken with an unmistakably aggressive tone.

Levi backed away from the call panel and smiled. Both muscle-heads wore expensive suits that were a little too tight around the chest. From the lump imprinted on the side of Meathead One's chest, it was clear he had a piece in a shoulder holster.

"I'm here to visit a friend."

"Sir, we're house security. What's your friend's name?"

"Vincenzo Bianchi."

Meathead Two smiled and motioned for Levi to raise his arms—inadvertently showing him the gun tucked into an in-waistband holster under his suit jacket. "I'll need to pat you down."

Levi placed the bag of pastries on a table beneath the call panel and raised his arms.

The meathead ran his hands through Levi's overcoat, exposing his brace of throwing daggers. Levi didn't wait to be asked; he removed the brace and handed it over.

The large man dumped the weapons next to the pastries.

The pat-down continued. If nothing else, they were being thorough. Levi took the opportunity to scan the names on the call panel.

"No wallet or ID?" the meathead said.

"No, I travel light."

Meathead One motioned toward the door. "All right, get out of here. There's nobody here by that name."

The two men's smiles made it clear that they were enjoying themselves at Levi's expense. They were full of shit.

Levi pointed at the call panel. "Is that why one of the buttons has a 'DVB' on it? Don Vincenzo Bianchi, I believe."

Meathead One's leering smile turned into a glare. "You're done here, sir. I suggest you leave."

Levi motioned toward his daggers and pastries. "And my property?"

Meathead Two growled. "It's no longer *your* property." He pulled out his pistol and aimed it at Levi's face.

In a swift and sudden motion, Levi twisted the man's wrist, swept his feet out from under him, and snatched the gun as it fell from his hand.

The heavy thud of the man's head hitting the marble floor echoed through the lobby.

Before Meathead One could react, Levi trained the muzzle on him. "Arms up or I swear I'll drill a new hole in you."

The man glanced at his unmoving partner, and his jaw muscles tightened. Slowly, he raised his hands.

Levi placed the barrel on the hollow of the man's throat and whispered menacingly, "Buddy, I don't even need to shoot you to kill you. This barrel is on your suprasternal notch. Just a little shove and I'll crush your windpipe—and you'll choke and die. Seen it happen many times; it's not pretty. Just be calm, and everything will be fine."

Levi slipped his hand under the man's jacket and withdrew a nine-millimeter Beretta from the shoulder holster.

He took a step back and pressed both the Beretta's takedown lever and latch release button. The slide popped forward and Levi tossed the gun onto the floor in several pieces.

"How the—"

Levi motioned with the first man's gun toward the call panel. "Call Don Bianchi. He and I are old friends."

The guard hesitated.

Levi tightened his grip on the pistol but maintained his distance.

"Listen, I know you're doing your job, but trust me, your best move right now is to call the Don. Move slowly, and don't get cute."

The guard nodded and pressed a button.

A man's voice spoke from a speaker on the panel. *"What's up?"*

"Mr. Minnelli, we have someone here to speak to the Don."

"What the hell's wrong with you?"

Levi called across the lobby. "Frankie? Is that you?"

"Ya, who's this?"

"Here's a clue: I fixed you up with your first girlfriend."

There was a pause. *"No, fucking way. Levi? Is that really you?"*

"Ya, it's me. Give this *stunad* the word that I'm okay. I need to talk to Vinnie."

Frankie must have put his hand over the receiver, yet his muffled voice still broadcast over the panel's speaker. *"Vinnie, you won't believe who's back in town."*

There was almost a minute of silence before a new voice came on the line. *"Levi, is that really you?"*

"In the flesh. I like the new digs. You've gone upscale on me."

"Holy shit, it is you. Where the hell have—no, never mind. Tony, send this guy up."

The guard glanced at his unconscious partner and looked like he was about to throw up. "Um, Don Bianchi. Tony is, uh ..."

"Vinnie," Levi said, "these *momos* you got guarding your place, I'm sure they're good guys, but they need to be taught a few lessons. I'm sorry, but Tony tried to play rough, and he's taking a nap right now."

"Shit, Johnnie, what'd you guys do?"

The meathead shifted uncomfortably. "I'm sorry, Don. But Tony, he's been out for almost five minutes, and this guy, he tore my gun apart like it was a toy."

"I swear, if you weren't my cousin's brother-in-law ..."

Levi cut in. "Vinnie, it's okay—"

"No, it's not. I'll send some boys down to pick up Tony. Johnnie, you escort the fixer up to my place."

"And Vinnie," Levi said, "you might need to get your man an x-ray. I think I heard something pop in his wrist."

Laughter erupted from the speaker. *"You haven't changed much, have you?"*

Levi shrugged. "You know me, Vinnie. I'm a counterpuncher."

The speaker turned off with a click, and the elevator doors slid open. Three well-dressed men walked into the lobby, stood by the unconscious guard, and glanced at Levi. "Sir, we'll take care of this."

With a nervous tremor in his voice, Johnnie motioned Levi toward the elevator doors. "After you, sir."

"My god, you look like you did twenty years ago!"

Levi patted his friend's face and laughed. "You don't look so bad yourself."

The two men hugged and kissed each other's cheeks.

Levi panned his gaze across the large, well-appointed parlor filled with ornately carved wooden furniture, beautiful paintings, and a museum-quality marble statue of the Venus de Milo. He whistled in appreciation. "This place doesn't look too bad either."

"This place?" Vinnie waved away the compliment. "It's a family joint." He motioned toward some chairs by the fireplace. "What's it been? Eleven … twelve years?"

"You got it. About twelve years."

Levi walked over to the fireplace and studied the pictures on the mantel. One of them filled him with warm memories. It was of Vinnie, Levi, Mary, and Vinnie's girlfriend at the time, all of them at Jennings Beach. Two sets of lipstick prints were on the photo—one just above Levi's head, the other just above Vinnie's.

"My god," Levi said. "We were so young back then. What ever happened to this blonde knockout on your arm? What was her name?"

"Oh, you mean Phyllis? I married that knockout a year after you disappeared on us."

Levi took a seat on a comfortable leather-upholstered chair. "I'm sorry about vanishing like that. It's really good to see you again."

Vinnie took a seat facing him, leaned forward, and motioned toward the picture. "You disappeared soon after your Mary passed, no?"

Pressing his lips together, Levi nodded.

The Don patted Levi on the knee and sighed. "I'm sorry about that. She was a good lady."

"Yes, she was. I took a long time mourning her passing, and I know I kind of fell off the face of the Earth, but I'm back now."

"You interested in coming back into the business?" Vinnie cocked an eyebrow.

"Well, I'm not sure. I actually came to see you. I have a favor or two to ask. One might be a big one." Levi glanced at the two men standing at the entrance to Vinnie's parlor.

Vinnie turned to the men and snapped his fingers. "Charlie, Frankie, can you give us a bit of privacy here? I'll call you when I need you."

The men left the room and closed the doors behind them.

Vinnie took on a serious tone. "Anything I can do for you, it would be a personal favor to me if I could help. Just ask."

"I appreciate it, Vinnie." Levi rubbed the side of his chest where the stitches were driving him nuts. "Let me start from the beginning.

"After Mary died, I literally wandered the world like a bum. I was lost and needed to find myself again." He sighed as emotions stirred within him. "Maybe I was feeling guilty because deep down, I think Mary might have taken her own life because we all thought the cancer was going to kill me. Anyway, that's where I've been all these years. But I finally decided to come back.

"I actually visited my folks' place, if you can believe it."

Vinnie smiled. "Is that what that beard is all about?"

"In part. Actually, I haven't owned a razor since I left the States."

Vinnie nodded for Levi to continue.

"I hadn't been back long when I discovered that New York State had managed to seize all of my assets. They did it all legal-like. I've got copies of the paperwork, but I was wondering if any of your government contacts might be able to look into that. See what really happened. They shouldn't have been able to siphon my funds without a death certificate, but they obviously did."

"Shit, you mean your house and—"

"The house, the bank account, hell, even the trust fund I'd originally set up for Mary. It had around three million in cash."

"Damn, they really wiped you out." Vinnie shook his head. "I'll see what I can find out for you. Obviously, I can't promise anything."

"I appreciate that, but there's another thing. This one might be a bit more political."

Vinnie snorted. "More political than the scumbag politicians in New York? This I got to hear."

"You know me, I'm cautious. I keep my nose clean, and I don't get involved in things that'll get me into too much heat. Also, I'm not the type to make enemies. But somehow, I've gotten someone's attention.

"If you can believe it, it was on the same day I learned that I didn't have a pot to piss in anymore. When I came home from the bank, I found two kids dead at my parents' farm. Sliced from ear to ear."

Vinnie's mouth dropped open.

"Within minutes of me finding their bodies, the cops showed up, picked me up as a suspect, and tossed me in jail. Turns out someone called my name in as the murderer."

"No shit." Vinnie sat back, his expression darkening.

"Well, I think the fix was in, because I was put into general population just after I was booked, and a bunch of Russians tried to kill me in my cell."

"Russians? Are you sure?"

"I'm positive. They mentioned someone named Vladimir having sent word to them. I can't for the life of me think of why anyone in the Russian mob would want a piece of me, but I was wondering if you might know anyone who knew someone."

Vinnie rubbed at the side of his face. "The Russians." He spoke as if the words left a bad taste in his mouth. "I can have someone reach out and see what's going on. We don't really do much business with them, if you know what I mean, but we occasionally talk. I'll do what I can about seeing if there's a contract and who's opened it."

"I really appreciate it."

There was an awkward tension in the air. The Don brushed away some non-existent dust from his slacks. "Okay, so you asked for a few things. Now I have a few things to ask you." He gestured to Levi's outfit. "You're looking a mess. Are you up for coming back on with the family?"

Levi was about to respond when Vinnie held up his hand.

"Wait, before you answer. I could really use an adult to straighten up some of these *momos* I've got here. They're good men, but they're hotheaded and need discipline. There's something about the way you are that helps others stay calm around you. They need that influence." Vinnie gave him a lopsided grin. "You somehow managed to teach *me* how to think about things before acting. I'm just not good on the front line. Deep down, I'm still that eighteen-year-old Sicilian hothead you met on Mulberry Street. I'm better at the business end nowadays."

Levi studied his friend's face. He was being completely sincere, and they'd never broken each other's trust. "I'll be honest, I'm not really sure if I want to get back in the mix yet. I literally just got into town today."

"If you're fresh in town, why not stay here?" Vinnie leaned forward and looked Levi in the eyes. "You'd be doing me a personal favor if you stayed."

"Vinnie, this place is beautiful, but I can't exactly afford—"

"What, are you insulting me now? For you, the place will be on the arm."

Free? Levi couldn't take such charity. He was about to argue when Vinnie shook his finger.

"Let me do this for you. You don't have to decide anything. For a friend, I would do this. But you've saved my life more than once. The least I can do for you is help you out in your time of need."

Levi nodded. A surge of warmth filled him as he clasped hands with his longtime friend.

"It's settled." Vinnie launched up from his chair and yelled, "Frankie, get your ass back in here!"

The double doors swung open and two mobsters walked in with tense expressions.

Levi stood, and Vinnie wrapped an arm around his shoulders. "Go kick out that no-good cousin of mine from the third-floor suite—"

"Vinnie," Levi protested, "I don't want anyone kicked out on my account!"

The Don burst out laughing. He gave Levi's stomach a light jab. "I'm kidding, you *mamaluke*." He turned back to Frankie. "Go talk to Lola and have her set up one of the empty suites. Levi's going to be staying with us."

Frankie shot Levi a smile. "That's great news." He turned and walked briskly from the room.

Charlie, who was more fat than muscle, cleared his throat. "Don Bianchi, Tony Montelaro is waiting outside the room. Did you want to see him?"

Vinnie nodded, and Charlie leaned outside and motioned for someone to approach.

Levi suppressed a smile as Meathead Two entered the room, his left arm in a sling.

The man spoke woodenly, as if he'd memorized what he was about to say. "Don Bianchi, I'm sorry for—"

"I don't want to hear it," Vinnie growled. He hitched his thumb toward Levi. "I owe this man my life, and you attacked him. You actually think I want to hear what you have to say?"

Levi put his hand on Vinnie's shoulder and whispered, "Let me handle this, okay?"

Vinnie glanced at Levi, then nodded and pointed at Tony. "Tony, you better listen to every word this man has to say, or so help me God, you'll regret it."

Tony looked even more uncomfortable as Levi walked over to him.

Levi pointed to the man's wrist. "I'm sorry about that. Is it broken?"

The big man blinked as if not sure how to respond. "No, it's just popped out of joint. Doc snapped the bone back in. He said I can't use it for a month."

Levi had to look up at the man; he was a good four inches taller than him and likely outweighed him by at least fifty pounds. "Listen, what happened downstairs, nothing personal, you hear me?"

Tony nodded, stiff and wary.

"Remember how you pulled your piece out and shoved it in my face? Next time, don't do that when the guy's in arm's reach." Levi pointed at Tony and then at himself. "I mean, let's be real. You're huge. If it comes to pure strength, you could probably tear me in half, right?"

Tony nodded again, his chest inflating slightly.

"But I'll bet you didn't even see what happened when I had you take a little nap."

A troubled expression on Tony's face confirmed Levi's guess.

"Your problem is you're too used to being able to use that strength. You got cocky." Levi patted Tony's chest and smiled. "Listen, having an attitude is good. I like a big attitude—it sometimes keeps you from having to do things you don't otherwise want to do. But cocky is another word for careless. As soon as you think you've got things under control, someone like me comes along."

Vinnie snickered as he fixed himself a drink at the nearby wet bar.

Levi continued. "I'd bet you a million dollars you wouldn't have guessed some bum off the streets like me, dressed the way I am, could have taken you down. Don't feel bad. One of my best tricks is not looking dangerous." He leaned closer to Tony and stared up into his eyes. "Looks can be deceiving."

Vinnie sat on top of his desk and pointed a glass filled with an amber liquid at the large man. "Tony, even on your best day, Levi would wipe the floor with you."

Tony's face darkened.

Levi shot Vinnie a look that said, *"You're not helping."*

Levi knew what the typical Italian mobster was like. They had a code that they followed. Not everyone had the same code, but there was one. However, one thing they all had in common was an ego. And the quickest way to piss one of these guys off was to make them feel like shit.

Levi cleared his throat. "Listen, what the Don said, that's not a knock against you. I'm just really good at a few things. Luckily, we're on the same side." He patted Tony on the shoulder and smiled. "Right now, you've got everything it takes to be a really dangerous guy. If you listen to me, I'll teach you how to think under stress, be more effective in how you use what God gave you. I'll drill into you the difference between being cocky and being confident. You've probably already learned that putting a gun to someone's face isn't the smartest move." Levi pointed at the man's injured wrist. "Just don't make mistakes, and you'll get there."

Vinnie took a swig of his drink. "Tony, you're one lucky bastard that our friend here doesn't hold a grudge." He pointed at Levi. "I want you to meet the family's fixer and my consigliere. He's been gone a long time, but now he's back. You're going to start taking your cues from him. Understood?"

"Yes, Don Bianchi." Tony looked at Levi. "Sir, what should I call you?"

Levi shot a glance at Vinnie, who'd conveniently forgotten that he hadn't agreed to be a part of the family business again. He looked back at Tony and sighed. "Just call me Levi. It's less confusing that way."

Vinnie hopped off the desk and motioned Tony away. "Get out of here, and get some rest."

Tony backed out of the room.

The Don walked over to Levi. "Levi, I saw that look you gave me. Trust me, I'm not going to get you into any trouble. We don't do business here anyway. This is a family place."

Which really meant the building was a mob-run establishment.

Levi placed his hand on the back of Vinnie's neck and gave it a playful shake. "You know I'm loyal, but understand something. There's things I'll need to follow up on that may not have anything to do with the family. I need you to really understand that, Vinnie."

Vinnie smiled. "So, you're part-time, then."

Levi laughed and gave his friend a one-armed hug. "Fine, consider me in, but part-time."

CHAPTER EIGHT

Madison removed her headphones when her supervisor walked into her office. He sat on the opposite side of her desk and betrayed no emotions as he asked, "So, we lost Yoder's signal?"

"Unfortunately, it seems so." She withdrew a printout from her desk drawer and laid it between them. "Depending on weather conditions, we sometimes get gaps in signal reporting, but we haven't gotten a signal since late yesterday."

"Where was he when the signal dropped out?"

Madison flipped to the last page and ran her finger down the timeline listing a long series of GPS coordinates. "He was still in New York. The signal bounced around a bit, but somewhere near Bowery and Delancey Street."

"Little Italy?"

"Yup." Madison patted the headphones draped around her neck. "Speaking of which, I was listening to a call received at a priority-one number, and I think it might be about our guy. It's in English."

Maddox raised his eyebrows. "Oh, really? Let's hear it."

Madison disconnected her headphones and clicked play on the audio recording.

"Da?" said a man with a Russian accent.

"Dmitri?" The second man was clearly American, with a New York accent.

"Yes. Long time to have talking to you."

"Did you receive the e-mail I sent you?"

"I did. I'm not knowing about that name, but I will look for you and call you back."

"Listen, if there's a contract, we'd take it as a favor if it gets wiped clean."

"I understand. But why this man? Is he one of yours?"

"He's protected. Dmitri, just look into it and let me know what you find out, okay?"

"It's important to your family?"

"It is."

"Fine. I study this and getting back to you."

"That sounds great."

The message ended, and Maddox drummed his fingers on the desk. "So, you think that was about our guy."

Madison pursed her lips. "It's a long shot, but if I break down what we just heard, we've got someone who has a pretty stereotypical New York Italian accent calling a known Russian mob asset.

"They were pretty careful about what they said, even down to using an e-mail to communicate the name of whoever they were talking about. The Italian guy mentioned a contract, which I presume refers to someone with a price on their head. He wanted whoever that was to get cleared from the contract."

Madison shrugged. "It certainly *could* be Yoder they were talking about, though it's hard to tell. And it's hard to imagine an Amish farmer associated with the Italian Mafia. But then again, he wouldn't be my natural pick as a target for the Russian mob either."

Maddox grinned mischievously. "You're right, it's hard to know for certain. But this might help." He pulled a folded sheet of paper from his suit jacket and pushed it across the desk. "I've had the NSA tracking keywords for me on a couple cases. Open that up and take a look."

It was a printout of an e-mail. "Well," said Madison, "the sender's address is blacked out, I presume that's because it's a domestic source. Destination is an e-mail at a dot-gov-dot-ru address, which looks like a Russian government target. And ... holy crap!" Her mouth dropped when she saw the body of the message. It consisted of only two words: *Lazarus Yoder.*

Her boss had a satisfied expression on his face. "Maddie, I think we've got some rather interesting connections developing."

"Wait a minute." Madison's mind raced with the new data. "If we have a mob contact in Russia getting e-mail at a Russian government address, that means ... that means the mob and the Russian government aren't necessarily on different teams."

"The lines are definitely getting blurred." Maddox tapped on the desk. "I'm going to walk some of this up the chain to get some warrants for additional taps. I'll see what else I can learn." He pointed at Madison. "Do we have anything on the hitter?"

"Actually, yes. I checked only twenty minutes ago, and her signal had popped up again. If you can believe it, we're now getting a signal from Nepal."

"Really?" Maddox considered this for a moment. "I think I have an idea, but I'm not sure how you're going to like it."

Levi couldn't remember the last time he'd slept so well. When had he ever experienced a mattress with a four-inch-thick pad of memory foam that supported him from head to toe?

Never.

He'd turned off the alarm clock a good thirty minutes ago, but lingered in bed to enjoy this unfamiliar comfort. Two thousand square feet on the eighth floor of a newly refurbished Park Avenue building. It was hard for him to accept that he was living here.

The door to the apartment beeped as its lock electronically disengaged. Levi sat up, and the firm but luxurious mattress adjusted beneath him.

Two sets of footsteps entered the apartment, but only Frankie appeared in the bedroom doorway. He pressed a button on the bedroom wall. "Rise and shine."

A hidden motor whirred, opening the drapes and letting daylight splash across the room. Levi blinked at the sudden brightness.

The night before, Frankie had taken him into the security room and added his fingerprints to the building's security database. He hadn't told Levi that his own fingerprint *also* opened the apartment door.

"Let me guess," Levi said. "*Anyone's* finger works on that door?"

Frankie grinned as he peered through the floor-to-ceiling window. "No. I'm head of security, so I can get into any of the rooms." He stepped to the doorway and gestured to someone in the living room. "Mr. Wu, the light should be better in here."

Wearing only boxer shorts, Levi flung aside the covers and hopped out of bed. "Mr. Wu?"

An elderly Asian man appeared beside Frankie. He carried a leather duffel bag and had a measuring tape draped around his neck.

"This is Mr. Wu," said Frankie. "He's going to be measuring you for some decent clothes."

Levi stretched his arms, the stitches on his side pulling annoyingly at his skin. He turned to the diminutive man who'd set his bag on the bed and had begun rummaging through it. "Mr. Wu, do you have tweezers and a pair of scissors in there?"

The wrinkled man glanced at him with a quizzical expression. "Of course. But I don't need that yet."

"Can I borrow them for a second?"

With a huff, the man dug through his bag and placed a long pair of tweezers and some thread nippers on the bed.

"Perfect." Levi grabbed them, walked over to the dresser-drawer mirror, and stood sideways next to it.

"What are you doing?" Frankie asked.

It was an awkward angle, but Levi pulled at one of the stitches with the tweezers, snipped it, and slowly pulled the knotted thread out of his skin. Aside from the two pinprick holes in his flesh from the stitch, the wound looked like it had healed.

The tailor muttered something in Mandarin that Levi thought meant "crazy man," then walked over to him. "Let me do it before you hurt yourself."

Levi handed the tools to the tailor, and Wu set to work removing the eighty-nine remaining stitches.

Frankie shook his head. "So, how'd you sleep?"

Levi looked out the window and onto the street. "What can I say? I slept like someone staying in an eighth-floor suite on Park Avenue."

"Well, I'll let you explore the apartment on your own time, but I wanted to let you know a few things first. Vinnie has some rules about folks staying here. There's a dress code—"

"And that's where Mr. Wu comes in?"

"Exactly. We want folks in here to keep up appearances—makes us fit in better with the neighborhood. Your fridge is empty right now, but Lola's going to call you in a bit to try and figure out what you like to eat and stock up the fridge for you. You're family, so you can pretty much ask for whatever you want, it's cool. For some of the regular *momos* who pay to be in here, they get a list to choose from."

"I'd been wondering about that." Levi looked through the doorway into the living room, which was tastefully decorated and filled with fine Italian leather furniture. "How can you guys afford this? I'm guessing the family has the entire building?"

Frankie gave Levi a lopsided grin. "Believe it or not, we make a pretty tidy profit on this place. We've got two hundred apartments in here, but only about thirty are like this. The rest are smaller apartments for connected guys that can afford the rent and want more access to things."

"Are you going to tell me what it costs?"

"Well, the made members get a reduced charge, but for the rest, there's a $250,000 initiation fee, and fifteen g's per month to keep people producing."

"Nice chunk of lettuce. And people pay that?"

"We've got a waiting list, if you can believe it. It's kind of a status thing."

Levi whistled appreciatively. "Nice."

Mr. Wu plucked the last stitch. "Okay, all done playing doctor. Now I can do *my* job."

Levi looked into the mirror and rubbed at the faint pink line where he'd been cut. "Awesome."

Mr. Wu took the tape measure from around his neck and motioned for Levi to raise his arms.

As the old man took Levi's measurements, Frankie pulled a brick-like package from the inside of his suit jacket and placed it on the nightstand. "That's an advance on your salary—"

"Hold on," Levi said. "I haven't done anything to earn it yet. I'm not taking charity!"

Frankie waved Levi's comment away. "Don't be a *stunad*. You think Vinnie's lost his mind and is just tossing C-notes left and right? I'm sure he's looking at it as an investment on future work. Besides, you'll need to pay Mr. Wu, and eventually get yourself a piece and other supplies. It'll take a while before we set you up with IDs and a bank account. Unlike before, more of the family income is coming in legit, so we even have direct deposit nowadays and use a real accounting firm. In the meantime, I'd suggest using the safe in your walk-in closet.

"Oh, one more thing. I ran your prints and did a spot check with NICS. With the help of some of our friends downtown, we should be able to get you a concealed carry permit pretty easy, and with a little bit more paperwork, we can get reciprocity in forty-five states. That'll take a while because of the damned feds. They can't do anything quickly. Anyway, hold off on getting a piece until we get that taken care of, *capiche*?"

Levi felt a wave of emotion hit him. He swallowed hard as he realized just how lucky he was to have these guys looking out for him, even after him being gone for so many years. Like a real family.

Mr. Wu laid the measuring tape back around his neck and scribbled in his notebook. "I'll start right away. You should have your first two suits late tomorrow."

"Wow, that's pretty quick."

"Don't let Mr. Wu fool you," said Frankie. "He's got a bunch of Chinese elves locked away in his workshop working around the clock."

The older man cast Frankie a mischievous grin. "We don't use elves. The Chinese use mogwai almost exclusively. Much more reliable."

Frankie snorted. "Just don't feed those bastards after midnight. I saw what happened in *Gremlins*."

Mr. Wu grumbled "stupid Hollywood movies" in Mandarin. He pulled a shoe catalog out of his bag and place it on Levi's bed. "I assume you need shoes, Mr. Yoder, so take a look. When I bring the suits, I'll bring samples of the ones you like so you can try them on."

"Thanks, Mr. Wu." Levi turned to Frankie. "Hey, do you know if Esther from the neighborhood is still in business?"

"Esther?"

"You know, big old Jewish lady, runs a sporting goods store."

Frankie's eyes widened with recognition. "Oh, *her*. Ya, Mrs. Rosen is still around. You need something?"

"I'll go visit her myself. I want to look into something kind of special."

A bell chimed as Levi opened the door to Rosen's Sporting Goods, and a woman's voice rang out from the back. "I'll be with you in a minute!"

The inside of the place had changed since Levi had last visited.

Gone were the big racks of seasonal clothing, and in their place were rows of everything from archery to weightlifting equipment. And there was a lot of it. At five thousand square feet, the store was larger than most in the old neighborhood.

A pimply-faced teen scanned a woman's purchases at a nearby counter. The woman's preschooler occupied himself by trying to bounce his new basketball.

The voice sounded from the back once more. "What kind of

meshuggener are you? Stop *kvetching* about it and just *schlep* the trash to the dumpster like I told you to this morning!"

With a smile, Levi followed the familiar voice, and quickly found its source.

A short, heavyset woman with her graying hair in a bun stood with her back to him. Her hands were on her hips as she watched another pimply-faced teen, a twin of the one at the cash register, struggling to drag a large plastic trash bin out the back door.

"Is that your grandson?" Levi asked.

"You think I'd put up with such if he weren't a blood relative?" The woman glanced over her shoulder, then froze at the sight of Levi. "Oy, my God!"

Esther rushed him, gave him a bear hug, and swayed from left to right, all the while speaking in rapid-fire Yiddish, none of which Levi understood.

"It's good to see you too, Esther."

The elderly woman held him at arm's length and patted at his freshly shaved cheek. "I'm so happy to see you again. I heard you were back in town."

"Oh? How's that?"

The woman tilted her head, which emphasized her double chin. "What, you don't think I hear things?"

"Let me guess: you talked with Nonna Romano."

Esther's eyes widened. "How'd you know?"

Levi hitched his thumb toward the front. "I saw a bag from Nonna Romano's bakery on the shelf behind the sales counter. "When an Italian nonna and a Jewish bubbe get together, well … few things that happen are left undiscussed."

"Are you accusing us of being gossips?" Esther raised an eyebrow and gave Levi a good-natured glare.

He handed her a small plastic shopping bag. "I brought you something."

Esther peered into the bag and groaned. "Oh, you wicked man. Entenmann's chocolate frosted doughnuts. Now I *know* you want something."

"Well, I was interested in—"

"Hold that thought." Esther raised her hand and yelled toward the front of the store. "Ira, make sure you and Moishe greet the customers and help them if they need it! If someone comes looking for me, tell them to wait! I'll be in the back."

She turned to Levi and motioned for him to follow.

They walked to the rear of the store, past the grandson who was dragging the now-empty bin back inside.

Esther led Levi to a desk in the far corner of a supply room, and plopped down in front of it. She pointed at the chair next to her, and Levi took his seat.

"*Nu*, what are you looking for?" Esther said. "I know you weren't much into selective-fire weapons, but I'd be doing you a disservice if I didn't tell you I can get you a really good deal on some MP5s that I stumbled into. Integrated suppressor, retractable buttstock, and a three-position trigger group. I know it's a German brand, but those Nazi bastards are pretty good with their craftsmanship."

"Nazis? I don't think the Germans nowadays—"

"Listen, just because they don't claim to be Nazis, doesn't mean they aren't. So, how many do you think you could use?"

Levi smiled. Esther hadn't changed a bit. For her, there were Nazis behind every bush, no dessert she'd say no to, and never a moment when she wasn't pushing a sale. It was all part of her special charm.

"Believe it or not," Levi said, "I'm not looking for a gun right now."

"No? Then what do you need? Explosives? I don't have any C-4 in stock, but I heard about some M112 demolition blocks that need a home. I can send out some feelers, if you like."

"No. I was wondering if you're stocking any bulletproof vests. Good ones?"

Esther nodded. "Of course I do. Are you looking for soft or hard?"

"Something I can wear under a suit or regular clothes."

"Well, I have some nice class-3A armor that'll stop a .44 Magnum." Esther patted his hand excitedly. "Oh, and if you're interested, I got something brand new. It's a vest that gives you ballistics protection as well as edged and spiked weapon protection. Along with the layers of Kevlar, this armor has titanium-gold mesh weaved into it, a totally new alloy. It's lighter than steel mesh and about four times as tough. The stuff's new, but they claim it's thin enough to wear under clothing.

"It also has a nice calfskin leather underneath that should make it very comfortable. One thing though, I'll need to get your measurements—it's a made-to-fit custom job."

"How much does that cost?" Levi asked.

Esther gasped and put her hand to her chest. "Price? Why does price matter when it's your life we're talking about?"

Levi tilted his head and narrowed his eyes at the hard-nosed business woman. A good fifteen seconds of silence passed before she breathed heavily, scribbled a number on a piece of paper and handed it to him.

Levi gulped at the number she'd written. "I'm sorry, maybe you have something different that's almost as good? Maybe something half the price. I can't afford that."

"It's your life, *bubbaleh*." She frowned. "Oy, I just can't stand the thought." She retrieved the paper, wrote a new price, and pushed the paper back toward him. "I can't have your life on my conscience. I'll give it to you for my cost."

Levi suppressed a smile. Amazingly enough, the number she'd originally quoted had been cut nearly in half. It wouldn't surprise him if Esther was still making a killing even at the new price. "Deal."

Esther smiled, and they shook hands. "Is there anything else you needed?"

"I need one more thing." From a hidden strap under his newly purchased windbreaker, Levi pulled out one of the knives he'd gotten from Denny. He laid it on the desk. "A replacement for this."

Esther picked up the knife and gave it a look of disgust. "What kind of blue-light special Mickey Mouse crap is this? Please tell me you're not using this for anything."

"That's why I'm here. I need something decent." Levi motioned toward the pad of paper on the desk. "Here, let me draw what I'm looking for."

Esther handed him a pencil, and he drew a picture of what he needed. "I want the balance to be here"—he pointed—"and the handle to be wrapped in paracord. I want the blade to be folded steel, something high carbon, like 420."

Esther scoffed and shook her head. "What's this knife for, peeling apples or fighting? What are you using it for?"

"I want it balanced for throwing, but figure I'll need it for slashing, attacks, pretty much what you might expect. Also, I'll need four of them."

She pursed her lips and studied the drawing. "I wouldn't go with the 420 steel if I were you. I've had some customers complain about chipping with the 420 if they hit something hard. You might consider using 1055 with proper tempering. It'll be tough as hell. No, wait—I think the new Japanese YXR7 would work even better. It's a matrix steel, and it's very chip-resistant due to the absence of large primary carbides."

Levi couldn't help but smile at the technical knowledge pouring out of this Jewish grandmother. Who'd believe an older woman running a sporting goods store was a relatively major arms dealer?

"Anyway, if you're up for learning how to maintain them properly, I think you'd do well with either the YXR7 or the 1055, though I think the YXR7 edges the 1055 out. I've got a friend on the West Coast who's been hand-forging blades like this for almost forty years. He's been working with these new forging processes. I can give him a call, but it might take a few weeks before he can turn it around."

Levi nodded. "That's fine, I'll go with your recommendation. What's it going to cost?"

Esther stood and motioned for him to follow. "Let's go back to the front. I can't trust Ira and Moishe alone together for much more than ten minutes before I start worrying they'll burn the place to the ground. As to the cost, let me call my friend in Washington State first and see if he can do it in a reasonable time. He's the best I know. Once I confirm the delivery time, we can talk price."

"I trust you, Esther. Just give me the bill and have a little pity on me price-wise. I'm only just getting back into the swing of things."

Esther patted Levi on his back as they returned to the front of the store. "*Bubbaleh*, I'll be fair with you, like always."

A bell chimed as the front door opened, and a tall Asian man entered the store. He wore a button-down shirt with long sleeves that were rolled midway up his tattooed forearms. He carried a shopping bag in his right hand, and his left pinkie was missing a knuckle.

Yakuza.

Levi had seen members of the Japanese crime syndicate in Japan, but he'd never heard of them coming to the US, much less Little Italy.

Esther waved at the man. "Hiro. I'll be with you in a second."

With a nod, the mobster pulled something from his bag and set it on the sales counter. The tension drained from Levi as he realized it was only a gift basket. Colorful ribbons and clear plastic covered a neatly-arranged pile of mochi, a Japanese dessert made from glutinous rice.

"Does that have the sweetened bean paste in it?" Esther asked.

Hiro shot her a smile.

She groaned and shook her head. "You boys are going to be the death of me."

Levi sipped at his seltzer. It was still early in the afternoon, and there were only two other customers sitting in the bar, both sitting at a table on the far side. Levi had just given Denny the summary of his latest problems.

"So, you don't know who's got it in for you?" Denny asked.

Levi shook his head. "Not yet. Believe me, I wish I did—then there'd be something for me to focus on. As it is, I'm kind of poring over my life and reexamining what I'm doing with it."

"Listen, man." Denny wiped a spot from one of the bar's glasses as he looked toward the street. "If there's anything I can do for you, just let me know."

"Nothing I can think of at the moment, but I have some folks looking into things for me. If I get a lead that you can help with, trust me, I won't be bashful."

Denny leaned across the bar and whispered, "I don't know about bashful, but I've been watching the window while you've been talking. There's a chick who's passed by three times, and every time, she peeks in our direction. For some reason, I'm not thinking she's looking for this brother's attention."

Levi turned. A tall slender woman stood beside the bar's window. She was dressed in a stylish dark-gray pantsuit that did a good job of showing off a nice figure, but could still be considered business attire. Straight black hair ran down to the middle of her back. Something about her curves, the hair, the mocha complexion, maybe even the eyes reminded him of girls he'd seen from Polynesia. But this woman had a more delicate bone structure. At the moment, her focus was on her phone.

"Her?" Levi said.

"Yup. Sister's not from around here, I can tell you that. She looks Hawaiian or something."

The woman put her phone in her purse and opened the door to the bar. She walked straight up to Levi and withdrew a thick envelope from her handbag. "Mr. Yoder, I was hired by a messenger service to give this to you."

The hairs on the back of Levi's neck stood on end. "I'm sorry, but I don't remember ever seeing you before, and I've got the memory of an elephant. How do you know I'm the person you're looking for?"

The woman's bland expression wavered.

A look of concern?

She smiled. "Well, I was shown a picture of you with a beard. Since you've shaved, I wasn't exactly sure if it was you. But your blue eyes are kind of hard to mistake."

Levi returned the smile. "I suppose I should be flattered." He motioned toward the bar. "Just leave it on the bar. I'll take a look at it in a bit."

The woman placed the envelope on the counter and pulled out a cell phone still in the manufacturer's box. "I'm also to give you this. It's a prepaid phone, set up with an international calling plan. I was told that the letter in the envelope explains what to do with the phone."

Levi withdrew a twenty-dollar bill from his pocket and offered it to her.

She waved her hand at the money and smiled. "I'm sorry, but I can't take that."

"Why?"

"It's against company policy."

"Sorry about that." Levi put the money back in his pocket. "Is there anything you need me to sign?"

She put the phone on the bar and began backing away. "No, I was told to just leave it with you."

"Hey, one more thing: how did you know you could find me here?"

The woman glanced at her watch. "Sorry, but I have another delivery that I'm already late for." She opened the door and walked out.

"Weird," Denny said.

"Very."

Levi leaned back against the bar, watching the entrance. There was no way a messenger service would have found him at this place—unless they'd been tracking him.

"Denny, do you have the stuff you need to run prints?"

"You mean prints off of her delivery? Sure thing. Be right back."

Levi turned back to examine the items on the bar. The envelope was plain white, with no markings. The phone was in a factory-sealed box and had no other markings aside from the brand of the phone and details of the pre-paid data plan.

For a moment he felt tempted to go after the woman, but some sixth sense told him that she was probably already long gone.

Denny returned with latex gloves and a small plastic case. He put on the gloves, opened the case, and began sprinkling a fine black powder onto the envelope.

"Were you able to run down where those tracking devices came from?" Levi asked.

"Yes and no. They're definitely government-issue, but they're kind of generic, so I don't know what agency might be using them."

With what looked like a delicate paintbrush, Denny lightly brushed away some of the powder. Two clear fingerprints appeared on the front of the envelope.

"Nice," Levi said.

Using a clear adhesive tape, Denny transferred a copy of the print to a small square of white paper. "These are clean prints. You want me to try and get an ID on her?"

"Yes, just in case. I'm guessing she's a cop or a fed or something. I suppose I'll know more when you open the envelope for me."

Denny rolled his eyes. "Why am I doing the dirty work?"

"You're better at this than I am."

"Well, at least you recognize my skills."

After Denny had transferred both prints—as well as a third he got from the back of the envelope—he took up a penknife from the case and carefully sliced the envelope open. He extracted a photo and a folded letter, and began dusting both for prints.

The photo was of a woman in a black trench coat stepping off a plane. She wore dark oversized glasses and had long shockingly bright red hair.

"Two more prints from the letter," Denny said. He transferred them to other squares of paper. "I'm thinking these prints on the letter are different than the ones from that girl." He put all five fingerprint samples in the plastic case. "I'll go scan these in while it's quiet in here. I have a friend from school who can run things through the FBI's database. It'll take at least a couple hours. If nothing shows up there, I'll dig around. I might find someone who might have access to government personnel files. If that chick's a cop or a fed, we should be able to find out."

"Thanks." Levi pointed at the partially folded letter. "Am I okay handling this now?"

Denny nodded. "Yup, go ahead. I've got what I need." He took the fingerprinting case and walked toward the back.

"Levi, you need anything?" Carmen called from the far end of the bar.

He shook his head and shot her a smile as he grabbed the letter and unfolded it. As he scanned the typewritten words, a chill raced up his spine.

Enclosed is a surveillance image of the person responsible for the deaths of Jebediah Yoder and Jacob Miller.

Last known location is in the Dolakha District in the Janakpur Zone of Northeast Nepal, approximately 125 miles east of Kathmandu.

A round-trip flight has been booked in your name, departing from JFK tomorrow morning. Flight details are enclosed on the second page.

The enclosed phone will receive updated GPS coordinates upon arrival to Nepal with further details.

The decision is yours.

"Holy hell," Levi muttered to himself. He flipped to the second page, which detailed the flight's itinerary. Flight out of JFK, connecting in Abu Dhabi, landing in Nepal. All totaled, nearly seventeen hours in the air.

His stomach burned, rage building within him. He didn't think of himself as a chauvinist—quite the opposite—but he had trouble imagining a woman slitting an eight-year-old's throat from ear to ear just to get to him.

And why would someone give him this information? What were they expecting him to do?

He turned his attention to the phone. It probably had a tracking device. But at this point, did it even matter?

When Denny returned, he nodded toward the opened letter, his eyebrows raised.

Levi gave him a *be my guest* gesture.

Denny read the letter, then looked up at Levi. "So? What are you going to do?"

"If I were smart, I'd rip this up and throw it away. It feels like a setup." But he couldn't just walk away. The image of his cousin and a dead neighbor lying in the dirt flashed into his mind's eye. He could feel the tension building inside him.

He grabbed a pad of paper and a pencil from the bar and wrote, *"Can I borrow that Faraday cage of yours? If this phone's bugged, I don't want it tracking me to my apartment."*

Denny gazed suspiciously at the boxed phone, then shot Levi a thumbs-up. He disappeared into the back and returned a moment later with two boxes, one larger than the other. He put the phone in the smaller box, which was made of copper mesh, then put the mesh box inside of what looked like a cooler. He snapped the lid shut and handed it to Levi. "Call me a bit paranoid, but just in case that thing was recording audio, it's now in a sound-proof box. It can't send anything, and more importantly it won't hear anything to record and send later."

"Want me to drop these boxes off on the way to the airport?"

"Bar closes at four a.m., so if you tell me you're buzzing by at six, I'll stay late." Denny smiled. "So, I guess you're going?"

Levi hopped off the barstool and drank the rest of his seltzer. "Well, my visa is still good for entry into Nepal, since I was just there a couple weeks ago. I'll call the airline when I get home and double-check everything. If it all checks out … I suppose I've done stupider things before."

Denny leaned across the bar and bumped fists with Levi. "Man, be careful. If I get anything before tomorrow morning on those prints, you want me to call?"

"Yup. If I'm being set up, I'd really like to know whose neck to choke."

CHAPTER NINE

Madison and Jen sat in the conference room, waiting for Maddox. His laptop was already hooked up to the projector, and the screen at the front of the room showed two images of Lazarus Yoder.

Jen pointed at the images. "Isn't that Yoder without his beard? Do you know where we got these pictures?"

"I took the one on the left, where he's sitting at a bar. The other one, I have no idea. Looks like he's at an airport security check. Has to be recent, since he doesn't have the beard."

Jen's eyes widened. "You surveilled him? Are you serious?"

"Actually, Maddox had me deliver some stuff to him."

Jen tilted her head and stuck out her lower lip. "Well, what was he like? Is he as good-looking in person?"

"You really have a one-track mind, don't you?"

"Come on. You have to admit that's as pretty of a face as any you've ever seen."

Madison shrugged. "Oh, he's definitely nice to look at, but there's something about him." Yoder's piercing blue eyes still haunted her. She'd felt as if he could see right through her. "I'm sure my mind was playing tricks with me, but it felt like he had a finely tuned bullshit detector and knew I was full of it from the moment I walked in that bar. I don't know … he felt dangerous."

The door beeped, and Maddox entered and took a seat next to his laptop. "Good morning, ladies. We've got a lot to talk about." He hitched his thumb back toward the images projected on the screen. "We'll talk about Mr. Yoder in a bit. First things first: I've asked you two here because I've gotten both of you cleared to work on a compartmented project with a codename of 'Arrow.' Obviously, we have very tight controls on who is read in, but your names have been added to the project access controls, and you should be able to access the Arrow files as of this morning. Let me brief you on the basics.

"For quite some time, the agency has been tracking the activities of a Russian mob boss known only as 'Vladimir.' We don't have a voice print or even a last name—other members of the Russian mob have been scrupulously referencing him only by his first name. As far as we know, Vladimir may not even be his real name, and it may in fact be a code word.

"But this name continues popping up, and it is commonly linked with mention of the Mount Yamantau site, located in the Ural Mountains."

"That's where Yoder's hitter traveled to."

"Exactly, Agent Lewis. That and the association with our elusive Vladimir in prior voice transcripts have made this Yoder fellow and his links to the Russian mob much more interesting. It's also why you're being read into Project Arrow.

"Let me start from the beginning.

"On March tenth, 1956, an Air Force B-47 went missing somewhere over the Mediterranean.

"Very few people are aware that the plane had been loaded at MacDill Air Force Base with a nuclear payload. Two Mark 15 nuclear bombs, with a combined yield estimated to be 3.4 megatons of TNT.

"Until very recently, the aircraft and its payload were both labeled as missing."

Madison remembered a moment from more than five years ago. It couldn't be the same incident. Could it?

Maddox pointed at her, as if reading her mind. "That's right, Agent Lewis. It was only a few days ago that I learned that you, while you were still with the Navy, were involved in helping the agency discover and dive on the missing B-47. It was during that dive that we learned the nukes had been separated from the wreckage. And from the intelligence we've been able to gather, we believe that those nukes are now in the possession of the Russian mob."

Jen gasped. "What in the world would they want with nukes? Sell them on the black market?"

"That's part of this project's mission. Gather intelligence about where our missing assets are, and if possible, understand who's behind the theft and what motivates them."

Madison leaned forward in her chair. "What does that have to do with Yamantau? I did some digging on it, and from what I could gather, it seems like it was suspected of being a Soviet-era nuclear research facility as well as a bunker in case of nuclear war."

Maddox nodded. "That's all correct. However, the intelligence we've been able to gather so far has indicated that elements of the Russian government are reactivating something they called 'Perimeter.' We believe that the Perimeter system is based out of a military base located inside Mount Yamantau."

"What's Perimeter do?" Jen asked.

"The principle behind the Perimeter system is simple. The Soviets were afraid that if at any time the leadership was killed or lost communication with their nuclear missile silos, a system would be able to retaliate automatically in the case of a nuke being dropped within the Soviet border."

"Oh, crap." Madison felt the hairs on her arms stand on end. "You don't think anyone would set off a nuke in their own country to start World War Three, do you?"

"That's the problem." Maddox pressed his lips together. "We can only guess at what's going on and what the motivations are. That's why we need more intelligence. However, I will say that we've run what intelligence we have past our war gamers, and they've come up with a scenario that should send chills through us all."

"Someone in the Russian mob could be trying to use our own weapons to trigger an automatic launch of the Russian nuclear missile defense system, which we believe currently stands at over 850 intercontinental ballistic missiles, capable of hitting anywhere in the continental US

"The secretary of defense has been informed of this scenario, and he's briefed the president."

Maddox leaned forward and tapped his index finger on the table for emphasis. "Agent Lewis, Agent Lancaster, it doesn't get more serious than this. We've been activated to investigate, using *whatever resources* are at our disposal."

Jen's back stiffened. "Have we tried talking to the Russian government about what we know? I mean, why would anyone want to do what those war gamers are proposing? It sounds crazy."

Maddox sighed. "It's complicated. From what we can tell, the Russians have their own internal factions warring with each other. Some of them want to rekindle the Soviet Union and relive the past, while others are truly looking to reinvent Russia into a modern, capitalist society. Still others may want nothing more than to turn the US into a nuclear wasteland.

"They know one or two nukes would never accomplish that, but if they can create a scenario where the *entire Russian arsenal* is launched against us at once …"

The room fell silent as Maddox's words hung ominously in the air. Jen looked as if she wanted to spit nails.

"Agent Lancaster," Maddox continued, "I need you to spend the next week reading through all of the Arrow files. Get yourself familiar with everything we know about the political climate and the actors involved. I'm arranging for you to go to the Russian embassy under diplomatic credentials in ten days. We have a few other agents already embedded there, but I think we may benefit from having you there."

Jen's serious expression hadn't changed. "You're talking about mingling with the political apparatchiks of the Duma or the Federation Council."

Maddox nodded. "Before you leave, I'll want you to formulate a plan and run it by me. I'll help as much as I can from here, but once you're on location, you'll be undercover as an embassy staffer. This is the big leagues. Are you up for it?"

"Absolutely."

"Good. We'll be highly dependent on any on-the-ground intel we can get."

Maddox then turned to Madison and hitched his thumb toward the images of Lazarus Yoder. "Agent Lewis, tell me: what was your impression of Mr. Yoder?"

"He's smart. Really smart. And cautious. He wouldn't even take the package out of my hand—he asked me to leave it on the bar."

"Well, he obviously ended up opening what you gave him, because the image on the right was taken early this morning at JFK airport.

"Agent Lewis, I need you to keep your eyes on this Yoder guy as well as the hitter we've sent him after. The cell phone you gave him has a tracking device in it; I'll send you the tracking information right after this meeting. But it will be a day before he's back on the ground."

"You've sent Yoder after the hitter?" Madison tilted her head, uncertain if she'd heard him right. "What if he kills her?"

"A calculated risk," Maddox admitted. "However, our profilers believe that Yoder, given instructions, will try to stay within the lines. And besides, I think he's smart enough to realize that if he does kill her, we'll drop the dime on him. I don't know what Nepalese prisons are like, but Chinese ones are pretty unpleasant."

"Can I ask what we're asking him to do?"

"When he arrives at his destination, we'll give him the current GPS location of the hitter. We'll ask him to track her down. If necessary, immobilize her. And by using the cell phone we provided, he'll be able to activate a calling beacon for extraction."

Judging by the expression on her face, Jen was as surprised by this as Madison was.

Maddox continued. "We'll have a Blackhawk ready with a team to extract them both. Once we have the hitter, Yoder can return to the States on his own recognizance and we'll see what can be learned from the hitter. As far as we know, she's a direct associate of this

Vladimir character. If we can get her, it may crack this case wide open."

He paused. "Do either of you have questions?"

Jen shook her head. "None from me."

Madison felt a sudden pang of guilt as she glanced up at the pictures of Lazarus Yoder. They were using him, and it all somehow seemed unfair.

She turned back to Maddox and shook her head. "No questions from me."

Maddox stood. "Okay, we're done for now. Go over the Arrow files. You'll need to know them backwards and forwards."

As Madison returned to her office, she couldn't help but feel dirty. Yoder hadn't asked to be involved in this, yet she'd played a part in pulling him into it.

She swallowed hard against the sour taste in the back of her throat.

As Levi walked down the stairs from the gate at the Tribhuvan airport in Kathmandu, he found himself facing a malodorous scrum of men and women of all ages fighting to get a prime position near the luggage conveyor belt.

Pushing his way through the crowd, he grew an appreciation for what it must feel like for toothpaste to be squeezed from its tube. Thankfully, he hadn't checked a bag. He'd brought only his small backpack containing a jacket and a single change of clothes.

He shoved his way through the baggage claim area and stepped outside, where a chill wind made the pungent smell of diesel coming from the nearby rat's nest of taxis a bit more tolerable. The taxi brokers swarmed around him, yelling prices for rides into town. Levi ignored them, retrieved the cell phone he'd received at the bar from his pocket, and flipped it open.

After a minute of searching for a cellular signal, he finally managed to snag one bar of service. Almost immediately, he received a series of texts.

. . .

Mr. Yoder, welcome back to Nepal.

This phone has been updated with the latest GPS coordinates of the target. Launch the app located on the home screen, and it should act as a compass, guiding you to the target's last known location.

The location will not be exact. You will have to use the photo to locate the target.

Once you've spotted her, press the up and down volume buttons at the same time.

An extraction team will arrive within the hour and take you and the target to a US-controlled facility. From there, you will be returned to your point of origin, and the target will eventually be brought to justice.

Levi noted how the "welcome back" implied the people behind the text knew he'd been to Nepal previously.

Of course they did. They were CIA.

Before Levi left the States, Denny had managed to ID the two owners of the fingerprints. The woman who'd delivered the package was a former explosives expert and diver in the Navy, who now worked as an intelligence analyst for the CIA. Denny had been thorough and had even obtained her military discharge papers. The fingerprints on the letter belonged to a long-time agent named John Maddox.

Despite the cloak-and-dagger nonsense he'd seen on TV, Levi knew the CIA was simply an investigative arm of the government focused on gathering intelligence outside the US. So why had they decided to get him involved? Why didn't they just have an agent grab this woman themselves?

Maybe they figured they'd have in him someone who was really motivated to get the job done—seeing as she'd killed members of his family and set him up to take the fall for it. Levi smirked as he walked farther from the crowded airport entrance. On that note, they were probably right. He was *very* motivated to find this bitch.

Yet he still felt a nagging doubt in the back of his mind. He couldn't be sure this woman had actually killed those kids. He'd have to know that for sure before he tossed her to the wolves.

He launched the customized locator app on the phone, and a compass appeared. It spun for a moment, then pointed east, indicating a distance of nearly 220 kilometers. That was roughly 140 miles.

Levi waved at one of the nearby taxi drivers.

Three men immediately swarmed him, all of them shouting various numbers.

"Taxi, sir, six hundred rupees!"

"No, five hundred fifty rupees!

"I do sir for five hundred rupees!"

Levi raised his hand. "Hold on." He pressed a button on the app to bring up a road map. The target was just outside a small town he'd been in only several weeks ago. "I need a ride to Jiri."

Two of the men waved dismissively and turned away, while the remaining taxi driver's face was scrunched up as if deep in thought. When he spoke, it was without his prior enthusiasm. "Thirty-five thousand rupees, sir. Best deal."

Levi glanced over his shoulder at the swarm of taxi drivers just outside the baggage-claim area.

"Sir, can do thirty thousand rupees. No more deal."

Levi faced the short Nepalese man and said with finality, "I'll go twenty-five thousand rupees. Not one rupee more."

The man pressed his hand to his chest as if having a heart attack.

Levi maintained a neutral expression.

Apparently realizing that his feigned heart attack was getting him nowhere, the man slumped his shoulders. "Okay, twenty-five thousand rupees. Go right now."

Levi smiled.

As Levi walked into the market in Jiri, he shoved the cell phone back into his pocket. The damned thing had long ago lost all signal, and without a reliable GPS sync, the tracking application was worse than useless.

Jiri was nestled at the foot of the Himalayas, yet it had some of the amenities of larger towns, such as a small rundown hotel, a colorful market, and even a bank. It occasionally hosted eco-tourists who wanted a taste of hiking in the Himalayan countryside.

But even though the entire town was bathed in bright colors, and the strong scent of curry from one of the food vendors wafted through air, the market was quiet. The crowds weren't aggressive, the vendors weren't hawking their wares at the top of their lungs, and what he'd come to think of as the ever-present sound of children yelling or crying simply wasn't there.

It set him on edge.

He approached one of the fruit-stand vendors. Since many of the signs were written in Devanagari, the script used in India, he asked in Hindi, "Do you speak Hindi?"

The gap-toothed man was probably in his late twenties. He looked Levi over from head to toe and responded in English with a British accent. "My Hindi is terrible. Do you speak English?"

Levi chuckled as he showed the man the picture of the mysterious redhead. "I'm looking for a foreign woman who might be in town or passed through in the last day or so. Did you by any chance see someone who might resemble her?"

The man studied the picture, then shook his head. "Sorry, mate. I just got back from the capital this morning with supplies, so I really can't help."

"Okay. Thanks anyway."

With his senses on high alert, Levi walked through the market, on occasion asking passersby if they'd seen the woman in the picture. All he got was confused looks and shaking heads. For over two hours, Levi strolled through the town, searching for his elusive quarry, before he finally got a lead.

It came from one of the eco-tourists who'd just come out of a bar, smelling of beer. When Levi showed the man the picture, he pointed to the southeast and said in English, with a distinct Spanish accent, "Near the Everest Base Camp trailhead. I saw a woman that might be her. She had a blue backpack."

"Thanks."

Levi fast-walked nearly a quarter mile to a vendor area just outside the trailhead. Almost immediately, he spotted a woman wearing a blue backpack. She was roughly five and a half feet tall, fit, and wearing hiking gear. But when she turned, Levi saw that she had blonde hair and was likely in her late sixties.

Not the person he was hunting for.

With a sigh of frustration, he turned away from the crowd at the trailhead and panned his gaze across the sparse collection of vendor stands on the east side of town.

His attention was drawn to a dark-haired woman who'd just bought a small bag of loose-leaf tea. He walked toward her.

The woman brushed back a thick lock of her dark hair that had fallen into her face. He froze as their eyes met.

Her coffee-colored eyes widened, and a smile appeared on her tanned face.

Levi felt unsteady on his feet. It was as if time had stopped.

No—it was as if time no longer had any meaning as Levi stared at the woman: a ghost from a dozen years ago.

His heart raced and his skin felt clammy. He barely managed to croak the words in Farsi: "How can it be?"

The woman standing not more than fifteen feet away from him was the spitting image of Mary.

But he'd watched them lower his wife's coffin into the ground. It couldn't be.

With a familiar smile that threatened to melt Levi's heart, she approached and extended her hand. "Hello, my name is Katarina. You look very familiar; do I know you?" She spoke in Farsi, the language of Iran. Mary's native tongue.

Levi took a deep breath and blew it out slowly. *It isn't Mary.* There were tiny differences. The nose was a touch straighter. This woman's lips were fuller.

He shook her hand. "I'm sorry, my name is Levi." He hadn't used the language much in over a decade, and the words didn't flow like he wanted. "You look so much like someone I knew."

Katarina laughed and once again flipped hair away from her face. "Well, I hope that's not a bad thing. Are you here as a tourist?"

"You look just like my wife," Levi blurted without thinking. His mind still reeled as he stood in front of Mary's doppelganger. "She passed a long time ago," he added.

The woman reached out and touched his arm. "I'm so sorry, that must be hard." She glanced at his hand and took a step closer. "Are you re-married?"

He shook his head and felt his cheeks grow warm. "No. I'm just in the country for a few days and wanted to explore a bit."

Katarina looped her arm around his and gave it a squeeze. "Well, would you mind exploring together? I never imagined I'd meet someone here who could speak my language."

For an instant, Levi struggled, knowing he had a task that needed completing.

The woman gazed up at him expectantly. It was hard to reconcile how another person could look so much like his wife. It couldn't be possible, but here she was. He'd never met any of Mary's family. Could Katarina be related?

"Sure," he said finally. "Let's explore. Did you have anywhere in mind?"

She began walking, leading him toward a gently sloping trail. "I heard of some ruins, a very old Buddhist temple not so far away. It's a bit of a climb if you're up for it. In fact, I just bought some Persian tea —maybe we can have tea up at the temple?"

Levi had been to that temple before. He'd spent the night in the secluded mountaintop location. His face burned with awkward embarrassment as he imagined spending time with this woman in such a place. Nobody else around.

He smiled. "Sure, let's go."

Levi lay on the cracked-stone floor of the abandoned temple. A cool breeze blew through the ruined building, and shadows danced crazily as the wind swirled around a small campfire burning in the courtyard, sending dried pine needles skittering across the floor. But despite the chill in the air, he felt warm with Katarina's naked body pressed against him, her right thigh draped over him like a blanket.

He leaned his head against the top of hers and breathed in the scent of lavender—probably from her shampoo.

She stirred, gazed up into his face, and smiled. "That was really nice." His seductress arched her neck and gave him a kiss.

"It was." Levi returned her smile.

Katarina ran her fingernails lightly along his naked chest. The edge of one of the nails was ragged, having broken during their lovemaking.

When her fingers wandered below his waist, he squirmed, the burning from the scratches on his back reminding him of how rough-and-tumble the past few hours had been. It was like nothing he'd ever experienced with Mary. Not better, just very different.

"So, Levi, now that we know each other in such a personal way, tell me more about yourself. Who is this man I have with me?"

He chuckled and kissed the top of her head. "I guess it's kind of complicated. I'm from America, if you hadn't guessed from my accent."

She leaned up on her elbow and looked down at him, completely unfazed by their nakedness. "Yes, I kind of figured that much."

Levi had always struggled describing what he did for a living. He'd never told Mary the entire truth—although he never lied, either. "I fix other people's problems."

Katarina smiled. "Like a plumber?"

"Not quite like that. Sometimes people have problems that others can't help them with, so they turn to me."

She lazily ran her fingers up the side of his chest. "Interesting. So you clearly have more than just the talents I know about." She let out a husky laugh. "Are you Muslim?"

"No. Let's just say I was raised in a Christian home, but I'm not exactly a religious person. My family is Amish, so I'm pretty much the opposite of what they are. I just try to do what I think is right."

"Amish…" For a moment, Katarina held a pensive expression. "Is Levi a normal Amish name?"

"Well, my given name is Lazarus. But I've been using Levi ever since I left home."

For a moment, Katarina's eyes became glassy, as if she'd almost come to tears over something.

"What's wrong?"

She shivered and shook her head. "Nothing." She smiled reassuringly and patted his chest. Pushing herself up from the hard floor, she grabbed at her clothes and said, "It's getting cold and late. Let's have some tea before we put out the fire and go back into town."

As Levi gathered his clothes, she began making tea with a small kettle she'd carried in her backpack, a bottle of water, and the loose tea she'd bought. By the time Levi was lacing up his hiking boots, she was already pouring two steaming mugs.

Levi approached her and lay his hand on her back. She jolted and cursed as she tipped over one of the mugs.

"Sorry about that—didn't mean to startle you."

Katarina handed him the unspilled mug and poured a fresh one for herself, emptying the kettle.

The aroma of the tea was different from anything Levi had had before. It had an almost bitter scent that reminded him of something he couldn't quite place.

Katarina lifted her mug in a salute. "To health."

Levi lightly tapped his mug to hers. "To new friends."

Despite the warmth of the tea, she drank hers almost in one gulp, then watched him expectantly.

Levi blew on his tea, then downed the bitter concoction, doing his best to hold back a grimace. Not only was it bitter, he'd never been a fan of tea without all of the leaves strained out of it. He swallowed hard, but even so, one of the leaves tickled the back of his throat.

Katarina looped an arm around his neck and pulled his head down for a deep but quick kiss. "I have to go to the bathroom. I'll be right back, and then we'll go back into town."

She turned and was almost immediately out of sight. The crunch of her boots on the gravel outside the temple faded beneath the crackling of their dying campfire.

As Levi waited for her to return, he sat down by the fire. His skin was tingling, and he suddenly felt a bit dizzy. His eyes danced along with the movement of the flames, and nausea cramped his gut. He felt his heart rate increase, and hot beads of sweat erupted on his forehead.

Am I getting a fever?

He scooted farther from the fire, Levi lay down on the broken stone floor and waited for the world to stop tilting at odd angles.

The coolness of the floor helped.

A lethargy washed over him. His arms and legs felt as if they weighed a ton. Even his eyelids grew heavy.

When he closed his eyes, the world stopped spinning, but his heart thudded in his ears. The sound was loud, like a bass drum blasting through his consciousness.

The beat slowed.

His senses grew fuzzy, and Levi lingered in a state of half-consciousness, not sure what was real and what wasn't.

And then he heard footsteps.

Cold fingers pressed against his throat, and the smell of lavender permeated his senses.

Katarina's voice cut through the darkness as she whispered in Russian, "Vladimir sends his love."

CHAPTER TEN

A thick stream of bitter liquid dripped into Levi's mouth and down his throat.

He swallowed involuntarily.

Within moments, spasms rippled through his stomach. He launched into a sitting position, vomiting up whatever he'd just swallowed—along with everything in his belly.

"I'm surprised you drank it," said a man's voice. It echoed within the abandoned temple. "After all, you must have smelled the poison."

Levi was on all fours, still heaving.

"To tell you the truth, I'm surprised she didn't slit your throat, just to be sure she did you in all proper-like. If I were an assassin, that's what I would have done. Easy-peasy."

The memories of Katarina, the intense, almost desperate lovemaking, the bitter tea, and her final words … they all came rushing back as Levi wiped his mouth and turned toward the voice in the shadows.

"Who are you?"

A man hobbled forward, but in the darkness, it was almost impossible to make out much more than his silhouette. He was dressed in the robes of a Buddhist monk, yet spoke English with an odd accent—

almost British, but not quite. "I believe you were looking for me, and it seems like I got here just in time."

Levi's stomach gurgled with pain, and his limbs still felt as if they weighed tons. But he turned to get a better look as the monk came closer.

The monk wore a patch over his right eye, and it was clear by the wooden stump projecting from under his robes that he had at some point also lost a leg.

"I'm sorry, your holiness, but I don't remember you." Levi spat, trying to rid himself of the bitter taste in his mouth. "Did you give me something that made me throw up?"

"I did. It was the juice of carapichea ipecacuanha, a root native to your hemisphere, but one I've found to be quite useful over the years." With a steady hand, the monk reached out and touched the side of Levi's face. "My boy, you are lucky beyond words that I reached you here in time. That woman..." He scowled. "She used enough poison that, were it not for what you are, you'd be dead ten times over. And if I hadn't come along to help you rid yourself of what remained, even *you* would have died. Why did you drink it? Even I smelled it from where I was watching."

Levi's mind swirled. Katarina had tried to kill him, and her final words, the mention of Vladimir ...

"I'm an idiot." He shook his head, and sat back, feeling nauseous and furious at himself. "And thank you. I'm sorry, but ... my memory is shot. I guess I just don't remember who you are."

"Nonsense." The monk chuckled and sat with one leg tucked under him, his wooden one extended forward. "About a month or so ago, I received word that an American traveler was looking for me. At the time, I wasn't sure why you'd be looking for me, but now that we have met, I'd say it was fortune that put us in the same place at this time. I've been watching you. You and I are bound by destiny, much more so than I think you understand. The monks know me as Amar Van. Perhaps that helps?"

Levi gasped. It had only been a handful of weeks since the end of his wandering phase, but it felt like a lifetime ago. "My god, that's right." Despite feeling like death warmed over, he smiled. "I heard about you in India. One of the gurus I knew, he spoke of you with the highest of reverence and claimed I must seek your guidance. I'll admit I feel a bit silly now about it, but I was wandering the world at the time, aimless, not really sure where I belonged. But I think I've found my way."

The monk shook his head. "Getting yourself killed by a beautiful yet evil woman is not finding your way." He studied Levi with his one good eye. The starlight peeking in through the temple's broken roof reflected off the monk's bald head and face, giving him an almost ghostlike appearance. He didn't seem much older than fifty, but the strength of his voice and the way he held himself suggested a younger man. "What was your guru's name?"

"Sinjali. He's from a small village in northern India."

"Abhiram Sinjali?"

"Yes."

"I knew him when he was but a little boy at his grandfather's feet. He saw in you what I see today, and thus he sent you my way. Wise advice on his part, and wiser still on yours, for we have now met. I'm sure you have questions, especially given your situation. Let's get started."

Situation? Nearly being killed by someone he'd allowed to get close? That was a "situation"?

Levi frowned as the monk's words sank in. Guru Sinjali was in his eighties. There was no way Amar Van could have known him as a boy. "Did you say you knew Abhiram Sinjali's grandfather?"

"I did." The monk gave him a warm smile, as if he knew what Levi was thinking.

"But the guru I'm talking about is in his eighties. We must be talking about different people."

"Maybe." The monk shifted his weight slightly. "Let me explain a few things about who you are. I don't expect you to understand what I'm saying at this moment, but in time, I think you'll grow to appreciate these words.

"First of all, I can hear things that few others can. I'd wager that your vision and hearing are better than most. Same with your sense of smell. You'll realize that whether it's the bird rustling in the tree or the scent of an animal in the forest, we have become one with our surroundings. Furthermore, I'd wager your reflexes are also faster than those of most of your peers. You've probably begun to grow conscious of this difference—you've experienced times when the world seems to move at a pace slower than normal?"

Levi nodded.

The monk continued. "Colds and other common maladies don't touch you; your health is quite robust. You heal quickly from common injuries." He motioned toward the spot where Levi had thrown up. "With the exception of poisoning yourself, you are largely immune to getting sick. However, don't allow yourself to be fooled. You're much more resistant to these things, but you're not invincible."

The monk flipped his eye patch up to show an empty eye socket where the lid had been stitched shut. "You're not immune to permanent harm, either. Things lost will not be regrown." He patted at the wooden prosthetic attached to the stump of his leg.

"Your memory is nearly perfect. I'm sure at first it seems natural, but if you think on it, you'll realize it's unusual. If you try, you can almost certainly recall the precise details of, say, a menu in a restaurant you went to years ago. I can do this, and I'd wager you can as well.

"You'll learn over time that the gift you've been given—or maybe it's a curse. I suppose it doesn't matter, really, which one it is. Either way, it's a burden you'll carry for a long time.

"I've lived with this for longer than you can possibly imagine. I can't explain how or why it has come to pass. I've visited with doctors, and they cannot explain it. Oh, they certainly want to study it, but I don't think there's yet an explanation that medical science can give. This thing that we share makes some aspects of our lives terribly difficult. The ones we love, they all grow old and die." The monk's expression turned somber, and he pressed his lips together into a fine line. "That's truly the most terrible part of what we share."

Levi considered what the man had said. Some of it made absolutely no sense, but other parts ... they were too close to the truth.

"Amar Van," Levi said. "It means 'Immortal One' in Hindi. Is that what you're claiming you are? Immortal?"

"No. We can certainly be killed. The poison that woman used on you could certainly have done it. As it is, you're going to feel terrible for weeks, maybe even months, until your body regenerates enough to evacuate and replace the damaged cells." The monk leaned forward and patted Levi's knee. "Listen, it's only fair I tell you my story, because as the first to bear this, I feel responsible for you. I have no idea how you received this thing, but I can smell it on you. It's almost like the way an animal can recognize its own kind by the scents in the air. This is how I knew what you are. I'll explain to you what I know, and for now, I assure you, you'll think me insane."

With Levi's stomach rumbling its unhappiness and the bone-weary lethargy sapping his strength, he sat back and tried to focus on the old man.

"My given name is Narmer, and my story starts in a different time, in a place that you'd call Egypt…"

It was nearly dawn as Levi staggered into the Nepalese town of Jiri. He'd spent most of the night on the mountaintop listening to a crazy man speak of a time from ancient history as if he'd lived it himself.

In the condition he was in, Levi had had no choice but to suffer through the man's improbable tale of delusion. But as the hours ticked away through the night, he'd slowly gathered enough strength to stand. And eventually, when the monk's tale was complete, Levi's legs were just strong enough to carry him down the mountain, one shaky step after another.

It was vengeance that drove him forward. Vengeance and fury. He'd smashed the useless cell phone against the rocks of the temple, vowing not to let the CIA track him any longer. In his mind's eye, he saw Katarina's face and was furious with himself. *How can I possibly have thought she looked like Mary?*

That woman had tried to kill him. Knowing her true nature, it wasn't difficult to believe that she'd killed two innocent kids at his parents' farm.

He would deliver retribution. Not only for her, but for this Vladimir.

He stuck his hand in his pocket and felt the hard remnant of the fingernail he'd found on the floor of the temple. He hoped it would serve as a sample of her DNA. He would find her ... and then he would find Vladimir.

Levi raised his hand at a nearby taxi. Without giving the driver an opportunity to say a word, he pointed west. "Kathmandu airport."

"Yes, sir." The taxi driver scurried to open the passenger door, then eyed Levi with a concerned expression and took him by the arm. "Sir, you don't look well."

It took every ounce of willpower Levi had to keep from heaving uncontrollably in front of the man. "I'm fine. Just get me to the airport."

With the driver's help, Levi staggered the few feet to the open car door, leaned heavily against the doorframe, and fell into the back seat.

The driver got in the front seat. "Thirty-five thousand rupees to Kathmandu airport, sir. Okay?"

Levi let his head flop back against the seat. "Fine." He didn't have the energy to haggle.

"Okay, sir."

The car lurched forward, and Levi rested his eyes, immediately falling unconscious.

Madison scrolled through the GPS hits they'd intercepted over the last thirty-six hours. They'd gotten nothing from Yoder or the hitter in that time.

Her stomach ached as she scrolled back up to the last known hit for the two signals and typed in the GPS coordinates. "Lazarus, where are you?" She'd lost track of them both somewhere between Nepal's capital city and Jiri.

Feeling helpless, she slipped on her headphones and turned back to her never-ending list of calls, scanning them to see if anything new had come in over her lunch break.

Four new intercepts.

She clicked on the first call.

"Misha, have you heard from Karl? It's late and he hasn't come home—"

She clicked on the next call, leaving the prior one on her "to do" list.

"Dmitri, tell him it's done."

Madison sat up straight as she recognized the woman's voice. She had listened to the hitter's earlier call at least a dozen times—she would recognize that voice anywhere.

"Why are you calling from this number? Is it secure?"

"I had an issue. I think I was being tracked through my phone, so I disposed of it."

"Fine, we'll arrange a replacement. What's done? Did you find the monk?"

"No, not him. Yoder. He's been taken care of."

Madison's mouth dropped open, and a gasp caught in her throat.

"Well done. Vladimir will certainly be pleased. What about the one you were sent to look for?"

"I couldn't find him, but after I took care of Yoder, I didn't want to risk being in the area much longer, should the body be discovered."

"Understood. Are you coming back in?"

"I'm almost there. Will be in later tonight."

"I'll let him know."

The call ended, and Madison ripped her headphones off and threw them on the desk. She slumped against the back of her chair, feeling an overwhelming sense of guilt.

"He's been taken care of," Madison repeated aloud. Hot tears blurred her vision.

Lazarus had been within arm's reach only a few days ago—healthy, vibrant, and alive. And now …

"He's been killed," she whispered to nobody in particular. *Because of us.*

Because of me.

Wiping the tears from her eyes, she stiffened her resolve and pressed her phone's speed-dial button for Maddox.

"Hey Maddie, what's up?"

"We need to talk. I think we've lost an asset in Nepal, and I think we've lost our tracking device on our hitter."

"Shit. Okay, I'll be right there."

Madison hung up and blew her nose.

This wasn't the first time she'd dealt with someone's death, but it was the first time she'd ever felt such an emotional reaction to anything at work.

She dabbed at her face. She didn't want to look teary when her boss walked in.

"He was associated with the mob. These things happen." She said it aloud, and it was true—but it didn't make her feel any better.

She felt as if something had died in her along with that blue-eyed man.

The flight into LAX was terrible; the poison was still working through Levi's system. The flight attendant noticed him staggering back and forth from the airplane bathroom, and arranged for him to have a wheelchair waiting for him at the gate.

He protested, of course—out of pride, obstinance, or perhaps simple stupidity—but in retrospect, he was grateful she didn't listen to him. He felt glad to not have to walk through the airport. He was seriously ill and had to face it.

And having a wheelchair in an airport proved to be an amazing experience. Levi quickly learned that people in wheelchairs went through customs and security much faster than everyone else. Even so, it took a full two hours before he managed to get himself into a taxi.

He told the driver to take him to the nearest emergency room.

Within minutes of his arrival, the doctors had him stripped down, wearing a hospital gown, and lying on a bed under warming covers. For a while, he passed in and out of consciousness, but eventually the effects of the poison were too much, and he fell asleep.

He woke, what felt like a very short time later, to find that someone had inserted an IV in his right arm and hooked him up to monitoring equipment. A nurse was placing two fluid-filled bags on the IV pole, and the equipment emitted a quiet beep with each heartbeat.

A doctor walked in with a chart in his hand. "Mr. Yoder, I'm very glad you were smart enough to cut short your travel home and come in. I'm Dr. Keller, the attending physician. Let me tell you something, it's a miracle you're alive right now. You *should* be dead. I frankly can't explain how you made it on a trans-Pacific flight and survived with what's in your system right now."

Levi felt a warm sensation crawling up his arm where the IV was pushing fluids into him. "What's wrong with me?"

The doctor pulled open his chart. "You have severe cyanide toxicity." He pointed a pen at the IV running into Levi's arm. "We're pumping you full of stuff that should help tremendously. I've administered a Cyanokit containing hydroxocobalamin, along with Nithiodote which is a solution of sodium thiosulfate and sodium nitrite. Both of those should help your system metabolize the cyanide into a form that you'll be expelling through your urine. I've also pushed an anti-emetic into your IV, so that should help with the nausea you complained about. You're extremely dehydrated, so we're also pumping you full of saline to help flush all of this through your system."

"How long will it be before I'm feeling less like someone who should be dead?"

Dr. Keller chuckled. "I still can't believe you're *not* dead with these lab results. We're going to take another sample of your blood after this treatment gets a chance to infuse through your system and see how things are trending. Either way, a nurse is going to be here in a bit to run a catheter. I'm admitting you overnight for observation, but I hope you'll be feeling better very soon. Maybe a day or two; it all depends on your bloodwork."

The room tilted a bit, and Levi lay his head back. He motioned toward his clothes, which had been stacked on a chair. "I want to make sure …"

A wave of nausea hit him, and he gritted his teeth.

"Mr. Yoder, don't worry about your belongings. The nurses will put everything in a bag, and it will be brought with you to your room. I'll go work on the admitting paperwork right now and see you in a couple hours, okay?"

Feeling weaker than he ever had in his life, Levi closed his eyes. "Thank you."

Scenes from the past few weeks flashed through Levi's mind.

Blood pooling around two innocent children lying in the dirt.

Katarina toasting to his health.

The delusional monk claiming he was much more than what he seemed.

The faceless image of a man he'd never met. Vladimir.

That man wanted him dead, and Levi had no idea why.

His mind reeled with the possibility that Vladimir might have people in this hospital waiting to finish Katarina's failed task.

Will I survive this? Levi wondered as the world went dark and consciousness fled.

CHAPTER ELEVEN

Levi dried off from the shower, wrapped a thick terry-cloth towel around his waist, and walked over to the bathroom mirror. It had been two weeks since he'd been poisoned, and even though the nausea was gone, he still felt relatively weak. He'd lost nearly fifteen pounds.

Vinnie had been out of town when Levi came back from Nepal, but when his friend came to the apartment yesterday to visit, he wouldn't take no for an answer. His friend arranged for Levi to see a local doctor. His appointment was in two hours.

"You should be dead."

The LA emergency room doctor's words still rang in his ears, and scenes of that night in Nepal flashed through his mind. Katarina's face haunted him, their frenzied lovemaking, her toasting to "his health," and his ultimate poisoning.

He'd been totally suckered.

He'd smelled something off coming from the mug of tea. And he'd ignored it. *I should have known.*

And then the words of that crazy monk, the one who claimed he was older than dirt itself. *"The ones we love, they all grow old and die."*

Levi leaned over the sink and studied himself in the mirror. His face was a bit gaunt from the weight loss—not emaciated, but he could tell that he'd been sick. But his eyes shone brightly in the bathroom light. At age forty-two, his dark hair showed no signs of going gray. No bags under his eyes, nor any signs of crow's-feet.

He lifted his right arm and looked at the side of his chest where he'd been sliced open by the Russian. He no longer saw the pink line where he'd been cut. No scar, no blemishes, nothing.

"You heal quickly from common injuries," the monk had said.

Shaking his head, Levi turned away from the mirror and went to get dressed.

Levi cradled the phone on his shoulder and stared out the window at the snow flurries. "Hey, Lola. I don't seem to have a phone book in this place. Do you think it's possible for you to call up a taxi for me? I've got an eleven a.m. doctor's appointment at Mount Sinai Medical Center."

"Of course, hon. Is it the one on First Avenue?"

"Yes."

Lola was the ultimate example of the voice not matching the person. Her voice was grating and harsh—a smoker's voice, though as far as he knew, she didn't smoke. Yet in person, she was a nicely padded woman in her sixties who was always smiling and would happily talk your ear off about anything, if given half a chance.

"I'll take care of it," she said. *"And I'll have one of the boys call you when they get there. Just take care of yourself, you got me?"*

"I'll go downstairs and wait."

"Now don't you give me any lip. I said wait. I don't care how tough you are, you've been sick. And besides, it might take a while. It was snowing earlier, and the traffic's a mess. You stay put and relax, you hear me?"

Levi chuckled. "Yes, Mom."

He'd interacted with Lola even back in the old neighborhood. She was Frankie's godmother—or maybe aunt, he wasn't sure. But like all the Italian women he'd known, she had her mothering and domestic side, and then there was the side that would throw a shoe at you if you got out of line.

"That's better. Just sit tight. I'll have one of the boys let you know when they get here."

Levi hung up and flexed his hands. He noticed the thin white mark on his right hand—the scar from when he was a kid and cut himself on some tin roofing. Unlike the scar on his side, this scar remained.

Levi opened and closed his fist, watching the muscles in his forearm flex and relax, the tendons showing clearly. Veins bulged in his forearms.

During his training in Japan, his fists had pounded on bundled tatami mats thousands of times.

Tens of thousands of times.

He'd stayed up late at night, while everyone else was asleep, loosing his frustrations on those bundles of reeds until his fists were bloody.

But as he studied his knuckles now, he didn't see even a blemish.

How could that be?

Why would he still have obvious scars from when he was a kid, but nothing from more recently? Nothing on his knuckles, nothing on the side of his chest.

Levi thought once more of Amar Van, the monk.

No, not Amar Van. That's what the other monks called him. *He* said his name was Narmer.

What the hell kind of name is Narmer?

Not Russian, certainly not Indian or East Asian.

He looked over at the computer on the desk. He'd never even turned it on before. He'd spent the first eighteen years of his life without electricity, so it wasn't much of a surprise that he'd never become fond of computers. But now there was something he needed to know.

He leaned forward and pressed the red power button on the front of the machine.

The machine beeped and whirred, and the monitor displayed a logo as the computer did whatever it was programmed to do. The logo looked different than the ones he'd seen in the past.

Was it a new version of Windows?

He barely even knew what that meant.

The logo disappeared, and the screen showed all sorts of tiny images. Then the word "Google" popped up, with a small box beneath it.

Levi stared at the mouse with suspicion. He'd used a mouse before, in the New York public library. When Levi had first come to the city, the library had astounded him—he'd never imagined so many books in his life. And then computers replaced the card catalogs that he'd become accustomed to—and that was how he learned what little he knew of computers.

Levi put his hand on the mouse and moved the little arrow on the screen until it hovered over the "Search Google" text. He pressed a button on the mouse, typed "Narmer," and hit the enter button.

The screen changed, providing him with a list of "hits" that showed references to his query. Something called Wikipedia showed up at the top, and he clicked on it.

The screen changed yet again, and Levi's eyes darted across the text.

Narmer was an ancient Egyptian king of the Early Dynastic Period. His identity is the subject of debates, although the dominant opinion among Egyptologists associates Narmer with the pharaoh Menes, who is renowned as the first king and unifier of Ancient Egypt.

Levi frowned. Whoever the monk was, he was trading on the name of a famous pharaoh.

He scrolled down the page, quickly absorbing the text. But when an image came up, he froze.

He recognized the item in the picture.

It was a golden cross with a loop on the top. The web page called it an ankh.

He quickly read the text beneath it.

Egyptian gods are often portrayed carrying the ankh by its loop. It is also an ideograph symbolizing life.

His mind raced back to the bank vault.

The tumors throughout his body.

The words spoken by the doctor in the Sloane-Kettering Institute: *That man in the waiting room doesn't have a thing wrong with him.*

The side of his scar-free chest.

His knuckles.

"Son of a bitch!"

The phone rang, and he grabbed the receiver. "Yes?"

"Hey, it's Tony. Your taxi guy is waiting for you. I'll make sure he don't leave. Come down when you're ready."

"Thanks, Tony, I'll be right there."

He hung up the phone and glanced once more at the picture of the golden ankh before turning off the computer.

He waved dismissively. "It's got to be some kind of screwed-up coincidence."

Levi signed into the patient reception area at the Mount Sinai Medical Center on First Avenue just before eleven o'clock. Before he could even find a seat in the crowded waiting room, his name was called by a nurse wearing blue scrubs.

He walked around a man being wheeled through the reception area and approached the blonde nurse who held a door open for him.

She wore an amused expression. "You're looking pretty good for a zombie." She led him down a back hallway and into an examination room, where she pointed at a high-armed chair. "Go ahead, take a seat and extend your left arm for me. I'll need to find a good vein."

"What was that about a zombie?" Levi asked.

The young nurse laughed, her cheeks reddening. "Sorry, I was just kidding. It's just that when Dr. Romano got your medical records from LA, he was pretty sure you couldn't be among the living."

She tightened a rubber tube around his upper arm and tapped with her gloved hand on a vein on the inside of his elbow. She rubbed an alcohol swab on the bulging vein and, with a practiced motion, pierced his skin with a needle that had a long thin tube attached to it. She then pushed a vial into the end of the tube.

Levi's blood spurted into the sealed tube.

With a practiced maneuver, she swapped out the filled tube and replaced it with another. Midway through it being filled, she released the makeshift tourniquet.

"How long will it take to get the results from the lab?" Levi asked.

The nurse withdrew the second vial and set it on the counter with the first. She placed a wad of cotton gauze against where she'd punctured him, withdrew the needle, and secured the gauze with several loops of a rubberized bandage. "It won't take long. The doctor wants it back right away. I'll take these vials to the lab, and I'll be right back to finish getting your other vitals."

As she was leaving, Levi blurted, "Do you think I can have my hearing and eyes checked real quick?"

"Of course. I'll be right back."

"Okay," the nurse said, "read the letters where my finger is pointing."

Levi had his hand over his left eye and peered at the eye chart. "P E Z O L C F T D."

"What?" The nurse stared at the chart. "Where did you get that from?"

Levi pointed at the chart. "At the bottom."

The nurse leaned down and squinted. "Damn. Okay, switch eyes and tell me what's the lowest place you can see."

Levi moved his hand over his right eye. The letters were clear. "P E Z O L C F T D."

The nurse shook her head and scribbled something in his chart.

"So, what'd I get, twenty-twenty?"

"No." The nurse continued writing.

Her shy smile was infectious. She was short, with a pretty face and a pear-shaped body. A diamond ring was on her left hand. She gave off a wholesome, good-natured vibe. Someone who liked to laugh. Such a different type of person than that creature who called herself Katarina.

Mary had been like this nurse. Happy. Wholesome. Their lives had been full of laughter.

"Why is it that 'no' is the only answer I get from all the women in my life?" Levi asked.

"I hardly believe that for a second." The nurse's cheeks reddened. "You're not twenty-twenty. Try twenty-ten, both eyes. Frankly, I'm not sure if I ever had anyone test at twenty-ten before. I had a couple kids do twenty-fifteen, but those were kids, not a forty-two-year-old adult. That's pretty impressive."

"And how'd the hearing test turn out?"

"Oh, with that you're an over-achiever as well." The nurse flipped through his chart. "We do a lot of hearing tests at this location, both for older people and for young kids. If there's any hearing issues, we usually see a sensitivity drop-off at higher frequencies—you know, as you get older, it's pretty normal for our ears to get less sensitive to certain higher pitches. But you don't seem to have *any* sensitivity loss. On the contrary, you're probably one of those who can actually hear a pin drop."

"So—I'm in good shape then?"

"I'd say! Your vision is twenty-ten, which means you can see stuff at twenty feet as well as most normal people can see it at ten feet. Basically your vision is about twice as good as people with what we think of as perfect vision. And your hearing is even better than that. Your sensitivity even at high frequencies is ridiculously good. I'll have to ask around and see if anyone has seen results like yours, but I wouldn't worry too much about needing a hearing aid just yet." She winked at him and teased, "All I know is that I'm not about to whisper things while you're in the building. You'd probably be able to hear it."

Levi rolled his eyes as the nurse set his chart on the counter and told him she'd be right back.

The monk's voice echoed in his head. *I'd wager that your vision and hearing are better than most.*

"Shut up," Levi grumbled.

A man in a lab coat knocked on the open exam door and walked in. "Mr. Yoder, I'm Dr. Romano." He shook Levi's hand. "How are you feeling? The nurse told me you were concerned about your hearing and vision." He picked up Levi's chart and began flipping through the pages.

Levi shook his head. "I was mistaken."

"Well, that's good to hear—no pun intended." The doctor grinned.

The nurse walked in and handed some papers to the doctor. "The labs just came in."

"Excellent." Dr. Romano began flipping through the lab results. "Well … I'd have to say you're looking pretty good. You're a shade on the low side with your iron levels, but I suppose after what you've been through, that's not unexpected."

"I'm down about fifteen pounds."

"How are you feeling overall? Has the nausea subsided?"

Levi nodded. "I'm not feeling sick anymore. Just maybe more tired than I'm used to."

"That's likely from the mild anemia." The doctor made a few notes in the chart, closed it, and stared directly at Levi. "But I think someone up there is watching over you, Mr. Yoder. You've recovered remarkably well. Now that you're rid of the nausea, I recommend you start focusing on your diet. Give yourself three full meals a day, try to mix in some dark leafy vegetables, beans, or even a nice big steak. You do that, and I think your iron levels should shoot right back up to normal, and you'll be feeling fine."

"That's it? The cyanide is flushed out of my system?"

"Yep, that's it. As far as I'm concerned, you're a walking miracle—but judging from your vitals and the blood work, I think the poisoning is thankfully, something you're done with. Did you have any other questions or concerns?"

"Nope, I think I'm good." Levi stood and shook the doctor's hand.

The doctor smiled and bowed his head slightly. "If you get a chance, tell Don Bianchi that Carmine Romano sends his best."

"I'll do that."

It suddenly dawned on Levi why he'd just been seen by the chief physician at Mount Sinai with practically no wait. Being a friend of the Don had its benefits.

A handful of mob associates were working out in the basement of the Helmsley Arms, the building that Levi now called home. Floor-to-ceiling mirrors were mounted on the walls, and state-of-the-art workout equipment ranged from stationary bikes to treadmills to a series of weightlifting stations.

Most of the crew were rotating through the weightlifting stations, but Levi found himself in the center of the gym, squared off against a 125-pound heavy bag hanging by a chain from the ceiling. Beads of sweat poured down his face as he performed a series of snap kicks, the heavy thwacks of his shin against the canvas echoing loudly across the gym.

It had been over a month since he'd returned from Nepal, and even now, he wasn't one hundred percent. He wasn't yet back up to his normal weight, but he was working hard to build up his stamina.

Tony Montelaro, the man whose wrist Levi had popped out of joint, set aside two forty-five-pound barbells and pointed at the bag. "Want me to hold it?"

Levi gave him a nod, and the big man grabbed the bag, steadying its gyrations.

With an ever-increasing pace, Levi sent a barrage of jabs, kicks, and punches at the now-steadied target. His hits grew in intensity, forcing Tony to brace himself against the onslaught.

After nearly two minutes of nonstop attacks, Levi finished with a spinning back kick that knocked Tony two steps backward and left Levi breathing heavily.

His muscles aching, Levi grabbed a towel and wiped his face. The heat from the exertion made him feel better than he had in a long time.

"Holy crap."

Levi turned to see that the others in the gym had stopped working out and were staring at him. "What?"

Tony chuckled and rubbed at his chest. "I'm just glad I wasn't that damned bag."

"Amen," said one of the other bull-necked mobsters. "I ain't seen nothing like that before in my life. Freaking Tasmanian devil is what that was."

Levi smiled and patted Tony on the shoulder. "Thanks for holding it for me." He pointed at the man's wrist. "Feeling better?"

"Yup. Doc said for me to start slow, so I'm keeping my bench press under two-fifty for now."

The elevator at the far end of the gym slid open, and Frankie stood in its doorway. He caught Levi's attention and motioned for him.

Levi gave Tony a playful jab to his heavily muscled arm before walking over to Frankie. "What's up?"

"Let's talk outside."

A minute later, the two men were on the street outside the apartment building. "Frankie," Levi said, "my workout clothes aren't exactly made for forty-degree weather. Why are we talking out here?"

"Let's just say I feel better talking out here."

Levi stuck his hands under his armpits as they started to walk.

"Levi, we managed to track down the bastard who was behind the state messing with your finances. He's retired now, but he was some higher-up in the New York Department of Taxation and Finance. Hell, once the bastard broke up the trust you'd arranged to pay your bills, he managed to pick up your house for the price of a year's worth of unpaid property taxes. He then flipped it for a big profit."

"You're shitting me. Are you sure?"

"No doubt about it. The same guy's signature was all over your stuff."

A surge of heat coursed through Levi, and his face flushed with anger. "I need a name and address. This is personal, so let me handle this my way, you understand?"

Frankie gave Levi an evil grin. "I figured you'd say that. When I told Vinnie, he just about hit the roof. Let's just say if there's anything you need, the family will lend whatever muscle is necessary."

"I appreciate it." Levi's mind churned. "So, tell me again why we're talking out here? What are you worried about?"

Frankie scowled. "You were still recovering, so I didn't bother you about it. But a couple weeks ago, I began suspecting one of the connected guys of playing more than one side. I bugged his place, and ... well, let's just say he's out. But I found a bug in his room, and it wasn't one of ours. Until we're sure the place is clean, I'm not risking talking any business in there."

Frankie didn't spell it out, but Levi knew that the guy they had kicked out was by now lying under a few tons of garbage at the dump. That was the price for working for one of the other families or trying to collect evidence for law enforcement. That's just how things worked in these rackets.

That was also where Levi drew the line. He didn't get involved in the dirty side of the business. He stayed clean. He'd always imagined himself as kind of like Tom from the Godfather movies: the family's *consigliere*. He was the cool-headed one who helped with strategies or fixed issues that couldn't be addressed with brute force.

But there were two big differences between him and that fictional character. First, Levi wasn't a lawyer. And second, Levi didn't mind *bending* the law. It was breaking it that he wasn't interested in.

He and Frankie had rounded the block and were heading back toward the apartment building. "Frankie, if you're interested, I know somebody who can do a security scrub on the place. Back in the day, I used to work with this guy's father, and he never failed me. This kid's a chip off the old block, just higher-tech. More modern. I'll vouch for him. He knows the score."

Frankie rubbed his hands briskly together and shoved them deep into his pockets. "I was going to ask if you knew someone. Yeah, hook me up with your guy. And I'll give you the name and address of that finance guy."

"Is he living in the city?"

"Nah, he's got a big place out in Connecticut. A freaking mansion on the sound, if you can believe it."

Levi smiled. "So he's probably got cable."

Frankie gave him a sidelong glance. "I'd guess so."

"Do we have anyone who works for the cable companies over there?"

Frankie paused at the entrance to the Helmsley Arms. "I think we can maybe dig up some friends over there. Why?"

Levi smiled. "Let me take a look at the address. I have a few ideas."

CHAPTER TWELVE

Levi shrugged his shoulders, trying to release the tension he felt as Angelo, one of Frankie's men, drove him through the nighttime streets of Fairfield. The electric car glided silently through a posh neighborhood of multi-acre estates within sight of the Long Island Sound.

"It's kind of eerie how this thing makes no noise," Levi said.

Angelo patted the dashboard. "Brand new Tesla Model S. I love this thing. Not only can I get to a job without even a whisper of engine sound, I can jam the accelerator and be outta here in no time flat."

"I can only imagine what they'll come up with next."

Levi scanned the area—examining the homes, the streetlights, what cars were parked outside, anything that might matter. It was two in the morning, so most of the houses' lights were off. None of the houses on this part of the street had fences. They probably figured with all the land around them, why bother?

No fences was good.

"Let's stop here," Levi said. "Our target is a couple blocks north on this street."

"You got it." Angelo pulled the car to the side of the road and rolled forward so that they were in the shadows between two streetlights.

The two men hopped out. Levi watched approvingly as the wiry driver closed his car door behind him without a sound. Angelo was a street soldier for the family, so he knew how to work at night.

As they walked nonchalantly toward the home of their target, Angelo leaned closer and whispered, "Mr. Minnelli told me to help you out. Are you going to fill me in on what we're doing?"

"I'm going to give someone some cable problems, that's all. I just need you as lookout."

Breathing in the salty air, Levi felt a surge of nervous energy. It was near freezing, and he caught a whiff of someone using their wood-burning fireplace.

He slowed as they approached their target: a large, multi-story home on the street corner. There was at least a one-hundred-and-fifty-foot stretch of lawn between the sidewalk and the metal box on the side of the house.

It was just like the cable guy had told him.

Levi gazed up the wall and along the roofline to a cluster of floodlights. He shrugged off his backpack, unzipped it, and took out a soccer ball.

"What in the world are you going to do with that?" Angelo asked.

"Watch."

Using a sideways throw, Levi whipped the ball toward the house. It landed in the grass, hopped a few times, then rolled along the slope toward the house. The floodlights kicked on, bathing the west side of the property in a brilliant, purplish-white light.

"Shit, motion detectors," Angelo whispered. Levi sensed the man's tension as he shifted his weight from one foot to another.

"Shh." Levi crouched on the sidewalk as the ball slowly rolled to a stop. He raised a hand to his brow to block the glare, and spotted a white rectangular box just underneath the lights. The motion sensor.

He dug into the backpack once more, pulled out a paintball gun, and took aim at the small plastic emitter just below the floodlights.

He pulled the trigger, and with an uncomfortably loud noise, the pressurized CO_2 sent a paintball flying at nearly three hundred feet per second. A plastic *thwap* sounded as the paint pellet struck its target.

Levi sent two more quick shots downrange, covering the sensor in black goo. With each shot, Angelo cringed at the noise. "Man, why aren't you just using a silenced .22? It's quieter than that damned thing, and it would be more accurate."

"I'm coming back to this place later," Levi whispered. "If that thing's hooked up to an alarm system inside, it'll probably freak out if the motion detector suddenly stops working because it got a bullet through it."

Angelo looked doubtful. "You think that paint's going to let you get past the motion detector?"

Levi smiled. "Not everything is as it seems. Let's just say those paintballs are a special formula. It should hopefully confuse things—"

The floodlights winked off.

Levi motioned for silence as he waited in the dark, listening, focusing all of his senses for anything out of the ordinary. It was dead quiet. Even the light breeze had expired, leaving Levi with only the sound of his own heartbeat.

Levi put away the paintball gun and handed Angelo his backpack. "Stay here and keep an eye out for any movement in or out of the house," he whispered. "It shouldn't take me more than a minute or two."

Angelo nodded.

With a nervous flutter in his stomach, Levi moved forward. He wasn't sure if what he'd done had worked. Esther had claimed the contents of the paintballs were formulated to be much thicker than normal, and the metal flakes in the paint would also bamboozle many of the motion detection technologies.

But you never knew with these things.

With a pair of wire cutters in one hand and a set of lock picks in the other, Levi casually walked across the lawn, the partially frozen grass crunching underfoot.

Despite his relaxed outward appearance, Levi was ready to sprint if he needed to. He hadn't come here to get stopped by a motion detector.

A smile crept across his face as the floodlight ignored his approach.

The paintballs had worked.

Levi knelt in front of a metal box at the side of the house. On the front was a sticker reading *Frontier Communications*. The box was locked with a simple cam lock that he could have taught any third-grader to pick.

He extracted a tension tool from his lockpick set, stuck it in the slot, and before he could even select a pick, the tumbler began turning.

He barely suppressed a laugh as he flipped open the box.

He found the coaxial cable connection and unscrewed one cable from the other. Then he relocked the box, gathered up the soccer ball, and calmly walked back to Angelo.

Step one was complete.

A wiry man dodged in and out of range, a serrated kitchen knife in his right hand.

The man lunged at Levi.

Levi blocked the knife hand with his forearm and clinched the mobster's arm. He pressed hard into the base of the assailant's wrist while bending it forward.

The man grunted, and the knife fell from his hand.

Levi let go and hopped out of reach.

"Damn, my fingers just went numb." The mobster cast a pained grin at Levi as he rolled his wrist back and forth.

"Lots of nerves bunched up at that spot," Levi said. He turned to the other half dozen mobsters gathered in the basement gym of the apartment building. "Just remember, block, twist, and use your leverage against the attacker's arm and wrist." He shifted his stance, putting his right leg behind him. "Also, remember to pay attention to your opponent's stance. Whatever leg is in the back, that's the arm they'll lunge with."

Standing with his right leg in back, Tony pantomimed a lunge at nobody in particular, but with his left arm. He then switched and lunged forward with his right and shook his head. "I'll be damned."

Levi took a seat on the floor of the gym and began stretching.

One man began practicing the blocking technique Levi had just shown them. "Are there other tricks you can teach us?" he asked.

"Sure. But how about I make you guys a deal. You all practice blocking knife attacks with each other. Whoever ends up mastering that, I'll teach you something else from my bag of tricks. Oh, and when you're practicing, none of you *momos* use real knives, you got me? I don't want to hear from Mr. Minnelli about you guys accidentally stabbing each other. Just use a stick or something."

Tony walked to the weight rack and began curling forty-five-pound dumbbells. "Hey Levi, do you mind if I ask a business-type question?"

Levi noticed the uneasy expression on Tony's face. "It depends. Go ahead and ask; I can't guarantee an answer."

"Well, Mr. Minnelli told us all not to talk to you about the details of some of the jobs we do. You're not involved in that side of the business. But can I ask, what does a fixer really do?"

The other men suddenly turned toward Levi, and the place went quiet. None of these guys had likely been "made men" when Levi had last been associated with the family, so they wouldn't know about his arrangement with the Bianchi family.

Levi tilted his head to the side and cracked his neck.

"That's an okay question to ask. Let me make it real simple. Think of me as the Don's *consigliere*, his advisor. I don't get involved with a lot of what you guys do, but I take care of special things. I fix situations that need fixing."

"Can you give—"

"Hold on, Carmine." Levi held up a finger and grinned. "I was going to give you an example. Sometimes, the family needs help getting some information that we can't otherwise use muscle to get. I'm pretty good at accessing places I have no business being in and learning about stuff that others can't.

"Everyone ignores the ragged old man standing on the street corner, smelling like piss, as he watches people stroll by.

"Nobody cares about the waiter in a fancy Wall Street restaurant. They don't think about him listening to conversations he shouldn't hear.

"Well, I've *been* that waiter and that old man, and lots of other things. I'm pretty good at sniffing out rats or getting information when nobody else can.

"I fix problems that most of you guys never knew existed.

"And sometimes, I even help fix problems for people who simply can't help themselves. There's lots of bad things happening on the street, as you guys all know. Sometimes I'm the Angel of Death; other times I'm just an angel."

Levi panned his gaze across the room. He had everyone's attention. Some of them were nodding with inscrutable expressions. "Does that help explain things?"

Tony chuckled. "Can you please give me a warning when the Angel of Death is coming? I don't want to be anywhere in the five boroughs, if you know what I mean."

Levi winked. "Just keep your nose clean, stick to the family rules, and I don't think you'll ever need to worry about that." He glanced up at the wall clock. "Okay guys, I've got to go."

Denny had called earlier saying he had some information for him. And this was one appointment he intended to be on time for.

Levi sat on a folding chair next to Denny's desk as he waited for the electronics genius to sort through a stack of FedEx envelopes. He glanced at his phone and frowned. "You don't get any signal in here."

Denny pulled one of the envelopes from the stack and laid it on his desk. "Of course not. I couldn't do some of my work if I didn't have a place that wasn't isolated from all the stray signals in the outside world."

Levi shrugged and shoved his phone back into his pocket.

"I've got what you were looking for." Denny squeezed open the envelope, and several papers fell out along with a tiny Ziploc bag containing a ragged piece of fingernail with red polish. "First things first." He nudged the fingernail toward Levi. "That thing just gives me the creeps. You can have that back."

The hair on Levi's neck stood on end as he stared at Katarina's nail. She'd been a huge lesson to him about people … and about himself. He'd made that mistake because of how much she looked like Mary— and he'd allowed that vulnerability to cloud his judgement. That was a mistake that had nearly cost him his life.

He grabbed the baggie and shoved it into his pants pocket.

Denny slid the photo across the desk and pointed to a smudge of lipstick. "They managed to swab the DNA they needed from where your wife kissed the photo. I'm impressed."

Levi had borrowed the photo from Vinnie—the same photo he had seen in the Don's parlor. It was the only thing he knew of that might have Mary's DNA on it—and he wasn't about to dig up her body to follow one of his hunches. He smiled at the youthful faces staring back at him from a bright and sunny day a lifetime ago. A time when things were a lot less complicated.

"Well, you've had me wait nearly a month," Levi said. "What's the results?"

"Sorry about the time, but the only guy I trusted not to screw things up was really swamped." Denny picked up the two sheets of paper and handed one to Levi. "They sent two copies of the report."

As Denny talked about the technical details of the report, Levi looked it over. The banner on the top of the paper indicated the work had been done at some biotech company out of Boston. Below that were all sorts of numbers and terms he wasn't familiar with.

Denny read the summary line aloud. "We successfully extracted sufficient DNA from a portion of the ripped cuticle and from the lip impression on the photograph for analysis. The results indicate that both were female of Middle-Eastern origin. The two DNA samples are related, fourth cousins or closer." He put the printout down. "Were those the results you were looking for?"

Levi shrugged. "Frankly, I'd begun to think I'd imagined their similarities. But if the two were related, it could very well be that they looked a lot alike."

"It's definitely possible." Denny tapped on the report in front of him. "And it did say fourth cousins *or closer*. Who knows—maybe sisters or something."

Levi leaned forward. "Can I hire you to hunt something down for me?"

"Sure. What do you have in mind?"

"I need to find this woman, or at least find out where she's been. All I know about her is that she called herself Katarina, and that's probably not her real name. She looked like she was in her mid-twenties, and she spoke Farsi, but now that I've had time to think about it, I don't think it was her daily language. Something about the pacing of how she spoke was off. I'd wager she grew up speaking the language, so she was fluent, but she probably moved away afterwards, maybe as a teen, and didn't use it much if at all afterwards. She also speaks Russian, if that helps. Maybe an Iranian who moved to Russia in her teens."

Denny scribbled notes on the back of his copy of the DNA report. "I'll see what I can do. What can you tell me about Mary? You know, maiden name, place of birth, parents' names, et cetera. I'll probably start from there and work my way outward."

"Her given name was Maryam Nassar, and she was born in Iran. I think in Tehran, but I can't be one hundred percent sure. I don't know her parents' names, but she told me they were professors of some kind. I never knew what they were professors of. She never spoke of any brothers or sisters, but they may exist—I just don't know."

"That's fine. I'll see what I can find out, but I can't promise anything. Some of these Middle-Eastern countries are pretty good with computerized records, but others … not so much."

Levi sat back in his chair and drummed his fingers on the desk. "Denny, before I start talking to you about the next topic I came here for, I want to make sure you and I are on the same page. You know the type of people I work with, right?"

Denny's expression turned serious. He nodded.

"Well, the one thing they value the most is trust. They need to trust their people. If that trust's ever broken, well … bad things happen. There's no room for second chances with these people." Levi leaned forward again. "So, my question to you is this: can I trust you to do a security-related job for them, and in turn, can *they* trust you, knowing the consequences of breaking that trust?"

For just an instant, Levi saw in Denny the same expression that Gerard Carter, Denny's father, used to give him when Levi asked him something that bordered on the absurd.

"Levi …" Denny hitched his thumb back toward the countless shelves of high-tech electronic equipment behind him. "If the FCC or any other government agency ever knew I had half of this stuff, they'd stick me in a hole so deep I'd never see the light of day. I don't know what you're asking of me, but as to whether or not my word is good? Let's just say I'll swallow a bullet before I'd knowingly break someone's trust."

Levi smiled, and they bumped fists. "I just wanted to be clear. Because so far, it's been just you and me dealing with things. If I bring in any of my associates, you're no longer Gerard's son. It's business. Serious business."

"You mentioned it's security related?"

Levi nodded. "I'll put someone in touch with you. His name is Frank Minnelli. He's one of—"

"I know who Mr. Minnelli is." Denny smiled and ran his hand through his closely cropped afro.

"Well, I don't know the details, but I'm suspecting he's got a bug problem. The electronic type. Probably needs an entire building swept. Maybe new computers, I don't know. But it's probably not a small job, if you know what I mean."

Denny's voice thickened a bit. "I really appreciate this, Levi. Trust me, I'll make this problem go away."

"I wouldn't expect anything less." Levi tossed his friend a wry smile. "Oh, and one more thing. Another favor."

"Shoot."

"Well, let me be blunt." Levi rubbed at the back of his neck. "I need something that's almost certainly not off-the-shelf. Imagine if you were a guest in someone's home. You don't have much time nor any real skill with computers, but you wanted to scrape as much information from their computers as you can and be able to walk away without it being obvious what you did. You have some thoughts?"

"What kind of information are we talking about? Credit card information? Passwords?"

Levi shook his head. "Nah, nothing like that. I'm thinking e-mails. Any kind of incoming or outgoing communication with the rest of the world."

"That should be a piece of cake. Do you want to leave any back-doors behind?"

"I don't even know what that means."

"You know, like a virus to see what the ongoing communications are and stuff. It's like a gift that keeps on giving."

"Frankly, I don't *think* I need that. I'm expecting that the communications I'm hunting for happened years ago."

Denny held up a finger and stood. "Wait one second, I think I've got something that should fit the bill." He turned, walked past several rows of shelves and disappeared behind a wall of boxes.

Levi heard the sound of a box being ripped open, and moments later Denny came back with a finger-sized device.

"I think this is what you need. I just got this one in. It's an updated version of a pretty standard hacker's toy."

It looked to Levi like a standard USB thumb drive.

Denny handed it to Levi. "Stick that into almost any computer and just turn it on. It'll automatically run some software that'll scan the machine for .PST files as well as a whole list of other files. It also has a database of zero-day Windows exploits that will rip through the OS registry searching for the rest of what it needs. If we're lucky, he's got auto-logons for things like Gmail and Hotmail and such, and we'll be able to pull that information too."

Hefting it, Levi studied the generic-looking black plastic device. "And how long does that all take?"

"Well, that's a USB 3.0 device, so its data transfer rate is pretty reasonable. For any offline e-mails like Gmail and such, it's almost instantaneous, because it'll just grab the user IDs and passwords and store them on the device. For the local e-mails, it just depends on how much data there is. It's got a bi-color LED on the end there"—he pointed— "that'll flash red while it's transferring and turn green when it's done. Could take as little as a few seconds or as long as a few minutes."

Levi turned the object over in his hand. "So just plug it in, wait for the green light, and done?"

"Well, done enough. Bring the dongle back to me and I'll help you sort through the fiddly bits and see what we have."

"What if he has more than one computer?"

"That's got a one-terabyte flash chip. Just keep plugging it into whatever computers you find. I doubt it'll run out of space. It's only copying what it absolutely has to have, and the data will be saved in different folders."

"Perfect. How much for this?"

Denny shook his head. "How about we settle up at the end of the month. Depending on how much Mr. Minnelli wants me to do, maybe no charge."

Levi chuckled at the excitement in Denny's voice. He was still young, no more than his early thirties, and he was looking for opportunities to prove himself, earn the same type of reputation his father had achieved—or maybe even one day exceed it.

"Listen to me," Levi said. "Depending on what you learn tracking down this Katarina person, I might be asking you for a tech package like your dad used to put together for me."

Denny's eyes widened. "So you're totally back in? 'The Fixer' is back in business?"

Levi shrugged. "It's what I do, but—"

"Oh man, and you want me to be your Q?"

"My what?"

"Dad used to talk about you like you were some 007 and he was your gadget supplier. You know, Q from the James Bond movies."

Levi stared at Denny for a moment, then began laughing.

"What?" Denny replied with mock indignation. "Q was the coolest character of all time."

"You do realize that Q stands for quartermaster, right?"

"Of course." Denny waved dismissively. "Well, now that I know you're back in action, I have things I was thinking of making and … let's not talk about it now. I'll go work on them and I'll show you when they're done."

Levi stood and shook Denny's hand. "And I'll have Frank Minnelli call you." He pocketed the USB dongle. "You'll be hearing from me within the week about this toy. I'll need your help sorting through whatever it's captured."

"I look forward to it."

Not nearly as much as I'm looking forward to meeting this politician, Levi thought.

CHAPTER THIRTEEN

Madison read the latest Arrow report received from the Russia opera-
tives. Jen had filed this one.

*I just attended a private party held in the Federation Tower. Lots of
politicians, high-end prostitutes, and business elites were there. Let's
just say I was at a disadvantage with the amount of silicone in the
room.*

Madison put her hand under her nose to suppress a laugh. The report
read exactly like Jen spoke.

*Vladimir Porchenko, one of the leaders of the United Russia political
party, was surrounded by a phalanx of bodyguards. I couldn't get
anywhere close to him, but I overheard people talking about Kosvinsky
Mountain. Something about bringing it online. I heard roughly the
same thing from two separate members of the Duma.*

I did some further research, and the Russians deny that anything exists over in Kosvinsky. In fact, when I called someone, they denied it so hard, they 'let slip' that Mount Yamantau was where nuclear research was being done.

I've not dropped the Yamantau angle, but my gut's telling me that there's factions of the political glitterati that want us to pay attention to that location. It feels like misdirection. I'm still in Moscow, and both Yamantau and Kosvinsky are in the middle of nowhere. We'll need resources to follow up on those locations.

I'll have another report within seven days.

Madison's desk phone rang, and "John Maddox" showed on the caller-ID screen. She picked it up. "Hello?"

"Hey Maddie, you got a minute?"

"Sure."

"We've had a development on Project Arrow. There's a good likelihood that some of our team may be drawing closer to one or maybe even both of our missing items.

"You've got a background as Navy EOD and are diver-qualified. How comfortable are you with your EOD side?"

Madison sat up straight. "I graduated near the top of my class on all parts of my EOD training."

"Great. Our nuclear asset analysts agree that the best way of handling the Mark 15 nuclear capsules will be to disassemble them on site and remove their uranium cores. That means bypassing the trigger mechanism and whatever else you run into. What if I told you that I'm thinking of sending you undercover on a recovery mission?"

Madison grimaced. "John, I definitely want to go, but I'll be honest. My CBRN training covered a variety of WMDs, but I need more information on the Mark 15. That thing's been out of production since way before I was born. I need schematics and—"

"Of course. I've arranged for you to get special training at Fort Lee in New Jersey. They have a mockup of the Mark 15 there and someone who can give in-depth training on it. One thing I need you to

understand ... this would be a Non-Official Cover assignment, and you know what that means."

A NOC was an undercover assignment with no official ties to the government. If she got caught, there wouldn't be a guarantee of acknowledgement.

"I understand."

Maddox's voice changed timbre. He sounded more official ... more serious. *"So, you're good with the training, and in the case that the mission is a go, you're good with going as a NOC?"*

"I am."

"Then pack your things tonight. I'll make the arrangements. You and another read-in member will be on a flight north to Fort Lee. Training should be only a couple days, and by then we'll likely know more about what the next steps are."

"I really appreciate your confidence in me. Thank you."

"Maddie, listen to me. I wouldn't assign this to you if I didn't think you were up to it. Now go home and get yourself packed. I'll call you in a couple hours."

As Madison hung up, her skin tingled with nervous energy. Her first undercover assignment, and she might be defusing a nuclear bomb. Who does that?

She smiled.

"This is going to be awesome."

On Levi's first visit to the property in Fairfield, Connecticut, he disconnected the fiber optic cable. It must have worked like a charm, because this morning, he got the call he was waiting for.

He was picked up by a tall, fat, Italian guy named Larry. They piled into his Toyota Tercel, drove to his work, and picked up a Frontier Communications work van. Levi dressed in a spare workman's uniform in the back of the van, and they drove north.

As they pulled up in front of the six-thousand-square-foot house, facing south toward the Long Island Sound, Larry looked nervous. He had beads of sweat on his forehead.

For a moment, Levi felt sorry for the guy. Who knew what the family had on this guy or what he'd been told? Maybe he was only cooperating because he'd been threatened. Levi wasn't about to ask.

"Larry, listen to me. This is just a walk in the park. This place is wired for cable and internet, right?"

Larry nodded. He was pale, and looked like he might pass out.

Levi snapped his fingers and motioned from Larry's eyes to his. "Follow me on this, Larry. You're going to test the connections on the cable boxes. That's something you normally would do, right?"

"Y-yes." The man nodded emphatically, and his second chin wobbled out of sync with the rest of his head.

"While you're doing that, I'm going to ask where the computers are that are using the internet. I'll say I'm testing the internet connections where they hook up to the computer. Again, not that unusual. Right?"

Larry nodded again.

"Good. I'll then go outside and hook the cable connection back up. Things will just start working again, I'll finish testing the internet connections, and we'll get out of there. You following me?"

Larry looked uncertain. "Is that it?"

Levi smiled. "That's it. Afterward, you'll take me back to the subway station you picked me up at, and we're done. We good?"

The man wiped his forehead and gave Levi a weak smile. "Yup. I'm good with that. Are you ready to go?"

"I am." Levi opened the door on the passenger side of the van and hopped out. He stuck his hand in his pocket and fingered the gadget Denny had given him. "Now let's get to work. This poor guy needs his cable back on."

It was busy at the bar, and Carmen grumbled when Denny took Levi to the back room.

"Is Carmen going to be okay with the front?" Levi asked.

Denny waved dismissively. "She's just bellyaching. If she really needs help, she'll buzz me or call her sister in. They only live a few blocks away."

In the hidden storage room, the electronics whiz stuck the USB device into a laptop and began typing. Levi watched over his shoulder.

"So," Denny said, "I assume my little toy worked as expected?"

"Pretty much. My guy had three different computers. Two of them were already on, and when I stuck that thing into the slot I found in the back, the red light came on, then flashed green a little bit later. The third I was kind of worried. I turned the machine on, and it took a long time before the red light turned on. But eventually it did, and the green light followed soon after."

Denny's fingers flew across the keyboard. "Well, looks like it did something. I see three folders, which is good. Give me a second."

A window popped up with a "C:\" prompt. Denny talked as he typed. "I'm merging the records that were scraped off the machines. Looks like we've got two .PST files. That means the guy was running Microsoft Outlook. I've got a filter for that and a crack for any password encoding. And it looks like we've got a Gmail account. Oh hell, even an AOL account. I'm surprised they still have those. Give me a second. I'll use a Tor browser to burrow into Gmail and download whatever he has stored in there. Then I'll grab the AOL stuff."

Levi only understood bits and pieces. "What's a Tor browser?"

Denny's fingers continued flying across the keys. Other windows popped up and download bars flashed on the screen. "Are you familiar with what an onion router is?"

"Nope."

"Well, first of all, Tor stands for 'The Onion Router.' It's kind of a play on words, since onions have layers, and the hacking community is big on sending messages wrapped in a bunch of layers of encryption. With a Tor browser, you unwrap one layer of a message's encryption to figure out where it needs to go, and then another layer, and so on and so forth until the message has been processed. Anyway, a Tor browser is a browser that lets you send and receive stuff through a network of these onion routers. It's a browser to keep people from knowing who's looking at your stuff. Hackers use it, folks that surf the dark web use it, hell, journalists are nowadays using it to talk to their sources."

"So, it keeps your computer anonymous? They don't know where you are or who you are?"

"Exactly." Denny pulled up a final window and cracked his knuckles. "Okay, we've got a database with … man, almost a quarter million emails. This goes back quite a ways." He turned to Levi. "What do we want to look for?"

"Well, how about my last name. There can't be too many hits on that. Do you have anything on that?"

Denny typed "Yoder" at the search prompt of the database he'd created and clicked on the "search" button. A progress bar inched its way along. When it was complete, several emails popped up.

Denny opened them one at a time, then shook his head. "Doesn't look like these are talking about you at all. A couple of other Yoders, it seems."

"You're right. Let's try something else." Levi's mind raced. "How about my old home address?" He gave Denny the address of his old house, and Denny ran the search.

This search went more quickly, and resulted in only one email.

Levi skimmed the content. It was a notification of default from the taxation and finance office for his old house. Probably what the bastard had used to arrange to scoop up his property for practically nothing.

"Any other ideas?" Denny asked.

"How about Maryam Nassar?"

Denny typed the name. "M-a-r-y-a-m N-a-s-s-a-r?"

"Yes."

He hit "search," and the computer paused for a moment, then came back with a single e-mail. Levi's heart began to thud. He hadn't really expected to get a hit on that.

"Well, it looks as if we have an e-mail to a Thomas Gambini." Denny clicked on the message.

.   .   .

A package cleared US customs, coming from Cairo, addressed to Maryam Nassar. Intercept the package. Do not open it. Someone will come by and pick it up.
—Vladimir

Could this be the same Vladimir who Katarina mentioned—the same one the Russians in the prison talked about? It was, after all, a common name.

"Can we tell where that e-mail came from?" Levi asked.

Denny pointed at the screen. "See the .ru at the end of the e-mail address? We can't be certain, but that would indicate that it came from Russia. Hold on, I can look at the metadata and see what IP address it came from."

The computer whiz typed a long string of numbers. "No doubt about it. Just did a reverse IP lookup. That IP address came from a host in the Russian Federation. Even though this e-mail's over a dozen years old, I think the Soviet Union had already broken up by then. Looks like it came from somewhere in Moscow."

"Can you get an address?"

Denny shook his head. "Nah, especially with how old this e-mail is. The IP address has probably switched hands several times. I can only get you the city. Sorry."

Levi patted him on the shoulder. "That's fine. This helped a lot."

He knew who to ask about this Vladimir guy. He lived a little over an hour away in a mansion, enjoying his cable TV.

"Have you made any progress on tracking down Katarina yet?"

"Sorry, Levi, not yet. I'm working on it, but unfortunately, there's not a lot of useful stuff online in Iran—none of their birth records or anything. I'm looking to see if I know anyone who might know someone in the area. We might have to manually go to whatever passes as their records office to get a clue."

"If you don't have any luck with that, try searching in Russia. There can't be that many Nassars in that area. Maybe Katarina has a trail that can be picked up over there."

Denny spun his chair around to face Levi. "I'll do that. Hey, and thanks for hooking me up with Mr. Minnelli. I'll be over at your guy's place probably for a week just doing a room-to-room sweep. He asked me to go over everything, including the computers and their phone system. It's going to take a while."

"Hey, no problem. Like I said before, just make sure you do what you say you're going to do, and everyone will be happy."

"Don't worry. I'll get you guys squared away."

They both stood and started back toward the bar.

"Is there anything else you needed?" Denny asked.

Levi thought for a moment, then nodded. "See about getting a tech package ready for me. I'll e-mail you a list of the things I need, but you probably know the drill. It needs to fit in a briefcase, and I need to be able to go through customs and airport security with it."

"When do you think you need it?" Denny placed his finger on the biometric reader on the wall. The door clicked open, and as soon as they had walked through, it closed automatically behind them.

"Well, it depends on how quickly you can find this Katarina person. I'll have to check with a few people, but I figure … a week, maybe two? I'm heading after her one way or another."

They walked into the bar, surrounded by the noisy din of raucous laughter and conversations. "I'll keep you posted," Denny said.

Levi waved at Denny, blew a kiss to Carmen, whose face contorted as she struggled to keep a smile from ruining her icy glare.

As he hiked toward the nearest subway station, his breath shot out in steamy jets. He now only had one thing on his mind.

What connection did that thieving ex-government worker have with his wife?

Levi and Frankie's driver pulled the car into the driveway of the mansion and parked next to an unmarked, white-paneled van. A gigantic man who looked like a family associate was waiting beside the van.

Levi glanced at Frankie. "I'm guessing you guys aren't going to let me take care of this myself?"

Frankie pointed at his chest with an innocent expression. "This wasn't my call. Turns out this Gambini guy has some connections with one of the other families, and Vinnie didn't want to take any chances."

As the big man opened the rear passenger door, Levi had to crane his neck to be able to take in just how huge this guy was. He was maybe six foot ten and surely in excess of three hundred pounds, all of it muscle.

The man nodded a greeting as Levi and Frankie stepped out of the car. When he spoke, it was with a surprisingly high-pitched voice. "Mr. Minnelli, everything's been prepared."

"Thanks, Paulie."

As the three men walked toward the front door of the house, Levi felt the icy talons of the winter breeze blowing bitter cold against his cheeks.

Frankie noticed Levi's frown and patted him on the shoulder. "Don't worry. This is your thing—you handle the interrogation. We're here just to make sure there's no problems." He turned to the walking mountain of a man and asked, "Is he the only one in the house?"

Paulie nodded. "His wife lives in Florida during the winter, and the mistress went out shopping. I've got someone keeping track of her. He'll make sure she's out for as long as we need her to be."

Levi could tell that the giant man was one of the family's capos. Sort of like an officer in the army, he was responsible for arranging things when a task needed more than one or two people to accomplish. Clearly, Vinnie wasn't taking any chances with this Gambini. The guy must really have friends in high places for Vinnie to intercede in this way.

As they stepped up to the front doorstep, the ten-foot-tall oak doors were opened by two men Levi had seen in the apartment building, but had never talked to.

The men stepped back, and the group walked into a large, breathtaking foyer. It was circular, with twenty-foot ceilings, marble floors as far as the eye could see, and carved wooden accents. Whoever built this place had spared no expense.

At the room's center, a large "G" was inlaid in the floor with red granite, done in a script that reminded Levi of the calligraphy he'd seen on fancy wedding invitations.

"Let me introduce you," Frankie said. He motioned toward the men who'd opened the door. One was tall and lean, the other was short and stout with bushy eyebrows. Levi couldn't help but think, *Laurel and Hardy.*

"The tall thin guy here is Carlo, shorter guy is Angelo." Frankie tilted his head to the giant man. "And you've met Paulie. Vinnie's asked him to help handle certain details."

Frankie patted Levi on the chest. "Boys, this here's Levi, our fixer. He's going to run the interrogation." He glanced at Laurel and Hardy. "You guys are ready with what you'll need to do, right?"

Both men nodded.

Levi noticed that they were wearing surgeon's gloves. Probably trying to avoid leaving fingerprints.

"So," Frankie said, "where is Mr. Gambini?"

Carlo motioned for everyone to follow him. They walked past a grand living room and into one of the offices Levi had visited not long ago when he was disguised as a cable repairman.

A man in his late fifties was sitting on a hard-backed chair, his wrists and ankles were bound to the chair. Several loops of braided nylon rope were tied tightly across his chest, and a long strip of gray duct tape covered his mouth.

So, this is Thomas Gambini.

Levi approached. Gambini didn't show fear. In fact, he looked defiant. As if to say, *"Do your best, I ain't talkin'."*

Levi focused on Gambini, letting the rest of the people in the room fade away. There was no Frankie, Carlo, Angelo, or Paulie. It was just him and the man he needed answers from.

Gambini was a large man. He'd probably worked out a lot during his life. He still looked strong enough to cause a fair number of people issues in a bar fight, but he'd grown soft—age had gotten the better of him. And his wealth had likely insulated him from worrying much about anything.

Levi smiled as he pulled up a chair.

"So, you're Thomas Gambini. I've never heard of you before." Levi reached forward and ripped the tape off Gambini's mouth.

The man yelled a string of profanities. "You guys don't know who the hell you're fucking with."

Levi leaned forward and gently placed his hands on the back of the man's clenched fists. "You're right. Tell me who I'm messing with."

Gambini glared, his breathing growing rapid. Levi could feel the man's pulse racing. He was nervous.

Good.

"Who are you people?" Gambini snapped. "What the hell do you want?"

Feeling calmer than he'd ever imagined he would, Levi spoke in a soothing tone. "I just have a few questions for you, that's all."

The man shook his head. "There's no fucking way I'm answering shit. You've picked the wrong guy—"

Levi slammed his knuckles into the back of both of Gambini's fists. He felt the tiny bones in the man's hands splinter.

The man screamed. Bubbles of spit collected on the edge of Gambini's mouth as he breathed hard, gritting his teeth.

Levi placed his palms onto the man's broken hands and studied Gambini's face. He saw the worry creep into Gambini's expression. All the while, he felt the heat coming off the man's injuries as blood began pooling and the swelling began. Any motion in Gambini's hands would aggravate the injury and send shooting spears of pain into the man.

Already, beads of sweat collected on his forehead.

Again, Levi spoke with a calm, soothing tone. "This is how it's going to work. I'm going to ask you questions. You're going to respond. If I don't like your answers, something's going to break." He patted the backs of Gambini's hands. The man winced. He was in a lot of pain.

Excellent.

Purple splotches were already spreading across the backs of

Gambini's hands, and the swelling was becoming obvious. "Mr. Gambini, I have begun by breaking things that can get fixed. Your hands may not be feeling so great, but they can be fixed. Trust me, I know how to break things that no surgeon can ever make whole again —so don't test me."

From the corner of his eye, Levi spotted Frankie standing at the corner of the room, watching. He had a shit-eating grin on his face and was whispering to one of his men.

Gambini's defiant expression had vanished. In its place was the look of a man who was ready to talk.

Levi patted Gambini's cheek and smiled. "Are you ready for a question?"

Gambini nodded.

"What do you know about someone named Vladimir?"

Gambini's face went pale. His lips moved, but no sound came out.

Levi leaned closer, placed his thumbs on the inside of Gambini's elbows, and squeezed the pressure points.

Gambini lurched against the ropes binding him. The veins in his neck bulged as a raw scream of pain issued from him. He sounded like a lost soul being banished to hell.

Levi maintained the pressure even as Gambini's face turned deepening shades of red. Most of the white in the man's left eye turned red as a capillary burst.

Finally, Levi released the pressure.

Gambini's body went limp.

The others in the room shifted in and out of the periphery of his vision, but Levi's attention remained focused on the man in front of him.

"Listen to me, Mr. Gambini. I know that had to hurt. My next move will involve a nerve below your waist. I should warn you that once I start in on that, you may never be able to leave the house without a diaper on. How about this? You tell me what you know about Vladimir, and I'll let you go. That's it. No strings." He gave his voice a menacing tone. "What do you know?"

Sweat poured off Gambini's face as he stared wide-eyed at Levi.

His one red eye made him look like an undead monster from a pulp novel. But he said nothing.

Levi began to reach toward the man's waist.

"No! Stop …" Gambini finally broke. "I don't know much. But I'll tell you what I know."

Levi leaned back and gave a slight nod.

"He's the first one who got me hooked up with some deals at the Port Authority," Gambini said. "I was in debt up to my eyeballs. It was so bad, I was looking into bankruptcy. Then he came along with a solution that seemed too good to be true. They needed someone to help with an audit and help with cooking the books on some transactions I was overseeing anyway. It was so easy, and I was paid in cash. That's how it all started. Occasionally, one of Vladimir's men would visit— you know, the leg-breaker types." Gambini glanced at the others in the room. "They'd show up when I was having trouble with some of the IT people.

"At first I really didn't know what was going on. I really didn't. But he arranged for accidents to happen to people who were becoming issues. I knew that if I ever crossed him, I'd be a grease spot."

Gambini scanned the room as if hoping to find a sympathetic face. He found none.

"Those Russians, they were all over the docks a decade ago. In the end, I managed to get an arrangement made where I was getting protection from the Colombo family in exchange for tax assistance, if you know what I mean. They pushed the Russians out, and that's really all I know. It was probably the worst handful of years in my life, being associated with those guys."

"What's he look like?" Levi asked.

"I never saw him. He called … or I think it was him. I don't really know. He sometimes used e-mail, but usually he just sent one of his goons if things needed to be done."

"And what does that have to do with Maryam Nassar?"

Gambini looked confused. "Who?"

Levi closed his eyes and took a deep breath. When he opened his eyes once more, he was the epitome of calm. "Maryam Nassar. At some point, Vladimir asked you to pick up a package that was addressed to her."

The man's eyes widened with understanding. "Oh, shit. That was a long time ago. Ya, I remember that. That was a total clusterfuck. I was supposed to intercept a package that had just cleared customs, but for once in my life those bastard postal guys were running early and had already left with the package.

"I checked the customs manifests and drove all the way out to some suburb where that bitch lived. I could tell that the mail had already been delivered in the neighborhood because some folks were taking mail out of their mailbox.

"Anyway, just as I got to the house, she was pulling out of the driveway, so I followed her.

"She stopped at the bank and went in. When she came back out I showed her a badge that I normally carry—just in case. I asked her where the package was. The fucking whore just walked right past me and got into her car."

Gambini's hands had swollen into the size of oranges, and he grimaced as he wiggled swollen fingers that looked like Vienna sausages.

It took all of Levi's will and focus to keep the venom from his voice. "What happened after that? Did you get the package?"

With a snarl of disgust, Gambini shook his head. "I followed her on the highway. She'd pulled off on some side street, and I kept flashing my lights and honking at her to pull over, but she just sped off. I came up around the bend, and if you can fucking believe it, the crazy bitch blew right through a guardrail and into a ravine."

Levi's heart raced. He had to focus on his breathing in order to remain calm.

"I had no idea what Vladimir would do if I didn't get that damned package, so I actually parked near the broken guardrail and climbed down to look for it in the wreckage.

"The car was flipped over, and it turned out the bitch was still conscious, though there was blood everywhere. I asked her where the package was as I searched the car. All she did was respond in that Arabic crap they all speak—"

"Did you call an ambulance?" Levi asked, his body tensed with pent-up aggression.

"Why the fuck would I do that? She's just some whore towel head that—"

Levi's fingers shot out and instantly crushed Gambini's windpipe.

The man's eyes bulged. He gasped for air, but got nothing. His body bucked violently in the chair.

This scumbag was the last person Mary ever saw.

Levi sent a fist across Gambini's cheek. The sound of bone snapping echoed through the room.

Finally, Levi let his rage loose. He pummeled the man. Bones broke. Blood splattered across Levi's face.

And the next thing he knew, two men were pulling him away.

"He's done, Levi!" Frankie shouted. "Snap out of it!"

With every inch of his body quivering with rage, Levi shrugged out of Laurel's and Hardy's grip. "I'm cool … I'm cool."

Someone handed him a wet towel, and he wiped his hands and face with it. The towel came away streaked with blood, and despite the burning hot rage still bubbling within him, a chill ran through him.

He'd killed a man.

But Mary had died because of what this man had done.

He'd *deserved* to die.

Levi looked down at the dead man … and he felt his anger shift.

The only reason Mary was speeding was because she was afraid.

And the only reason Gambini had done what he'd done was because *he* was afraid of retribution from a Russian mobster named Vladimir.

It all made tragic sense—yet Levi felt no better now than he had ten minutes earlier. There was no closure. The responsible party hadn't really paid any price.

He breathed in the coppery scent of blood.

Frankie's voice took on an authoritative tone. "Angelo, Carlo, go get the supplies. We need to get rid of the body and sanitize this place."

He patted Levi on the shoulder. "Our friend here hasn't made this any easier. Just make it happen."

Levi closed his eyes, wishing he had a mental image of Vladimir to focus on. He concentrated on his slowing his breathing until his rage subsided.

Then he opened his eyes.

Gambini's face was unrecognizable; his misshapen head hung at an impossible angle. There was blood splattered everywhere.

Levi had allowed himself to lose control a few times before, but it had never resulted in anyone's death. Today had changed everything.

He turned to Frankie, feeling a surge of guilt. "I'm sorry about that. I just ... I lost control."

Frankie hung his arm over Levi's shoulder and laughed good-naturedly. "I didn't think you had it in you. I know Vinnie's talked about your temper, but man ... that's something to see."

Levi shook his head. He wasn't necessarily mad at himself for killing Gambini. The bastard had deserved it. He was mad at himself for losing control. "Still, it shouldn't have happened."

"Are you fucking kidding me? If that douchebag had done that to my Carlita, I'd be giving the guy transfusions just to keep him alive so I could keep torturing him for the next week." Frankie pointed at the bloody body. "Come on, you know pounding the shit out of him ... it had to have felt great."

Levi smiled, but inside, he felt a sense of moral outrage. He couldn't let something like this happen again.

When Carlo and Angelo returned, they were covered from head to toe in white plastic coveralls, and were laden down with bleach, chemicals, and other cleaning supplies.

Carlo handed Frankie two sealed bags of clothes. "Before you put those on, Angelo's got to spray both of you two with some of that cleaning solution of his."

As Levi began unbuttoning his bloodstained shirt, Gambini's final words replayed in his mind.

She's just some whore towel head ...

Killing Gambini had been wrong, but Levi knew that some part of him, deep inside, had enjoyed it. On principle, he hated violence; it wasn't his way. But this guy earned what he'd gotten.

He turned to Frankie, who was also getting undressed. "You want to know if it felt great? What can I say, Frankie. The guy hurt one of mine; I just returned the favor."

Frankie laughed like a hyena. "That you did, my friend. That you did."

CHAPTER FOURTEEN

As the apartment building's elevator doors opened on Levi's floor, he let out a drawn-out yawn. It had been a stressful day, and he was ready for a hot shower and a nap. He headed down the hall toward his apartment.

Up ahead, a man stood near the open door to one of the apartments. He wore a finely tailored, dark-gray, pinstriped suit. He was about five foot nine, with a muscular build. His voice carried down the hallway as he yelled, "What the hell are you doing in my apartment, you fucking monkey?"

Levi felt annoyed. He'd had enough drama for the day.

"What's going on?" he asked as he stopped beside the stranger. He looked into the apartment.

Denny was inside. He had a screwdriver in his hand, a disassembled computer on the desk, and a look of concern on his face.

The stranger huffed beside Levi. "I just moved in, name's Leo. Do you know who this jigaboo is—"

A resounding thwack sounded as Levi threw all of his weight into an open-handed smack against Leo's cheek.

Leo yelled, "What the hell!"

Levi shoved the man face-first into the wall. "Shut up," he growled.

Several doors opened in the hall. A few heads poked out, looked toward the scuffle, then vanished. They didn't want to get involved.

"You need any help?" a voice called.

Tony was approaching from the elevators. He'd probably just gotten off his security shift.

"Call Mr. Minnelli!" Leo shouted. "I shouldn't have to—"

Levi shoved Leo's face harder into the wall. "Tony, call Frankie. This trash needs to get taken care of."

Tony pulled out his cell phone and walked back toward the elevator.

Leo pushed away from the wall. Levi gave him two quick hard shots in the kidneys, shoved him back against the wall, and levered his arm behind him. "Move again and I'll break it."

He shouted into the apartment. "Denny, you okay?"

"I'm fine. I was just upgrading some of the hardware like Mr. Minnelli asked me to."

Leo tried to plead his case. "Listen—"

Levi cut him off. "Not another word. You're staying right where you are, with your mouth shut, until Frankie arrives."

Only a couple of minutes passed before Frankie and Tony came rushing down the hallway. "What the hell's going on?" Frankie yelled.

Levi let go of Leo, who shouted, "This crazy asshole just attacked me for no reason!"

Frankie turned to Levi with a tired expression and sighed. "I just got back to my apartment, didn't even get a chance to take a shit, and I get called for this?"

Levi pointed at Denny, who was now standing in the apartment's doorway. "Let's just say that I'm walking to my apartment and stumble into this moron yelling at Denny for being in his apartment, calling him a monkey and—"

"He *what?*" Frankie's face flushed red. Without warning, he punched Leo in the gut.

Leo doubled over, only to have his face collide with Frankie's knee. Blood burst from his nose.

"This isn't how we are in our home, you fucking animal," Frankie growled.

Levi watched with a sense of satisfaction as Frankie grabbed Leo by the lapels of his now-bloodstained suit and punched him yet again in the gut.

Leo fell on all fours and puked up whatever he'd eaten earlier that day.

"Now get up and apologize to that man," Frankie said.

With a groan, Leo wiped his mouth and staggered to his feet.

Frankie whispered, with an ominous tone, "And I swear to God, if I'm not convinced you mean it, you're out of here."

Leo pressed his hand against his ribs as he coughed to clear his throat. He stepped toward Denny, who had been looking wide-eyed at the entire scene.

"Sir," Leo said, "I don't know what I was thinking." He wiped away the blood streaming from his broken nose, only to spread a red streak across half of his face. "I sincerely apologize for getting upset and calling you names. It wasn't right, and it won't ever happen again."

Frankie made a disgusted sound. "Tony, help get this asshole to the doc. He's making a mess of this place."

As Tony took Leo away, Levi gave Denny a fist bump. "Hey man, seriously, are you okay?"

Denny chuckled and shook his head. "You guys are crazy, but I'm fine. Trust me, I've heard much worse from better people. Try being the only black guy in a differential equations class full of white entitled assholes who've probably never seen a public school student before."

Frankie stepped over Leo's puke and shook Denny's hand. "Listen, I'm really sorry about that. The guy's brand new here, but I take responsibility. I don't cotton to none of that kind of racist bullshit in here."

"No worries, Mr. Minnelli." Denny tilted his head toward Levi. "Like I told him, I've heard worse."

Frankie patted Denny on the shoulder. "Well, either way, just know that's not how we are. You have any issues, you just let me know. I'll take care of it."

Levi nodded at the stained carpeting. "Want me to call someone about that?"

Frankie groaned. "Aunt Lola's going to kick my ass for this."

"So …" Denny hitched a thumb toward the disassembled computer. "I'll just get back to work."

Frankie pulled Levi away from the apartment and lowered his voice. "I forgot to mention it before, but let's you, me, and Vinnie get together upstairs. Figure about seven tonight."

"Sure. Is it business or just social?"

Frankie leaned closer and whispered, "We've got some unfinished business having to do with Gambini."

Levi tilted his head. "Okay … I'll see you then."

Frankie patted Levi on the shoulder, mumbled something about Aunt Lola, and walked back to the elevator.

Levi poked his head into Leo's apartment. "Hey, Denny, if you need anything, I'm at the end of the hallway."

With a motherboard in one hand, a screwdriver in the other, and a penlight shining in his mouth, Denny nodded an acknowledgement.

Levi continued toward his apartment—finally.

Frankie's words echoed in his head. *We've got some unfinished business having to do with Gambini.*

What could possibly be left to talk about regarding Gambini?

A loud knock on the front door woke Levi and sent him lurching into a sitting position. The clock read 6:29, and right at that moment it ticked over to 6:30 and the alarm went off.

Levi shut off the alarm, swung his legs off the bed, and staggered from the bedroom, wearing only boxer shorts. "Who is it?"

"It's Denny. Can I come in to upgrade—"

Levi opened the door. "Come on in." As he turned back to his bedroom, he said over his shoulder, "Sorry, not trying to be rude, but I'm supposed to be meeting with Frankie and the Don in half an hour."

"No worries." Denny closed the door behind him and made a beeline for the computer on the desk in the living room. "Sorry about being so late, I was hoping to finish by five, but clearly that didn't work out. This should be pretty quick though. I'm adding a customized Anonabox to your network connection and some configuration changes to your software, like that Tor browser—"

"These upgrades are all for anonymous internet access, right?" Levi asked as he shrugged into a tailored button-down shirt.

Denny plugged the network's RJ-45 cable into a fist-sized black plastic box and hooked Levi's computer to it. "I'm impressed you remember. I always thought you were a technophobe."

"Not really." Levi put on a freshly pressed pair of slacks. "It's not that I don't care for technology, I just didn't grow up with it like you did. Remember, I lived my first eighteen years on an Amish dairy farm. We didn't even have electricity. And besides, I've got a pretty good memory; it seems I can pretty much remember anything I see."

As Denny booted up the computer, he asked "What do you mean you remember anything you see?"

Narmer's words replayed in Levi's mind. *Your memory is nearly perfect.*

"I don't have an explanation for it, really. But I've noticed that I can remember even the littlest things, if I think about it hard enough. It's almost like using a VCR and scanning through the tape."

"Nobody uses VCRs anymore."

Levi sat on the living room sofa and slipped his feet into a comfortable set of calfskin loafers. "Well, you know what I mean."

Denny looked doubtful. "Are you seriously saying you have an eidetic memory?"

"Eidetic?"

"You know, photographic memory."

Levi shrugged. "I suppose."

Denny picked up a paperback off the desk: *Monster Hunter International.* "Have you read this?"

"Yup, finished it last night."

Denny flipped to a random page. "Okay, chapter fifteen, how does it start?"

Levi closed his eyes and imagined turning the pages. It felt like the days when he'd flip through a library's card catalog, searching for a book. When he got to the page that read "Chapter 15" at the top, he zeroed in on the text below the chapter heading.

He cleared his throat. "'Julie! We have gargoyles on the roof. At least two of them,' I shouted into my cell phone."

Denny's mouth fell open. "Holy shit, man. You really do have a photographic memory! Were you born like that?"

"I don't think so." Levi frowned as Narmer's voice grumbled in the back of his mind. "I just started noticing I could remember things that I'd seen, you know, like license plates and stuff."

He felt a sense of regret as he thought of the elusive monk. Could he really have been telling the truth about everything? It couldn't be possible—could it? Levi didn't even like to think about it.

A chirping sounded from Denny's pocket, and he pulled out his cell phone. He tapped on it, then smiled.

"What?" Levi asked.

Denny turned his phone toward Levi. "Do you recognize that picture?"

A chill raced through Levi as he looked at the woman in the picture. She was a young version of Mary ... but she was not Mary.

Definitely not Mary.

He nodded.

"Awesome." Denny tapped on the screen and studied it for a moment as he read. "Well, it seems like Katarina Nassar was a student at the University of Moscow eight years ago. That was a picture from her student ID. The rest of the student records aren't online. I think to get anything more, we'll need someone to go there and do some digging."

Levi walked over to Denny and gave him a kiss on both cheeks. "You're the man." He pointed at Denny's phone. "Can you get me a hard copy of that?"

"Sure, no problem. I can even get it laminated. I'll do it tonight when I go back to my office."

Levi glanced at his watch. He needed to get going. "Denny, I need that tech package I asked you about in the next week or so. Can you do it?"

"Sure thing. I've almost got everything put together. Just working out the bugs on one of the new items." Denny glanced at the calendar on his phone. "It's Tuesday now, so … I can have it all put together by Friday night. Does that work?"

"It does, and thanks. I've got to go. You okay with whatever you need to do in here without me?"

"Yup, no problem. I'm just swapping out your phones and computer connections. I'll test everything out, but you shouldn't notice much difference. I'm uninstalling your regular browser, but just click on the onion icon and that'll get you to the internet anonymously."

"I think I understood half of that." Levi smiled ruefully. "Listen, sometime in the near future, you're going to have bring me into the twenty-first century on my computer skills. But for now, I'm out of here."

As he walked to the elevator, Levi felt a growing sense of purpose. Katarina was just a piece to a tragic puzzle. A means to an end. There was really only one final target, and it frustrated him to no end that he didn't even know what the man looked like.

Vladimir had a lot to answer for.

Hey, Jimmie. Hey, Luca. Hope I'm not late."

The thickset mobsters were seated on either side of the double doors to Vinnie's parlor on the penthouse level. They popped up from their chairs as Levi approached.

"No, sir. Right on time. The Don's expecting you."

They opened the doors, and the warm sound of opera enveloped Levi as he walked into the huge, lavishly appointed room.

Vinnie was sitting in a plush leather chair, his eyes were closed as he savored the sounds of the aria playing through hidden speakers in the walls, his right hand moving with the notes of what Levi thought was one of Puccini's greatest works.

Ma il mio mistero è chiuso in me;
il nome mio nessun saprà!
No, No! Sulla tua bocca
lo dirò quando la luce splenderà!

The powerful operatic voice suddenly halted, and the Don turned in Levi's direction. "You're right on time."

"I see you are still a lover of Puccini."

"Not just Puccini, it's that feeling of sound penetrating my being …" Vinnie walked over to the wall, flipped a switch and the fireplaces on both sides of the room crackled to life. "I seem to recall you gained a fondness for opera as well."

A door opened on the far end of the parlor and Frankie walked in.

Levi shrugged. "For me, I prefer it live. Something seems to be missing when it's recorded."

Vinnie glanced at Frankie and nodded. He motioned for Frankie and Levi to join him by his executive-style desk—the only real furniture in the room that wasn't a chair. "Okay guys," he said, "let's get down to business. First things first, someone's got their phone on. Turn everything off."

Frankie patted at his suit coat and frowned. "Mine should already be off."

"Well, someone's got *something* on. Levi?"

Levi pulled his cell phone from his pocket and showed it to Vinnie. "Not using it, if that's what you mean."

"No, you have to actually turn the damned thing off all the way. Your buddy, what's his name—"

"Denny," Frankie volunteered.

"Yeah, Denny." Vinnie pointed at a new pyramid-shaped device on the desk. It looked like it was carved from black stone, but at its peak was a tiny red light. It looked like a piece of random art. "Your buddy Denny hooked me up with this thing. It tells me if there's any signals being broadcast in the room. You know, if someone's wearing a wire or has a cell phone that's powered on and could be listening."

"Denny put another one of those in the front lobby," Frankie added. "He said it'll even detect electrical fluctuations from things like a wired mic. I tested it, and it seems to work like a charm. That guy's pretty good."

"I'm glad he's working out," Levi said as he turned his phone completely off. "I used to work with his dad, and that guy was a freaking genius. Denny's a chip off the old block, just a higher-tech version."

Vinnie stepped over to a minibar built into the wall behind the desk and poured a thick amber liquid into two crystal tumblers filled with ice. He then squeezed on the handle of a large metal canister—an old-style soda maker, the kind that ran off CO_2 cartridges. It gave out a loud whooshing sound, and Vinnie squirted freshly made seltzer into a tall glass.

When they all had their drinks, and the pyramid's light shifted from red to green, Vinnie said, "Okay, now we can talk." He motioned toward a group of chairs huddled near one of the fireplaces. "Let's have a seat and get comfortable."

Levi studied his friends' expressions as he sat back on the dark-brown leather chair. They were both amused about something. "Okay, what's the big mystery? What's up?"

Vinnie cleared his throat and gave Levi a toothy grin. "I heard about what happened today with that asshole, Gambini."

"Ya, well—"

"I didn't believe it until I saw it," Frankie exclaimed. He hitched his thumb at Levi. "You'd always said if he got going, he had a real temper on him, but I thought you were full of crap—until today."

Vinnie smiled. "Did I ever tell you how I met Levi?"

"I don't think so. I remember the first time you and him came to my mother's house." Frankie's face almost split in half, his grin was so wide. "You had a black eye, and you'd brought this bearded mook to the house." He glanced at Levi. "No offense. Oh, and I remember my sisters *so* wanted to know who the brooding blue-eyed rabbi was."

"Rabbi?" Levi laughed. "What's it with everyone thinking I'm a rabbi? I'm not even Jewish."

Frankie shrugged. "Eh, when you're wearing a beard and dressed all in black, what do we know?" He turned back to Vinnie. "Anyway, I swear any time you brought Levi over, my mom would lock my sisters up. That's pretty much all I remember."

Levi gave Frankie a puzzled look. "Why in the world would your mom worry about me coming over? I wasn't about to do anything to your sisters."

Frankie laughed. "I think it wasn't *you* she was worried about. It was mostly Regina. She just went on and on about your pretty blue eyes."

"Enough about your sisters," Vinnie said. "They were always a pain in the ass." He tilted his head toward Levi. "I knew about his temper because that's how we met. I was getting my ass handed to me by three guys from the neighborhood and out of nowhere, this rabbi—"

"Oh lord." Levi rolled his eyes.

"Levi came out of nowhere with fists flying and pretty much tore the three Lorenzo brothers new assholes."

"I remember that." Levi grinned. "I saw three guys beating on one guy and something in me just sort of snapped. I don't cozy up to bullies. In fact, I hate them. I guess I haven't changed that much over the years."

"Well, I don't know about that, Levi." Frankie sipped at his drink. "Not sure what you learned on your parents' farm, but that trick you did with the elbow on Gambini ..." He looked at Vinnie. "I'm telling you, the guy's eye just turned red like a freaking tomato."

"That's not a trick," Levi said. A surge of anger rushed through him. *That asshole killed my wife.* He took a deep breath and let it out slowly. "That stuff can just happen if you cough or go through something stressful—"

"Okay, enough with that," Vinnie interrupted. "About this Gambini guy, I had some people do a few things." He patted the air in Levi's direction. "I know you don't want to know about the details of what we do, but in this case you're directly affected, and you're up to your eyeballs anyway. Remember how we found out what that bastard did with your house and the money you'd set aside? Well, we found it."

Levi was confused. "You found what?"

"Your money," Vinnie said. "All of it. And more. Tell him, Frankie."

Frankie's expression was a bit more subdued than Vinnie's, but the smile at the corners of his lips was unmistakable. "Well, it turned out that Gambini had most of his assets in offshore accounts. And let's just say that with a few pieces of information that we managed to dig up on our friend Thomas Gambini—and a few faked documents here and there—we managed a transfer of funds from Gambini's accounts to one of our shell accounts in the Caymans. We managed to recoup everything." His smile widened. "We've got the sale price of your house, plus interest, sitting in an offshore account waiting on you. *And* we figured out that right around when the state claimed the assets in your trust fund for its own use, that money somehow managed to end up in one of Gambini's slush funds. We have that as well."

Vinnie leaned forward and put his elbows on his knees. "Normally, we'd take a ten percent cut on anything we have to get involved with, even from made men. But given the situation, and you're as close to family as it gets, I ain't gonna take a dime. I'll call Irving to make arrangements. We can't dump all that cash into your accounts right away, otherwise you'll have the IRS breathing down your neck, but give us about six weeks and we'll siphon the money into something you can access."

Levi felt a smile stretching across his face. This was a huge relief. He'd been feeling like a freeloader of late; the family had been nothing but understanding regarding his financial issues, but it was the first time he'd ever taken money from others in his life and he hadn't been comfortable with it.

He focused his gaze on Vinnie. "You keep the money from the trust fund. I can't take it."

Vinnie looked as though Levi had just said he was an alien. "Are you nuts? It's your money."

Levi shook his head. "It isn't. I set up that trust for Mary. It was supposed to pay her expenses over the rest of her life, and I just can't. You keep it, with my blessing. Use it for whatever you need."

"Levi, I'm not sure you understand," Frankie interjected. "We already got stuff out of Gambini. Trust me, Vinnie and I are pretty happy about the whole arrangement. The part you're getting is just the share you're owed. We've already gotten our taste."

Levi's mind raced. He'd never imagined he'd get the cash back, and he'd already adjusted to that reality. Somehow, money didn't seem as important as it once did.

"It's blood money," he said. "It's Mary's money. And I won't take it. I'll take the funds from the house—that's something I bought before I met her, so I kind of feel okay about that. The rest..." He shook his head.

Vinnie reached over and patted Levi's knee. "Hey, I understand what you're saying. But I don't feel right about it."

"Listen." Levi gave Vinnie a wry smile. "I'm not crazy. I really appreciate this, but I wasn't expecting to ever see any of my money again, and … this is what I want. Buy your girl Vanessa a Barbie or something."

Vinnie stared at him for a long five seconds before lifting his glass. "Okay. I'll set aside the trust money for a year. If at that time, you still feel the same way, I'll honor your wishes."

Levi lifted his seltzer, and the three of them tapped glasses and said *"salud"* simultaneously.

As he sipped at his seltzer, Levi turned his gaze to Frankie. "Do you know anyone I can get legit IDs from?"

"IDs? What kind you need?"

"A passport. I just don't want to use my name."

"I think I know someone."

Vinnie cut in. "Is this because of the Russian thing?"

Levi nodded. "Those guys probably think I'm dead. I'd like to keep it that way. However, I got a lead and I need to follow it."

"Listen to me." Vinnie leaned forward, sipping at his amaretto. "Those guys went totally silent on me after we asked about you. That's not normal. I usually get the professional courtesy of responses from other organizations. There's something not right going on over there, and you need to be careful. I can't guarantee anything over in that part of the world, you *capiche*?"

"I know, and I normally wouldn't go, but—"

"Hey, I understand. Someone over there has Mary's blood on their hands just as much as Gambini did. *And* that bitch that nearly killed you and took out those two kids at your parents' place." Vinnie tapped the side of his head with his index finger. "I pay attention. Nobody does that and gets away with it." He set his glass on the arm of the chair. "What can we do to help?"

"All I really need is a legit passport that'll get me through customs and back. The rest I can take care of myself."

Frankie made a clacking noise with his tongue and shook his head. "You need more than that. I'll talk to Irv and get a credit card or two in your assumed name. Do you know exactly where you're going?"

"I've got a lead that starts in Moscow. After that, I'm not sure. I'll follow the trail."

Vinnie pointed at Frankie. "Once you get him the passport, he'll need a visa and flight information to get the visa rushed. Get him some comfortable seats, if you know what I mean. Even with all that, it'll probably be a week before all that's taken care of." To Levi, he asked, "Are you sure there's nothing else?"

"I'm good." Levi stood. "I just need to get a decent night's rest. I'll have a lot to do before I'm on my way."

Vinnie and Frankie both stood. They hugged and kissed Levi on both cheeks.

As Levi left the parlor, Vinnie called across the room. "I'll have Phyllis light some candles for you at Saint Ignatius."

Levi returned to his apartment thinking, *I'm not sure an entire candle factory's worth of candles will help with what I need to do.*

CHAPTER FIFTEEN

In the supply room of Rosen's Sporting Goods, Levi shrugged into the bulletproof vest Esther had handed him.

"*Nu*, what do you think?" she asked. "It's about five pounds, and the weight should carry evenly across your shoulders. Does the calfskin feel good against your skin?"

He rubbed his hand along the vest and twisted his torso to the left and right. It was amazing how thin yet sturdy it felt. "I like it. It's comfortable." He grabbed the white undershirt he'd laid across the back of Esther's chair and slipped it over the vest.

Esther wiped her hands across his shoulders, smoothing out the wrinkles in his T-shirt and shook her head. "*Bubbaleh*, you'll need to buy one size bigger if you're wearing this. It looks tight."

Levi slipped on his shirt and began buttoning it.

Esther took a step back and eyed him from head to waist. "You know what? It looks okay. You might want something bigger during the summer, otherwise I think you'll end up *schvitzing* like crazy."

"Well, spring is still a couple months away, so I have some time." He tucked his shirt into his pants.

Esther held out a supple leather contraption that looked almost like a shoulder holster. "Go ahead and try that on. I'll help you adjust it."

Levi shrugged into the leather harness. It looped comfortably over his shoulders and fit almost perfectly. There were two leather sheaths on each side of his chest, angled so that he had easy access to the knife handles, but positioned so they wouldn't imprint if he wore a suit jacket.

Esther circled behind him and tugged on one of the adjustment straps. "There, that looks good. Is it comfy?"

Levi lifted his arms up and down. The harness moved easily. "It's great. Now the important part: you said my knives were in?"

Esther pulled open the top drawer of her desk and pulled out a polished oak box with gleaming brass hinges and clasp. She set it on the desk. "My guy really outdid himself. Here, take a look." She flipped open the latch and lifted the lid.

Levi smiled when he saw the four gleaming blades set in form-fitted recesses coated in red velvet. He lifted one dagger and hefted it in his hand.

The balance felt good.

So did the weight.

Esther turned on the gooseneck lamp on her desk and aimed it at the knife in Levi's hand.

He smiled at the faint ripples of the craftsman's handiwork. Staring down the length of the blade, he nodded with approval at the edge geometry. The paracord-wrapped handle felt very comfortable in his hand.

Satisfied, he seated the blade in its scabbard, then did the same with the other three knives.

"Can I test them?" he asked.

Esther pointed uncertainly at a long wooden board leaning against some boxes. "I suppose you can throw it at that, but please don't miss. I've got some other orders in those boxes."

Levi donned his suit jacket and buttoned it like he normally would.

The daggers felt comfortable in their sheaths.

He reached into the V-shaped opening in the front of his jacket and was able to extract the first knife without the hilt getting caught on his lapel.

He threw the knife. It flew end over end toward the target. Before it had even hit, Levi threw the second. Then the third and the fourth.

Each one hit the wood with a satisfying thunk, one right next to the other.

"Oy, you've done that before!" Esther gasped. She patted at her chest.

Levi walked over to the target and yanked out one of the knives. He studied the tip of the blade and scanned the razor-sharp edges. He saw not even a blemish. "Esther, these are really nice. Thank you."

Esther said something in Yiddish.

Levi tilted his head at her. "What?"

"Oy, you *goyim*." She sighed and gave him a crooked smile. "I just said, 'Use it in good health.'"

Levi bent down and kissed the grandmotherly woman on her cheek.

Esther waved her finger at him. "Don't think being nice and sweet will get you a deeper discount than I already gave you. As it is, I can barely sleep at night with how little I made on this deal."

Levi inspected each of the knives, put them in their sheaths, and picked up the box. "Do you know anyone selling professional makeup supplies? I used to get stuff from a Broadway makeup artist I knew, but she doesn't seem to be around anymore."

"One second, let me get my book."

They walked into the front of the store. One of Esther's twin grandsons sat on a stool reading a paperback. It was still early morning; Levi had probably been the only customer so far today.

Esther pulled a black, leather-bound notebook from behind the register. "You're not talking about glamour shots makeup or broadcast TV stuff, right?"

"No, I need supplies for the kind of stuff you use for Halloween. Liquid latex, stippling sponges, prosthetics, the works."

Esther put her address book on the counter and turned it so it was facing him. She pointed at a name. "Go talk to Louisa and tell her I sent you. She doesn't deal with the public—she's some big-shot head makeup artist for a movie studio—but I'll bet you she has what you need."

Levi glanced at the name and phone number, closed his eyes, and was able to see the page as if he were still staring at it. "Thanks, Esther, I'll give her a call."

He turned to her grandson. "Ira, you enjoying the book?"

The boy looked up from the novel and gave him a crooked smile. "Yup, it's pretty cool. Oh, and I'm Moishe. Ira's ten minutes younger and acts ten *years* younger."

"Moishe, be nice," Esther grumbled, and ruffled his hair. Then she handed Levi an envelope. "The bill's in there."

Levi peeked in the envelope and widened his eyes. "I don't suppose you take checks?" he joked.

She tilted her head, and her double chin wobbled. "I don't suppose you'd like a swift kick in your *tuchus*?"

He smiled. "I'll stop by later today and bring cash."

"Good. I'll see you then."

As he stepped outside into the cold, his breath coming out in streams of steam, his phone vibrated. He put it to his ear. "Yup."

"Levi, it's Denny."

"Hey, Denny, what's up?"

"I've got your stuff ready ahead of schedule. Come by whenever you're ready."

"Awesome. I'm actually in the neighborhood. Is it cool for me to come over now?"

"Sure. See you in a bit."

Levi turned toward the bank. He'd now need the cash for both Denny and Esther.

Whenever he'd gotten a tech package from Gerard, Denny's father, it had always felt like opening up a Christmas present. The older man always tossed in a few extra interesting goodies. Levi suspected that Denny would try hard to be as creative as his dad had been.

His palms began to sweat with anticipation.

~

Levi spent the better part of the day with Denny in the back room of Gerard's, talking through all of the items in his new briefcase of goodies—everything from run-of-the-mill items—like lockpicks and surveillance microphones with built-in high-frequency transmitters to more sophisticated technology.

Denny flipped open a laptop, and the screen displayed a Windows logo. "As you can see here," he said, "it looks like a normal computer. But it's actually a Trojan horse. Watch."

He closed the lid and pressed a hidden button in the back. This time when he opened the lid, it revealed the inside of the base of the computer.

"This is the working battery," Denny said, removing an oblong object that occupied nearly the entire bottom of the case. He pressed a button on each side of the battery, and it opened, revealing a hollow interior. "It's a custom-molded lithium-ion battery, but as you can see, the inside is shielded and you can store all sorts of goodies in it if you need to."

"So you mean I could have a gun or plastic explosive inside that and nobody would know?"

Denny smiled and pulled from his pocket the thinnest double-barreled handgun Levi had ever seen. "I was thinking of these when I designed the battery case. The inner cavity of the battery is .665 inches and this little guy is CNC machined to be exactly that width."

He slipped the gun into the battery case, pulled another from his back pocket, and placed that one in the case too. They fit perfectly. He resealed the battery and handed it to Levi.

Levi shook it. Nothing moved whatsoever. He gave it back to Denny. "What's it shoot?"

"They're both set up to shoot .45 caliber. Those are 255-grain over-pressure rounds. Trust me, they'll give you a hell of a kick. Two shots each." He placed the battery back into the laptop, resealed the case, and placed it into its recessed spot in the briefcase. "There's no safety, but it's got a ten-pound trigger pull, so I wouldn't worry about an acci-dental misfire."

Levi drew out one of his new throwing knives and showed it to

Denny. "Any thoughts on how I could get this on a plane? I'm not keen on checking any baggage, if you know what I mean."

"I figured you might ask me something like that." Denny ran his fingers along the edges of the briefcase. "Notice how the walls of the suitcase kind of taper out a bit? The problem is, they'll run this through their x-rays, and if there's anything suspicious, they'll tear it apart. So we can't exactly shield the briefcase from being scanned—they'll just open it up. But along the *edges* of a metal briefcase, they're not expecting anything to be there other than the metal side walls. Well ..."

Denny held up his hands and waggled a pair of gold rings, one on each of his ring fingers. "I've got neodymium magnets embedded in these rings. If I put the magnets right here and here ..." He put the rings on specific spots on the sides of the briefcase, and the inside walls of the briefcase popped open, revealing a thin hollow space all along the edges.

Levi laid his dagger in the hollow. He squeezed the side of the briefcase, and it sealed shut with a metallic click. He smiled. "It just barely fits."

"And it's completely sealed, so if anyone even thought to look, the x-rays don't show anything but the case itself." Denny unlocked the hidden compartment again, and Levi retrieved his dagger. "Obviously you'll need to wrap those in foam or something so they don't slide around."

Denny picked up another item from its recessed spot in the brief-case and handed it to Levi. It looked like a somewhat bulky cell phone.

"What is this, and why is it so heavy?" Levi asked.

"I took a standard commercial sat phone and added some of my own tricks to it." Denny held up an identical copy of the phone. "I've added an automatic handshake between these two phones. When you call me or I call you, nobody's going to be able to tap into the conver-sation. I've got military-grade encryption programmed into this, and I've got the phones changing the random seed for each and every call based on a synchronized atomic clock. I figure if the NSA puts their whole Utah Datacenter on this, they *might* be able to crack it in a couple months—and that would be for just one message. I've also added a location scrambler, so anyone trying to track you will see you hopping all over the place.

"I also preprogrammed my number on that phone, but it's good also for insecure calls if needed."

Levi put the phone back into the briefcase.

Next, Denny pulled out what looked like an ordinary belt and a plain black baseball cap. "These two are sort of my pride and joy. Put them on. You can just put the belt on over your clothes for now."

Levi cinched the belt around his waist and slipped the baseball cap on his head. "This cap's got something poking my scalp."

Denny clipped a wire from the belt to the back of the hat. "The belt is wrapped around a molded flexible battery pack, and the hat … it needs a bit of explanation. Let's just say it'll tell you when someone is watching you."

"It what?"

"Let me demonstrate." Denny turned away from Levi. "Those things you're feeling on the inside liner of the hat are little wire posts. They're spaced out evenly around your head and you'll feel a little tingle from one or more of them if someone starts staring at you."

Levi narrowed his eyes at the back of Denny's head. "Bullshit. There's no way."

Denny turned around and stared at Levi for several seconds.

"I don't feel anything—"

Suddenly Levi felt a weird tingle coming from the front of the hat. He turned his head, and the sensation traveled, always stimulating the wire post that was closest to Denny.

Grinning, Denny walked a full circuit around Levi, keeping his eyes fixed on him the entire time. The tingle on Levi's scalp shifted with his movements.

"That's amazing. Does this work in a crowd?"

Denny nodded. "I've got a circuit built into the wiring to limit the number of false positives. Think of it this way: In a crowd, everyone is looking everywhere. People's eyes are always landing on you and then shifting away. You'd only want to know about it if they were focused on you and not moving away.

"I tested it outside with Carmen helping out. I even eliminated false positives from mirrors and stuff, because a mirror isn't going to follow you around."

"How does it work?"

Denny unclipped the hat from the belt and showed Levi the film-like electronics encircling the hat's lining. "So, you've seen how at night, when a light shines into an animal's eyes, you see an eerie glow reflecting off of them, right?"

Levi nodded.

"Well, humans don't have that same reflective property, at least not to that extent. For our retina to reflect light, we need something brighter. You've seen what happens when there's a camera flash."

"You mean that red-eye effect?"

"Exactly." Denny pointed at a series of tiny tube-like projections that barely poked through the lining of the mesh cap. "What I have here is something that's a bit nuts, because if you could see the light, your head would probably look like it was a 360-degree flashlight it was so bright."

"What do you mean?"

Denny pressed his lips together. "Okay, so we normally can only see light at certain wavelengths. Let me start simple for a moment. We probably all learned in school about ROY G BIV, the colors of the rainbow starting at red and ending at violet. That corresponds to light at wavelengths of roughly 700 to 350 nanometers. The bigger the wavelength, the closer to red, the shorter, the closer to violet. That's what our human eye can detect. But that's not the limit of the light that exists. For instance, that hat is sending out a bunch of light in every direction at roughly 1550 nanometers. Deep into the infrared spectrum. Each of the tiny lasers in there sucks up a good amount of power, and even though you aren't feeling it, the laser's aim is tilting up and down at about twenty times a second.

"So what you have is basically a hat that's projecting light that nobody can see in all directions. It's strong enough to hit things and bounce off. That's where my electronic filters comes in. I'm heavily filtering what comes back and trying to alert you only if I've detected a signal bouncing back that seems to be following you."

"Does it work from a distance?"

"It should be good out to about a hundred yards. Anything more than that, I'm currently squelching, because the reflection gets dicey."

Levi removed the belt, and Denny put both items back in the case.

"So, let me get this straight," Levi said. "I wear that, and it spits light out that nobody can see in every direction. If someone's looking at me, the light is going to bounce back, and the hat has sensors that will alert me."

Denny smiled. "That's probably a lot better description than I gave. That's exactly what it will do. However," he held up his index finger, "I would only use this during the day, and only if you don't think someone is using any kind of night-vision goggles around you. If they are, you'll stand out like a freaking lighthouse."

"Makes sense. Don't use it at night."

Denny gave Levi a Ziploc bag with two gold rings in it. "Those should fit you." He patted the open case and asked, "Do you have any questions?"

Levi shook his head and pulled a thick envelope out of his suit jacket. "That's what you asked for plus a little more."

Denny hefted the envelope and fist-bumped Levi. "Hey, man. I really appreciate it. So, when are you taking off?"

"I'm waiting on the visa to clear, but should be any day now."

Denny held up his copy of the sat phone. "Well, I'll have this on me the entire time. Anything you need, just let me know and I'll do everything I can to help."

"Trust me, I'll probably be calling before you even realize I'm there."

Denny closed the briefcase, handed it to Levi, and they both began walking back to the bar. "What's your next stop?" Denny asked as he pressed his finger on the biometric sensors embedded in the tiles of the wall. The hidden door cracked open.

They walked into the bar. Several people glanced in their direction as Carmen was busy serving customers.

"I've got to go buy some makeup."

"Makeup?" Denny raised an eyebrow.

"You got something against makeup?" Levi deadpanned.

Denny laughed. "No man, if that's your thing, you do you."

One of the men at the bar turned to Denny and grumbled, "You said you were going to get some Red Stripe in. What's the story on that?"

"Howie," Carmen interjected, "I already told you it's on order from the distributor and it just hasn't come in yet. Chill out."

"Listen, Howie," said Denny. "Because you've been waiting so patiently, you and your friends get ten percent off today's bill."

The grizzled old man smiled and turned to Carmen. "Double shots of your best whiskey for me and the boys."

Carmen gave Denny a withering glare.

Levi patted his friend on the shoulder and headed out the door. It was almost time.

Madison walked into her supervisor's office and sat in the chair across from Maddox. He was drumming his fingers on his desk, and from his grim expression, it was clear he was stressed.

"It sounded serious," she said. "What's up?"

"It is serious. We just got intel that Russia's Perimeter program has been activated. Someone's moving the nukes to some 'final destination,' and people at the very top of our organization and beyond are shitting bricks."

"Do we know where they're taking the nukes?"

Maddox shook his head and pushed an envelope toward her. "No, but I'm sending you to Moscow, and I'm having some people meet you at the airport baggage terminal. They'll take you to a safe house that'll serve as a base of operations."

The envelope contained a new passport with her picture and a current visitor's visa for the Russian Federation. "My name is Nicole Cole? Are you serious?"

Maddox shrugged. "Hey, I didn't pick the name. Remember, you're going in as a NOC, so we're not taking any chances on your ID being compromised. You're just a happy-go-lucky American citizen visiting Moscow as a tourist. No official cover means no official paperwork is being filed for this on your behalf. Obviously, your ID will check out, but that's about it. It'll give you room to maneuver and should hopefully keep the FSB from sniffing too hard at you."

FSB was the successor to the infamous KGB, and they tended to keep track of anyone coming and going from the embassy.

"Do we have any leads at all? Did we manage to track down that Katarina person?"

Maddox smiled and turned to his computer. "On a related note, we did have an interesting development occur just recently."

Madison leaned forward and watched the monitor as he typed. "Everything associated with the Arrow project has been given top priority throughout the intelligence community. We're scanning all faces in public terminals and airports. And guess what got flagged last night?"

He hit enter, and a video appeared on the screen. It was of a well-dressed man walking through an airport security check. His face was partially obscured, but something about his profile … the jawline and hair …

She gasped. "No way. Is that Yoder?"

Maddox hit the space bar, and a crystal-clear image of Lazarus Yoder popped up on the screen. "That came off of a passport scanner at JFK."

Madison felt a rush of electricity. "That's without a doubt Lazarus Yoder. Holy crap, he's not dead."

"That seems to be the case." Maddox gave her a crooked smile. "However, the passport scan wasn't for a Lazarus Yoder. It came back as a Ronald Warren, checking in for an Aeroflot flight to Moscow. First-class passage."

"Ronald Warren?"

"I know. We both know that's Lazarus Yoder, but the records match. The passport is valid and shows his photo as a match. I checked. I've got folks looking into it, but I did another query this

morning and got a hit just before you got here. Take a look at this."
Maddox pressed the spacebar again. An image appeared of a man
sitting in a wheelchair. Lazarus Yoder. He looked haggard, and
Madison could almost feel the pain he was in.

"That was from a couple months ago at LAX," Maddox said.
"Somehow we managed to miss him coming back into the country
from Nepal. Maybe it was because he didn't finish his scheduled flight,
but either way, it looks like Yoder is alive and well."

"He must have been injured or something. Why was he in a
wheelchair?"

"No idea. But whatever the hitter did, it looks like it took a toll on
him. Our profiler thinks he's heading to Moscow for payback."
Maddox leaned forward in his chair and smiled. "Yoder can ID this
Katarina woman, and she can likely lead us to Vladimir. I've got
people who are waiting on his flight to land. Hopefully, by the time
you're in-country, we'll have a much better idea of where to go."

He added, with a hint of concern, "Maddie, you again might end up
face to face with this guy at some point. Be careful. This guy is some
kind of operator, and he has resources." He tapped a few more keys,
returning to the passport photo. "That's a face I'd expect to see walking
the red carpet or on some men's magazine, but don't be fooled. He may
look like the guy next door, but he's almost certainly out to kill, and he
probably won't care who gets in his way. If we can turn him, he'd
become a good asset that we can exploit, no more than that. Right now,
he's probably our most promising lead. Hell, he may already know
who this Vladimir is. And even if he doesn't, he's going after someone
who we know *does*."

Madison grasped her new passport tightly. "When am I leaving?"

A look of guilt flashed over Maddox's face, but was quickly
replaced with a stone-like expression. "I've got you booked on an Air
France flight out of Dulles at 6:35 this evening."

Madison's eyes widened as she glanced at her wristwatch. "Shit, I
only have—"

"I've got an FBI car waiting outside for you. They'll get you home
and through the traffic in time."

"FBI?"

"I told you, this has way more attention than you can imagine." Maddox stood. "Do you have any questions?"

Madison stood and shook her head.

To her surprise, Maddox reached across the desk and shook her hand. "I'll see you soon. And Maddie, I can be reached twenty-four seven. Now go. They're waiting for you just outside the front entrance."

Madison raced out the door.

CHAPTER SIXTEEN

Flying first-class for the first time in his life, Levi had taken advantage of the most important amenity it provided: the "do not disturb" button on his seat. It had allowed him to plan out his sleep so that he woke just as they began their descent.

Now, with the leather strap to his carry-on bag looped over his shoulder and his briefcase held tightly in his left hand, he shoved through the crowds in Sheremetyevo International Airport.

As he exited the main terminal, he was hit with a gust of bitter-cold air. It was well below freezing, and tiny stings of sleet blew into his face. The odor of diesel was overwhelming.

A man in a suit jogged toward him, waving a hotel sign with "Ronald Warren" printed on it.

"Sir, Mr. Warren." The man was panting, and his cheeks were red from the cold. "I've got your car. I'm Eugene, the driver from your hotel." He spoke English with only a slight accent.

Levi frowned. "I didn't ask for a car."

The man looked taken aback. He pulled out a printed sheet, glanced at it, then showed it to Levi. "Sir, it was prearranged by your travel agent. This is the order. You *are* Ronald Warren, are you not?"

Levi examined the printout. It included a scanned copy of his passport—with his picture—and his arrival itinerary, including the flight and even his seat number. It was all printed on hotel stationery.

"My travel agent." Levi chuckled as he imagined Frankie booking the flight and hotel. "I suppose he forgot to tell me about the car."

The man held out his hand. "Sir, I can take your bag. The car is parked in the express parking lot nearby, if you'll follow me."

Levi tightened his grip on his briefcase and carry-on and shook his head. "Don't worry about the bags. Let's get out of the cold."

"Yes, sir." The driver pointed at the sand-covered asphalt as he crossed the walkway to a large parking lot. "Be careful—it may be icy."

A minute later, Levi was settling into the back of a brand new Mercedes S-Class sedan. The scent of the plush leather seats enveloped him as the driver started the car and turned on some soft classical music. Levi relaxed as they weaved smoothly through the airport traffic, got onto the M11, and headed toward downtown Moscow.

Speaking in Russian, Levi asked, "So, Eugene, is that really your name?"

The driver's eyes widened. He smiled and replied in Russian. "Oh, you speak Russian very well. Of course, in my mother tongue, Yevgeny is my name, but I was taught that Eugene was the equivalent in English, so I use it for non-Russians. I think it's easier for Americans and Europeans to pronounce, don't you think?"

"You're probably right. Americans especially would have trouble with foreign-sounding names, trust me. How long until we get to the hotel?"

"It's shouldn't take long. Maybe half an hour. Did you want me to get you a table for dinner at the hotel? They have a very good Italian restaurant on premises."

"No, that's okay."

Levi glanced at his watch, which he'd already adjusted to local time. It was too late to go to the university.

"Yevgeny, this is my first time in Moscow. If tomorrow I need to get a taxi, is there anything I need to know?"

"I would suggest arranging with our concierge in the hotel. They can help with all of that."

"What if I'm not near the hotel? In America, I can find taxis in downtown areas easily."

Yevgeny shook his head. "You can't do that here. The taxis are not something you can easily get just by waving. However, it should be okay for you, since you speak Russian. When we get to the hotel, I'll give you a list of the taxi companies. Whenever you need a taxi, you call their dispatcher, and they'll send a car to your location."

It took a bit longer than the half hour Yevgeny had estimated, due to traffic, but Levi enjoyed the chance to relax, and soon enough he was walking into the lobby of the hotel.

Frankie sure hadn't spared any expense. The lobby was a huge expanse of marble, with Roman-style columns climbing up to a thirty-foot ceiling. It was at least a hundred-foot walk to the front desk, and on the way he was asked multiple times if he needed any help with his luggage.

Considering that the last time Levi had been in Russia, he'd had nothing but the clothes on his back, he found it hard not to be awed by his new surroundings.

"Good evening, Mr. Warren." A tall blonde woman behind the front desk greeted him in near-perfect English and gave him a toothy smile. Her name tag said "Tiffany," but underneath it, "Tatyana" was spelled out in Russian. Her fingers flew across her computer keyboard. "I hope your ride from the airport was comfortable. I have your room prepared."

She held out her hand. "Can I please see your passport and the credit card you'd like to use to secure any incidental charges."

Levi handed her the passport and an American Express platinum card under the name Ronald Warren. She made a copy of the passport, swiped the card, and talked about the amenities in the hotel as she continued typing.

Levi turned away from the front desk and panned his gaze across the lobby, paying particular attention to the faces of the people hovering near the entrance.

Without turning around, he asked in Russian, "Tatyana, do you know of anywhere I can buy used clothing?"

"I'm sorry, but I'm not sure I heard you correctly. Did you ask where you can buy *used* clothing?"

He turned back and saw her perplexed expression. "Sorry. In America, they have places where people donate clothes they don't use anymore, and other people buy them. Does Moscow have anything like that?"

Tatyana shook her head. "I don't think so." She held up a finger. "One second, let me ask someone else." She picked up a phone and spoke briefly with someone. A half-smile appeared on her face, and she grabbed a local map as she hung up.

She drew a circle around a location and showed it to Levi. "If you look here, there are places near Lubyanka. There are some stores that sell 'vintage' clothing. Maybe that is what you're searching for?"

Even Levi had heard of Lubyanka. It was infamous as the place where KGB headquarters was located, but given how Russia had changed since the Soviet era, it was probably the location of Maserati and Ferrari dealerships today.

Levi smiled and handed her a one-thousand-ruble note, which was roughly the equivalent of eighteen dollars.

"Oh." Her eyes widened, and she shook her head. "That's not necessary." She pushed the bill back across the front desk.

He placed his hand on hers and smiled. "You didn't need to get me the information I asked for. Just take it, and thank you."

Her face reddened as she took the money. "How many key cards would you like?"

"Just one."

Levi closed his eyes. He still had a solid image of the people he'd spotted in the lobby.

Tatyana handed him his key card in an envelope. She pointed at the room number she'd written and said, "Just take the elevators to your left. It's on the fifth floor. I hope you have a nice stay at the Four Seasons and in Moscow."

He leaned forward and whispered, "How much longer are you working tonight?"

Her cheeks reddened once again. But her surprised expression quickly changed to a pout. "Unfortunately, I just started my shift. I won't be done until the morning."

Levi smiled, reached into his pocket, and removed a two-thousand-ruble note from the wad of money he'd exchanged back in JFK. He pressed the bill into her hand. "I'll be down later. If you can, please let me know if anyone asks about me."

"Oh, but we would never give out room numbers—"

"I know. But if anyone asks, try to remember what they look like. Okay?"

Before Tatyana had a chance to reply, Levi headed to the bank of elevators and pressed the up arrow.

As he waited for the elevator to arrive, his stomach fluttered, and the hairs on the back of his neck stood on end.

He had the distinct feeling he was being watched.

It was two in the morning, and the streets of Moscow were dead. Madison tilted her head and tried stretching the stiff muscles in her neck.

"Rough flight?" Agent Don Jenkins asked as they walked toward the warehouse.

"The flight was fine, it's just that I got stuck in the middle seat between two guys who were the size of sumo wrestlers."

"I know what that's like."

Madison had landed in Moscow only twelve hours ago. She'd met with Don and two other agents at the airport, and from there was transported to the safe house, a nondescript home in the outskirts of Moscow. She was briefed on the latest intel and then caught a few hours of sleep.

Now she huddled in her jacket outside the warehouse while Don withdrew a set of lock picks. She kept watch, peering through the gloom; the nearest streetlight was fifty yards away.

From somewhere in the distance came the sound of water lapping against a shore and the grinding of chunks of ice wearing against each other. *The Moscow River.*

Their intel sources believed that the missing nukes had been brought up from the Black Sea through a variety of water channels that led ultimately to the Moscow River. Those nukes were supposedly stored in one of the dozens of warehouses along the waterfront.

She heard the soft sound of metal sliding against metal, and then a click.

"Got it."

Don cracked the door open. They walked inside and quietly closed and locked the door behind them.

The warehouse was pitch black. Don's disembodied voice whispered, "Okay, let's do this and get the hell out."

Madison shrugged off her backpack and pulled out her night-vision glasses. She was fumbling with its strap when Don whispered, "Here, let me help you."

She felt his hands on hers as he twisted the device in her hand.

"Okay, slip it on."

Madison lifted the device over her head, and Don turned the switch on. An olive-hued world suddenly glowed brightly in front of her. The warehouse was huge—easily a hundred feet deep and triple that in width.

Don was already retrieving the fast-neutron detector from his backpack. Madison had received a briefing on the high-tech nuclear material detector before leaving the States; it was essentially what the US ports used to scan cargo ships—except it was portable. It looked a lot like the metal detector Madison had at home, but instead of a flat circular detector on the end of the pole, it had a wrist-thick cylinder-shaped wand.

Madison pulled her own detector from her pack, extended the telescoping pole, and locked it in place. "So," she whispered. "How do you want to do this?" She panned her arm across the vast expanse of the warehouse.

"The guys on the pier will start showing up around five, so we're out of here in two hours. Let's stay within each other's sight, just in case anyone shows unexpectedly." He waved her to the left side of the first aisle, and he went to the right side of it, sweeping his detector over the shipping containers from top to bottom.

Madison slowly ran the far end of her detector from the base to the top of the metal container. She paid careful attention to the tiny LED near the handle. It would light up only when in the presence of radioactive material.

Madison's shoulders were on fire as she unlocked the pole and collapsed the detector back to a size that would fit into her backpack. Two hours of searching, and they had found nothing.

Don grimaced. "This sucks, doesn't it?"

"Yup. How many more of these warehouses are there?"

"Lots, unfortunately. But that's not what I was talking about. It sucks holding that damned stick over your head for a couple hours. Don't know about you, but I'm not sure if I can feel my arms anymore."

Madison stretched her arms to the ceiling and shrugged her shoulders, trying to clear the lactic acid buildup from her muscles.

As they stepped out into the pre-dawn, they removed their night-vision glasses and stowed them in their packs. Don knelt at the door with lock picks in hand as Madison kept watch. Her cheeks stung from the bitter cold, and she breathed into her hands.

The metal clicked, and Don whispered, "Okay, it's locked."

They walked away from the warehouse, following the path of the river. They'd parked a half mile away in one of the public parking lots. A few flakes of snow began to fall, and Don buried his hands in his pockets. His face was practically obscured by the jets of steam he was breathing into the air.

"So," Madison said. "Is this what you've been doing ever since you got here?"

"Pretty much. Glamorous, right?"

She snorted.

The wind carried the sound of voices, and they both looked up. Don held out his arm, and Madison recalled their pre-mission discussion about what to do if they encountered anyone. She looped her arm around his, making it look as if they were just a couple on an early-morning stroll.

Under one of the few streetlights along the river's edge stood a group of teenage boys. They were laughing loudly, and appeared to be drunk.

"Be careful," Don warned.

The cold that had been seeping into Madison vanished as she strode purposefully forward, avoiding eye contact with the unruly teens.

"Hey!" one of them yelled.

Madison and Don increased their pace slightly, ignoring the group.

One boy ran into their path and yelled, "Do you have any spare change?"

They tried to move around him, but the other three ran up to them. "Don't ignore us, you bitch!"

"Hey," said another, leering. "Maybe she has something *more* to offer."

"Enough," Don growled at them in perfect Russian. He pointed toward the street. "Leave us alone."

"Or what?" The tallest, most muscular teen pulled out a knife and grinned. "Give me your money."

Another boy stepped up to Madison and petted her hair.

Madison felt her heart rate increase as she tensed.

And then chaos erupted.

Madison twisted the boy's arm and kicked his feet out from under him.

A baton appeared in Don's hand, and he slammed it into the tall teen's wrist, sending the knife flying.

A third teen raced toward Madison and was met with a side kick in the chest that sent him staggering.

Don raised the baton at a fourth teen—and the boy spun away and ran. The other young thugs followed suit.

But one of them, staggering drunk, went too close to the riverbank. He fell in with a splash.

"What was that?" Don asked, his voice laced with concern.

Madison muttered a string of obscenities. She dropped her backpack and shrugged out of her coat.

"Wait," Don said, "what are you—"

She raced to the shore, grimaced, and dove into the water.

The freezing temperature almost squeezed the air right out of her lungs. Her skin burned with cold as she grabbed a handful of the sinking teen's hair.

In the Navy, she'd drilled repeatedly in Arctic conditions to maintain her dive certifications.

She'd hated those drills.

She half-swam, half-walked back to the shore, dragging the semiconscious teen behind her.

A moment later, Don's arm wrapped around her waist, lifting her from the water. He grunted as they both dragged the sputtering teen up onto the shore.

Madison scrambled up the river's embankment, her skin burning with cold. She grabbed her jacket from the sidewalk and wrapped it around her as the teen staggered away. He was apparently drunk enough not to be affected by the cold. She could only hope he was alert enough to get inside before hypothermia set in.

Don hefted her backpack in his hand. "Okay, that officially sucked."

Madison zipped up her jacket and hopped up and down on her feet, trying to get her blood flowing into her extremities again. "Why couldn't that asshole have just face-planted on the sidewalk?" She took the backpack from Don. "C'mon. We're both wet and miserable. Let's get to the car."

Don began jogging, and Madison followed alongside. "You know,"

Don said, "I wouldn't have said a word if you'd let Darwin just sort that kid out."

Madison shook her head. "I don't need that little shit on my conscience."

As they ran alongside the river, Madison scanned the rows of warehouses. She worried they might never find what they were searching for. And with the Perimeter system activated, would someone actually be crazy enough to set a nuke off, triggering what might end up being World War 3?

"We've got to find those nukes," she murmured.

Levi stepped out of the taxi and hoisted his backpack over his shoulder. On the street behind him, an impatient driver blared his horn, and on the sidewalk, an old woman pushed a cart dispensing a deicing agent.

He could have taken the train directly to this location for significantly less money, but it would have made things a lot easier for anyone who wanted to follow him. He still had the nagging suspicion that someone was watching him—but he wasn't sure if it was real or just part of his overactive imagination. Luckily, he had the cash, so taxis were the most practical option.

Even though the crisp morning air carried the ever-present scent of diesel, Levi breathed in deeply. He relished the enticing smell of fried piroshkies—the Russian version of fried bread, usually stuffed with something sweet or savory.

He was standing on Lemonosovsky Prospekt, a street that intersected the Moscow State University campus. This was where Katarina had been a student, and somewhere on this campus, there had to be records of her time at the school. Those records were now the key to finding her—and getting to Vladimir.

His boots crunched through the morning snow as he walked north across Lomonosov Square. He adjusted his cap, feeling the tiny spike-like protrusions against his scalp. The wire powering the cap snaked through his shirt, out of sight—especially since over his shirt was a hand-me-down trench coat with large lapels flipped up against the cold and wind. This coat hadn't been fashionable in the Soviet Union since the eighties—and maybe not since the forties or fifties in the US—but it kept Levi warm, and hid the things he didn't want seen.

He'd talked to Tatyana earlier that morning. She'd said that nobody had come to ask about him. That was good. What had amused him was that, as he walked away from the front desk, the metal spike at the back of his hat zapped him with a persistent message, telling him that someone was staring at him.

Tatyana.

At least he knew it was working.

As he approached the statue at the center of the square, he stopped a passing student. "Excuse me, where is the administration building?"

The girl squinted at him through Coke-bottle glasses. "You have an interesting accent. Where are you from?"

"Vladivostok," Levi lied. "I'm late for a meeting at the administration building. Do you know where it is?"

She pointed north. "Across the square, the big building straight ahead."

Levi thanked her and continued forward. A twinge on the back of his hat told him someone was watching him. Probably the girl.

As Levi walked into the administration building, an odor greeted him. It reminded him of when he'd gone to the New York Public Library's main branch on Fifth Avenue. The smell of age. It was unmistakable.

He found it oddly pleasant.

He followed the signs to the registrar's office. Another student was already waiting outside the office, so Levi stood in line behind him.

The man sitting behind the counter pointed and groused at nobody in particular. "Damn cameras acting up again!"

Levi tilted his head to look at what the man was complaining about. He had pointed to a monitor with a view of the hallway—but where Levi stood was a blob of shimmering light. Almost as if …

It had to be his hat.

He remembered what Denny had told him about how he'd look to anyone wearing night-vision goggles. *You'll stand out like a freaking lighthouse.*

He made a mental note that he had the same effect on some video cameras.

Levi finally made it to the front of the line.

"Yes?" The man behind the counter looked as if he'd swallowed a lemon and his patience was on a razor's edge.

"I'm trying to contact a former student and wanted to know if there was some kind of forwarding address."

The man grunted and waved dismissively. "I only have current student records. You'll need to go to the archivist. Section A, ninth floor."

"This building?"

The man motioned for the next in line, and a student brushed past Levi.

As Levi turned reluctantly away, another student in line motioned down the hall. "Sir. Section A is in the main building. You'll find the stairs on the left."

"Thanks."

The route wasn't as easy as the student made out. Levi had to find his way through the maze of corridors that led back to the main building, climb nine flights of stairs, then walk through yet another maze before he reached the first sign that pointed him toward the archivist.

On the way down the hall, he passed an elevator. *Would have been nice to know that was there.*

When at last he reached the archivist, he found himself standing before a long wooden table piled high with thick folders. On the other side of the table, an older woman was putting folders into a file cabinet. Despite her age—she had to be at least seventy—she had the sturdy build of someone he could imagine wrestling bears when she was younger. She moved with purpose and surety.

"Excuse me, is this where I can find old student records?"

The woman turned toward him. "I suppose. What do you need?"

Levi glanced at her employee badge. Anya Voriskova. The picture on the badge showed a much younger version of the woman. She'd clearly worked at the school for decades.

"Anya. That's a beautiful name." He gave her his best smile. "I was wondering if you could—"

"Why?"

"Why what?"

The woman huffed loudly, leaned into the open file drawer, and shoved it closed with a metallic thunk. She shook her finger at Levi. "Don't you think that by being nice I'll somehow forget that you're just using pretty words to get something you probably shouldn't get. So why are you asking for whatever you're asking?"

Levi pouted just a bit for effect. "I just thought the name was quite pretty."

The woman's gruff demeanor softened just a bit, but the metal stud on the front of Levi's cap felt as if it were trying to zap a new hole in his skull as the woman stared unblinkingly at him.

"Well," Levi continued, "my wife died recently, and she didn't really get along with most of her family, except for one niece, to whom she wanted to give a small inheritance. Unfortunately, I don't have an address for the niece—or anyone on my wife's side of the family. But my wife's niece went to this school a number of years ago. So I'm looking for a forwarding address or something so I can try to reach her."

The woman's gruffness dissipated, and she looked downright sympathetic as she patted Levi on his upper arm. "I'm sorry for your loss. What's the name of the student?"

"Katarina Nassar. I'm not exactly sure what year—"

"Pfft." Anya waved dismissively as she sat at a computer terminal. "With these new computers, they can help me find the record right away."

She typed for a moment, then shook her head.

"I see here that she graduated with a Masters in Ancient History. Quite an interesting choice. But there's no address. That's quite strange. One second."

The woman wheeled her chair across the floor and scanned the wall of filing cabinets. She selected one of the dozens along the rear of the room and pulled open a drawer.

"Are these all the student records?" Levi asked. The room was huge, and it was filled with almost nothing but filing cabinets.

Anya laughed without looking up from what she was doing. "Not even close. These are just the records for the last ten years. We used to create microfiche records, but now everything is being put on the computer. Your niece's files are somewhere in between. Some of the years didn't make it on the computer, so that's why—found it!"

With a manila envelope in her hand, she rolled back to the table and laid open the student record. She ran her finger quickly through the Cyrillic text. She clearly was able to skim much faster than Levi could; she'd flipped to the second page before he'd even finished translating the first paragraph.

Finally, she landed her finger on a spot and nodded. "Here we go. Her application records came from a very expensive secondary school here in the north part of Moscow. And they include a home address." She looked up at Levi and frowned. "I'm not supposed to let you have personal information about a student without some kind of signed authority." She turned the folder around so it faced him, winked and said, "I'll be right back."

She walked toward the back of the room and began poking through a pile of papers.

Levi smiled as he read off Katarina's home address. In his mind, he scanned the image of the map Tatyana had shown him last night. Katarina's address was in the far west of Moscow. Probably an hour's drive or maybe even more.

He turned the file back around just as Anya walked back to the table. She gave him a crooked smile. "I'm sorry I couldn't give you what you needed."

"Thank you." Levi leaned over the table and gave the old woman a kiss on both cheeks.

She smiled and shooed him away. "Go, go find your niece, you…" She left the rest unsaid.

As Levi headed down the hall, he heard the chime from the

elevator ahead. A tall, balding man in his fifties exited and passed Levi on his way toward the archivist. Levi rushed to the elevator and caught the door just before it closed. He pressed the button for the ground floor.

Just as the doors were about to slide closed, a hand jutted between them, and the balding gentleman entered the elevator with a sheepish grin. "Wrong building."

The hairs on the back of Levi's neck stood on end. The man looked familiar.

Levi took a step back and focused his mind's eye on the people he'd seen since arriving in Russia. His mental video recorder fast-forwarded as he hunted for a match.

Just as the elevator reached the ground floor, Levi's pattern matcher clicked onto the scene. This man had been at his hotel last night.

As the doors opened, the man gestured for Levi to go first.

Levi shook his head and smiled. "I forgot something upstairs."

The man hesitated, then stepped out.

Levi pressed the button for the eighth floor. The moment the doors slid closed, he opened his backpack and pulled out a small bulb syringe and clear tape. He uncapped the syringe and squeezed the bulb, blowing fine black dust on the button with the "9" on it.

He pressed the clear tape onto the button, then tore a piece of white paper out of a notebook, removed the tape from the button, and placed it on the white paper.

It was a perfect fingerprint.

He stepped off the elevator at the eighth floor, capped the syringe, and put everything away but the paper. He took a close-up picture of the fingerprint with the sat phone. Then he typed in the address from Katarina's records, and hit *Send*.

As he began walking toward the stairs, his phone buzzed. Levi answered.

"Okay," said Denny, *"I see what you sent me. Let me guess, you need me to run it through NCIC? IAFIS? What?"*

Levi spoke in a low, hushed tone. "Not sure who it might be.

Maybe FSB. Maybe CIA. Could be Russian mob. Maybe nobody important at all. I'm not sure. Just let me know what you find."

"The print looks good, I'm already sending it out. I can't tell you how long though. And I might not get anything. But I'll let you know either way."

"That's fine. Do what you can."

"And the address? What do you want me to do with it?"

"Let's start with the owner and maybe the purchase history. But I'll take anything that comes up. Thanks, Denny."

Levi hung up and began devising a plan.

The balding man might be absolutely nobody, and Levi was being paranoid.

Or he wasn't being paranoid and he was being followed.

He couldn't risk being followed, not with his next move.

It was time to use some of his old tricks.

CHAPTER SEVENTEEN

It was just before noon, and Levi had again just finished sweeping his hotel room for bugs when his sat phone vibrated. Denny.

"Hey, Levi. I've got information on that address you gave me."

Levi's eyes widened. "Damn, that was quick." He placed the wand-shaped bug detector back into the briefcase. Nobody had placed any listening devices in his hotel room since he'd left.

That was good.

Denny's voice crackled over the sat phone. *"Who do you think you're dealing with, an amateur? The address is some big old house built in the 1840s. Definitely not a low-rent district. It's owned by a Russian historical society."*

"Do you think that's legit?"

"The records I can see go back around fifty years without any changes, so yeah. I'll look into this society place and see what their story is, but it might take a while. I'm not sure if that stuff's accessible electronically."

"So nobody named Nassar owned the house. This might all be a wild goose chase."

"Well, I don't know what to tell you. I'll dig into this historical

society and see what the story is. Maybe the Nassars were into history and owned classic homes."

"Did you by chance get anything on the fingerprint?"

"Not yet. For some of the databases, I have to pull in some favors."

"Sorry, I know. Just—"

"I'll send you a text the moment I hear something definitive."

"Thanks. Oh and by the way, that hat of yours. Let's just say it does strange things to security cameras too."

There was a full two seconds of silence on the line before Denny responded. *"Oh, damn, that makes sense. Some cameras will detect a wider range of wavelengths and—"*

"It's okay, I don't need to understand it, I'm just letting you know."

"Thanks, man. Keep safe."

Levi ended the call and thought about the next part of his plan. He had everything he needed. All of his clothes lay on the side of the bed he didn't sleep on. These included the ones he'd purchased in Lubyanka Square. That area had changed. The Lubyanka building still housed the successor to the KGB, now known as the FSB, but the area around it had been overrun with high-end shops. The shop that Tatyana had found for him was perfect, although the prices were outrageous.

The old Soviet-style, out-of-fashion clothes were set aside for his upcoming trip to Katarina's house. The scuffed and heavily used walking cane with the brass wolf's head for a handle—another of his Lubyanka purchases—lay with them.

He stripped to his waist as he walked over to the bathroom counter where he'd arranged the makeup and costume products that he'd brought from New York. He turned on the overhead sunlamp for additional light.

He couldn't remember the first time he'd put on a disguise, but ever since he was a kid, he'd learned that he had a knack for voices and imitating others—and changing how he looked felt like a natural extension of those skills. He'd lost count of how many times he'd gone in disguise as an old man to watch people he knew. He enjoyed it. It gave him a picture of what they were really like.

It was like he was peering into their souls.

But he hadn't done this in a dozen years, and he felt a touch of anxiety as he stared at himself in the mirror. With a deep breath, he frowned at the image staring back at him and murmured, "Might as well get this over with."

He wet his hair in the bathroom sink and smoothed it back so that it lay tight against his scalp.

Then he ripped open a package containing an untrimmed latex skullcap. While gazing into the bathroom mirror, he carefully laid the thin, flesh-colored cap on his head and adjusted the fit. With a small pair of sharp scissors, he trimmed the edges, leaving just enough overlap with his skin to apply spirit gum and glue the edges down.

Tilting his head back and forth and side to side, he examined his work. The cap fit well and didn't bunch up anywhere.

So far, so good.

Using a stippling sponge, Levi dabbed several layers of liquid latex along the edges of the skull cap. That always gave him a more seamless appearance. He then applied a colored mask grease with a stippling motion over the entirety of the skull cap.

Levi nodded at his bald self. "Now we need some hair."

He opened a package of crepe wool and began teasing apart the braid that it had come in. Actors tended to use the cheap stuff that was made of vegetable fibers, but Levi wanted a more realistic look, so he'd asked for actual plaited wool. He applied adhesive along the crown of his bald cap, cut a four-inch segment of the teased wool, and carefully placed the cut end against the tacky glue. After waiting a moment for the glue to dry, he repeated the process until he had a semicircle of hair on the crown of his head.

With a liberal application of translucent powder, he removed the shine from any exposed glue. He carefully combed the hair and, using an electric shaver, contoured it a bit so that it lay correctly.

Finally, he looked into the large mirror and smiled.

Not bad.

He extended the magnifying mirror that was mounted to the wall on a flexible gooseneck attachment. "Now for some aging."

He opened the jar of foundation and applied it with a wedge-shaped sponge in a thin coat across his forehead and cheeks, and along his throat. This changed the opacity of his skin and acted as a base layer to apply his other changes.

When he was satisfied with his work, he grabbed a makeup brush with a plum-colored shader, tapped it against the powder-based makeup, and applied shadow to his temples, the hollows of his cheeks, his forehead wrinkles, under his eyes, and along some lines on his neck.

He didn't even bother looking in the larger mirror anymore. He was beginning to feel at ease with the process. Having done this hundreds of times over the years, he'd learned that there was an art—or at least an instinct—to the makeup process. It was one of the skills he'd acquired that he felt particularly proud of.

"I guess if I ever want to change vocations, I could always go the makeup artist route."

Using another brush, he applied highlights to his cheekbones, nasal folds, and forehead wrinkles.

As he continued, the process got quicker.

He softly blended the wrinkles to ease the contrast between the highlights and shadows. He dabbed on a maroon effect, which gave the illusion of broken capillaries on his nose, upper cheeks, and forehead.

He added a few subtle aging spots on his face and hands. He spent a little more time with the backs of his hands, highlighting the blood vessels and making the overall effect more complete. As a final touch, he did a few makeup tricks to simulate bushy eyebrows.

When he was done, he stood back, studied himself in the large mirror, and smiled.

He cleared his throat and said in a gravelly, aged voice, "Damn, I could give Brezhnev a run for his money, couldn't I?"

Levi walked slowly, leaning slightly on his cane as he traveled through the hotel lobby. Since nobody in their seventies would be lugging around a backpack, he instead held tightly onto a large shopping bag that contained his backpack. A ratty sweater was draped over the top of it.

Whenever he was in disguise, Levi tried to *feel* like the person he was emulating. The aches of stiff joints, or the leaning due to back spasms—these became part of his character. Even being a little bit crotchety had served him well in the past.

The doorman opened the door for him, and as he stepped out into the cold, another rushed up to him and asked in Russian, "Sir, may I help you with your vehicle?"

Levi pointed with his cane at a cab and grumbled, "I called a cab. Name is Komarov."

The bellman rushed to the taxi, and Levi hobbled slowly after him. Under the direction of the bellman, the taxi pulled up closer.

"Mr. Komarov, let me help you with your bag," the bellman offered.

Levi held the bag close to his chest and shook his head.

The bellman opened the taxi door, and Levi allowed himself to fall into the back seat, making a production of dragging his right leg into the car along with his cane.

The cab driver turned to him. "You need to go to Nikolina Gora?"

Levi nodded.

As the driver waited for the car in front of him to move, Levi noticed two men standing on the far end of the hotel entrance, smoking. One of them was the balding man he'd seen twice now, once when he'd checked into this hotel, and once on the elevator at the school. The other man looked like he'd come out of KGB central casting. If a movie needed someone with a humorless, stone-faced expression, heavily muscled, and over six feet tall, this guy would have been perfect.

The taxi lurched forward, and Levi watched as his tails turned to study someone who had just walked out of the hotel.

Levi rolled past the men and he suppressed a smile.

They didn't have a clue.

The traffic was astonishingly light for midday in the Russian capital. The taxi soon pulled onto Highway A106, and the driver quickly had the tiny four-cylinder car going the speed limit.

"How long until we get there?" Levi asked.

The cabbie glanced at his navigation device. "Eh, I'd say forty minutes. The traffic is very light today. A big snow was supposed to come, but it ended up turning north."

Levi leaned back, closed his eyes, and wondered who those guys at the hotel were.

They might end up being trouble.

As the taxi rolled slowly along the street, Levi's eyes flicked back and forth in amazement. The homes here made Gambini's mansion look like a hut. Most of the homes were on ten or more acres, and all were sprawling mansions done either in an ultra-modern style or in a classic Victorian style. Opulence surrounded him.

The taxi stopped at the entrance to an older-style home. It was blocked by a large iron gate with an intercom.

"Can you wait a moment?" Levi said to the cabbie. "I want to make sure someone is there."

The driver failed to cover up his look of annoyance as he nodded.

Levi stepped out of the car and hobbled to the intercom a little quicker than he had at the hotel.

He pressed a button on the intercom, and a moment later a voice crackled through the speaker.

"Yes?"

Levi leaned in. "I'm here trying to find a Katarina Nassar."

"Who are you?"

"I'm an uncle of hers. I'm trying to find her, but I've had difficulty doing so. My wife died recently, and she left Katarina a small inheritance. Is she there?"

"She doesn't live here anymore, but maybe I can help you. I will open the gate."

A loud buzz erupted from the intercom, and the metal gate swung open.

Levi waved the taxi driver away and began hobbling up the nearly quarter-mile driveway.

The house and grounds were well tended. The snow had been cleared from all the walkways, and either the roof was heated or someone had actually swept the snow off the red tiles. When Levi at last reached the front steps, the double-door entry cracked open.

A tiny middle-aged woman in a maid's uniform appeared at the entrance and smiled as he hobbled up the stairs. "Please, let me take your coat so you can get comfortable."

Levi peeled off his coat and handed it to her. But when she glanced at the bag, Levi shook his head. "I'll keep this. Thank you, my darling."

"Helena. My name is Helena. And yours is?"

"Mikhail Komarov at your service, lovely Helena." Levi gave her a little bow.

Helena smiled and motioned for him to follow. "Gustav is in the sitting room. He's the one you talked to."

They walked through a large foyer with parquet wood flooring. There was polished wood everywhere, and it gave Levi a warm feeling. The place was lovingly cared for.

If Katarina had lived here, she came from a wealthy family. All he knew of Mary's family was that they were academics, and that almost never meant wealth.

Helena led him to a warm room with a large fireplace. Sitting on a hard-backed wooden chair before the fire was an old man who couldn't have been less than eighty. He maintained an erect posture, but his chin had dipped into his chest, and he'd fallen asleep.

Helena cleared her throat. "Gustav, Mr. Komarov is here."

The old man started awake. As he turned toward Levi, it was evident that the man suffered from severe cataracts. The gray hue was obvious even from twenty feet away.

Gustav was blind.

The old man motioned to a chair opposite him. "Please, sit. You must be cold."

Levi walked cautiously, keeping in the character of a man in his fading years. As he sat, he gazed across the room at a portrait of a man and woman. "Gustav, is the splendid painting hanging on the wall an image of you and your wife?"

The old man smiled and shook his head. "No, no. Not at all, Mr. Komarov—"

"Please, call me Mikhail."

"Mikhail. That's a picture of my long-time employer, benefactor, and friend—and his lovely wife."

"Employer?" Levi smiled. "No offense, but you seem of an age where employment would be a thing of the past."

Gustav laughed heartily, then erupted with a fit of coughing. "You'd think so."

"Excuse me." Helena's tiny voice alerted them to her presence as she carried in two cups of steaming tea. "It's time for your tea, and Mr. Komarov, I assume tea is okay for you as well?"

"Of course." Levi took the cup and set it on a stand next to the chair.

"Thank you, child." Gustav carefully felt for the cup on the table where Helena had left it, and took a careful sip.

Helena vanished nearly as quickly as she'd appeared, and Gustav picked up where he'd left off. "The man you see in that painting, he's the true owner of this home. But that is another story. Do you have time? It might help explain some of what I know and don't know of your Katarina."

Levi leaned forward attentively. "Of course, I have time."

Gustav smiled, his yellowed teeth a sign of his advanced age. "Well, the story started almost eighty-years ago. I was fifteen when I was hired by Dr. Boris Petrushenkov and his wife, Katarina. Back then, we still had stables and horses and such on the property. I was tasked with maintaining the grounds and exercising the horses."

"What did Dr. Petrushenkov do?"

"Oh, you haven't heard of him? No, I suppose you wouldn't have. I would guess that you have heard of Howard Carter, the British archaeologist?"

"I think so. Isn't he the man who discovered the tomb of King Tutankhamun?"

Gustav pointed a gnarled finger toward Levi. "Exactly right. Back then, that was all anyone could talk about. So I felt bad for Boris, because he too was an archaeologist. His wife as well. And neither ever got credit for the things they did. They'd both discovered many new things in Egypt, and many relics in our Russian museums are there because of Boris and Katarina's work.

"Alas, one day they came back from one of their travels and they'd both contracted tuberculosis. It wasn't like it is today, when you can take a pill and your problems go away. Back then, tuberculosis was a deadly disease.

"Still, they didn't let the illness stop them from working; they were both quite dedicated. I remember being very worried when they left for their next trip; I'd never seen Boris so ill. When they returned six weeks later, Katarina was barely able to breathe, but by some miracle, Boris seemed to have recovered.

"Such things happen on occasion. For instance, I never got sick. Others in the household did, but I seemed to have a natural immunity to that horrible disease."

Gustav paused to sip at his tea.

"Anyway, it was only a few days later that Katarina passed. Other than when my poor dear Misha died, I'd never felt as grief-stricken. Let me tell you, Katarina was an angel on this Earth."

Gustav wiped at his rheumy eyes and took a deep crackling breath.

"Boris never truly recovered. Certainly, for years he played at life, he took ridiculous risks, but the light had gone out from behind his eyes. I could see it. It was about fifty years ago that Boris took a trip down to Egypt, like he so often did, and that was the last time I saw him."

Levi pitied the old man. "Did Boris have children?"

"Sadly, no. He and Katarina never had children, and he never remarried. I truly believe his heart was broken after she passed."

"But I thought you said he still owns this house? I assume if you've not seen the man in fifty years, he's probably passed as well…"

Gustav smiled. "You're thinking, 'Who pays the bills? The salaries for Helena and the others you've not met?'"

"Well, I suppose so."

The old man shook his head. "I honestly don't know. I long ago expected to receive notice that it was time for me to find another employer. But I've been waiting fifty years, and every month I get money deposited into the same account. When someone leaves, they are replaced. I don't truly understand, but that's what leads me to why I buzzed you through the gate. Katarina Nassar was one of those people who came and then left."

Gustav sipped at his tea and shook his head. "I remember the day she arrived, a little over eleven years ago. My eyes had begun failing already, but I could see her enough. She was a pretty young girl, maybe eleven or twelve. She arrived with just the one suitcase, and she had difficulty speaking our language.

"I remember the tales Boris used to tell of the women in Egypt. Beautiful beyond compare, dark complexion, hair, and eyes, and a mysterious air about them. I'd never met anyone from anywhere other than Russia, but Katarina was all of that and more. She barely ever talked, even when I knew she'd mastered our language. She listened, and on occasion I saw her laugh, but there was a sadness about her. I felt sorry for her.

"She attended a private school and then university. And then one day, she never came back. Just like Boris."

Levi's mind raced with questions. Who in the world was paying for all of this? And someone had sent Katarina here. Could it have been Vladimir? Was the Russian mob paying for this house? But if so, why?

"Did Katarina ever talk about anyone outside the house?" Levi asked. "I'm trying to find her so I can give her the inheritance."

Gustav shook his head. "I don't think so. At least not around me."

"I heard her speak of someone." Helena stood at the doorway of the sitting room.

Levi turned and raised his brows.

"She was a dear girl," Helena said, "but I think she was afraid of Gustav. Maybe of men. She spoke of an uncle in the city. I don't think it was you, the name isn't right—"

"Vladimir?" Levi asked.

"Yes!" Helena snapped her fingers and nodded emphatically. "That was it. She spoke of an Uncle Vladimir on a few occasions."

Levi's heart began to race. "Did you ever see him?"

"No. I made breakfast for her every morning, and then a car would be sent to take her to school. It would drop her back off after school, just in time for dinner. Only on rare occasions did she leave for the weekend. I assumed it was to stay with her uncle, but I never wanted to pry."

"Did you ever learn why she came here?" Levi asked Helena. "Why not stay with her uncle instead?"

"All I know was that her parents had died. I think it was in an accident. But like I'm sure Gustav told you, she was sent here."

"And how did you end up here, Helena?" Levi asked.

She shrugged. "I answered an ad in the newspaper. I think I was the first to respond—"

"You were," Gustav said.

"And I got the job. I've been here almost twenty-five years."

Levi smiled and shook his head. "And yet you've never met your employer?"

Helena pointed at Gustav and cracked a smile. "He thinks he's my employer. But the truth is, we all do what is needed here. I'm paid well, and I'm happy. What else do I need to know?"

Levi felt a vibration coming from the bag lying next to his leg.

Gustav held out his cup in a trembling hand. "Let's toast to your finding Katarina, and I pray she's found happiness."

Levi picked up his tea, which had cooled a bit, and touched cups with Gustav. The man drank deeply, but Levi suddenly felt uneasy. He sniffed at the cup; it smelled of the pungent black tea he'd drunk hundreds of times. He sipped at it lightly and tasted the pleasant and mild tannic quality of the brew.

It was just tea.

And these were just innocent people getting by as well as they could.

His bag vibrated once again, and Levi's anxiety ratcheted up a notch. Denny was trying to reach him.

He stood. "Gustav, Helena, thank you so much for the fire, the conversation, and the information. I think I have what I need to keep looking. Thank you."

Gustav waved in his direction and smiled. "It was good talking to you, Mikhail. I hope you find her."

"Do you want me to call you a car?" Helena asked.

Levi shook his head. "I'll do it. I've got a phone."

As Levi walked down the long driveway, he dug out his phone and looked at the text on the screen.

Call me.

He hit the speed dial and put the phone to his ear.

Before he even heard the first ring, Denny's voice came through. *"Levi, I've got an ID on that fingerprint for you. You ready for it?"*

Levi approached the gate, and it automatically yawned open. "Hit me."

"It belongs to someone named Harold Wilson. He reports to a John Maddox over at Langley. He's a CIA spook."

"Maddox. He was one of the fingerprints on that envelope."

"Not on the envelope, that was a Madison Lewis. Maddox's print was on the letter itself. Both this Wilson and the Lewis woman report to Maddox. They must love you to keep such close ties."

Levi stopped on the sidewalk, thinking. "You don't by chance have Maddox's phone number, do you?"

"No, but I do have the direct operator number for Langley. You want that?"

"What am I supposed to do, call a public operator and tell her that one of the most secretive organizations in the world has a spy on my ass and I want to talk to the spy's manager?"

"Well, it might work, though I probably wouldn't phrase it exactly like that. Besides, it's not a public operator. It's an operator in the CIA —big difference."

Levi laughed. "That's ridiculous. But okay, text me the number. Oh, and one other thing. I got more information on the house and Katarina. Evidently she's had a so-called 'Uncle Vladimir' ever since she was a kid. And the previous owner of the house was a man named Boris Petrushenkov who vanished some fifty years ago. Nobody who works at the house has heard from him since, but someone continues to pay them, and they don't know who. Oh, and get this. Boris's wife died of TB, and you know what her name was?"

"No clue."

"Katarina."

"That's weird. All right, I've written this stuff down. Not sure if I'll find anything, but if I do, you'll know right away."

"Thanks, Denny. Text me with the number. I'll see if I can get ahold of him, and then who knows what's next."

"Good luck."

The line went dead.

By the time Levi had finished calling a taxi dispatcher to arrange for a pickup, Denny had texted him the number for the CIA.

Levi dialed the number and after two rings, someone responded. *"Office of Public Affairs, Central Intelligence Agency."*

"Hello, I'm not sure if this is the right number, but I need to be dispatched to an employee at the Langley location. His name is John Maddox."

"Who may I say is calling, sir?"

"Tell him it's Levi Yoder."

"One second, sir." After putting him on hold for a bit, the operator came back on the line. *"Sir, I'm connecting your call."*

The phone rang once, and a brusque voice answered. *"Maddox. Who is this?"*

"Listen, John, you know who this is. You're the same guy who sent me on a fun trip to Nepal. And you've got some bald-headed guy named—"

"Okay, that's enough. This isn't a secure line."

"Exactly. Your people need to stop following me, or I might just send an anonymous message to our friends in Lubyanka. Am I understood?"

Levi heard Maddox breathing through gritted teeth. There was silence on the line for a full three seconds. *"Why does this call seem to be coming from the middle of the Antarctic?"*

"Am I understood?"

"Can I ask one question?"

"Go."

"Would you be willing to talk with two of my people? You've already met one of them."

"Explain to me how that's at all in my best interest."

"What we're doing is critical to our nation's defense—"

"Don't try to give me some patriotic horseshit—"

"I'm not, but I am afraid you may inadvertently be involved in something that's a national security issue. I swear to you, I'll pull the surveillance team as soon as I get off the phone. But we'd like to talk."

Levi paced. He wished he could see Maddox's face—then he'd be able to gauge how full of crap the man was. Over the phone, it was hard, though the man sounded sincere.

"You need something from me," Levi said.

"Actually, I think we might both be after the same thing, but likely for very different reasons. Will you meet—"

"Have them meet me at Club 21 on Tverskoy Boulevard in two hours. I'll make a reservation for three under the name Maddox."

"Two hours is a—"

"Two hours or not at all."

"I'm extending an uncomfortable amount of trust ... fine, I'll make it happen."

A taxi turned onto Levi's street, and he waved at it.

"As long as you aren't trying to screw me, you don't need to worry about me. Club 21, two hours."

Levi disconnected the call and hunched over as the taxi rolled in front of him. "A slight change of destination. How long would it take to get to Club 21 on Tverskoy Boulevard?"

The driver tapped the address into his navigation system. "One hour and fifty minutes."

Levi got in the cab and handed the man a five-thousand-ruble note. "Another one of those if you can get me there in one and a half hours or less."

"Sir, tighten your seat belt. This will be an interesting ride."

Levi smiled as the driver floored the accelerator and raced through the residential area.

He thought back to what Maddox had said. *Actually, I think we might both be after the same thing, but likely for very different reasons.*

How could he and the CIA be after the same thing?

The ride was not going to be nearly as interesting as the dinner.

CHAPTER EIGHTEEN

When Jen walked into the safe house carrying a large duffel bag, Madison gave her a bear hug. "I didn't think we'd see each other in-country."

Jen lifted Madison off her feet. "It's good to see you too. Do you know why Maddox had me rush over here?"

Before Madison could answer, her sat phone rang. Both women put their ears to the receiver.

Maddox's voice crackled. *"Maddie, is Jen there?"*

"Yes, she just arrived. We're both listening. What's going on?"

"We've had a development, and I need you two to be somewhere in less than an hour—"

"John," Jen interrupted, "you realize by my coming here, I've compromised the safe house, right?"

"Of course I know that. I have to assume the FSB followed you from the embassy and is right now calling someone to figure out what this place is and why one of their assignees just went there. But it had to be done. I'm having a car come by to pick you both up, along with your stuff. They'll drop you off at your destination and will then take your things to another safe house. Now let me go over what's happened.

"Yoder contacted me to tell us to lay off the surveillance—and this guy knows way more than he should. I think we can use this to our advantage. He's agreed to talk with two of my people, and I'm banking on the two of you."

"Why us?" Madison asked.

"Don't think this is being sexist or any of that bullshit, but our profiler thinks Yoder's more likely to cooperate with a woman than a man."

"Did you actually pay someone for that advice?" Jen remarked snidely. "I could have told you that for free."

"Anyway, I need you to get him to cooperate. We intercepted some fresh intel that indicates our person of interest is likely at Kosvinsky Mountain. We also suspect she knows where the stolen packages are."

"And Yoder knows what she looks like," Madison thought aloud.

"Exactly. Not only that, we believe he's highly motivated to find her, so we have that to induce him to cooperate. I have interrogators at a black site on standby. We need to know what she knows. And most importantly, we need those missing packages."

"Even if he agrees to work with us," Jen said, "then what? That place is like twelve hundred miles away on the edge of Siberia or something."

"There's a small airfield on the north side of a tiny village called Kytlym. I can get the three of you there with equipment in under six hours. That'll get you about fifty kilometers east of the mountain. You'll need winter survival gear. Our information says you won't get past the main entrance, but we have GPS coordinates and a map of a tunnel used by maintenance workers. We've got uniforms and IDs that should get you through."

Feeling a bit shaky about the plan, Madison looked to Jen, whose expression suggested she had the same misgivings.

"We believe this Yoder guy will be a straight arrow if we play it straight with him. Obviously, you can't tell him about the packages, but how much more you say, I'll leave up to you. Ladies, it's now your call. If you're not up for it, we'll pull you out, no harm, no foul. Otherwise we have little time to spare."

Feeling a surge of adrenaline, Madison shrugged. "What the hell. You only live once."

"Agent Lancaster?"

Jen nodded. "Let's do this."

"Okay. A car will be picking you up in five minutes to take you to meet Yoder. He's set a reservation under my name at a place called Club 21. I looked it up, it's swanky. After that, I'll arrange for a plane to be fueled and ready whenever you give the go-ahead. Good luck and God bless."

Maddox hung up.

Jen opened her duffel bag and began tearing through various outfits. "We're trying to convince Blue Eyes to work with us and Maddox gives us only five minutes to change? Fuck!"

∿

Levi's cab driver earned his money, getting him to Club 21 ten minutes ahead of his aggressive deadline.

At first, the tall, dark-haired hostess with a model's face and body was very disagreeable about making the table available early. But with sufficient financial motivation, she became very helpful. She gave Levi a blinding smile. "The private table is ready whenever your guests arrive, Mr. Maddox. If you like, I can seat you now."

"Thank you, Elena, but no." Levi motioned toward a dark corner near the entrance. "I'll just wait here."

∿

Madison and Jen hurried along the street toward the restaurant.

"How are you going to play this?" Madison asked.

Jen smoothed out her black miniskirt and adjusted the swooping neckline of her tight red blouse. Madison wished she had the guts to tell her that she looked like a hooker.

"We're here early," Jen said, "so we can both read him and figure out the best approach. Even though Maddox tried to act cool about this, I could tell he was spooked."

"Wouldn't you be? Some guy we're tailing calls you and says, 'Lay off'?" Madison grimaced. "Yup, I think that's official territory for wondering who the hell we're dealing with. How'd Yoder even know to call him?"

The bright sign of Club 21 appeared in front of them, and they walked inside.

The hostess at the reception stand gave Jen a look that could curdle milk. In Russian, she asked, "May I help you?"

Jen smiled and shook her head. "We're a bit early. There's one more coming." She turned to Madison. "Let's wait over in the corner."

Madison nodded politely at an elderly man who was already waiting there. He was bent over with age, leaning heavily on a cane. She felt sure she'd never seen him before, but ... those eyes.

Recognition dawned on her.

She smiled at Levi, and he gave her a wink. They shook hands.

"Nice to see you again," Madison said. She looked around the front part of the restaurant. "This is a nice place."

Jen clearly had not recognized Levi Yoder. She gave Madison a look as if to say, *What are you doing?*

The hostess approached with three menus in hand and smiled coquettishly at Levi. "Mr. Maddox, if your party is ready, I can seat you."

Levi held out his elbow to Madison. She looped her arm around his and laughed at Jen's stunned expression as the hostess led them to the back of the restaurant and seated them in a private room.

Levi's voice exhibited the strained shakiness typical in a man of advanced years as he said in slightly accented Russian, "Elena, can you please tell the waiters to give us five minutes? I want some uninterrupted time to talk with my associates before things start."

"Of course. I'll close these doors for you." The hostess pulled on a hidden latch on each side of the doorway and drew the pocket doors closed.

With a sense of wonder, Madison watched as Levi pulled a wand-shaped device from his shopping bag and ran it over each wall and under the table. He glanced apologetically at Madison and Jen. "If you will, can you please lift your arms for me?" He now sounded much more like the man she'd talked to in the bar.

Madison lifted her arms, and Levi ran the device up and down her body. At no point did he touch her or act improperly.

Jen studied him as he wanded her. "So, that's all makeup? Even the bald head?"

Levi chuckled as he placed the wand back into his bag and settled onto a seat facing them. He motioned toward the door. "They'll be here in a minute; let's go ahead and order. Get anything you like—it's my treat." He picked up the menu. "I hear the steaks are very good."

Madison paused for a moment as she studied the man. If she didn't know better, he looked exactly the part of a harmless Soviet-era retiree. Tearing her attention from Levi, she focused on the menu and her eyes popped when she saw the prices. Converting from rubles to dollars in her head, she observed that even the cheapest appetizer was over twenty US dollars.

Jen shook her head as she read aloud the English translation for one of the choices. "Steak frites grilled, shallot confit, vegetable tian, french fries, with bordelaise and bearnaise."

"Sounds good," Madison remarked.

"But I don't understand what half of that even means," Jen complained.

"It's a pretty standard ploy at high-end restaurants." Levi said matter-of-factly. "They make it sound fancy, when in fact what you just read could easily be described as 'steak and fries with baked vegetables and some sauces.'

"Everything is like that in this country. I wouldn't be surprised if you went to a McDonalds here and instead of chicken nuggets, fries, and ketchup, they described it as 'tender morsels of free-range organic chicken with a heritage wheat crust, served with pommes frites and a sweetened heirloom tomato reduction.'"

Madison covered her mouth as she laughed.

A light knock sounded on the doors, and they slid open, revealing a waiter with a tray full of appetizers. Madison's stomach grumbled as the man laid the items on the table while giving a full description of each.

"Our first appetizer is our Japanese A5 beef skewers. You'll find six skewers of the highest quality beef, rubbed with our own house seasonings and seared to a perfect medium rare. It is served with a choice of two dipping sauces, a vanilla honey mustard sauce and a teriyaki barbecue glaze.

"The second appetizer features our finest beluga caviar and blinis. Served with it are savory and sweet blintzes, salmon roe, chopped egg, scallion, and crème fraiche."

The third plate was placed almost directly in front of Madison. It was a still-steaming loaf of the darkest bread she'd ever seen and a large silver bucket of pickles.

"The third appetizer is a specially made black bread with fried onions inside. It is served with freshly churned butter and fresh pickles."

Levi nodded approvingly and asked the waiter in Russian, "Do you speak English?"

The waiter responded in heavily accented English. "Yes, I learned in school. Are you ready to order?"

Levi nodded to Madison and Jen. "Ladies first."

Jen ordered in perfect Russian. "Your steak frites? What cut of meat is it?"

"It's a ribeye steak."

"I'll take that, but I'd prefer it with no pink inside."

The waiter seemed taken aback. "You mean well done?"

Jen nodded.

Madison also ordered in Russian. "I'll have the same, but I'd prefer mine to still be mooing."

The waiter laughed. "Rare it will be, and I'll ask the chef to make sure it has extra moo."

"I'll have the same as the ladies," Levi said, "but make mine medium rare."

"Very well, excellent choices. What about drinks?" The waiter turned to Jen.

"Gin and tonic."

"And for you, miss?"

"An amaretto sour."

"And for the gentleman?"

"I'll have a seltzer."

"Anything else for anyone?" The waiter paused, then bowed slightly. "Very well, I will be right back with your drinks." He stepped out of the room and closed the doors behind him.

"Seltzer," Jen said. "I didn't think anyone drank that anymore."

"I'm old fashioned." Levi shrugged. "Anyway, I'm not big on alcohol. I'm a lightweight and I don't like feeling out of control. Your Russian is really good, both of you—probably even better than mine." Levi gave them a wink. "Then again, I suppose it goes with your jobs."

Madison felt the silent pause hanging in the air, and she had no desire to fill that gap.

"Anyway," Levi pointed at the foods arrayed on the table, "I wasn't sure what kind of foods you two might like to whet your appetite with, so before you two arrived, I pre-ordered a meat, fish, and vegetarian choice. I hope you don't mind."

"This all looks fantastic, thank you." Jen gave Levi a brilliant smile.

Madison couldn't remember the last time anyone she'd ever dated had even cared what her diet preference was. This mobster was surprising her. She gazed at the fuzzy-browed wrinkled man with male-pattern baldness and laughed.

"What's so funny?" Levi asked.

She shook her head. "Nothing. I just think it was really considerate of you. Let me be frank, I wasn't expecting that."

"What were you expecting?"

Madison shrugged. "I guess I don't know." She pointed at the food. "Thank you for this, it's really great. And I'm starving."

"Well, let's eat." Levi grabbed one of the skewers of meat before pushing the plate closer to Madison and Jen's side of the table. "The only time I've ever had this kind of steak is when I lived in Japan. Take a couple of these skewers—you'll thank me. Oh, and try it first without any dipping sauces. Just appreciate the meat. It's not like anything I've ever had in the States."

Madison took one of the skewers and slid the meat onto her plate. They were perfect cubes with uniform crispy browned edges—they looked like little works of art. She popped one of them in her mouth and moaned involuntarily. "Oh my god. It's like meat butter."

"Exactly!" Levi said. "Isn't it awesome?"

Jen made the same moan and covered her mouth. "Oh shit, you're right."

"I'm glad you like it." Levi smiled and grabbed a blini, which was really just a dollar-coin-sized pancake, and placed on it a dollop of sour cream and a tiny spoonful of caviar. He raised his handheld appetizer as a toast. "Listen, let's cut through the BS. You have an agenda—whatever it is your boss has told you to talk about—and we'll get to it before we leave this table. But for now, let's have a beautiful meal and talk about things."

"Things?" Madison said.

"Sure." Levi pointed at Madison. "What's your name?"

"Nicole," she said without hesitating.

Levi smiled. "Okay, Nicole, I believe in being blunt. You are both beautiful women. But you, I can't quite put my finger on. I've traveled to more places than you can imagine, but I'm having trouble placing you. You appear to be Polynesian, but I know you aren't. You almost look aboriginal, as in from Australia, but your bone structure doesn't fit. Let me guess: you're half Japanese, half Australian aborigine?"

Madison laughed. "You're close. Japanese and African-American."

Levi nodded. "Interesting. I can see that. I don't mean to embarrass you, but it's a unique and attractive combination."

Madison felt heat rise up her neck.

Levi turned to Jen. "And your name is?"

"Jennifer Lancaster."

Madison barely kept the shock from registering on her face. One of the things covert agents all learned was to not reveal their true identities when on the job. Maybe he already knew her name and it was a test, but still …

"Jennifer, I think you're a little easier to place. Blonde hair, I can see the roots aren't much darker than the tips, so I'd wager you're a natural blonde. You have a girl-next-door look, but an athletic build. I'd say Scandinavian descent. Maybe some German tossed in—no, I stick to the Scandinavian. Maybe Dutch mixed in somewhere."

"Okay, that's just weird," Jen said. "My mom's side of the family is Norwegian and my father's is Dutch."

Madison sliced a piece of bread off the warm loaf and slathered butter on it. "Can we ask *you* some questions?"

"Of course. It wouldn't be any fun if it was all one-sided."

"What do you do for a living?"

A crooked grin bloomed on Levi's face. "That's an excellent question. I'll have to answer that one carefully. I guess the best way to describe it is that I fix things."

"Like broken TVs?" Jen asked with a smile.

"No, not exactly." Levi pursed his lips. "The people I tend to fix things for have nobody else to turn to. The police are too busy, their lawyers are useless, and yet they still have a problem. Let me give you an example.

"There was a rumor about an important man who liked abusing little girls. This man had the politicians and police in his pocket. I won't name names, but let's assume this man was a member of one of the families."

"Mafia?" Jen said.

Levi grinned and continued. "One day, a little girl, no more than twelve, she filed a complaint with the police about her being raped by this man.

"Now, I happen to have some friends in high places as well. I heard about the complaint. I also heard how the police and hospital had 'lost' the rape swab evidence and closed the case.

"I don't like bullies. No, that's not right. I don't just dislike them, I *despise* them. So I began to pay attention to this man … the rapist. I learned a few things about him. I managed to get some evidence that couldn't get 'lost.' And then I had a conversation with a few people who were more important than that abuser. I showed them the evidence.

"The problem was fixed. Permanently."

Madison furrowed her brow. "Did you get paid for that?"

Levi turned to her with a confused expression. "By whom? The twelve-year-old? Of course not. Sometimes things need to be fixed, and there's nobody to pay the bill. These things happen on occasion."

Madison felt an upwelling of unbidden emotion. Her chest tightened, and she grew angry with herself for reacting to his story. It probably wasn't even true. Or was it?

There was a quick knock, and the doors slid open. Two waiters entered, one with their drinks and the other with plates of food.

Jen mouthed "wow" at her. Madison wasn't sure if the "wow" was about the food or what Levi had just revealed.

Levi raised his glass of seltzer. "To a beautiful dinner and a productive conversation to come."

After dinner, Levi talked with the two agents for nearly thirty minutes over coffee. They weren't telling him everything.

He drummed his fingers on the table. "Let me get this straight: you have a lead on the location of someone named Katarina. You're convinced it's the same one I'm interested in, yet you don't even know her last name. How is it that you even think we're talking about the same person?"

Madison, who still insisted on calling herself Nicole, pressed her lips together; she seemed to be struggling with what she could say or not say. "I've listened to some audiotapes of her. One was related to what happened at your parents' farm. We've also intercepted conversations regarding the lead we have. Same first name, and more importantly, the same voice."

So they have wiretaps on some key phone lines. That explained a few things.

Levi frowned. "Why are you so interested in her? I understand why *I'm* interested, but nothing that either of you have said makes any sense. You won't tell me what the national security issue is. There's absolutely no way you're going to convince me that some woman who killed some kids is so high on your list of things to do that you'll come out here to find her."

He waited for them to say more, but they were silent. So he asked them outright.

"Why is she of interest to you?"

Jen leaned forward. The top of her ample cleavage showed to good effect. "You're right. We actually don't give a shit about Katarina Whateverhernameis. She has some associates that we absolutely need to find. She's a means to an end. That's all."

Levi sat back, tilted his head, and smiled. His heartbeat increased and he felt a tingle on his fingertips as he drummed them on the table. "I take it you're looking for a male associate. Is that right?"

"Yes," Madison said.

"Tell me the man's name."

"We can't," the two women said simultaneously.

Levi shook his head. "Let me make this perfectly clear. Tell me the name, first name only. If it's who I think it is, I'll go with you. That means we're on the same team, and we go all the way together. If you won't tell me, then I think we can call it a lovely night."

The women looked at each other. Finally, Madison nodded, and Jen said, "Vladimir. I really can't say any more than that."

The two women watched Levi expectantly.

Levi considered his options. These women claimed to know where Katarina was. And while he had gotten some new information at her old house, it wasn't a lot. He could leverage their help.

He sighed. "Okay, ladies. You said there's a flight and cold-weather hiking involved. I suspect we'll all need a change of clothes."

"So you'll go?" Madison asked.

Levi nodded. "Yes. I have to go back to my hotel to change and pack a couple things."

Madison slid a piece of paper across the table. "That's the address of the private airport we'll take off from. Let's meet there at midnight."

Levi glanced at the paper. "Okay. Do you ladies need me to arrange a taxi for you?"

Jen shook her head. "We've got it covered." She glanced at her wristwatch and turned to Madison. "We have to go."

Levi stood and shook hands with both women. "Go ahead, I need to call up a taxi for myself. I'll see you at the witching hour."

As the women left, Levi's mind raced. He'd never given thought to the possibility of getting to Katarina with others in tow.

But if these women could help him get to Katarina—and then to Vladimir—it was a possibility worth exploring.

As to what would happen to Vladimir when they find him … that was something for him to worry about later.

CHAPTER NINETEEN

Madison bounced up and down on her toes, trying to keep warm as she gazed at the street running up to the private airport. Aside from the runway lights and the light coming from the cabin of the Pilatus PC-24 jet that Maddox had arranged for them, it was pitch black outside. The moon glowed silver in the cloudless sky, and the temperature had fallen to near zero.

Jen paced. "Do you think he's going to bail on us?"

"No idea. But it's midnight, and I don't see the lights of a cab or anything else. Yoder struck me as the punctual type."

"Shit, I'm freezing."

Madison glanced at her watch: two minutes after midnight.

"It's too late for traffic or anything else to be—"

"Shh." Madison waved for Jen to be quiet. "Do you hear something?" She strained to see, but it was too dark to make out anything beyond fifty feet.

Through the still night came the sound of gravel being crushed against pavement. And then a silhouette appeared in the moonlight—someone jogging directly toward them, dressed head to toe in black.

Madison's heart raced.

But as the jogger drew closer, and light reflected off his face, she breathed a sigh of relief, feeling her faith in Levi vindicated.

"Sorry I'm late." Levi panted lightly as he slowed to a stop. "I had the taxi drop me off about a mile away. I didn't want to take any chances of them reporting to the FSB about some American being picked up at my hotel and dropped off at an airport."

Madison shook her head in amazement. What kind of civilian would even think to take that kind of precaution?

Jen stepped forward and hugged Levi. "I'm glad you made it."

Levi held his arms out awkwardly, not hugging Jen back.

When she released him, he turned to Madison. "Good morning, Nicole."

Madison cringed internally at his use of the name. "Good morning to you too. Now let's get on that plane, because I'm freezing my ass off." She turned and climbed the steps into the cabin.

The passenger cabin was configured with six seats, three on each side, with extra space in back for their cargo. Madison claimed the first seat, Levi sat to her right, and Jen took the seat behind her.

As they strapped themselves in, the stairs were already lifting, sealing the cabin shut. The pilot stepped out of the cockpit door and used a flashlight to check the seal of the cabin door.

Apparently satisfied, he spoke to Madison with a mild southern accent. "Ma'am, traffic control will not authorize us to land at Kytlym, but I'll arrange for a 'malfunction' and an emergency stop on their runway. This isn't going to be a fast-rope mission or anything, but you'll need to clear the aircraft quickly just in case anybody comes to take a look. It'll be way early in the morning, so I doubt anyone will even be awake. Anyway, I'll delay as long as possible to get parts to fix the plane's so-called problem."

"How long do you think you can stall there?" Jen asked.

"It's a remote location, so four or five days. I'll see what I can do."

Levi turned in his seat and asked, "How close are we landing to the objective?"

Jen glanced at Madison, who nodded. "The landing strip is about fifty-five kilometers from where we're heading."

Levi shook his head. "Kytlym is pretty far north. Plan for not much more than two miles per hour hiking through the snow. That's a two-day trek, each way, assuming no issues."

"You know where Kytlym is?" Madison said, surprised.

Levi shrugged. "I might have studied a map of Russia at some point or another. So, your objective is Mount Kosvinsky. It's about the only thing west of that place in that range. I'm guessing there's some hidden base there you guys have information on?"

Jen's jaw dropped, but only for a moment. "No comment."

Levi rolled his eyes and laid his head back against the seat.

Madison turned to the pilot. "We'll try to make it back by day four. At worst, we'll come up with auxiliary exit plans."

"Okay then, everyone buckle up. We'll be cruising at forty-thousand feet and expect touchdown in just over three hours." He returned to the cockpit.

Moments later, the cabin lights dimmed, and the engines began spinning up.

Madison turned to Jen and Levi. "We better get some sleep while we can."

"Aww," Jen said, sticking out her lower lip. She looked fondly at the back of Levi's seat.

To Madison's amazement, Levi was already sound asleep, and apparently dreaming. His eyes were darting under closed lids. The serene expression on his face sent butterflies through her stomach. For all that this man likely was, and the things he'd probably done, at this moment she could imagine what he'd looked like as a boy, sleeping.

Jen leaned forward and whispered in her ear, "Tell me you don't think he's gorgeous."

The pilot pushed the engines to full throttle, and Madison felt herself shoved against the seat.

She closed her eyes and tried her best to get some rest.

∼

The team had made it two hundred yards from the airfield when they hit the edge of the pine forest. Levi motioned for a halt as the others trudged through the knee-deep snow after him.

"This sucks," Madison said. "We were told this area was supposed to have practically no snow."

"I'd kill for a pair of skis right about now," Jen added.

Levi sniffed the air and looked west. "Well, obviously your weather guys were wrong. Also, it's going to snow soon. I can sense the change in humidity."

Both women were wearing night-vision goggles. Madison lifted hers onto her forehead and stared wide-eyed at him. "How can you see anything?"

He panned his gaze across the landscape, noting the glistening shine off the snow. "I suppose my eyes are adjusted." He pointed at their legs, which were knee-deep in snow. "I suggest we get everyone on some snowshoes."

He drew a knife from under his jacket and scanned the nearby trees. Spotting a spruce, he chopped at some of the lower branches.

Madison watched as he gathered five finger-thick branches and cut them into equal sizes. "I take it you've made snowshoes before?"

He motioned her aside. "You're in my light."

"Oh, sorry." Madison stepped aside, then looked up at the star-filled sky. "Um …"

Levi chuckled as he pulled a loop of paracord from his backpack. "I'm kidding." He motioned for both of them to come closer. "Sorry, I've got a weird sense of humor sometimes. Anyway, it's actually really simple. Both of you, watch."

Jen and Madison gathered around.

"Five pieces of live wood," Levi said, "roughly the length of your elbow to the tip of your middle finger. Tie one end tightly together."

He tied the end and grabbed a shorter length of wood.

"Fan out the sticks and place your first cross-brace where your heel would go. Tie that across the five sticks."

He grabbed two more cross-braces.

"Now grab two more sticks of equal size and place them roughly where the ball of your foot would be. Bend and tie the cross-braces to the five sticks. And finally, bend the end of the sticks together and tie those up."

Levi held up a large oval shoe and smiled. "We just need five more of these to tie to our boots, and this hike'll go a lot quicker."

Madison and Jen flicked open their own blades and began hacking at the trees.

"Do you guys need any rope?" Levi asked.

"Nope," Jen replied. "But I wouldn't mind if you at least make sure I'm not doing this wrong. I can barely see my hands in front of my face."

Levi made quick work of his second shoe, then watched both women do a remarkable job imitating what he'd just done. It wasn't long before they had three serviceable pairs of snowshoes, and he proceeded to show them how to tie themselves on.

The women grinned as they walked with relative ease over, instead of through, the snow.

"This is *so* much easier!" Madison said.

Jen walked over to him at a brisk pace. One of her feet tilted into the snow, and he caught her as she slammed face forward into his chest.

"Make sure you don't forget to walk flat-footed," he warned them both. "You're just trying to keep your footprint as wide as possible so the snow will support your weight. As soon as you dig in the heel or toe of your shoe, you're going to sink."

Jen looped her arm over his shoulder as she regained her footing. Levi felt uneasy as she pressed her body against his. He slowly stepped back.

Madison walked over with an even gait, looking at Jen. "Are you okay?"

"I'm fine." Jen looked up at Levi. "Thanks for keeping me from face-planting into a tree."

"Of course. Now, can we talk through the objective before we get going? I'll start with a quick summary of what I know. We've got roughly fifty-five klicks west-northwest to travel. We're then supposed to glide in under assumed identities, hunt down Katarina ... and that's where it gets fuzzy. I'm guessing we're planning on taking her out without anyone noticing?"

Madison frowned. "If you mean *kill* her, no ..."

"Jeez, Nicole. What do you take me for?" Levi shook his head. "That's not what I meant. We both want some information out of her, and that's not going to happen unless we're among friendlies. So we knock her out or incapacitate her and drag her out of there and back to the plane. Then we get to some location you've not told me about. Is that the plan?"

"I'm sorry, Levi, I didn't mean—"

Levi waved her words away. "I'm just trying to get a feel for our plan."

"You guessed correctly," Jen said. "Priority one is get her out of there. We've got some stuff that'll knock her out. Assuming we get back in time for our exit plane, then we'll all go back to a to-be-determined site."

"For questioning, torture, or whatever," Levi said coldly.

Neither Jen nor Madison commented on this.

"Well," Levi continued. "I figure the terrain is going to get worse the closer we get to the base of the mountain. At best we have seventeen hours of tough travel each way. If we're carrying someone on the way back, maybe double the return trip. I suggest we don't stop until we're two or three klicks away from the objective.

"The tree line goes right up to the base of the mountain, so we should still be well into the woods, beyond what normal security sweeps might be done. If we manage to make that tonight's stopping point, we'll be close enough to be fresh when we get to the entrance you guys talked about in the morning. I'm guessing we're going to have a very long day, probably not stopping until at least midnight. What do you guys think?"

Jen had been nodding in agreement the entire time he spoke, but Madison looked perplexed.

"Levi," she said, "I think that's a great plan, but I have a question. You don't have to answer it, but curiosity is killing me. Have you been in the military before? I mean, you talk like some of the SEALs and other SF guys I know. You obviously know your way around the woods and the weather. You know counter-surveillance techniques that most civilians would never think of. Hell, you knew to reach out to my boss, and I have no freaking clue how that was possible. It's also little things, like you not saying *kilometers* but *klicks*, as if you've been leading soldiers for years. Who *are* you?"

Levi couldn't help but smile at Madison's plain expression of curiosity. She was a no-bullshit type of person. He liked that.

"Nicole, you keep having insightful questions, but I'm afraid there isn't really much to it. Any survivalist would know how to plan a trip or know about making snowshoes or detecting weather changes. I've lived almost a decade without a roof over my head, in the most godawful places you can imagine. I just sort of picked up a lot of what you're seeing. As to some of the other stuff, I must have absorbed a thing or two from one of my cousins who was an Army Ranger. He was one of the black sheep, kind of like me—being Amish and not living an Amish lifestyle. He died in Afghanistan in 2003."

"I'm sorry," Madison said.

"No need to be sorry." He shrugged. "It's not like you killed him. He was an impressive person. I guess it's fair to say he rubbed off on me a bit, though I've never led anything. I've survived things that I had no business surviving, though. I've seen people I love die. And frankly, if we're going to do this, I want to make sure we all get out in one piece."

Madison's face clouded with a strange expression. The dim starlight highlighted her cheekbones and framed her face beautifully against the dark backdrop of the woods. "I-I'm sorry," she said. "I didn't mean to pry—"

"Yet you did, and it's okay. I'd want to know about the person I'm traveling with as well. It's smart to ask." He glanced back and forth between the two women. "Are we in agreement with the plan? Push hard, camp for the night within an hour's reach of the target, and then push hard through the rest until we're all sleeping in our beds some-where safe."

Both women nodded. "Agreed."

Levi looked up at the sky. Recalling the star patterns in the northern hemisphere, he pointed west-northwest. "I believe we're heading that way, right?"

Jen pulled out her compass. She studied it, then looked up at Levi and shook her head. "Did you also swallow a compass when you were a kid?"

Levi grinned and began plodding through the snow-covered terrain.

It took longer than expected to reach their campsite. Levi shifted them away from a direct path, claiming they were downwind from a pack of wolves and wanted to stay out of their way. Madison thought he was imagining things until about thirty minutes later, when they heard the howls and barking.

The sounds came from where they'd have been had they not changed course.

As Jen put together the tent, Madison stretched, feeling her muscles scream with overuse. "Jen, you sure you don't want any help?"

Jen waved her off. "I've got it."

Madison put on her night-vision glasses and scanned through the darkness. Levi had been gone for nearly ten minutes, and she was feeling anxious.

What could he be doing?

She thought about how he'd just assumed an unspoken lead posi-tion in their group. At first she'd resented it, but by now, she'd become comfortable with him leading. She was somehow trusting him more than she could ever have imagined she would.

Jen, of course, had been drooling over him ever since she'd first seen him back at Langley, and Madison felt pretty sure the woman would do just about anything to put him as a notch on her bedpost.

Madison could never be like that, but she couldn't blame Jen for feeling that way. Levi was smart, seemingly kind, and oddly considerate of what they thought.

Good-looking, too. That was undeniable.

Footsteps sounded to her right, and Madison felt a disturbing sense of relief at seeing Levi walk back into their camp.

How he was able to even see what he was doing was beyond her. There was almost no light from the stars or moon; it was blocked by the thick forest canopy.

"That took a while—you constipated?" Madison joked.

Levi shook his head. "Not particularly. If you are, I can gather some spruce tips and make you a tea. It's high in vitamin C and should help regulate you."

She covered her mouth and barely held back a snort. *And he's funny.* Something about him just cracked her up.

Madison couldn't help be annoyed that she'd begun to feel overly comfortable in this man's presence. After all, he was a mobster. One of the bad guys.

Levi glanced back and forth between Madison and Jen's butt, which was up in the air as she pressed down on a stake to keep one of the corners of the tent down. "If you girls need to go to the bathroom, don't go more than fifty feet from our camp. I've got spring traps positioned on the perimeter, so if we get any nocturnal visitors, we'll have an early warning."

Jen turned. "We're three kilometers from the target. You think security would come out this far?"

"No, I'm talking critters like wolves or even maybe a bear that woke up early, though I think that's unlikely. If they're downwind from us, they'll know we're here. As soon as they cross one of those spring traps, we'll hear the snap of the stick and be alerted."

Madison adjusted her glasses and scanned the woods. "So, I'm guessing we're taking shifts on watch."

Levi nodded. "Anyone particularly want the first shift?"

"I do," Madison said quickly.

Levi glanced at his watch. "Okay, let's assume two hours each. Jen, do you want the next shift? If not, I'll take it."

"I'll take it," she said. "For not letting us become wolf chow, I figure I owe you four hours of uninterrupted sleep."

Madison grabbed a thin thermal blanket from her pack, wrapped it around her shoulders, and sat against the trunk of a large fir tree. Jen slithered into the entrance of the tent, then poked her head out and looked up at Levi.

"You can come in," she said. "I swear I won't bite."

Levi hesitated before following Jen in, and Madison suppressed a chuckle. The idea that Levi seemed reluctant to be in a tent with Jen amused the hell out of her.

Madison felt for her .45, which was seated comfortably in her shoulder holster. She silently prayed to whoever might be listening. "God, I hope I don't have to use it."

Madison tapped the bottom of Jen's hiking boot.

Jen bolted upright, blinking sleep from her eyes. She pouted at Levi as she scooted out of the tent. The man couldn't have been farther from her without being outside the tent.

Madison crawled into the shelter, taking Jen's place. She noticed Levi was breathing peacefully, yet he was shivering from the cold. Something about watching the man silently suffer pulled at her heartstrings.

She laid her thermal blanket over him and lay with her back toward him. As she closed her eyes, she sensed his shivering begin to subside.

Madison must have fallen asleep, because the next thing she knew, the blanket was on her, Jen was asleep only inches away, and footfalls sounded outside.

She crawled from the tent, feeling surprisingly well rested for having slept only a few hours.

In the pre-dawn light, Levi was stripped naked to his waist. Despite the cold, he was sweating as he performed a complex kata involving a spinning kick, punches, and deep sweeping lunges.

Madison watched the fluid motions, spellbound. It was hard to take her eyes off of him. Each move had a beautiful simplicity to it, but he performed them with immense strength and fluidity. It was like a dance.

He continued for another two minutes before coming to the end of the form. He bowed to nobody in particular, then turned to her. Steam was actually rising from his bare skin.

"Good morning," he said pleasantly.

"That was awesome to look at. Was that Wing Chun?"

Levi's eyes widened. "I'm impressed. Do you practice martial arts?"

"Certainly not like that. I'm not nearly that good."

Levi grabbed his undershirt from a tree branch and put it on. "What do you do? Can you show me?"

"No," Madison said quickly, feeling embarrassed. "I mean, it's not nearly as smooth as what you do—"

"Oh, come on. I'd love to see whatever you know. Different styles —it's kind of my thing." Levi gave her a slight pout. "Please?"

Madison stood and grumbled, "I can't believe I'm doing this in the middle of the woods."

Levi finished dressing, all the while keeping his eyes fixed on her, which didn't make her feel any less weird about it.

She did a few stretching exercises, then proceeded to one of the katas that began with several spear-hand thrusts. She then moved into high and low stances, and soon she lost herself in the movements of the exercise.

When she finished, she wiped beads of sweat from her forehead.

"You're beautiful."

Madison turned to Levi. "What?"

Levi's eyes widened, and for the first time, she saw him flush with embarrassment. "I'm sorry, I just meant that you move beautifully. 'I'm not nearly that good,' she says. 'BS', is what I say."

The tent flap opened, and Jen poked her head out. "I'm guessing it's time to get going?"

Madison was still replaying the *You're beautiful* in her head. She felt her cheeks burn. "Yup, let's eat some of those yummy protein bars and get going."

They were about a kilometer from the edge of the woods when Levi felt the vibration in his backpack. He opened it, pulled out his phone, and put it to his ear. "Denny, is this important?"

"Well, take a look at the picture I just got from one of the video feeds I tapped into."

Levi pulled up the image Denny had texted him. It showed a dark-haired woman exiting a building. His heart thumped loudly as he put the phone back to his ear.

"Um, that might be our girl. I can't be sure, the quality of the image isn't great, but it sure as hell could be her. Where is that?"

"That was this morning, coming out of the United Russia head-quarters building."

"What's United Russia?"

"One of the Russian political parties."

Levi glanced at Madison and Jen. "Shit. Denny, can you do me a favor? Give that image and that information to John Maddox."

"The CIA guy?"

"Yes. We've got conflicting information here, and I think we're trying to accomplish the same thing."

"Well, how about this. I'll send you a link to an anonymous drop box where I'll leave the bitmap photo. I'm not comfortable reaching out directly. Besides, I don't actually have his e-mail address."

"Fine, text me with the URL to the drop box and I'll do the rest."

"Listen to you, using 'URL' in the correct way. I'd almost think you weren't born in a seventeenth-century society."

"Funny guy. Thanks for the information, and keep me posted on anything else you find."

"Will do."

Levi hung up and turned to the other members of his team. "I need Maddox's e-mail address. It looks like we have an issue."

Levi watched the maintenance crew unload a pickup filled with wooden crates.

He'd reached out to Maddox and given him the new intel. Maddox promised to follow up, but insisted that their most recent intercept had said Katarina was waiting at the mountain site for a critical package.

A package that none of the CIA folks were willing to talk about.

Levi had considered just giving them a copy of the university ID and leaving it to them to finish what was probably a wild goose chase. But he decided to go along with them and see the current mission through.

He and the two women were dressed in uniforms that looked identical to those of the maintenance crew workers, who were now wheeling the crates into a concrete bunker built into the side of the mountain.

"Are you sure it's an entrance?" Levi whispered. "It almost looks like an outer warehouse or something."

"It's definitely an entrance," Jen insisted.

Madison nodded. "We have blueprints to the site, and it shows an entrance at this spot. But I agree, it looks like those guys are storing things in there." She pointed at the crew leaving the building, "And look, they're coming back out."

The maintenance crew closed the metal door, hopped onto the open bed of the pickup, and drove northeast along the road.

As soon as the truck turned out of sight, the team dashed across the road to the warehouse. But Levi felt a tickle on the back of his neck. His sixth sense was screaming at him that something was wrong.

He sensed a subsonic hum, just out of range for him to hear.

Jen led them toward the entrance and reached for the handle to the door.

Trusting his instincts, Levi launched himself at her. As he lifted Jen off her feet, an explosion of pain shot through him.

His muscles seized, and he fell face-forward into the dirt.

The last thing he felt was the burning in the soles of his feet as darkness overtook him.

CHAPTER TWENTY

With tears blurring her vision, Madison pressed on Levi's chest thirty times, tilted his neck, pinched his nose, and breathed twice into his mouth.

Jen groaned. "I think he broke my ribs."

Madison felt for a pulse, found none, and continued with the chest compressions. "Oh, please, Levi, don't die on me."

She breathed twice more into his mouth.

Suddenly Levi's body convulsed.

Pressing her fingers against his neck, she felt a weak thread of life. Her strength fled her as she cried, "Levi, can you hear me? Levi?"

His eyes fluttered, and he took a deep breath. Tears streamed down the sides of his face.

Jen scrambled over to them. "Oh shit, let's get him out of the open."

The two women dragged Levi back across the road. When he began convulsing again. Madison prayed aloud, "Please, God, don't let him die."

They dragged him several hundred yards past the tree line, well out of sight of the road, and sat him against a tree. He shivered violently.

Madison held him in her arms. "It's okay. I've got you."

"His lips are blue." Jen began rubbing his legs.

He suddenly kicked and leaned heavily against Madison, shaking his head.

"It's okay, Levi," Madison said. "She's trying to help."

He pulled out of her arms, still shaking. His eyes blinked rapidly and he shook his head. Through gritted teeth he began digging in the undergrowth.

"What's he doing?" Jen asked.

Levi seemed possessed as he pulled a knife from somewhere inside his shirt and began digging a line into the ground.

Madison pulled the shovel out of her pack. He grabbed it from her and began digging deeper into the half-frozen soil. His breath came in ragged gasps. He groaned, "Shelter … freezing …"

It suddenly made sense. "It's warmer underground," Madison said to Jen. To Levi, she added, "Please, let me help you."

Levi fell to his side, exhausted.

Madison took the shovel from his hand and began digging in earnest. Jen helped. Within minutes, they'd dug a three-foot-deep trench into the loamy soil of the pine forest.

Jen grabbed one of the thermal blankets and laid it in the trench. She looked terrified as she studied Levi. "He's going to die if we don't build a fire."

"No," Levi growled. "No fire. Too close. They'll smell it."

Madison helped Levi into the trench, then lay down alongside him. "Get the blanket out of my pack and lay it on top of us. Maybe my body heat will help warm him up."

Levi was incoherent as he lay against her, trembling like nothing she'd ever encountered before. She pressed his cold face against her and wrapped her arms around him.

As Jen tucked the insulating blanket over them, she grimaced with pain.

"Jen? Are you okay?"

"I'll be fine." Tears ran down her cheeks. "This is my fault. He might die because I was an idiot."

"It's not your fault. If you can, contact Maddox and tell him what happened."

Jen nodded and walked away.

Madison suddenly felt overwhelmed with emotion. She lay partially on top of Levi and leaned her cheek against his, holding him as tightly as she dared. Slowly, his shivering subsided, and the warmth of their bodies grew. The trench and the thermal blankets helped contain their body heat.

Levi's arms wrapped around her waist as he pulled her against him. With her lips next to his ear, she whispered, "It'll be okay. I've got you."

He tightened his grip ever so slightly. "Thank you, Madison."

Hearing him speak her name—her real name—broke something inside her. She began to sob.

Levi nuzzled his face into the crook of her neck and spoke in the weakest of whispers. "Let's not do that again."

Madison's tears fell onto him. "I promise."

Levi awoke to Madison lying next to him, sound asleep, in what could only be described as a grave. A light covering of tree branches and leaves served as a roof inches above them.

His upper body ached as if he'd had a car accident and hit his chest against the steering wheel. The soles of his feet were burned and swollen.

Where are my shoes?

"What happened—"

And then he remembered.

That subsonic hum. It was the same one he'd sensed many times before from transformers operating at high voltages.

"Levi?" Madison's face appeared in front of his, only inches away. The warmth of her breath mingled with his.

He smiled. "You really are beautiful, even up close."

Her eyes glistened with unshed tears. "How are you?"

Their bodies were pressed against each other, legs intertwined, the soft soil of the Russian forest serving as their bed. He couldn't imagine a more unexpected scenario to find himself in. "Alive, thanks to you."

"Do you remember what happened?"

"I remember hearing a transformer nearby, and just as Jen was about to touch the door, it dawned on me. I was at the wrong angle to reach her arm, so I dove at her. I'm guessing she—" His body stiffened. "Is she okay?"

Madison nodded. "I think you took the brunt of the shock. You literally knocked her off her feet with that tackle. Aside from some busted ribs, she's fine. She's holed up further back in the woods. You and I are still pretty close to the road, but buried like we are, unless someone literally steps on us, we won't be seen."

Levi replayed the actions of the maintenance crew in his mind. After the last of the crewmen had left and the door was closed, one of the men had briefly pointed at the entrance. No, he hadn't pointed … he'd almost certainly aimed a remote at the metal door, likely activating the security system.

I'm an idiot. I should have seen that.

It was only then that Levi realized it was dark outside.

"How long was I out?"

Madison rested her hand on his chest. "You've been going in and out of consciousness for most of the day. The sun went down a few hours ago."

Levi laid his head back against Madison's upper arm. He winced as he twisted to face her.

"Hey, don't hurt yourself."

She was lying on his right arm while his head lay in the crook of her left arm. Her head was slightly above his, a fine-featured silhouette against the leafy backdrop. He stared up into her eyes.

"What?" she said.

"I thought I'd dreamed it, but I remember you calling my name. Do you mind if I call you Madison from now on? That *is* your real name, right?"

She pressed her forehead against his, and before she could say anything, he shifted the angle of his face and gave her a light kiss on the lips. It was lingering, warm, and tender. It seemed to last forever, yet it ended too quickly.

She didn't push him away.

"I'm sorry about that." Levi let his head fall back against her arm. "I normally save that for the end of the first date. I don't have the energy for anything else."

Madison buried her face into the side of his and laughed quietly. "If you think me doing CPR on you is an acceptable form of a date, you need to learn a thing or two about dating."

"What can I say? I'm out of practice."

"Shh." Madison pressed a finger against his lips. "Get some rest. We'll see how things are as dawn approaches."

Levi wiggled his toes again and grimaced. The resulting tingling was similar to the painful prickly sensation that comes from a sleeping limb that's beginning to wake up. "Madison, I think my feet might have been burned by the electricity passing through me and into the ground."

"They were. The soles of your shoes were partially melted. Jen took them off, applied an antibiotic ointment, and dressed your feet. She's building a sled of sorts, and we're going to drag you back the way we came. And we contacted the pilot. He said he should still be there when we get there."

A wave of fatigue washed over Levi. He closed his eyes, enjoying Madison's warm embrace. He had almost forgotten what it was like to lie in someone's arms.

In his mind's eye, he saw Mary looking at him. She almost always had a stoic yet confident expression. He knew that she'd had a hard life before meeting him, leaving her family and everything she knew, though he knew of only some of the struggles she'd gone through. Yet there were those moments when she'd allowed herself to be vulnerable. To trust completely in him not to hurt her.

It had been those moments that had made him fall in love with her.

He'd lived for those moments.

Suddenly, her face morphed into the face of Katarina. He felt a strong revulsion about what he'd allowed himself to do with her. She'd broken through a barrier that he'd thought would forever be closed. And then she'd tried to kill him.

Yet he couldn't bring himself to hate her, even with everything she'd done.

Pity her, yes. But not hate.

He reserved his hate for one person. A faceless man. Vladimir.

And then, behind his closed lids, he pictured Madison's face.

So often she'd stared at him with distrust, or apprehension, yet for brief moments, he had seen a vulnerability there. It had reminded him of Mary.

Had she gone through tough times as well?

She'd saved his life.

She'd pulled him back from the brink.

He was strongly attracted to her. But she deserved better.

He already had his dead wife, a seductress he wasn't sure what to do about, and a man he knew needed to die all floating around in his head. Madison didn't deserve anyone with that much baggage.

Just as he was about to succumb to sleep, he murmured, "I'm incapable of having a relationship."

Levi smiled as he stepped on the balls of his feet, holding out his hands to steady himself. "Well, considering I died two days ago, I'm feeling pretty good."

Both Madison and Jen were watching with worried expressions.

"Levi," Jen said, "both of your shoes had a one-inch hole burned through them. The skin on your heels *can't* be healed yet."

She was right about that. While on the balls of his feet, Levi felt okay—but when he rocked back on his heels, the pain was almost unbearable. He knew he was pushing things too fast.

But he waved off her concerns. "I'm a fast healer. And besides, I fixed my shoes."

"Levi, don't be a jackass," Madison scolded. "We can take you the rest of the way."

Levi looked at the makeshift sled. They'd been dragging his butt through the snow-covered terrain for two days now. But while he'd been resting and healing, they'd been working themselves to exhaustion.

It was time.

"Listen, I widened the front of my snowshoe and put an extra cross-brace where the ball of my foot is. I'll put most of my weight on that. We'll make better time." He demonstrated his point as he walked confidently, resting most of his weight on the balls of his feet. "See?"

Madison and Jen looked at each other, shook their heads, and shrugged.

"I'm taking the sled with us, just in case," Jen announced.

"I'll be fine." He motioned toward the east-southeast. "You ladies want to take the lead? I'll follow."

Madison shook her head. "No, you go ahead so we can make sure your stubborn ass doesn't get itself into trouble."

Levi smiled and began marching toward the horizon.

∼

"We made it."

It hadn't been an easy journey by any stretch of the imagination, but they were back on board the plane. Madison wrapped both Jen and Levi in a hug.

"And I only died once," Levi quipped, grinning.

Madison smacked him on the chest and failed to keep a smile off her face.

As they settled into their seats, Jen tapped her on the shoulder and whispered, "Just got something from Maddox. It's big." She handed over her phone, which displayed a text message.

Kosvinsky site confirmed as a false flag.

Intercepted transmission revealing a new site fifteen miles east of Moscow.

Satellite monitoring has confirmed unusual activity at location six days ago.

On-site personnel have confirmed site as location of one of our missing packages.

Located thirty feet below surface of a lake.

Will have transport ready for J + M upon landing.

Arranging for additional dive equipment on site.

M will lead package neutralization and extraction.

Medical transport needed for L?

Madison's heart raced. One of the nukes had been found.

She gave Jen a fist bump and a thumbs-up. The mission was on.

She turned to Levi, who was staring at his phone. "Levi, Jen and I have something to do when we land. Maddox is asking if you need him to arrange transport to a hospital for you."

Levi shook his head without looking up from his phone. "I'm fine."

"I kind of figured you'd say that."

Levi turned his phone toward them. "Denny sent me another snapshot. It's definitely Katarina. You guys got some seriously bad intel regarding that damned mountain."

The snapshot provided a clear picture of an attractive brunette stepping out of a limousine. She had pouty red lips and a dark expression —and she was young, maybe mid-twenties. Madison would never have guessed the girl in this picture was capable of being an assassin.

"So, I guess I know where you're heading," she said.

Levi put the phone away. "I'll do my best to try and get her somewhere where we can talk. Do you by chance have something that will knock someone out quickly? Unlike in the movies, hitting someone in the back of the head isn't exactly reliable and can—"

"I've got something." Jen rummaged around in her backpack, then handed Levi a thumb-sized silver canister.

Levi turned the canister over in his hands, examining it. "It looks like spray deodorant."

"Uh, no," Jen said. "Using that as deodorant would be a mistake."

Madison grinned evilly at Jen. "I don't know, that would be kind of hilarious to see him use it as deodorant."

Jen rolled her eyes. "That's sevoflurane, Levi—a fast-acting anesthetic. I'd suggest spraying it into a cloth and quickly covering her face. You'll probably want to hold your breath while doing it. It's supposed to smell sweet, but I've never tested that."

The plane's engine revved and they began taxiing onto the runway.

Levi stowed the can in his backpack and turned to Madison. "In case I don't see you two again, thank you for everything."

Madison's throat suddenly felt thick with emotion, but all she could manage was a weak smile. She didn't want to think about it, but he was probably right. They might never see each other again.

The pilot pushed the engines to full throttle, and Madison was pressed back into her seat.

The flight to Moscow was going to be three hours.

Madison felt that was going to be far too short.

CHAPTER TWENTY-ONE

"I'm sorry it took so long, but their security was pretty good. I've exploited a zero-day backdoor into a commercial package the building's security system is using. I've now got root access."

"Whatever that is. Denny, I've been standing here for almost three hours freezing my nuts off, and I've seen no one of interest. You've got to get me inside."

Levi had landed five hours ago and had raced to Dubrovka Station as soon as he had changed at his hotel. For three hours now he'd been watching people come and go from the fifteen-story building across the street—the one that housed the headquarters of the United Russia political party. It was now five minutes to nine—the building's closing time.

"Here's the thing, I can't seem to reach the badge-reader access list from here. The controls and list aren't exposed to an external network."

Levi gritted his teeth to stop them from chattering. "Any suggestions?"

"Well ... I have prior badge scan logs on the system I can access. I can create you a badge that should work, but then I'd have to FedEx it

to you. So we're looking at a few days minimum. I'm assuming you want to get into that place right now?"

"Yes."

"Then you'll have to just walk in as a guest." Levi heard the sound of Denny's fingers clacking on the keyboard. *"Okay, I've added 'Ronald Warren' to the building's approved guest list. You'll probably need to show your passport. Do you even know what you're looking for?"*

"Not really, but I'm going to wing it. Thanks for your help. Let's hope this works."

He darted across the street, through the evening traffic and entered the building. In his suit and carrying his metal briefcase, he'd be able to pass as a businessman with Russian political interests.

An armed guard stood behind the front desk. With a look of annoyance, he declared in Russian, "The building is about to close."

"I was asked to come here for a late meeting."

The guard was a few inches shy of six feet, but with a bodybuilder's physique, he still cut an intimidating figure. He studied Levi warily. "Who is this meeting with?"

"Well, Katarina Nassar asked me to come, but I think she meant for me to meet not with her, but someone she works for."

"Mr. Porchenko?"

"Yes." Levi nodded. "She said he'd be coming late, but to let me wait in his office."

"Where is Miss Nassar?"

Levi shrugged. "I'm guessing with Mr. Porchenko."

"Your name?"

"Ronald Warren."

"An American? Can I please see your passport?"

Levi handed him his passport.

The guard typed something into his computer, then handed the passport back and pointed to his left. "Mr. Porchenko's office is on the fifth floor. Take the elevator up and you can wait there in the lobby."

"Thank you."

As Levi turned, the guard said, "The security station closes in a few minutes. You can let yourself out, but keep in mind if you do, you won't be able to get back in until the morning."

"Thanks again." Levi's heart thudded heavily as he hurried to the elevators.

~

Levi's smile couldn't have been larger as he held the fundraising pamphlet for United Russia in his gloved hand. The bottom of the pamphlet was signed by the party leader, Vladimir Porchenko.

Couldn't be a coincidence.

"The bastard," Levi said to nobody in particular. "I've got you."

With a last name, he could track this man down. But a politician? The head of a political movement? Could that really be the person he was looking for?

Could a major figure in Russian politics actually be an underworld boss?

Across the organization's lobby was a closed office door with the name "V. Porchenko" on it. Levi tried the door.

Locked.

Levi pulled out his lock picks.

It was a simple pin and tumbler lock. He stuck a torque wrench into the slot and probed with his pick. Scraping the pins while putting just a little bit of pressure on the tumbler, he felt the pins begin clicking into position. Finally, the lock turned.

He stashed the picks and entered Vladimir Porchenko's office.

Levi's senses tingled as he detected the faded scent of lavender. The same scent Katarina's hair had been perfumed with.

She'd been here, and not long ago.

The office was enormous, easily thirty feet square, and it was filled with what looked like priceless artifacts from ancient civilizations all across the world: pottery with faint hieroglyphs, African tribal masks, jade artifacts from China, and a collection of beautifully preserved new-world obsidian arrowheads. On a stand at the far end of the office was a six-foot-long log carved with symbols that looked like runes from a J.R.R. Tolkien novel. The log was nearly three feet thick and had to weigh over a thousand pounds.

A huge sandstone desk dominated the center of the room. It looked like an ancient druid altar. In fact, maybe it was precisely that. Its surface looked worn down as if by millennia of exposure to the elements, and those dark stains … they might even be evidence of ancient blood sacrifices.

"What the hell is this guy into?"

More importantly, could there be anything in here to convince him that this was in fact the same Vladimir who had tried to have him killed? The Vladimir who'd had those innocent children killed at his parents' farm?

The Vladimir who had Mary's blood on his hands?

Levi opened a file cabinet drawer at random and began flipping through folders. Most of the files were in Russian, unsurprisingly, and even though he could speak and understand the spoken word at full speed, reading was troublesome. He had never really gotten used to the Cyrillic alphabet, and he felt like a third-grader when reading it.

Still, he got the gist pretty quickly. Most of it was gibberish about politics.

Levi scanned the office once again. This guy was supposed to be a mobster.

How can that be, when he's so out in the open?

Levi felt anxiety course through him as he realized this guy might not be the one he was looking for. And even if he was, the man would be very careful.

He wouldn't keep records of mob business here. Too easy to find. There would be nothing here about assassinations. Nothing about the guys Gambini said Vladimir had working at the docks.

Levi huffed with frustration and continued flipping through the files, not even knowing what he was looking for.

He paused when he reached a file that contained x-ray films. He pulled one out and held it up against one of the lights in the ceiling.

There was some text at the bottom.

. . .

Sample: Unidentified (V. Porchenko)
   Vacc: 30 kV
   Mag: 3,000kx
   Bright Field(BF)-STEM image

The image itself showed several instances of dots arranged in complex patterns. A line was drawn to signify the width of one of the objects: "2nm."

Levi had read enough science journals to know this must have come from a scanning electron microscope. The "2nm" signified two nanometers, which was more than a thousand times smaller than the width of a hair.

"What the hell is this?"

Levi studied the typewritten sheets accompanying the x-rays. He didn't understand many of the words—probably science or medical jargon. He understood the Russian word for "blood," though. Maybe this had something to do with an infection?

He studied the second x-ray film, which looked a lot like the first, except the dots now looked more like uneven blobs. It was almost as if the objects from the first film had melted.

Levi froze as he heard elevator doors slide open out in the lobby.

A man's voice groused, "You need to talk to these people. Leaving the lights on like this—it's just a waste."

The office door opened, and a tall, middle-aged man with dark hair and piercing gray eyes appeared. At the sight of Levi, he stopped short.

"Vladimir, why are you just standing there?" A dark-haired beauty walked past him—then gasped.

Katarina pulled out a gun before Levi could draw a dagger.

The near-deafening report of the gunshot echoed through the room as Levi dove behind the giant log.

How in the world could she have missed? Levi drew his dagger and peered around the log.

He couldn't believe what he saw.

Katarina was still standing just inside the doorway, the gun hanging limply in her shaking hand. But the man she'd walked in with lay slumped on the floor.

She'd shot him.

Katarina spoke in barely above a whisper. "How are you alive, Levi?" Katarina glanced at the man she'd shot. "He'd have killed me if he knew you were still alive."

"Katarina, put the gun away. Look, I'm putting my knife down." Levi stood slowly, laying the throwing dagger on the log and holding his hands to the sides—though he was careful to keep his right hand hovering near the dagger.

"You killed my parents." She raised the gun and aimed at him, but her finger was off the trigger. "I need to know why. Why'd you do it?"

Levi shook his head, confused. "I don't even know who your parents were."

"That's a lie," she growled, her voice shaky with emotion. Fear? Anger? Both?

Levi pointed his chin in the direction of the doorway. "Is that Vladimir? Did he tell you I killed your parents?"

Katarina nodded.

"I don't know who your parents were, but my wife, Maryam Nassar, was killed by one of his men."

Katarina's mouth fell open. The gun wavered. "Maryam … how can that be?"

"My wife came from Iran a long time ago. I think you two might be related."

Katarina lowered the gun. "My aunt's name was Maryam. My father's sister." She pressed her non-shooting hand against her stomach. "And … I'm pregnant."

Now it was Levi's jaw that dropped. "By me?"

Katarina grimaced. "Who else? *Him?* You think I'd keep something that pig impregnated me with?"

Behind her, Vladimir's eyes flickered. He wasn't dead. Levi could tell by the fit of his shirt that he wore a bulletproof vest. Still, being fired upon at such close range, the man probably had some broken ribs.

Katarina continued. "Since I was twelve, how many abortions have I had because of him?"

A gunshot blasted through the room, and Levi's face was splattered with something wet.

Blood.

A second gunshot, and Levi felt the bullet strike him in the chest like a sledgehammer.

But Esther's wunder-vest had done its job. Had it not been for that, he'd be dead.

He threw a knife through the cloud of smoke, rolled to the side, threw another, and pulled out a third knife. When he heard the metallic clatter of a gun hitting the ground, he raced past Katarina's unmoving body, which had fallen across the altar, and to the doorway, where Vladimir was on his feet, slumped against the doorframe, coughing up blood. A gun lay on the floor beside him.

Levi kicked the gun into the lobby and looked into the eyes of the man he'd come to murder.

Both of his knives had struck home.

One had skewered the man's arm, passing cleanly between both bones, and pinned him to the wooden doorframe. The other had struck at a downward angle, at the juncture of where the collarbone and neck meet.

The spot just above Vladimir's own bulletproof vest.

Levi studied Vladimir, the man who'd caused him, and so many others, so much pain.

To his shock, he recognized him.

But it was impossible.

"Boris Petrushenkov," Levi said.

Boris. The man who had employed Gustav at the house where Katarina had lived as a child.

A man who had vanished fifty years ago.

Vladimir's eyes widened. He coughed up more blood. "So you know my little secret. And who are you?"

"How is that possible? You must be over a hundred years old."

"One hundred and twelve, actually. The land of Egypt has many

ancient curses. Oh, my angel Katarina. How many years ago I swore at
your deathbed that I'd join you in heaven. I'm so sorry. This damned
curse, it's ruined me." He closed his eyes and groaned. "I should have
died with my wife decades ago, yet here I am. With those that I held
close betraying me." The man glared at the younger Katarina, whose
body was splayed across the altar, blood pouring from her wound. "A
fitting end for that lying bitch."

Levi tightened his grip on his knife. "You killed Katarina's parents,
didn't you?"

Vladimir sneered. "They stole something precious from me."

He thought back to the ankh he'd retrieved from the international
package. It suddenly all made sense. Mary must have received the
package from relatives, maybe even with the intent of keeping it from
Vladimir. That package, that ankh, was what Gambini had been after,
and why Mary had visited the bank that same day. She'd placed it in
the safety deposit box just before he found it.

Vladimir continued staring at Katarina with an expression of cold
malice. "Thieves. They deserved what they got. Buried in the tomb
they discovered. But it wasn't me that killed them."

No. You just gave the order.

Vladimir winced and shifted his gaze back to Levi. "Why are you
here?"

"I wanted to meet the man who killed my wife," Levi growled.

"Then you have the wrong man. The only person I've ever killed
was that cheating bitch behind you. Was she your lover, perhaps? Did
she bed you and leave you?" Vladimir appeared not to have any clue
who Levi was. "So what? I had her when she'd had no other. I've had
her hundreds of times since. She's nothing."

Vladimir's shirt was now soaked in his own blood, his complexion
was pale, and he was almost certainly going to bleed out. It wouldn't
do any good to call Maddox.

"It was one of your men," Levi said. "Maybe you remember
Thomas Gambini?"

Vladimir smiled. "I remember everything."

He moved his hand toward his neck, and Levi moved his dagger so it was only inches from the man's left eye. "Leave the blade where it is."

Vladimir lowered his hand. "Thomas Gambini, you say." His teeth were stained with blood. "He was the crooked tax director in America. In New York City. I didn't ask him to kill anyone. You've got the wrong person."

"No, you didn't ask him to kill anyone. But you sent him after something else."

Vladimir's eyes widened. He sniffed the air, and his eyes rolled to the back of his head.

"You! That Nassar bitch. Damn that whole family to hell!" The man's voice was hoarse with emotion. "I can smell it on you. You're the one with the Pharoah's curse. My Katarina could have been cured! I've spent my life trying to find such a thing again, and you have it inside you. Damn you!"

Despite his rage, Vladimir began to laugh. Blood spurted through his nose and dribbled out the side of his mouth.

Levi heard Narmer's words in his mind. *You'll learn over time that the gift you've been given—or maybe it's a curse. I suppose it doesn't matter, really, which one it is. Either way, it's a burden you'll carry for a long time.*

Vladimir sneered. "I'll see you in hell." His knees buckled, and he collapsed, dangling from the arm that remained skewered to the doorframe. His chest stopped rising and falling and a shroud of silence fell over the room.

Levi felt for a pulse.

There was none.

Levi retrieved his knives, cleaned them, and put them back in their sheaths.

It was over.

Yet Levi didn't feel any better.

He looked down on Katarina's broken body and shook his head.

There was no joy in having finished this job.

As he walked back to Vladimir, he noticed something poking out of the man's closed fist. A bit of black plastic. Levi pried the man's fingers open—and heard a click behind him, from the direction of the log.

In Vladimir's hand was what looked like a car's remote control, with a single button. Vladimir must have been holding the button down, and then Levi opened his fist....

A dead man's switch.

Levi hurried over to the log. What had he activated? Whatever it was, it couldn't be good.

He knocked on the polished wood and heard a deep thud.

The log was hollow.

He ran his hand along the smooth carving until he felt a slight give. He pushed, and the top half of the log lifted up on an oiled hinge.

The log was lined with some type of metal shielding and in the hollowed-out cavity was a long metal cylinder. Welded to the cylinder was a fist-sized oblong metal box with a digital timer.

The red LED was counting down, from seven minutes and twenty seconds.

Levi's heart thudded in his chest.

Oh shit.

~

Despite having been at the bottom of an ice-covered lake for the last half hour, Madison felt a warm sense of elation as she climbed onto the shore lugging a fist-sized metal box with dozens of wires trailing from it. She ripped her dry suit's mask off and high-fived Jen.

"We did it!" she whispered.

It was late at night and they were less than a quarter mile from a residential neighborhood. Other agents emerged from the water, steaming silhouettes in the darkness, lugging the two stages of the nuclear capsule from the lake. A van waited, its engine idling, and they began the loading process.

Madison held up the electronic timer. "Now we've just got to find its twin."

Suddenly, LED numbers appeared on the device. It began counting down from eight minutes.

"What the hell?" Madison gasped. "Did someone here just do something to turn this on? Are you guys playing a prank on me?"

The other agents, who were disassembling the primary and secondary stages of the bomb, shook their heads.

Madison struggled to get out of her dry suit. Maybe contact with the water had shorted the device. As she finished, Jen's phone buzzed on her belt.

"Hello?" Jen paused, and her eyes widened. "Oh, shit. She's right here. Hold on." She handed the phone to Madison. "It's Levi."

"Levi? It's good to hear—"

"Madison, listen: I'm in a fifteen-story building that houses the United Russia political party. I'm in Vladimir Porchenko's office. Our targets are deceased, long story, but more importantly, I'm staring at what I think might be a bomb. It's counting down, currently at six minutes and forty seconds. I know you're former EOD, I've read your DD-214, I'll explain someday. Any suggestions?"

Madison looked down at her own timer. It was running on the same countdown.

She began pacing, and tried to keep the panic from her voice. "Levi, listen to me very carefully. Tell me exactly what you see."

"I see a metal cylinder, it's roughly six feet long, has a three-foot diameter, and no obvious way to open it. That's about it, other than there's a box about the size of my hand with a countdown going on. It's welded to the top of the cylinder. Should I just run for it and let it go off or—"

"No, don't go anywhere. It won't do you any good." Madison closed her eyes and took a deep calming breath. "Levi, that's a two-stage fission-fusion nuclear bomb."

"You're shitting me. Okay, what can I do?"

Levi sounded remarkably calm. Madison would be freaking out if she were him.

"I suppose at this time, it can't hurt to admit that I just defused one of these twenty minutes ago. You don't by chance have a plasma torch to cut through the metal case?"

"No, all out." A metallic gong sounded over the line. *"It doesn't seem very thick; I can try cutting it open with one of my knives like a can opener. Will this thing blow up if I do that?"*

"It shouldn't. Let me give you a really quick explanation of what you've got there.

"That's a two-stage bomb, but the first stage is really what we focus on. It goes off, then the rest goes off. It basically consists of a sphere of uranium with a pit of plutonium plunged into it. That's the fission part of the bomb. Surrounding it are roughly a hundred equally spaced high-explosive charges connected with gold wire. They're all set to go off at the exact same time. Basically, the explosives are shaped to compress the fuel so that a fission reaction will start.

"If anything goes awry, like one of the explosives doesn't fire or the timing is off, you'll get a fizzle, which means the fission reaction won't start, and neither will the fusion reaction, and you in essence have a dirty bomb blowing radioactive crap from there to kingdom come.

"But let's assume it all goes correctly. From there, it just gets worse. X-rays from the primary bomb are reflected by the case, and it critically heats the foam around the entire package into a plasma, compressing the secondary and kick-starting the fusion reaction. A big boom."

"Okay. I've got barely more than five minutes, so let's stick to what I need to do. You're sure that me using brute force to open this won't set it off?"

"Do me a favor, do it carefully and not near the timer. It shouldn't be shock sensitive, but let's not push our luck."

"Understood. Okay, I'm putting the phone down. It's on speaker."

Madison winced as she heard several gunshots.

"Levi! Are you okay?"

"I'm fine." His voice sounded far away. *"I think I just destroyed some museum piece. However, I don't think the druids are going to miss it. I needed a hammer."*

Madison hopped up and down in the cold as a loud pounding came over the line. Levi was apparently hitting the nuclear device with a hammer.

Four minutes left.

"Okay, I've gotten through the case. I see a maze of wires going into something that looks like a soccer ball or some abstract geometric art."

"Great—you're looking at the primary, the thing that looks like a soccer ball. There should be wires running into each of the panels—those are the high-explosives charges I told you about. Now, as quickly as you can, *don't cut*, but *pull* the wires out of the explosives."

"So, this isn't exactly how I've seen them do it in the movies ..."

"Levi, no jokes. Please be careful. Any spark can set off one of those pieces of high explosive, and even if it doesn't set off the nuke, it'll ruin your day, believe me. Just carefully pull out each wire and try not to have the exposed parts of the wires touch anything. Remember, no sparks."

Levi took a deep breath. *"Here goes nothing ... that's one wire. No boom. Two."*

As Levi continued to count off the wires pulled, Madison kept an eye on the countdown timer, which was moving all too quickly.

When the timer hit a minute thirty, Levi had pulled only about half of the wires.

"Levi, you only have ninety seconds. You have to move faster."

Jen wrapped an arm around Madison and whispered, "He'll be fine."

"Eighty ..."

The timer counted down below thirty seconds. Madison's voice cracked. "Thirty seconds. Please hurry."

"Ninety ..."

Madison and Jen squeezed each other's hands as they watched the timer count down.

Twelve seconds.

"Ninety-five ..."

Four seconds.

"Ninety-eight ... "

The countdown timer next to Madison hit zero, and its wire leads sparked.

"Levi! Levi! Are you there?"

Silence hung heavily in the air.

Madison felt as if her heart had stopped.

"I'm here."

Madison blinked away tears as she sat back on her heels.

Jen spoke into the receiver. "Levi, Maddox has someone en route to your location to help with the cleanup."

"So this is what you guys were going after the entire time? No, wait, let me guess: 'No comment.'

"Listen, guys, this has been fun and all. Uranium, plutonium, and such. My leather gloves are now shredded by that damned gold wire. I don't even want to think about what would happen if TSA did any bomb detection swabs on me.

"But I'm not waiting around for your guys. I'll wedge something in the front door when I go so they can pick this crap up, but if you don't mind, I'm getting out of here."

He clicked off.

A man in the truck yelled, "We're all loaded up. Let's go."

Madison hopped into the back with Jen, who gave her a fist bump. "It's done. Both packages are taken care of."

Madison nodded, yet her stomach felt tied up in knots, and she wasn't even sure why.

Jen leaned against her and whispered, "You know he likes you a lot. I have a radar for that kind of thing. And it was painfully obvious he had zero interest in me."

Madison shook her head. "It doesn't matter, really. Even he said he's incapable of having a relationship, and frankly, how could I? You heard him. He killed two people tonight."

Jen shrugged. "I don't know. There might be a good reason for that. He's a good man, Maddie. Deep down. I can tell."

Madison sighed. "That's what makes him killing those two so hard. It's something I can't reconcile."

Jen patted Madison's leg. "Well, leave those thoughts for later. We just saved the freaking world from disaster—I think we can chalk that up as a success. We need to celebrate."

Jen was right. Madison should feel proud of what they'd accomplished.

So why did she still feel so sad?

Madison sat in a conference room with Jen, Don Jenkins, and a handful of other agents who'd all been part of project Arrow. Four weeks had passed since the conclusion of the mission, and now Maddox was giving the AAR, the After Action Review. They walked through what had worked well and what could have been improved, and focused on any critical issues they'd encountered.

"Did anyone have any other questions before I get to the last part of the AAR?" Maddox asked.

One of the agents asked, "Did we ever figure out what Vladimir intended to do with the nukes?"

"Unfortunately, we weren't able to glean much from Vladimir's office, and it's hard to get into the mind of a madman. Without more information, your guesses are probably just as good as mine. I *can* report that when news leaked of his untimely death, his cabal of political apparatchiks scurried into the recesses of the Russian political system, not unlike so many cockroaches when the lights are turned on.

"However, we did get some intel about the Perimeter program. Vladimir had enough influence to get that Russian program reactivated —but with his death, Perimeter has been deactivated, and we have our missing payloads back on US soil."

Maddox placed a small velvet box on the table in front of him. It was the kind of box that usually held an agency award.

That got everyone's attention.

Maddox gave everyone a crooked grin and shook his head. "This isn't for any of you folks, I'm afraid, though I think some of you deserved it. There's only so many awards that go out. But right now I want to talk about the actions of one of our assets."

Madison tilted her head. Assets were typically non-agency personnel, though sometimes equipment might be considered an asset.

"We've gotten the forensics analysis back regarding the incident that resulted in two deceased: Katarina Nassar and Vladimir Porchenko. It appears that an MP-443 Grach, a Russian pistol, was fired twice. One shot hit Katarina Nassar in the back, killing her instantly. We believe the other shot was intended for one of our assets, Lazarus Yoder.

"We say this because the spent bullet, a 7N21 AP 9mm round, was found on the floor, and its deformity showed that it did hit a target. The bullet had Kevlar fibers on it as well as microscopic scrapes of a titanium-gold alloy. We suspect Mr. Yoder was wearing a custom-built bulletproof vest, since we're not aware of such an item being available commercially.

"It was confirmed by gunshot residue analysis that Vladimir Porchenko was the shooter."

Madison swallowed hard. *So Levi didn't murder her.*

"Vladimir Porchenko also wore a bulletproof vest, but he received two stab wounds—one to the right arm, pinning him to a doorframe, and a deeper one where the neck meets the shoulder. The latter wound cut several key blood vessels and caused Mr. Porchenko to bleed out.

"Based on blood spatter and wood damage, the forensics team believes that the knife that pierced between the ulna and the radius of the right arm was thrown. And since that pinned arm was the same arm Mr. Porchenko used to shoot with—as determined by gunshot residue —we know the knife attack was *after* the shooting.

"It is therefore the opinion of the forensics team that Mr. Yoder was not responsible for the death of Miss Nassar, and was acting in self-defense in causing the death of Mr. Porchenko."

Maddox continued, talking about Levi's calm and resourceful actions in disarming the bomb, and how he stayed in the building—despite what he'd said to Jen on the phone—to let in the CIA personnel and lead them to the scene.

But Madison heard little of this. She was busy holding back tears, thinking about how she had misjudged the man.

She caught Jen watching her. Her friend flashed a sympathetic smile.

Finally, Maddox opened the velvet box and revealed a medal. "And with that, the agency awards Mr. Lazarus Yoder the Agency Seal Medal. It's a way for the agency to award non-agency personnel who have made significant contributions to the agency's intelligence efforts."

Maddox looked at Madison and Jen. "Unfortunately, I'm having difficulty determining how to get Mr. Yoder this medal. Agent Lancaster? Agent Lewis? Would it be untoward to ask if you can find a way to get this to him—or bring him to us, so I can formally present it?"

"I think Maddie should give it to him," Jen said.

Madison took a deep breath. The idea that she'd see Levi again both elated and terrified her.

"Agent Lewis, are you up—"

"I'll do it," Maddie said.

"Very well." Maddox closed the box, handed it to her, then turned to the rest of the agents. "That's pretty much it for the AAR. Good job, folks. I think we're done here."

As the agents filed out of the conference room, Maddox tapped Madison on the shoulder. "Agent Lewis, can you come to my office? We need to talk about a few things."

CHAPTER TWENTY-TWO

Levi sat with Dr. Nicholas Vasiliev, Professor of Pathology for Massachusetts General Hospital and head of the Diagnostic Electron Microscopy Unit. "Okay, Dr. Nik, what can you tell me?"

The doctor held out his hand. "Can you show me your finger once more?"

With a sigh, Levi put his index finger in the man's hand.

The doctor shook his head in amazement. "Absolutely no sign of the puncture, and we pricked that finger for blood samples just two hours ago. It's unbelievable. Levi, I know you've said you're not interested in investigating this further, but I'd be remiss if I didn't stress once again how important this might be to the advancement of the sciences. If you could let us study you, I'm sure we could arrange for housing, pay you, we'd do whatever it takes."

Levi shook his head. "Like I told you, I'm not here for that. I just want some answers about this." He tapped on the medical folder he'd stolen from Vladimir's office. "I don't understand what these papers are saying, but I want to know if I have what this guy had."

"Well, I'll be as blunt as I can be. I have absolutely no explanation for how your blood, muscles, tissues, even skin have these tiny abnormalities—"

"But what *are* these things? Is it a disease?"

"No. They're … they're something science has been working on, but has never achieved. We call these things nanites—basically tiny machines." He paused. "Let me put it this way. When Henry Ford put out the Model A, that was the epitome of travel and technology for its day. Right?"

Levi nodded.

"You've watched *Star Trek*, I assume. Those spaceships with warp drive and such, we can only imagine what that's like from a technological point of view. We have no idea today how to create such a thing. It's somewhere in the future. We *hope*.

"So now imagine I'm Henry Ford. What you've just done is bring me one of the space ships from *Star Trek*. You've proved to me what is technically possible, far in the future—and from where I stand now, with the technology I'm familiar with, I don't even really understand how these nanites work. But I can conceive of how they're possible."

Levi huffed with frustration. "So is it the same or is it different from what this other guy had?"

"It's the same."

"And why does one of the pictures show these 'nanites' clearly, and the next one shows them as blobs?"

"Your samples did the same thing. After five minutes or so, the nanites decompose. Why? I have absolutely no idea. Maybe they're keyed to the specifics of your body's environment? Temperature? Salinity? Other chemical or electrical characteristics of the human body? I'm only guessing."

Levi stood, gathered Vladimir's medical files, and held out his hand. "Give me all the records you've created about my visit."

The doctor looked as if he was about to cry, but he handed over the records. "This is everything, like I promised. There are no copies."

"Thank you. Dr. Nik, I refuse to be a guinea pig or a sideshow freak. I'm going to live my life, however long that is, and make the most of what I have." Levi handed the doctor a check. "Please put this toward future research in the name of the Nassar family."

As the doctor looked down at the check, his eyes widened. "My god."

Levi patted the man on the arm and walked out of doctor's office.

At the nearest nurses' station he asked, "Do you have a shredder?"

She nodded and pointed behind her.

"Do you mind if I use it?"

"No, not at all."

Levi fed each sheet of both his and Vladimir's records into the shredder. When he was done, he gathered up the shredded pieces and pushed them through once more. Then he swirled the bits of paper together with the rest of the material that was already in the trash.

He felt much better than he had in a long, *long* time.

One phase of his life was over.

As he left the hospital, he breathed in deeply. *Spring.* It was a time of reawakening, a rebirth from a harsh winter.

Maybe even a rebirth for him.

The ghosts of his past had been buried.

It was time to truly start over.

Levi flipped a coffee stirrer over his knuckles and sipped at his seltzer. Gerard's was nearly full, Denny and Carmen were busy serving their customers, and Levi felt comfortably anonymous.

The door opened behind him, and the wind blew in from the street, bringing with it the smell of spring and … something else.

He turned.

Silhouetted in the entrance was a dark-haired beauty he hadn't seen in months.

Madison was dressed in a black skirt, matching medium heels, and a form-fitting white blouse that contrasted beautifully with her milk-chocolate skin.

Levi swallowed hard, trying to remain cool, and motioned to the empty barstool next to him.

She smiled, walked over, and sat.

He returned her smile. "I'm glad to see you. To tell you the truth, I'm a bit *surprised* to see you."

She pulled a small velvet box from her purse and placed it on the counter. "I'm here for three things. First, Maddox asked me to find you and present this to you."

Levi eyed the box with curiosity. "How'd you know I would be here?"

"I didn't. This was the first place I stopped, and I got lucky."

He opened the box. Inside was a bronze medal with the CIA logo on the front. He turned it over and read the inscription aloud. "Agency Seal Award. This award is made to non-agency personnel for making a significant contribution to the intelligence efforts of the Central Intelligence Agency."

"That's what the agency considers to be an 'award,'" Madison said. "I wish it could be something more substantial."

Levi shook his head. "No, this is actually really nice. Frankly, I figured I'd be more likely to get handcuffs than awards from them."

"The agency doesn't do that," Madison said matter-of-factly.

"Oh, right. Not an enforcement division. That's more for the FBI and such."

Madison leaned closer and said in a hushed tone, "Don't you want to know my other reasons for being here?"

His interest piqued, Levi leaned closer to her.

She handed him a thick envelope.

Levi looked inside. It was full of hundred-dollar bills ... and a plane ticket.

"The cash is to pay for your time. The agency would like you to take a meeting with them; they have a proposition for you. The plane ticket is to get you there."

"A proposition? Are you involved?"

"I asked not to be."

Levi felt a twinge of regret. "Okay. You said you came here for three reasons."

Madison squirmed uncomfortably. "What are you drinking?"

"Seltzer."

She frowned. "There's a reason I asked not to be involved." She waved at Denny. "Bartender, we'll need lots more alcohol right here. I'm buying. Two double whiskeys."

Levi raised an eyebrow, but he waited patiently until Denny delivered the shots.

Madison downed one, winced, and motioned for Levi to follow suit.

He shook his head. "I don't need the alcohol."

Madison hesitated. He could see tears in her eyes, but they didn't fall. "Agency rules state that I can't date anyone I'm working with in any capacity."

For a moment, time seemed to halt. Reflected in Madison's eyes was a vulnerability that sent a shiver racing up and down Levi's spine. He recognized that look.

He hopped off his barstool and cradled her face in his hands. "It's a good thing we aren't working together."

Tears fell down her cheeks as Levi gave her a soft, lingering kiss.

Some of the people in the bar whistled loudly. Levi and Madison laughed and leaned their foreheads against each other.

Madison asked, "What about your 'not capable of having a relationship' thing?"

Levi wrapped his arms around her, burying his face in the crook of her neck.

"I lied."

PREVIEW - THE INSIDE MAN

"Pizza delivery."

The familiar voice broadcast through a hidden speaker in the small security office. A yellow LED on one of the security consoles flashed, indicating someone had sent an "open" command to the front gate.

Yoshi Watanabe checked the surveillance monitors that overlooked the sprawling apartment complex. One of the video feeds showed the north security gate sliding open, allowing the Domino's delivery person onto the property.

There was nothing unusual about a pizza delivery. Ten p.m. was a little later than normal, but not overly late, and Yoshi recognized the delivery man's voice—he'd heard the same voice several times a week for nearly a year. But this time, there was something about the way the driver had spoken that caught his attention.

Had the man's voice quavered just a bit?

The hairs on the back of Yoshi's neck stood on end.

He scooted his chair closer to the monitors and scanned the images for the delivery car. There were nearly two dozen different motion-activated video cameras dotted throughout the property, but it took only moments to find the Honda with a Domino's emblem on its side, parked in front of Building 3. There was no one in the driver's seat, yet a plume of exhaust came from the back of it.

Yoshi shook his head. "That's how you get your stuff stolen."

But then he spotted a gray blob lying next to the car. He zoomed in several times, and the gray blob suddenly turned into a person with bright-red hair.

It was the Domino's delivery guy. No doubt about it.

His heart racing, Yoshi flipped through Building 3's other cameras. He caught a man wearing a ski mask racing from one of the apartments, a child's limp body draped over his shoulder.

He checked the feed: first floor. And the man had run out of the third apartment from the end.

Yoshi's breath caught in his throat.

Apartment 1C.

That wasn't just any child. That was the granddaughter of Shinzo Tanaka, the leader of one of Japan's largest crime syndicates.

"No!" he yelled impotently at the screen, waking the other security guard.

"What? Who?" The bewildered guard was still blinking the sleep out of his eyes as Yoshi raced from the security office.

Sprinting across the courtyard toward the security gate, Yoshi grimaced when he heard the two-ton gate begin to move. He arrived in time to see the back of a late-model Honda fishtailing away from the apartment complex, the exit gate yawned open behind it.

Gritting his teeth, Yoshi spun on his heel and raced toward Building 3.

He was greeted by one of the security guards.

"Yoshi? What's going—"

"Shut up and call the police. There's been a kidnapping! Building 3, apartment 1C."

A chill raced up the middle of Yoshi's back. If they had gotten away with the child ... what had they done to her mother?

~

Ryuki Watanabe took the first available flight to Tokyo after his brother, Yoshi, called with the news. Ryuki had been instrumental in getting Yoshi placed at the apartment complex to watch over the girl, yet he couldn't let his brother take the blame. The kidnapping of Tanaka's granddaughter was his responsibility.

Now, late in the evening in downtown Tokyo, he waited alone in a conference room on the top floor of the Tanaka Building. He'd hoped that this day would never come, yet he felt unusually calm as he sat at the conference-room table waiting for the chairman to arrive.

He shook his head as he panned his gaze around the room. Ryuki preferred the traditional decorations of his Japanese ancestry: low-profile tables around which people would sit *seiza*-style, hanging scrolls with Japanese calligraphy, and silk-embroidered art. But Tanaka favored a Western style. The room smelled of the twenty black leather high-back chairs, and the long table they encircled was made of black wood that gleamed with a heavy polish. Ebony, perhaps.

The far door opened, and Shinzo Tanaka strode through the doorway. The man was in his mid-sixties, his bloodshot eyes betrayed his otherwise stone-like expression. Two bodyguards followed one step behind him, closed the door, and effectively blocked the exit.

Ryuki felt a surge of anxiety as he waited for his long-time boss to speak. As Tanaka's second-in-command, he'd known the man for nearly a quarter century, yet he'd never seen him look as haggard as he did this evening.

"Ryuki." The elder's gravelly voice was heavy with emotion. "How ... how did this happen?"

"I'm sorry." Ryuki bowed his head as he nervously traced the outline of the knife in his front right pocket. "It all happened very quickly. The man broke into the apartment, the child's mother was knocked unconscious, and the child was taken, all in less than a minute. The American police are involved, and I have our people looking into it as well."

Tanaka's face darkened as he pressed his lips into a thin line. "You promised me that my granddaughter would be safe in America."

"I did." A cool sense of resignation washed over Ryuki as he bowed before his boss. "I'm prepared to give a most sincere apology."

He drew from his pocket a knife, a packet of gauze, and a pristine white silken cloth, then laid them all on the table. He placed his left fist on the middle of the cloth with his pinkie extended, and bowed his head with a deep sense of regret. This was his first time ever disappointing the man. He prayed it would be his last.

Gritting his teeth, he picked up the knife, flipped open the razor-sharp blade, and sliced heavily across the last knuckle of his pinkie.

The knife sliced through the fibrous tendons, and he felt them snap like rubber bands. He tightened his core, and barely suppressed a grunt of pain.

When the deed was done, he used his right hand to bundle the severed tip of his finger in the white silk. His head still bowed, he gave the grotesque offering to Tanaka, who grimly accepted the apology.

The wound flared with heat, and Ryuki wrapped the injured finger with a gauze impregnated with a clotting agent. With a fresh cloth, he cleaned the blood from the table.

Finally, Tanaka pulled out a chair and sat across from him. "Ryuki, we must find my granddaughter. She's my son's only child."

Ryuki felt the man's pain even through his own. Tanaka had already lost his son—killed in the US in a drive-by shooting—despite keeping him from their life, just like Ryuki had sheltered his brother. And now the man feared he would lose his granddaughter too.

"I will get more of our people on this," Ryuki said.

Tanaka leaned forward and slid a note across the table. Ryuki retrieved it with his right hand.

"I'm giving you permission to reach out to the Italians in our American territory," Tanaka said. "There is one there that I'd trust with this."

Ryuki cringed at the slight. The implication was that he'd fallen out of trust, at least with regards to Tanaka's granddaughter.

"Before approaching him," Tanaka continued, "get permission from his superior. Promise whatever you need to acquire his help. I'll cover the expense." He stood, and the bodyguards opened the conference-room door. "Take the next flight and arrange this with the head of the Bianchi family from New York City."

Ryuki stood as well, and Tanaka placed his hand on his shoulder and squeezed. "Bring my granddaughter safely back to me, Ryuki. She's my only living heir." His tone brooked no argument. "Nothing else is more important."

Ryuki bowed, and Tanaka gave him a light shove toward the exit. "Go!"

As he strode quickly down the hallway, Ryuki unfolded the paper and looked at the English name scrawled on it.

He pressed the button calling for the elevator and wondered who Levi Yoder was.

Levi woke to the pre-dawn sounds of New York City rising from several stories below his Park Avenue apartment. With a luxurious stretch, he yawned and stumbled out of bed. It was just before five a.m., earlier than he normally liked to wake up, but as he padded his way out of the bedroom, he couldn't help but smile at what he saw.

Standing next to the wall-mounted bookshelves, bathed in the warm glow of an antique Italian lamp, was a statuesque woman in her early thirties. She was wearing nothing but one of his button-down shirts as she thumbed through a thick three-ring binder of old medical journals she'd pulled from a shelf. She had straight shoulder-length black hair and mocha-colored skin, both of which contrasted beautifully with the white shirt.

Last night was the first time he'd brought Madison to his apartment —an apartment owned by the Bianchi family, one of the largest of the New York Mafia families. It was a baby step into his secret world.

"You're up early," Levi remarked.

Madison looked up at him in silence for a few long seconds. A smile creased her delicate features.

"What?" He frowned as he looked at himself and then back at her.

"You're just cute. I didn't think anyone still wore pajamas to bed anymore." She tapped a finger on the binder. "You've got a strange collection of books. Is reading medical journals a hobby of yours?"

He shrugged, walked over to Madison, and kissed her on the cheek. "Good morning to you, too. Hopefully, you're good with eggs, because that's the only breakfasty stuff I have in the fridge. I'll go make us some ham and cheese omelets."

Madison huffed loudly. "Levi, don't ignore me. What's with all this medical stuff? It seems like odd reading material for someone to have unless, well, you know—you're a doctor."

Levi grabbed a carton of eggs from the refrigerator and spoke over his shoulder as he prepared breakfast. "Well, I'm obviously not a doctor. You know about how I had cancer a dozen years ago? Well, at the time, the docs all said it was a terminal case, yet obviously I managed to cheat death. But I eventually realized that I didn't come out of that time in my life totally unscathed."

"What do you mean?" Madison now stood at the entrance to the kitchen, and she sounded concerned. "Are you saying the cancer has come back? You haven't relapsed, have you?"

"No, nothing like that. It's hard to explain. Back then, so many things had happened at once: my wife died in a car accident, I had terminal cancer, and I was struck with a debilitating fever that really knocked me out. And then, suddenly, all on its own, the fever broke, my cancer had gone into remission, and that was when I noticed that other things were different too.

"The world seemed to be filled with more colors than I'd ever noticed before. The sounds that had always been there, muffled into the background, were more obvious to my ear. Hell, even the smells of the city were stronger and more distinct. At first, I wrote it all off as a strange side effect of the cancer. But after a while, some ... other things ... became hard to ignore."

"Like?"

Madison asked as she rested her chin on Levi's shoulder, watching as he deftly cracked eggs into a mixing bowl. He felt the warmth of her pressed against him and wondered how much he could say without her thinking he was nuts.

"Well, it was little things. Like I could remember random facts without even trying. For example, I could tell you that the restaurant two blocks north of here had chicken piccata on its Daily Specials menu ten days ago, and it was $10.99. The only reason I know that is because I was walking past the place and saw the sign. I can tell you the license plate number of the Uber driver who brought us here. Hell, I know the ticket stub number for the opera that I attended with a friend of mine two weeks ago."

Madison took a step back. "Are you serious?"

Levi poured the beaten eggs into a pair of hot skillets. "Yup. That's one of the reasons I started combing through those books, trying to figure out—"

"Why didn't you just go see a doctor?" Her voice took on an excited tone. "Are you seriously saying you can remember *everything* you've ever seen?"

Levi nodded as he sprinkled chopped ham and cheddar cheese onto the half-cooked eggs, and carefully flipped each of the omelets onto themselves. "Pretty much. Go ahead. I know you're dying to test me."

Madison reopened the three-ring binder, which was an assembled collection of old issues of the American Journal of Medicine, and flipped through the pages in one of the journals. "Okay, this one's from October, 2015. It's an article about fevers of unknown origin—looks like you bookmarked it. What's it say just above table one?"

With a flick of his wrist, Levi flipped both omelets over and sprinkled a bit more shredded cheddar cheese on top. In his mind's eye, he recalled the image of the green-hued medical journal and mentally turned the pages to the appropriate article. It had been one that had particularly intrigued him.

"Okay, how about I start with what Petersdorf did.

"Petersdorf also classified fevers of unknown origin by category, that is, infectious, malignant/neoplastic, rheumatic/inflammatory, and miscellaneous disorders. Fevers of unknown origin also may be considered in the context of host subsets, for example, organ transplants, human immunodeficiency virus, returning travelers."

He looked over his shoulder as he turned off the stovetop's flame, and Madison stared open-mouthed at him.

"Holy shit, that's amazing. Why haven't you become a doctor or something?"

Levi laughed as he grabbed two large dishes from the cabinet and slid a perfectly-cooked omelet onto each of them. "Maddie, it doesn't exactly work like that. Just because I can remember things, doesn't mean I understand everything I'm reading. I've got other books on those shelves about electronics, physics, and other subjects. So yeah, I can tell you what a resistor or a capacitor is, but I don't know beans about what to do with them. Well, maybe I sort of do, but not really."

"So basically you have a photographic memory."

Levi shrugged. "I guess. In those journals I learned that photographic memory—they call it eidetic memory—it's not really something adults have. Sometimes a real small percentage of young kids might have it, but it goes away before adulthood. The only instances of eidetic-like memory in adults were associated with people with some form of traumatic brain injury. And I didn't have anything like that—at least not that I know of.

"I don't know, maybe the fever, or the cancer, or both, did a number on me. Anyway, the memory thing does come in handy sometimes, but it's not exactly a key to being a genius. I'm far from it."

He sprinkled a few finely-chopped scallions across the omelets and motioned toward the dining area. "Let's get you fed. You've got a long day ahead of you."

Madison's gaze followed Levi into the dining room. "Levi, you're really full of surprises. I'm sorry, I should be helping—"

"Nonsense, you're my guest. Grab a seat; I'll go get some orange juice."

Levi hustled back to the kitchen and smiled to himself as he thought of the beautiful half-naked woman in his living room. It was strange for him to share private aspects of his life with someone. His biological family knew nothing of what he'd just shared, and his mob family only knew small pieces.

He couldn't help but wonder what the future might hold for the two of them.

~

Levi stood at the back of the common room in Harlem's YMCA with Carmine and Paulie, watching Madison leading her class. She wore a white gi with a black belt cinched around her narrow waist, and she was putting a group of nearly two-dozen neighborhood kids through several basic martial arts forms. Her students ranged from around five years old to late teens, and represented the rainbow of races and cultures that made up the neighborhood and New York City itself.

To Levi, Madison was the personification of grace and beauty in a slim five-foot-ten-inch package.

He had to admit, their relationship was complicated. To say they were friends was to make too little of it, but to say they were a couple ... well, it wasn't quite that either. They didn't even live in the same state—she lived in DC, he lived in New York City.

But it was their jobs that truly made their relationship complicated. After all, she was a covert operations officer for the CIA ... and he was one of the leading members of a prominent Mafia family. She didn't know that part, but she did know he was involved with some less-than-savory characters. And that was enough to make things awkward from time to time.

They'd met nearly a year earlier while Levi was overseas, taking care of some private business. He found himself in a situation that ended up forcing him to cooperate with people who turned out to be agents of the CIA—including Madison. He'd been smitten from the moment he first saw her.

It was hard to imagine a more unlikely pair. He wasn't sure where their relationship was going, but she had his undivided attention. That was undeniable.

"You know," said Carmine next to him, "if she really wants to teach kids, I could probably find her a nicer place uptown."

Carmine and Paulie were the mobsters who'd accompanied Levi here.

"Nah," said Levi. "She knows the guy who runs this place and wanted to do him a favor. The way I understand it, this guy saved Madison from an orphanage in Okinawa back when she was a kid, he got her together with her grandma who lives out in LA"

"Okinawa? She doesn't look Japanese ... no, you know, I take that back. I guess I kind of see it now. I figured she was Hawaiian or something. You know, like one of those hula dancer types."

Levi smiled. "Not even close."

His friends had certainly been surprised when he showed up yesterday at the mob-run apartment building with a girlfriend on his arm. They were naturally curious about her, especially since Levi tended to keep that side of his life fairly quiet, but he hadn't really talked to any of them about her yet.

"I think her mom was Japanese and her dad was a black GI," Levi explained.

"Nice," Carmine said, though following his gaze, Levi wasn't sure if he was talking about Madison or about the group of Latina moms who were across the room watching their kids practice karate.

"Is this what she does, teach karate?" Paulie asked.

Levi craned his neck to look up at Paulie, who stood nearly six foot ten. "This is just a hobby, something she's been doing since she was a kid. She works out of DC doing political analysis and stuff." Political analyst was Madison's official cover, since her real job title was strictly confidential. "We don't talk too much about work. It saves some awkward questions, if you know what I mean."

Paulie nodded. "Yup, it can be tough. My Rita and I have been married for almost ten years, and she still thinks I'm an accountant. It's just easier that way."

A door leading into the common room opened and a tiny Asian girl walked in. She couldn't have been more than five years old, and she wore a yellow dress with a wide black belt and puffy sleeves. Her black hair was pulled back into two ponytails, each of which was tied with a matching yellow ribbon. In her hands, she carried a small box tied with red ribbon. She scanned the room, and when her gaze landed on Levi, she walked directly to him.

With a sense of curiosity, he knelt so that he was eye level with her. "Hi there. Is there something I can I help you with?"

With a serious expression, she bowed and began speaking in rapid Japanese.

Levi blinked with surprise and wondered how she knew he'd understand her. After all, with his dark-brown hair, blue eyes, and a rather pale complexion, nobody would have confused him for Asian. But he had lived in Japan for a handful of years and was fluent in the language.

Levi smiled as the tiny doll of a girl spoke her memorized message.

"Yoder-san," the girl said, "my name is Kimiko and my father wishes you good health and prosperity. He hopes to invite you to visit so that you and he can talk in private." With both hands, she presented the box to him.

Levi took the box, returned her bow, and said in Japanese, "Thank you, Kimiko."

He untied the ribbon and opened the box. Inside was a stack of one-hundred-dollar bills and a rolled-up parchment. Levi thumbed through the stack of money and whistled with appreciation. Then he unrolled the parchment. It was a formal, handwritten letter, its Japanese calligraphy gorgeously done with a brush, in a traditional style.

Yoder-san,

I have contacted Don Vincenzo Bianchi, and he has given me permission to reach out to you.

I am Mr. Shinzo Tanaka's US representative and would very much like to have a meeting with you. I would not ask this unless I felt the cause was justified. There is an innocent life at stake, and I humbly request your assistance on behalf of my superior.

I've enclosed something to compensate you for your time. I hope to hear from you tonight.

Sincerely, Ryuki Watanabe.

The rest of the note was repeated in English, and gave an address and a time later that evening. It was signed with a reddish-brown thumbprint whose hue resembled the color of dried blood.

Levi looked at Kimiko with curiosity as she tapped at Paulie's leg. "Sir?" she said as she stared wide-eyed at the large man.

With an amused expression, Paulie leaned down. "Yes?" He spoke very softly with a warm and friendly tone to his voice.

"You're very tall," she said matter-of-factly, in perfect English. "Can I sit on your shoulder so I can touch the ceiling?"

Levi watched with wonder as the giant man engaged with the guileless little girl. For a man who could tear a person apart limb from limb, he was very gentle with Kimiko as he lifted her onto his right shoulder and stood.

Kimiko reached up, touched one of the ceiling tiles, and let out a peal of high-pitched laughter. "I did it!"

Laughing, Paulie carefully placed her back on the ground.

She held out her hand with a serious expression and shook hands with Paulie. "Thank you, Mister. I'm going to tell everyone at school about you, but I don't think they'll ever believe I saw a giant." The she shifted her gaze to Levi and again spoke in Japanese. "I have to go. My dad's driver is waiting for me. Maybe I'll see you later?"

"It's possible," Levi replied in Japanese.

The girl ran out of the common room just as the class began to disperse.

Levi felt a tap on his shoulder and turned to see Madison smiling at him. "You made a new friend?" She nodded toward the exit.

"I suppose so." He shrugged and gave her a peck on the lips. "We all done here?"

"Pretty much." Madison snaked her arm under his suit coat and around his waist, giving him a squeeze. "Though I think next time, you should teach the class with me."

"I don't know, I kind of like watching you do it. So—what time do you need to be at Penn Station?"

"I've got an early day tomorrow, so my train's scheduled to leave at three."

They walked toward the exit as the YMCA staff began moving the common room's furniture back into place.

Levi glanced at his watch and sighed wistfully. "Maddie, these weekends go by too quickly."

She tightened her grip around his waist and leaned her head against his. "I feel the same way. But hey, unless something happens, I should be off for two weeks right around Christmas. If you think you can deal with me for that long, we should plan something. It's only a little over a month away."

Carmine had already gone ahead to get the car, but Paulie had hung back and now chimed in. "You know, the wife and I had a really nice time at the Poconos for our fifth anniversary. The resorts are all probably booked, but I know a few people. I can probably get you guys into one of those two-story champagne tub suites and stuff. It's nice and romantic."

Madison bumped her hip against Levi's. "Hmm, romantic sounds nice." She gave Levi a quick kiss on the cheek. "Let me go change and I'll be right back."

Levi's gaze followed her as she darted past a few people talking in the hallway. He imagined what it would be like to be with Madison in a hot tub filled with bubbles.

He looked up at Paulie. "Okay big guy, if you have some strings you can pull, I'd appreciate it."

Paulie grinned. "Not that it's any of my business, but you two look good together. I think you guys should make a more permanent arrangement."

Levi laughed and shook his head. "It's complicated." He pictured the giant mobster playing the role of Yenta, the matchmaker from the Broadway play *Fiddler on the Roof.*

He glanced again at his watch. "Hey Paulie, can you go out there and make sure Carmine knows we'll need to head straight to Penn Station before going to the Helmsley? I've got to talk business with the don, and Madison can't be around for that."

Driving along Park Avenue, the sedan rolled just past East 86th Street and pulled up to a stately old building with two marble columns on each side of the entrance. The words "The Helmsley Arms" were emblazoned in gold leaf above the ten-foot doors.

As Levi hopped out of the car, the cool damp of the late fall in New York City hit him. The earthy smell of fallen leaves and exhaust filled the air, an unmistakable signature of when and where he was.

The doors opened as he approached the building's entrance, and Frank Minnelli, the head of security, stood in the doorway. The man was in his early forties, the same age as Levi, and dressed in an almost identical tailored suit.

He motioned to Levi. "Come on. We're waiting on you."

Together they walked past the two burly mobsters who were guarding the entrance, across the building's marble-floored foyer, and into the elevator to the top floor.

"So," Levi said, "I'm guessing someone reached out to Vinnie?"

The elevator doors slid open, and they started down a short wood-paneled hallway.

"You better believe it," Frankie said with a snort. "But I'll leave that for Vinnie to tell."

Two more mobsters hopped up from their chairs and opened a set of double doors. Frankie and Levi walked through into Don Bianchi's parlor.

Levi couldn't help but be amazed at how far up his friends had come since they all started out together in Little Italy over twenty years ago. The huge room had two fireplaces, was finished with ornately-carved wood paneling, and was well-appointed with beautiful paintings and a museum-quality marble statue of the Venus de Milo.

At the far end of the room, Don Vincenzo Bianchi, the head of the Bianchi crime family, sat at his large mahogany desk, wearing reading glasses and poring over a sheaf of papers. As the two men walked in, he motioned for them to approach.

"Come in, guys. Frankie, you and I need to talk about a few things, but first let's all get this Tanaka syndicate business out of the way."

Levi took a seat in one of the two reddish-brown leather armchairs in front of the desk, and Frankie sat in the other.

"Vinnie," said Levi, "what's this about someone getting your permission to reach out to me? Who are these people? Are they some new Asian outfit?"

"They're hardly new." Vinnie removed his reading glasses, tossed them on the desk and rubbed his eyes. "Frankie, how many made-men and connected guys do we have right now?"

Frankie frowned. "I think with Carlo Moretti last month, we're at a hundred twenty-seven made men, and I'm not sure on the complete number, but we've got right around one thousand earners in total."

The don drummed his fingers on the desk and turned back to Levi. "I got a call this morning from the number two guy in the Tanaka Syndicate. You might not have heard of them, but they're a pretty serious group out of Japan. In the last handful of years they've expanded beyond the island and have been muscling in on some of the Tong businesses on the West Coast. Heck, they even have a presence here in the city.

"Levi, you and I have both agreed that it's best you not be part of the day-to-day business dealings of the family, especially with some of the stuff you've been doing with the feds. But you know what we're dealing with when it comes to these other groups. Let's just say this Tanaka syndicate has ten times our manpower, and they've got resources everywhere."

Vinnie leaned forward and poked his finger in the air for emphasis. "They've made us an offer contingent on your helping them out with something. And it's a really serious offer."

"The message I got said something about an innocent life," Levi said. "Do you know what they want from me?"

Vinnie shrugged. "I have no idea. What I do know is these Yakuza types are vicious when angered, and I'm not interested in sending you into a meat grinder. This Ryuki guy, the syndicate's number two, he said that he'd guarantee your safety—that he just wants an opportunity to have a sit-down with you. He was extremely polite, like a lot of those Asian types are. But frankly, I don't like it.

"Levi, you and I go back to the beginning. I love you like a brother, and I'll tell you, I don't know what to make of this. This guy was really vague—he wouldn't even tell me why he was looking for *you* specifically. So what I'm saying is, if you don't want to go, you've got my complete backing on that. It's your call."

Frankie cleared his throat and frowned. "Levi, I did a little checking on this Tanaka syndicate—or tried to. Their main guy is a man named Shinzo Tanaka, but there's almost no record of him. I can see that he was denied entry into the US a handful of years ago, but that's about it. The man's a ghost. This Ryuki guy, his number two, is the same. No record. No beef with the local or Japanese law.

"But that's official records. Word on the street is different. There, everyone knows these two. And the word is, stay away from these Yakuza nuts. These guys make us look like choirboys." He jabbed his finger in Levi's direction. "So be careful. I can't read this one, and that makes me a little crazy."

Levi heard their warnings, but his curiosity was gnawing at him. Why did they want to talk to him specifically? How did that little girl manage to pick him out of a crowd of people at the YMCA? And how did she know he understood Japanese?

He looked at Vinnie and smiled. "Is the offer they gave for my help worthwhile?"

Vinnie returned the smiled. "I wouldn't have told him how to reach you if it wasn't a sweet deal."

Levi hopped up from his chair and rapped his knuckles on the desk. "In that case, I guess I shouldn't keep the man waiting."

AUTHOR'S NOTE

Well, that's the end of *Perimeter*, and I sincerely hope you enjoyed it.

For a long time, I'd written things geared for my kids to enjoy, mostly epic fantasy. However, it was never anything I took too seriously. I did it because it made my sons happy.

I'll freely admit that when I began writing adult genre stories, like this one, I felt like I'd turned a page in my writing "career."

Along the way, I'd made friends with some rather well-known authors, and when I talked about maybe getting more serious about this writing thing, several of them gave me the same advice, "Write what you know."

Write what I know? I began to think about Michael Crichton. He was a non-practicing MD, and started off with a medical thriller. John Grisham was an attorney for a decade before writing a series of legal thrillers. Maybe there's something to that advice?

I began to ponder, "What do I know?" And then it hit me.

I know science. It's what I do for a living and what I enjoy. In fact, one of my hobbies is reading formal papers spanning many scientific disciplines. My interests range from particle physics, computers, the military sciences (you know, the science behind what makes stuff go boom), and medicine. I'm admittedly a bit of a nerd in that way. I've also traveled extensively during my life, and am an informal student of foreign languages and cultures.

With the advice of some New York Times bestselling authors, I started my foray into writing novels. With my background, it's easy to imagine that I might focus solely on science fiction, but I'd note that I've always been a sucker for mainstream thrillers, especially those with international settings.

Truthfully, I hadn't intended to self-publish this novel. My intent was to send this to mainstream publishers. After all, I got lots of rave reviews from the traditionally published authors who'd read the manuscript. They were all very kind and a great source of encouragement.

I eventually did submit the story to acquiring editors at major publishers, and even though I'd received some interest from them, they all in the end felt it wasn't right for their particular audiences at that time. In hindsight, it's very difficult for an unknown author to "break into" traditional publishing, and for the acquiring editors, it's a big risk taking a chance on an unknown author. These are things I can fully appreciate.

Given that, I was faced with a choice of leaving the stories in a desk drawer and moving on with my life, or taking a chance and seeing if I could find the audience for my stories.

Obviously, I'm stubborn and chose the latter.

I'll assume that if you've read these last few paragraphs, you've only done so because you've read this novel in its entirety, and I've hopefully kept you entertained. If so, that means I've found you! You're that elusive "audience" that the publishers had said they didn't know how to reach.

Yay!

If I could ask anything from you, dear reader, it would be to please share your thoughts/reviews about the story on Amazon and with your friends. It's through reviews and word-of-mouth that this story will find other readers, and I do hope *Perimeter* finds as wide an audience as possible.

Again, thank you for taking the chance on a relatively-unknown author and reading his debut thriller. I should warn you, it's only the beginning.

It's my intent to release two books a year, one in the science fiction/technothriller category, and another in the mainstream thriller genre, similar in style to this book. In fact, this won't be the last time you read about Levi, it is my intent to have a series of Levi-based novels, and the next one is already in the works.

Given that, I should note that I have released another story at roughly the same time as this novel. A work of science fiction titled, *Primordial Threat*.

If you'll indulge me, below is a brief description of *Primordial Threat*:

The year is 2066 and the world is oblivious to the threat it faces.

The fate of humanity lies on the shoulders of Burt Radcliffe, the new head of NASA's Near Earth Object program.

He's been rushing the completion of DefenseNet, a ring of satellites that are both part of an early-warning system as well as the means to eliminate incoming threats.

Yet Burt knows that despite the world's best efforts, nothing can be done about the alert he's just received.

Coming out of deep space is a danger that's been approaching since the dawn of time. A black hole. An unstoppable threat that promises death for all in its wake.

Dave Holmes was a modern-day Einstein. As the original architect of DefenseNet, he'd had visions of this Primordial Threat before he disappeared, yet he'd left behind no details on how the problem might be solved.

Can Holmes be found, and if so, will his solution even work?

The world has less than a year to find out.

ADDENDUM

Broken Arrow:

In *Perimeter*, two nuclear devices have gone missing. This situation is often referred to in military jargon as a Broken Arrow.

In the real world, there are almost certainly several dozen nuclear weapons that have been lost and not reclaimed—and that's a conservative estimate, as most countries are loath to admit their real numbers.

For example, on October 3, 1986, the Russians lost a Yankee I-class submarine in eighteen thousand feet of water at the bottom of the Hatteras Abyssal Plain. It was reported that thirty-four nuclear weapons were lost in the incident.

Perimeter is based on an actual Broken Arrow incident. On March 10, 1956, a B-47 bomber launched from MacDill Air Force Base near Tampa was reported missing somewhere over the Mediterranean. No trace of it was ever found.

The Perimeter System / Dead Hand:

Soviet Russia did have a program known as "Systema Perimetr," or the Perimeter System.

This Soviet-era program was created to deal with a situation where Moscow lost communication with its nuclear silos. In the case of heightened security alerts, the system would be activated. If there were any nuclear attacks detected in the Soviet homeland, an immediate nuclear counterstrike would be initiated without the need for explicit authority from the central command.

This program was also known by the term Dead Hand.

It is rumored that this program still exists in post-Soviet Russia.

Nanites:

Though the specific applications of nanites in *Perimeter* are fictional, nanites themselves are not a thing of fiction. The engineering world has had the ability to create things at the molecular level for quite some time.

The best example of this is in computer CPU manufacturing. Today, we are mass-manufacturing electronics with processes dealing with trace widths as low as seven nanometers. That's more than a thousand times smaller than the width of the finest hair. An atom averages anywhere from 0.1 to 0.3 nanometers wide.

We've even been able to manufacture tiny machines at the nano-scale. Think of a nanite as a tiny robot. A nanorobot, if you will. Molecule-sized robots have been the promise of medicine for quite some time. The concept used in *Perimeter*, where these "tiny doctors" are able to repair the body (within reason), and fend off sicknesses, is not really as ridiculous as it might seem.

Today, it is already possible to synthesize nanites that can determine where they are, and deliver minute units of a medicine to the correct locations. For instance, if one of these nanites was carrying a drug meant to treat a specific form of cancer, it would also carry a sensor that would help it identify its molecular target.

The advantages of such a precision approach are obvious. Chemotherapies, by contrast, blast the entire body with poisons, damaging healthy cells along with the cancerous ones. Nanites could be "programmed" to target only the unhealthy cells.

Yet today we are not using nanites as tiny doctors. Why?

Many challenges exist—among them, the ability to manufacture these nanites in a sufficient quantity to do clinical testing. This is hugely expensive today, and frankly, that's the biggest technical hurdle.

But once that hurdle is crossed, the field is open for what could be a revolution in medicine, generating entirely new methods of treating cancer, other diseases, and even possibly halt the aging process.

ABOUT THE AUTHOR

I am an Army brat, a polyglot, and the first person in my family born in the United States. This heavily influenced my youth by instilling a love of reading and a burning curiosity about the world and all of the things within it. As an adult, my love of travel and adventure has allowed me to explore many unimaginable locations, and these places sometimes creep into the stories I write.

I hope you've found this story entertaining.

- Mike Rothman

You can find my blog at: www.michaelarothman.com
I'm also on Facebook at: www.facebook.com/MichaelARothman
And on Twitter: @MichaelARothman